D0916224

WEAPONS OF MASS DECEPTION

Also By David Bruns and J.R. Olson

Novels

Weapons of Mass Deception

Jihadi Apprentice

Rules of Engagement

Short Stories

"Death of a Pawn"

"Battle Djinni"

***

Find out more about Bruns and Olson at
www.twonavyguys.com

DAVID BRUNS
AND J.R. OLSON

WEAPONS OF
MASS DECEPTION

REEF POINTS
MEDIA LLC

This is a work of fiction. Names, characters, places, and incidents are products of the authors' imaginations or are used fictitiously and are not to be construed as real.

To Melissa and Christine

CHAPTER 1

Northeast Iraq, near the Iranian border
15 March 2003 — 0200 local

The Iranian was late.

Uday Saddam Hussein al-Tikriti shifted in the backseat of the black Range Rover. His face was calm, but inside he raged. He checked his Rolex again—the fifth time in as many minutes.

0200. *Two hours! This Iranian asshole has kept the son of Saddam Hussein waiting in the desert for two hours!*

He sniffed and wrinkled his nose. The bodyguards on either side of him, hulking men dressed in worn army fatigues—as per the Iranian's instructions—averted their eyes. The two men in the front seat stiffened and stared straight ahead.

"Out," Uday barked to the one on his right. "I will walk awhile."

"But, sir, the—"

"Shut up and let me out!" First they fart in his car, then they try to stop him from getting fresh air.

1

Stay calm. Father trusted you with this mission—not Qusay—because you are the favored son. Keep it together.

He brought his voice down to a conversational level, but kept the edge of authority. "You will walk with me, Baseer." His head of security exited the front passenger seat and waited for Uday to join him. The mountain air was sharp and clear after the stuffiness of the Rover. Uday breathed deeply, watching his breath steam when he released it. The very thinnest of crescent moons hung above them, casting a silvery sheen over the landscape. He moved to the Kia 2.5-ton truck, noting that the Iraqi Army emblems had been sanded off and the doors repainted.

He nodded to the men in the rear, waving his hand for them to stay seated when they tried to scramble to their feet. Most of the space in the truck bed was taken up by the cargo, plain wooden boxes lashed securely to the deck. Again, per the Iranian's instructions.

Why did his father even listen to this man? During the conflict CNN called the "Gulf War," when the Iraqi airfields were being pummeled by American bombers, this same man convinced his father the Iraqi Air Force would be "protected" in Iran. One hundred thirty-seven Iraqi fighter jets were flown to Iran. One hundred thirty-seven fighter jets never returned home to Iraq. War reparations, the Iranians claimed. Why would his father trust such a man?

He knew the reason: Saddam was afraid. Fighter jets were toys compared to what was in these plain wooden crates: weapons that would turn the world against him, if they were discovered on Iraqi soil.

No, Saddam had seen the Americans enter Afghanistan. Uday had watched his father obsessively flip the channels of his massive TV between Al Jazeera and CNN, sometimes watching both at once. He had seen the Americans lobby the United Nations with their pictures and their money and their threats. Saddam knew in his heart that it was only a matter of time. The Americans were coming, and this time they would not stop at the border.

Still, it made Uday's heart ache to think of the money they had sunk into the contents of these boxes. Had the crates been made of solid gold, they would not represent a tenth of the treasure they had spent. These few boxes represented decades of work. The smuggling costs alone to move the equipment into Iraq had been enormous—and that was before they'd built a single bomb. Uday let his eyes run over the boxes and the handful of men guarding them. A hot flush of anger rose in his throat.

And now they were giving it to the Iranians for safekeeping.

He shook his head, annoyed with his daydreaming. The men eyed him nervously. Most of them had never even seen Saddam, or his sons, in the flesh. The ten men in the Kia had no idea why they'd been selected for this mission and no idea what was in the crates.

With a final nod, Uday turned on his heel and strode past the Kia, hands clasped behind his back. The roadside ended in a steep cliff. He peered over the edge of the fifty-foot drop. He couldn't see the bottom, but he heard the trickle of water.

The mountain on the other side of the Kia climbed up less steeply in a jumble of rocks and shadows. He heard the distinctive yipping of a golden jackal in the distance, a sound any son of the desert would recognize immediately. They hunted at night, pursuing rodents or rabbits, and the occasional kid goat if the young shepherds weren't vigilant.

The sound of an approaching vehicle interrupted his thought. Finally! A black SUV rounded the bend at a crawl, lights extinguished. It came to a stop fifty feet from Uday, its exhaust smoking in the night air. Uday shot a hand signal to Baseer and began to walk slowly toward the new vehicle.

Behind him, car doors slammed as his protection detail—the four men he trusted most on the planet—fanned out to either side. He walked boldly up to the passenger's side door and put his hands on his hips to show the Iranian his displeasure at being kept waiting in the cold, filthy desert for two hours.

He could make out only two figures in the vehicle. A light flared in the passenger seat as someone took a drag on a cigarette. *That must be him*, Uday thought. The man smokes like a chimney, his father had told him, laughing at his use of American slang. He's never without a cigarette in his hands. Uday composed his face into an expression of irritation.

The purr of the lowering window seemed loud in the stillness of the night. Uday opened his mouth to speak just as the cigarette flared again. He choked back his outrage when he saw the man's face.

It was a handsome face, high cheekbones, noble nose and brow, strong jawline. His neatly trimmed dark hair was shot with distinguished gray and brushed straight back from his forehead. And yet there was a shadow behind the dark eyes that offset the handsome features. A shadow that made Uday, who as Saddam's son had seen and perpetrated all manner of evil in his life, fake a cough and avert his eyes from the man's gaze. The Iranian's brow twisted in what might have passed for sympathy. He held out a pack of cigarettes. Marlboros.

"Cigarette?" he asked.

The tenor voice was soft, tender, but it gave Uday a chill nonetheless. Uday shook his head and stepped away as the car door opened.

The Iranian was slim of build and slightly stoop-shouldered. He stretched, the lighted tip of the cigarette arcing into the sky as he reached his arms over his head.

Uday looked from the Iranian to his driver, who had not moved from behind the wheel of the Rover. "You brought only one man with you?"

The Iranian gave a low chuckle and brought his wrist to his lips, muttering a short burst of Farsi. The rocky shadows shifted as a platoon of heavily armed men moved into the clearing. Uday's heart skipped a beat. Iranian commandos.

Aware that his own men were watching him and desperate to regain some control of the situation, Uday adopted a tone of outrage. "How dare you?" he hissed in English, the tongue common to both men. "You bring these men into my country—"

The Iranian stepped close, so close Uday could smell the man's aftershave and the dead taint of cigarettes on his breath. "I am a cautious man, Uday, a trait you would do well to emulate. Stop this posturing and show me the weapons you need me to hide from the Americans." His voice was pitched low, for Uday's ears only, and his warm breath puffed against Uday's cheek as he spoke. He wheeled away and walked toward the Kia.

Uday followed, trailed by his four-man security team. Four of the Iranian commandos were still in place, weapons trained on the Iraqi contingent, mirroring their movement toward the big vehicle. The rest had disappeared.

The Iranian reached the back of the truck and said in flawless Arabic, "Get out." The ten soldiers, without waiting for a confirming order from Uday, piled out of the truck. The Iranian waited until they were herded away before he hoisted himself into the back of the Kia. One of his commandos came forward with a crowbar and a flashlight. He lowered the tarp across the back entrance and positioned himself between the truck bed and Uday's people.

Light seeped out from the edges of the tarp and a screech rent the air as the Iranian opened a crate. Minutes ticked by as Uday heard only faint rustlings from the truck bed. The light snapped off, but the tarp stayed down. *He's waiting for his eyes to adjust,* Uday thought. He flinched as the Iranian dropped lightly to the ground next to him.

"Everything is as it should be. That is good, Uday."

"And we will get these weapons back this time? Not like last time." Uday puffed out his chest. "I need assurances."

The Iranian's lips twitched. "Of course, assurances. All you need to do is call me."

Uday nodded, setting his chin in satisfaction. At least he had managed to do that much in front of his men.

The Iranian spoke to his men in rapid Farsi. The four commandos approached the Iraqi soldiers and ordered them to drop their weapons. When the Iraqi officer protested, the nearest commando jabbed him in the throat and the man went down, gagging. The Iraqi troops all dropped their weapons.

Uday's security detail shifted around him in a protective circle. He heard the metallic *snick* of weapon safeties being released. He wished he had brought more men. The Iranian walked between Uday's men and took his arm, gently leading him away from his security detail.

The Iraqi soldiers' wide eyes glimmered in the moonlight. One of them, no more than a boy, really, was crying softly, and Uday smelled the sharp stench of urine. Uday was aware that his men were watching him, waiting for a signal.

The Iranian drew his own pistol and cranked the slide back. He placed it in Uday's hand. The metal was cold and heavy against his sweaty palm. He knew from the weight and the grip that it was a Chinese semiautomatic, fitted with a suppressor. "Kill them," the Iranian said, his tenor voice almost seductive in softness. "It is necessary."

The officer fell to his knees, his hands clasped in front of him. "Please, I beg you. Spare us. Please."

"Kill them, Uday." The Iranian's tone was insistent.

Uday felt himself hyperventilating, his pulse pounding in his ears. Baseer caught his eye, urging him to comply with the Iranian's orders. Uday shot the Iraqi officer in the head, then glared at the Iranian.

"Satisfied?" he asked.

The boy on the end, the one who had pissed himself, tried to run, and one of the Iranian commandos cut him down with a three-bullet burst of suppressed automatic weapons fire.

The Iranian nodded to his commando team. "Finish it."

It was over in seconds. The soldiers, his security team—all dead. The Iranian commandos pushed the bodies over the edge of the cliff into the ravine until all that remained of Uday's men was a ringing in his ears and the acrid scent of the discharged weapons. Uday jumped at the Iranian's soft touch as the man reclaimed his weapon. Uday could feel his disdain, the way he dismissed Uday now—

The Iranian's posture stiffened, and his head snapped toward the rocks. He raised his wrist to his lips and spoke in rapid Farsi. An Iranian commando stepped onto the road fifty feet behind the Rover and made his way toward them, towing a struggling figure in white. He shook the boy hard before he threw him to the ground in front of Uday. He was all of twelve years old, dressed in typical shepherd garb and sandals. His eyes traveled up to meet Uday's and grew wide as he realized who he was looking at.

If he was going to kill me, I'd be dead already. Uday tried to still the shaking in his hand as he reached out to help the boy up.

The Iranian stepped between them, grasping the boy by the front of his shirt and jerking him to his feet. His other hand passed behind the small of his back and there was a flash of silver in the moonlight. A knife, Uday realized. The boy's body fell from the edge of the cliff like a rag doll.

The Iranian stepped close to Uday, the scent of aftershave and cigarettes now overpowered by the smell of blood. Uday shrank back.

"I am a cautious man, Uday." He barked out an order to his men.

The commandos disappeared into the night, except for one man who climbed into the Kia truck, started it, and drove it east toward Iran. The Iranian seated himself in the Range Rover, lit another cigarette, and, with a final look toward Uday, pulled the door shut. His driver wheeled the Rover around and headed back the way they had come.

Uday Saddam Hussein al-Tikriti stood alone in the desert.

CHAPTER 2

Chesapeake Bay, near Annapolis, Maryland
06 April 2003 – 1645 local

The April wind whipped across the yawl, filling the mainsail of the *Hornet* and heeling the boat hard to starboard. Midshipman First Class Brendan McHugh gripped the helm, a large stainless steel wheel, and leaned into the twenty-degree cant of the deck. They were making twelve knots easy. A brilliant sun lit the Chesapeake Bay and sailboats from the United States Naval Academy sailing regatta—the first one of the spring season—dotted the water around him.

He tugged up the zipper on the neck of his fleece. It was the kind of day he loved, the kind of day he would long for during the Dark Ages of the academic year, that stretch of time between Christmas holiday and spring break when the Annapolis weather turned gray and rainy and the full brunt of coursework consumed every midshipman's attention.

He tried to enjoy the moment, to live in the now. That's what

Mark would have said if he were here. Tears sprang into Brendan's eyes, and he was glad for the hooded Ray-Bans he wore. It would do no good to have Liz see him crying; she was pretty much a mess herself.

It was odd, the way he could almost feel Mark next to him. The funeral had been a beautiful service, but it wasn't Mark. The hymns, the flag-draped casket, the stillness in the vast space of the Naval Academy chapel broken only by the sobs of Mark's mother, Marjorie . . .

No, the Mark he remembered was sitting behind his right shoulder, feet propped on the bulkhead, cracking wise.

The first time he'd met Mark, Brendan had been a plebe, and not a very good one, either. It wasn't the physical routine or even the yelling that got him, it was the memorization. So much to remember and spit back in the face of any upperclassman who wanted to harass you. He had just come from a forty-five minute "training" session with Midshipman Second Class Fermit, a real ball-buster with bad breath to boot. Fermit had Brendan braced up and rigged—Naval Academy–speak for a favorite plebe disciplinary technique that required the trainee to pull his chin deep into his neck and hold it there with both hands. Not so bad for a few minutes, but painful after a half hour.

Fermit had caught him on some minor infraction, Brendan couldn't even remember what it was now, and jacked him up against the wall outside his room. He stalked in and out of his open door, wearing only a white T-shirt and uniform trousers, asking Brendan questions in rapid fire and Brendan getting more and more snarled up as his memory hit its limits. He'd already sweated through his uniform, and he wondered if he had a fresh shirt to change into before evening inspection. When Brendan got into this situation, he'd found the best strategy was to go "rope-a-dope" until the upperclassman tired of playing with his victim. But that wasn't working today.

"Name all the weapons carried on the F/A-18, McHugh." Fermit's breath was rank, but Brendan did his best not to react. The bastard probably stopped brushing his teeth to see if he could make plebes gag when he spoke to them.

"I'll find out, sir!" Brendan responded at the top of his lungs. Assholes like Fermit liked it when you yelled; it showed intensity. He got the added satisfaction of seeing flecks of his own spittle make Fermit back up a step.

"What? You can't name any, McHugh? You are a worthless piece of shit, McHugh. Why don't you just wash out now and save the taxpayers some money?"

"No, sir!" *Why don't you eat shit and die, you loser?*

"Name all the classes of destroyers in the Fleet, McHugh."

Brendan took a deep breath, ready to belt out another "I'll find out, sir," when he heard her. Liz's voice, high-pitched, musical with always the hint of a laugh behind it, floated down the passageway. "Go Navy, sir. Beat Army, sir."

As fourth-class midshipmen, or plebes, they were required to double-time through the corridors of Bancroft Hall, make only right-angle turns, and to "sound off" at every one. Her voice was getting louder and timed with her footfalls as she squared her corners. She was coming toward them. Brendan held back a sigh. She was coming to save his ass—again.

No, Liz, I can handle this dickhead, just stay away.

She appeared at the end of the passageway, a slim figure made smaller by her dark uniform. She squared the corner to face them, yelling out loud enough for Fermit to hear. "Beat Navy, sir!"

Had it not been more serious, Brendan might have burst out laughing. Fermit's face went white, his jaw hanging open as Liz trotted down the polished hall toward them. As a plebe at the Naval

Academy, everything—*everything*—centered on beating West Point at any event where the two schools competed. A plebe shouting "Beat Navy" was an insult akin to saying your mother had sexual relations with farm animals. Fermit's mouth worked open and shut a few times as Liz reached them.

"Plebe halt!" he screamed at her. Liz froze. Fermit blinked at Brendan as if wondering why he was there. "Shove off, McHugh. You, Soroush"—his trembling finger wavered at Liz—"up against the wall. Name all the classes of destroyers in the Fleet. Go." He bent over so his face was right in Liz's ear when he screamed at her.

Liz refused to meet Brendan's eye as he pushed off the wall and squared the corner. He could hear her rattling off the names of destroyers as he trotted away. He checked the clock. Twenty minutes until formation. He felt bad about leaving her, but there probably wasn't a question Fermit could think up that Liz couldn't answer.

He was almost at his door. A quick shower, a fresh shirt, and a review of some likely quiz questions before the evening meal were what he needed to clear his head. He would use that mnemonic trick Liz had taught him.

"Plebe halt."

Oh shit, not again. He froze.

"Come in here, McHugh."

Double shit.

The voice floated out from an open doorway to his left. He did a military turn toward it, ready for the worst.

"Don't just stand there, McHugh. Get in here."

Brendan trotted to the door and rapped his knuckles on the jamb. "Midshipman Fourth Class McHugh, requesting permission to enter—"

"For Christ's sake, will you get the fuck in here, McHugh? And stop shouting at me." Mark's black-stockinged feet were propped up on his desk and he was stripped to a white T-shirt and gym shorts.

His blue eyes were warm, adding to the power of his smile.

"At ease," he said.

Brendan went to parade rest, his hands crossed in the small of his back, senses on full alert. Mark's approach seemed relaxed enough, and he had a reputation among the plebes of the company as a "cool" upperclassman—i.e., not an asshole—but Brendan had never spoken to him.

"For fuck's sake, McHugh, *relax*. I'm not going to bite your goddamned head off. I'll leave that to dicks like Fermit." He spit out the second-classman's name like a bad taste in his mouth.

Brendan, still wary, allowed his hands to drop to his sides and his shoulders to ease down a notch. *Be careful—this is how they get you.*

Mark chewed his lip. "Fair enough," he said. "You don't trust me, and that's probably a good thing for your own survival. You're a hockey player, right?"

Brendan nodded. "Yes, sir," he replied in a normal voice.

"I'm recruiting for the sailing team. How about you crew for me in the off-season?"

Brendan's eyes must have widened because Mark laughed out loud and let the legs of his chair hit the polished floor. "No tricks, McHugh. I'm on the level. I need a crew and I think you'd do a good job. Plus, it gets you away from the Hall for a few overnights and weekends . . . away from that dickhead down there." He cocked his head toward the door to the hallway, where they could both hear Fermit screaming at Liz. His voice had reached a hysterical pitch, probably because she had answered all his stupid questions and he was frustrated.

Brendan nodded at Mark. "I'll do it."

"Good choice, McHugh," Mark laughed. "Shove off, I'm going to catch a catnap before dinner."

Brendan turned toward the door and placed his uniform cap on his head.

"Oh, and McHugh," Mark called to him. "Bring your friend, what's her name—Soroush? I can use her, too."

Brendan blew out his breath. Crewing for Mark had made his plebe year at the Academy bearable. It gave him and Liz a place to get away from the Hall for a few hours or a weekend. He owed Mark everything.

Screw the funeral. He would remember Mark the way he would have wanted to be remembered: sitting in the stern of the yawl, feet up, blue eyes hidden behind his Ray-Bans, a smile on his face from the last joke he had shouted out to them. Not as a closed casket.

Of course, all that was Mark before 9/11, the day that changed them all. Mark was a Marine first lieutenant when it happened, and he was part of the first wave of troops that entered Iraq. Overnight he went from carefree Mark to Marine Mark. The once-playful blue eyes turned the color of ice and the jokes became less frequent.

Brendan looked over his shoulder. Liz was hunched over a chart in the stern, her legs braced against the bulkhead for stability. She had been looking at the same chart for twenty minutes, a pencil loose in her grip.

"Hey, Liz, you okay?"

She raised her head, her eyes hidden behind sunglasses, but Brendan could see the tracks down her cheeks. The wind blew her short, dark hair across her face, but she made no attempt to push it away. She smiled at him. Well, she tried to smile.

It's okay, Lizzie. I miss him, too. That's what he should have said, but instead he plastered his face with a wide grin. "Any idea where we are?" he asked. That was Mark's favorite line.

This time she gave him a real smile. "Does it really matter? We're not in the Hall, are we?" They both laughed—for real—but Brendan felt the sting in his eyes again.

Her face froze. Liz stood, her finger pointing to the starboard side of the boat. "Man overboard," she screamed. Brendan saw a flash of red hair whip by the gunwale.

The crew reacted instinctively. As Liz kept her finger pointed at the target, Brendan brought the thirty-six-foot yawl around. The crew of eight called to one another, and Brendan took a mental tally of the missing voice. He needn't have bothered. From the red hair, he already knew it was Riley.

He swung the helm to bear on Liz's pointing finger, fuming to himself. The mainsail was down in heaps on the deck and he started the engine. Once the nearby boats saw that *Hornet* was able to recover their man, they kept their sails full and stayed their courses. Brendan watched the regatta flash by them.

Midshipman Fourth Class Donald Riley was his and Liz's attempt to pay it forward. Just like Mark had done with them, when he and Liz were named co-captains of *Hornet*, they agreed they would pick a plebe from their company to join their crew. It would be their way to give back, their memorial to Mark's generosity of spirit.

Riley was a terrible plebe, there was just no other way to say it. Brendan was only 5'10", but Riley was even shorter. And heavier, a lot heavier. The kid had been off and on "Sub Squad," Academy slang for the midshipmen who failed their quarterly PT tests, and without help from Liz and Brendan, he'd probably still be there. He was their project, and they'd picked a doozie.

Still, the kid had skills. With a near eidetic memory, Riley consumed information like most people breathed air, and some claimed his computer skills were hacker level. Unlike Brendan, this kid never had any issue with memorization, and his academic scores were tops in his class. But that wasn't what had made Liz and Brendan choose him.

Riley was one of the post-9/11 crop of midshipmen, the ones who never would have considered a military career had they not been touched by the terrorist attack. His uncle, a bond broker, had been in the World Trade Center when the planes hit. Riley never spoke to him about it, but Brendan had heard that his uncle managed to call their home answering machine minutes before his tower collapsed.

No, they'd made the right choice with Riley. What the kid lacked in physical prowess he made up for in guts.

Liz dropped her hand and picked up the tethered life ring. She swung it wide, and Brendan watched the orange ring arc over the chop toward Riley's pale face and red hair. Brendan killed the engine to stop their headway. Two more crew members took the rope from Liz and hauled Riley toward the boat. When he was close enough, they reached over the gunwale and hoisted Donald Riley into the cockpit.

The boy collapsed to the deck, splashing water over Brendan's Docksiders, his pale belly spilling out from under his shirt. One of the crewmen muttered "fucking Riley" under his breath and took a seat on the bench.

Liz whirled on him. "What's your problem, Richardson? Have you forgotten we're in a race here? Move it!"

The two crewmen scrambled forward to the winches as Brendan swung the helm and put them on a bearing to fill the mainsail again.

Liz knelt next to Riley. "You okay, Don?"

Riley sat up. His voice was hoarse. "I'm sorry, Liz. I just slipped and went off the side. It happened so fast . . ."

Liz held out her hand and pulled him onto the bench next to her. "Go get some dry clothes on, Don, and then we need you back on station. We're in a race here, or have you forgotten like those other knuckleheads?"

"No, ma'am. I'm on it." Riley gave her a bright smile. He slid forward and disappeared into the tiny cabin.

Brendan kept his face impassive as he watched from behind his dark glasses. He was going to miss her when they graduated, but she'd make a great officer—and besides, Marine green was a good color for her.

He watched Liz angle her body as the deck canted beneath their feet again. They had one of the faster boats in the regatta; if they kept this kind of speed on they might even place in the top five. She stepped back until she was next to Brendan. She bumped his shoulder with hers.

"Do you have any idea where we are?" she said softly.

"Does it really matter?"

CHAPTER 3

Al Jazeera was broadcasting live from Firdos Square in Baghdad.

Hashem had the sound muted, but the images on the screen needed no words. A US military M88 armored recovery vehicle was in the process of pulling down a statue of Saddam Hussein in front of thousands of screaming Iraqis. The iconic thirty-nine-foot statue, erected in honor of Saddam Hussein's sixty-fifth birthday, depicted the dictator with his open hand raised in friendship. But now there was a heavy chain wrapped around his neck and the statue leaned over at a twenty-degree angle. With a snap, the structure fell and hordes of Iraqis rushed to spit on the image and beat it with their shoes.

Baghdad had fallen.

Hashem had always assumed Saddam Hussein's forces would fall, but the speed with which the Iraqi forces folded surprised even him.

He shook his head and drew fiercely on the last of his cigarette before crushing it out in the overflowing ashtray.

A mere three weeks from the time the Americans entered the country until they took Baghdad. Unbelievable. CNN had taken to calling it the Battle of Baghdad. What battle? With a force that large it took almost three weeks just to drive there from Kuwait.

The crawler on the bottom of the screen said the whereabouts of Saddam and his two sons were unknown. Hashem wondered idly if he should have tied up all the loose ends from his last interaction with the Iraqi regime. No, he decided, killing Uday would have inflamed an already tense situation between their two countries. Still, with this latest news, the consequences would have been nil.

The door to the private room at the restaurant began to open, and Hashem shifted the ashtray to the sideboard, brushing cigarette ash from his suit jacket as he stood. His brother wore the robes of his office, the cream-colored *qabaa*. The garment fell from his thick shoulders, and a white turban framed his round face. Despite his fifty-one years, his beard was barely graying.

Hashem took a knee before his half brother. "Your Eminence, thank you for seeing me on such short notice."

His brother nodded to the guard at the door to leave them. "Hashem! Off your knees, my brother. Rise, please." He grasped Hashem's hand and pulled him to his feet.

Despite his kind protests, the obeisance was part of their routine. Aban always liked to be reminded of his office, and Hashem felt obligated to pay his respects to his elder brother, the holy man. So they played the game each time they met.

"Let me look at you." Aban grasped him by the biceps, holding him at arm's length. The older man stood a head shorter than Hashem, and even though thirteen years his elder, Aban's round face and youthful features made them seem much closer in age.

"You look like shit, brother." Aban shook his head. "It's those cigarettes. American cigarettes, no less!" He barked out a command. The door snapped open, and his bodyguard filled the doorway. Aban pointed to the overflowing ashtray. The man swept the refuse onto a tray and disappeared without a word.

Hashem licked his lips. He wanted a cigarette now more than ever. The sharp corner of the Marlboro package inside his jacket pocket pressed against his ribcage. To keep his hands busy, he poured the remains of his cold tea into the trashcan and drew fresh cups for himself and his brother.

Aban had seated himself at the table, his short legs spread wide beneath his robes, his belly sagging to touch his thighs. He pursed his lips as he watched the replay of the scene in Firdos Square. Every few minutes, Al Jazeera showed a split screen with a replay of the statue hitting the ground on the right side and some mindless commentator babbling on the left. They had cut the head from Saddam's statue now and were dragging it through the streets, where Iraqis, features twisted with rage, smacked the face of their former dictator with their shoes.

The muted Al Jazeera network cut to a White House briefing with the US Secretary of Defense. He cackled silently, peering over the lectern nearsightedly. The news crawler said: RUMSFELD CLAIMS "EXCELLENT PROGRESS." BATTLE OF BAGHDAD "AHEAD OF SCHEDULE." Aban's lips twisted.

"First the abomination of Israel at our doorstep, then we are labeled as part of Bush's Axis of Evil, now this. The American noose tightens, brother." As if making his point, he tugged at his collar. He took a loud slurp of tea and thunked the clear glass cup down on the tabletop. Tea sloshed onto the linen cloth. He turned to Hashem, his eyes fiery like when he gave his Friday sermons on television—Aban was famous for the length and ferocity of his Friday sermons. "Meanwhile, we make empty threats, religious protestations that ring hollow on the world stage. Allah wants us to be bold, to strike at the heart of this cancer . . ." He trailed off as he studied his brother's face.

"You have news for me, Hashem?" His voice took on a hopeful tinge.

"I have the devices, Your Eminence," Hashem replied. He could barely contain the excitement in his voice. "The weapons that will allow you to fulfill the will of Allah." It was all he could do not to laugh out loud at his brother's openmouthed response.

"How?"

"Saddam was terrified the Americans would find their weapons of mass destruction." Hashem nodded at the silent screen where Saddam's golden statue was falling for the hundredth time. Al Jazeera and CNN were rife with talk of the mysterious WMDs, but no one could find them. The Americans were rapidly becoming the butt of an international joke.

"It seems he had good reason to be concerned. Technically we are only holding them for safekeeping, but I think we can assume they are ours now." He laughed. In the first Gulf War, Iran had held Iraqi warplanes for "safekeeping." The Iranian Air Force still used those planes today. Safekeeping indeed. Still, there was a big difference between a MiG fighter and a nuclear warhead.

"Do the Americans know we have them?" his brother asked.

Hashem shook his head. "I took precautions." *I should have killed Uday.*

Aban's belly quivered beneath his robes, and he beamed at Hashem. "Brother, you are truly a man of your word."

Hashem knew what this could do for Aban's career if—when—they executed an attack. A strike against Israel would make Ayatollah Khomeni's shot to international stardom following the 1979 overthrow of the Shah seem like child's play. Aban would become a world leader overnight; President Bush would have his Axis of Evil words turn to ashes in his mouth.

Still, there was work to do before they were operational weapons.

Much work to do. He cleared his throat.

"There are complications, Aban," he said. "The Iraqis developed warheads, but their work was sloppy, rudimentary at best. It will take time to make them viable weapons and secure missiles and launching systems for them—outside normal channels, of course. In the meantime, I have established a base at—"

Aban held up his hand. "Please, do not say. For now, the less I know about this, the better. I trust you, Hashem, and that is enough."

Hashem swallowed his words. The hiding place was the best part of the plan.

He could recall the trip as if it were yesterday. Just the three of them: Aban, him, and their father. Hashem had been barely fourteen years old. His favorite memory of that three-week trip was listening to his father and Aban talk by the campfire about rocks and mining and uranium deposits. Aban had just received his PhD and was eager to show off his knowledge to their father. That trip was when Hashem decided he was going to be a geologist, too.

They made camp in the Zagros Mountains, a remote site, barely accessible by their four-wheel-drive vehicle. They found the cavern one afternoon during their second week: a vast space at the base of a mountain, half the size of a soccer pitch, with a level, sandy floor and an entrance large enough for their truck. He could see his father and brother even now, standing in the glare of the headlights speaking about the formation of the natural wonder in hushed tones as if they might wake some sleeping giant. His father put his arm around Aban's shoulders. At that moment, Hashem wanted nothing more than to be like his brother.

That trip was the end of innocence for Hashem in so many ways. Within the next year, his father was dead, the Shah had fallen, and Aban's always-present religious tendencies had bloomed into an obsession.

And Hashem was alone.

He entered university the next year, but he was not able to study overseas like his brother. By his sophomore year, he had been recruited by *Ettela'at* as an intelligence officer.

Aban was nodding at him, still smiling, and Hashem shook his head to clear it of these random memories.

"We have time, Hashem," he was saying. "As the Americans say, we have many balls in the air. We must be patient while the situation clarifies for us. Patience and victory are twin sisters; one does not exist without the other. Our greatest asset is our secrecy, brother. Above all, you must preserve that—especially in your international dealings." He placed his hand on Hashem's knee. "We must be prepared to wait—years, if necessary—for the right moment." Hashem met his brother's eyes. The Friday sermon fire had returned.

The plump hand tightened on his knee. "And above all, my brother, we must have contingencies. You have considered the possibility that our primary objective may not be possible?"

Hashem nodded. Israel was a hardened target and getting worse with every passing month. Soon the Israeli Arrow system, an advanced version of the American Patriot surface-to-air missile defense system, would be operational. In truth, the Iraqi weapons were low-yield, his expert told him no more than four or five kilotons each. Poor by international standards, but enough to destroy a medium-sized city—assuming it reached the target.

No, Aban was right: contingencies were needed to make a proper statement to the world.

"I will call Rafiq," he said. "Perhaps he can help."

Aban clapped his hands. "Hezbollah, an excellent idea!" His grin darkened and he narrowed his eyes at Hashem. "I'll leave it to you as to whether or not the bastard can be trusted."

Aban stood, and just like that, he became His Eminence again. His features took on the gravity of his office and he even seemed taller, slimmer. Hashem knelt again. Aban placed his hand on Hashem's head. "Rise, my brother. Please." He stared into Hashem's eyes, then kissed him on both cheeks. "You are an instrument of Allah, my brother. I have faith in you."

In spite of himself, Hashem felt a lump in his throat, and tears stung his eyes. He mumbled an inaudible reply, a flush of embarrassment creeping up his neck. His brother was the only man who could draw such emotions out of him.

Aban stepped away and called out. His bodyguard filled the doorway again. Aban snapped his fingers and pointed to the table. The bodyguard, a hulking man with a clean-shaven head and eyes set too close together, dropped an aluminum briefcase on the table with a thump. He stepped aside to let Aban pass, then followed the cleric out the door.

Hashem had a cigarette out and his lighter fired before the door even clicked shut. He drew deeply, letting the smoke calm his lungs, allowing it to trickle out of his nostrils before he blew a long stream at the ceiling. He smoked the entire cigarette and started a second before he laid the briefcase flat on the table. He carefully dialed the combination on the lock. 4-30-80. The date of their father's death. The locks made a loud clack in the empty room as he opened the lid.

Green and white bills, neatly banded and stacked, filled the case. He pulled one stack and flipped through the bills, letting the flutter fan his face. Hashem took another deep drag on his cigarette as he felt the sides of his lips curl into a smile.

American cigarettes, American dollars, American destruction. The symmetry was beautiful.

He reached into his breast pocket for his mobile phone and sent a text to a cut-out number in Lebanon.

While he waited, he stared at the silent TV screen, watching Saddam's statue fall again and again.

CHAPTER 4

United States Naval Academy Graduation, Annapolis, Maryland
23 May 2003 – 1400 local

Liz Soroush air-kissed her mother's cheek, careful not to let the older woman's makeup mark her dress blues.

The limo driver stood to one side, hand on the car door, a permanent half-smile on his lips. Liz's mother, elegant in a pink suit from some famous designer, tucked a stray strand of hair behind her daughter's ear.

"Congratulations, Elizabeth. I know you worked very hard." Her voice was soft, and Liz bristled at the unspoken regret in her tone.

We're not going to do this today.

Liz smiled at her own reflection in her mother's stylish smoky glasses. The US Marine Corps eagle, globe, and anchor insignia on her lapel and the second lieutenant bars on her shoulders gleamed in the May sunshine.

I did it. I graduated. I'm a Marine.

"Thank you, Mom. That means a lot to me . . ."

As usual, her father saved the day. He slid his arm around her, pulling her close. "Lizzie, you did it! I'm so very proud of you." His accent was still heavily salted with the tones of his native Iran. She folded herself into his thick arms, letting the scratch of his beard scrape her cheek.

Whereas her mother towered over both of them, she and her dad were the same height and build, thick and strong.

"Thank you, Papa," she whispered.

Fatima and Ahmad Soroush had left Iran in the late 1970s with their three sons in tow. Ahmad, an engineer, settled his family in Los Angeles, and through the Iranian expat community he found a good job with a local real estate developer. Within a few years, he was running the company. Money had never been an issue in the Soroush household, and Liz could have attended any university in the world.

She chose Annapolis.

Her closest brother was just finishing high school when Liz was born. Fatima Soroush might have had visions of her perfect little girl dressed in the latest fashion, but Liz might as well have been born a boy, for all the good it did her mother.

Liz let her father go. "You're going to miss your plane, Papa."

The old man's eyes were misty under his bushy eyebrows. "I know. I just wish we had more time."

She pushed him gently toward the open car door. "I leave for Quantico in the morning and I have a million things to do before then. Now go."

She waved as they drove away. She didn't really have that much to do, but she was looking forward to the graduation party at Marjorie's this afternoon, and five days with her parents was more than enough togetherness for one visit.

The parking lot outside the Navy-Marine Corps Stadium, where the US Naval Academy Commencement Ceremony had been held, was still a saluting madhouse from the thousand or so newly commissioned ensigns and second lieutenants filling the area.

She'd seen a few silver dollar salutes—it was tradition that a newly commissioned officer flipped a silver dollar to the first person who saluted them—and it made her smile. In a place like the Academy, tradition sometimes felt like a mindless repetition of outdated acts, but silver dollar salutes held a special place in her heart.

Liz finally made it to her car, still parked on the Academy grounds, her arm tired from all the salutes. Brendan leaned against the hood, his lean body clad in the US Navy service dress white uniform. An overnight bag lay at his feet.

"I left my car parked over at Marje's. Mind if I get a ride?"

"Sure," Liz replied. She searched his face, looking for some clue about how he was feeling. He met her gaze, but gave her nothing.

Liz got behind the wheel of her 1999 Honda Accord. Both the trunk and the backseat were packed with her gear for her drive to Quantico early the next morning, so the front seats were moved forward. She drove down Admiral's Row, the Academy housing for senior officers, and past the chapel. A newly minted ensign was just coming down the wide stone steps with his bride on his arm.

"And so it begins," Brendan said, watching the couple walk through a sword arch. Naval Academy midshipmen were not allowed to marry, but that restriction was lifted once they graduated. The Academy Chapel would be doing weddings every hour for the next week to keep up with the demand.

"They'll be divorced in a year and you know it," Liz replied.

"Maybe."

Liz made the turn past the parade ground, toward the back gate.

"Ever wonder about us, Liz?"

She let out her breath in a rush. Did she ever.

"We've been through this, Bren. You're a SEAL, I'm a Marine. We're going different places . . . and we're not going to get there together. Maybe someday, but we owe it to ourselves to make the most of our separate lives first."

Did she really believe that? Brendan McHugh was her best friend and sometimes boyfriend, but more than anything he'd been there for her for all of the last four years. The familiar scenery of the parade ground slid by the car window, maybe for the last time. No one made it through the Academy on their own, and she couldn't remember a day in her time here when she hadn't at least talked to Brendan for five minutes. Was she really willing to give that up? Her head said yes; her heart . . . she wasn't sure what her heart was telling her.

On the other hand, she knew this was her moment. The 9/11 attack had changed everything for them, and her path lay in a different direction than Bren's. They laughingly called the Academy the Boat School, but behind the chuckles, the mission was deadly serious. They were professional military officers now, and they owed it to their country to repay their training with dedicated service.

Brendan punched her on the arm. "You're such a hard-ass, Liz. You'll make a good Marine."

Marje met them at her front door. "Oh, thank God you're here. I need some help setting up. Get out of those uniforms and meet me in the kitchen." She wagged her finger at them. "No fooling around, you two. I need your help now."

Another benefit to her and Brendan's friendship with Mark had been the fact that his mother lived in the Annapolis area. The Academy had a sponsorship program that paired midshipmen with local families, and Marje had been glad to sponsor Brendan, Liz, and Don Riley.

Their bond only deepened when Mark was killed in Iraq. Her son's death had taken its toll. Her beautiful auburn hair was shot with gray, and the deep lines that radiated from the corners of her eyes and lips looked permanent.

But at least she was happy today. It was probably the first time since the funeral that Liz had seen her really smile. She kissed Marje on the cheek. "I'll just be a minute."

Liz retreated to a spare bedroom and carefully hung up her service dress uniform. She slipped on a pair of cutoff jeans and a white bikini top, and she finger-combed her hair as she made her way back to the kitchen.

"What can I do?" she asked.

Marjorie looked up from a plate of cold cuts she was fussing over. "Don just got here with a whole pack of people. Can you get a badminton game started? Anything to keep them out of the house while I get the rest of the food ready."

Liz trotted down the lawn to where a group was crowded around a cooler of beer and soda. The Severn River sparkled at the base of the property and she could make out the Academy buildings on the opposite side of the river.

"Alright, who's up for some badminton?" Quickly, she organized two sides and got the game underway. By the time Brendan and Marjorie showed up, the other team was losing badly.

"Ensign McHugh," she called, "I think that team could use some help."

Before Brendan could answer, a tall blonde girl reached out and snagged his arm. "You can play on my side," she said with a smile. "I'm Milli, by the way, with an *i*."

Liz rolled her eyes. "Twelve serving three," she called and swatted the birdie.

Having Brendan on the opposing team definitely helped even the score, but it soon became clear to Liz that "Milli with an i" was playing her own game—and it wasn't badminton. She stuck to Brendan's side and seemed to be always touching him. Liz felt a spark of . . . what? Jealousy? She'd just spent that last week telling Brendan they needed to live their own lives; she was not jealous.

On the next rotation, she found herself opposite Milli on the net. The girl was tall, with an easy elegance that reminded Liz of her mother. Her full breasts were barely held in check by her pink bikini top and her blonde hair was pulled back in a ponytail that ran halfway down her long back. The hint of a sneer on Milli's model-perfect face made Liz want to duck under the net and use her racket as a weapon of opportunity.

Brendan stepped in front of Milli. "C'mon, Lizzie," he taunted her with a wicked grin. "Let's see what you got."

Liz ignored him, biding her time. It took a few volleys before Don could feed her the perfect set-up shot. The birdie arced high, coming down right where she needed it. Brendan went airborne, trying to get his racket over the net, but it was out of his reach. Liz waited until the last second, then leaped and spiked it across the net as hard as she could. The birdie flashed past Brendan's shoulder and nailed Milli right on the forehead.

Liz smiled through the net at Brendan and shrugged her shoulders. "Sorry."

Liz relaxed into the worn cushions of the sofa and closed her eyes.

Marjorie's den was cool and dark, lit only by one floor lamp with a dim bulb. The party was done and it was just the four of them now: Brendan, Marjorie, Don, and Liz. Apart from the whisper of the ceiling fan, the only sound in the room was the occasional clink of ice in their glasses.

Marjorie raised her glass toward Mark's picture on the wall, his Marine officer portrait. A wooden triangle with a folded flag under glass anchored the collection. "What is it you military types always say? 'To absent friends?'"

"To absent friends," they all echoed softly.

Liz's gaze roamed over the photographs, settling on the picture taken on Mark's graduation day. In typical Mark fashion, he'd managed to modify the silver dollar tradition to suit his needs: the picture showed him flipping *two* coins, one each to a saluting Liz and Brendan.

Liz nudged Brendan with her toe and nodded toward the shelf. He lifted a square gift box from one of the lower shelves and pulled his chair closer to Marjorie.

"Marje?"

Her gaze still rested on the picture of Mark. She started when Brendan called her name.

"We have a gift for you," Brendan said.

"Oh!" Marjorie sat up quickly. The ice clinked in her glass as she set it on the floor. "For me? You shouldn't have." Her fingers plucked at the bright ribbon. "It's almost too pretty to unwrap."

Liz laid her hand on Marjorie's. "Take your time, Marje."

The older woman ripped off the paper to reveal a jewelry box. She snapped the lid open, and stopped. The room was silent for a long moment.

Don tugged his chair closer. "It's a—"

"I know what it is, Don," Marjorie said. "It's the silver dollar from Mark's first salute." She looked at Liz and Brendan. "Which one of you did this?"

"It doesn't matter, Marje," Liz said gently. "We gave the other one to Don."

"I can't accept this, guys," Marjorie said. Her finger ran across the polished face of the coin. Liz bit her lip. That coin had been in her pocket since the day Mark had flipped it to her, and her fingers had worn the features smooth. She sneaked a glance at Brendan. Just another thing she was giving up to follow her dream.

"Just try it on," Liz said. They'd had the coin set in a handsome circular setting with an eyelet at the top for a chain. She lowered the necklace over Marjorie's head. The older woman held it up in the light, her eyes tearing up.

She reached out and pulled Liz and Brendan close. "Promise me. Promise me you'll stay safe and come home in one piece," she whispered.

Behind Marjorie's back, Liz found Brendan's hand and squeezed it hard.

CHAPTER 5

Abu Hamam, Syria
15 June 2006 – 1715 local

The land greened around them as they neared the Euphrates River. Hashem cracked open the window of the Range Rover. He could smell the moisture in the air now, a foreign scent after the unending dust of the desert.

"How much longer?" he asked the driver.

The driver consulted his dashboard GPS unit. "Fifteen minutes, Colonel."

Hashem nodded and shut his window, the interior of the car suddenly quiet again. He turned to his passenger. The man stiffened. Hashem pretended not to notice.

This was the best they could send him? This bundle of nerves was an explosives engineer? He took a deep breath to calm himself. He knew the man was probably more nervous about meeting a Quds Force colonel than about the training assignment, but still the man's nervous energy filled the air with tension.

The driver turned off the main highway to a rutted side road. He hit a pothole, the impact ringing through the car. The man beside Hashem lashed out with a curse.

"Slow down, you idiot!" the man screamed. "Do you want to blow us all to hell?"

The driver's jaw tightened, but he said nothing. Hashem smiled to himself. Maybe this engineer would work out after all.

The road wound through a short stand of trees, the driver taking extra care to avoid the deep ruts. They rounded a bend and the narrow thoroughfare opened onto a broad meadow. In the center of the clearing, atop a small rise, sat a two-story house, white paint peeling from the concrete in patches. Hashem grunted in satisfaction. Rafiq had chosen well. The sight lines were clear in all directions for at least three hundred meters and there were no neighbors nearby. He saw the shape of a dish antenna poking above the facade. They even had Internet.

There was a movement on the roof, and then a glint as a man lowered a pair of binoculars.

The door of the house opened and a slim man exited. Hashem hadn't seen his half brother in years, but the man did not seem to have aged a day. The Rover traversed the last few meters, then swung wide so as to deposit Hashem directly in front of the door.

Rafiq stood back to let the driver open Hashem's door. The ritual gave Hashem a precious few seconds to size up his new partner.

Rafiq Aboud's mother had been a fair-skinned, blonde Lebanese woman. Her genes had lightened her son's complexion to the point where he could have passed for a generic European or even an American. He'd been educated at a small liberal arts college in the American Midwest—paid for by Hashem—and spoke English like a native.

Rafiq eyed him as Hashem stepped out of the vehicle and

stretched, clearly willing to let his older brother make the first move. His cool gray eyes—their father's eyes—locked onto Hashem's without hesitation. Hashem realized with a start that it had been a long time since someone had looked at him without fear. His respect for his sibling went up a notch.

"Salaam, brother," Hashem said, opening his arms.

Rafiq took a step forward. The man was half a head shorter than him, but his body was knotted and wiry beneath Hashem's hands. His every movement was precise, a calculated expenditure of effort. Rafiq's cheek was clean-shaven and moist when Hashem kissed him.

"Salaam," he said, his voice neutral. "I trust your trip was comfortable?"

Hashem grunted. He waved his hand toward the engineer, who offered a nervous nod.

"Perhaps a tour before I offer you some tea?" Rafiq said, lifting his eyebrow.

The engineer cleared his throat. "Colonel . . . um, may I suggest we take the explosives out of the vehicle . . ."

Rafiq called into the open doorway and two men hustled out of the building to the back of the Range Rover. Hashem pegged them as Hezbollah, and men with experience. His brother knew how to pick men as well.

The engineer lifted the rear hatch and ran his hand over the cargo, looking for damage. Satisfied, he stepped back and indicated for the men to take the unlabeled boxes. Rafiq pulled a smaller carton from the stack and opened it. A three-inch device with wires on one end and a covered detector on the other fell into his hand.

"Passive IR trigger," he said to the engineer. "You can teach my men how to make EFPs?"

The engineer nodded excitedly, his nervousness gone. "Explosively formed projectiles are my specialty, sir, and PIR triggers are the latest in remote detonation technology. I—"

Rafiq held up his hand to stop the engineer's chatter. The man's jaw snapped shut, and a look of worry crept over his face again.

Rafiq caught Hashem's attention and gestured toward the door. "Please, brother, let me show you our operation."

The interior of the house was cool. Hashem noted the AK-47s, loaded, adjacent to every window in the room. A long table with benches took up most of the space, and a small kitchen area occupied the far wall. Everything looked neat and clean. They passed into the next room, this one filled with bunk beds. Hashem did a quick survey: twelve bunks, all neatly made, and the floor swept.

A heavy steel door was set into the concrete wall. There was a loud clunk as Rafiq turned the handle and swung the door wide. He grinned at Hashem. "This was one of the reasons I selected this place for the training. Self-preservation in the event of an accident."

The room beyond might have been a high-tech factory assembly line or a university cleanroom. The space was lit with overhead florescent lights, showing six men huddled over workbenches. They all wore white lab coats over their clothes and their long hair and beards were covered. Latex gloves covered their hands, and on each wrist the men wore bracelets that connected them to their workbench. Hashem raised his eyebrows and motioned with his head to the wrist tethers.

"ESD protection. Electrostatic discharge," Rafiq said quietly.

The men looked up briefly, then returned to their work. A set of instructions, complete with pictures, was laid out on the table before each man. A tray of ingredients occupied the space beside each workstation.

Rafiq continued in a whisper. "Iraqi Shiite freedom fighters. They are learning the basics of making an IED—improvised explosive device. Of course, in the field they would not have these elaborate safety precautions, but in this room even a small explosion would have catastrophic effects." He grinned at Hashem. "Caution is a virtue, is it not, brother?"

Hashem nodded slowly. He had always liked Rafiq, but his respect for his younger half brother was quickly growing. His investment in this young man's education—university and otherwise—was paying off nicely.

The explosives engineer's eyes widened and a grin spread across his face when he saw the training facilities. His nervousness evaporated as he became an instructor, pacing the room, coaching his students, and smiling when they succeeded.

At the end of the second day, Rafiq insisted that the engineer test each man individually on his skill and speed at assembling each type of explosive device. When this was done, Rafiq pointed at two of the men. "You have one hour to build an EFP with a passive IR triggering device. We will test them tonight."

The chosen men exchanged glances then headed back to the workshop. The Iranian engineer started to follow them, but Rafiq stopped him. "They work alone."

The whole crew ate a leisurely dinner as the sun set. Rafiq demonstrated an easy manner with his men, laughing with their jokes, but Hashem noted that they deferred to him in all things.

The men being tested joined them halfway through the meal. Rafiq called to them as they entered the room. "Any trouble? The weapons are ready for testing?"

The first man spoke in a confident voice. "Yes, Rafiq. I am ready." The second man shifted his feet before nodding.

"You seem less confident, Kaleel. Do you need some additional time?" The movement around the table ceased as the men watched Rafiq. Hashem noticed his brother's eyes—the gray had turned hard as stone as they bored into the man's face.

"You are ready?" he asked again.

The man swallowed, but returned Rafiq's gaze steadily. "I am ready, sir."

"You are certain?"

The man nodded.

"Good." Rafiq clapped his hands, then gestured to the two open spaces on the bench. "Eat. We have a long drive ahead of us tonight."

It was full dark by the time they finished the meal and cleaned up. Outside, the thinnest sliver of a waning moon was just topping the horizon. Hashem's Range Rover idled in the drive with a battered pickup truck parked behind it. He and his brother rode in the Rover along with one of Rafiq's Hezbollah men.

Within a few minutes, they'd left the greenery that surrounded the river basin and entered the open desert. The Rover picked up speed on the highway, the driver keeping an eye on the pickup truck behind them. Hashem watched the sliver of moon climb higher in the sky.

Rafiq called to the driver to take the next left. He slowed and turned into a wadi, the headlights showing the barest trace of a road. As the minutes passed, the walls around them rose, but the trail smoothed out into a passable road. The Rover hit a large pothole, throwing Hashem against Rafiq. "Pardon, brother," Hashem said.

Rafiq turned in his direction. His eyes were bright, his mouth half-open as if in expectation of a surprise. "You will be pleased, Hashem. Very pleased."

He called to the driver to halt and opened his door, stepping out before the vehicle had stopped. He was armed with an AK-47, as was his Hezbollah bodyguard. Hashem's hands instinctively touched his 9mm Stingray-C and the ivory handle of his knife before he exited the vehicle.

With the headlights extinguished, Hashem's night vision returned slowly. Rafiq spoke in Lebanese with his two Hezbollah men, while the Iraqis milled about, talking quietly and smoking. Hashem sniffed the cigarette smoke and resisted the urge to pull out his own pack of Marlboros. The Iraqis who had built the IEDs stood near the back of the pickup truck, two dark shapes resting on the tailgate.

Rafiq clapped his hands for attention. "We go on foot from here. You two"—he gestured at the Iraqis—"carry your devices. And follow us at a safe distance."

The group trudged deeper into the canyon, separating into small groups: the Hezbollah men with Hashem and Rafiq, the Iraqi trainees trailed by the Iranian engineer, and finally the two Iraqis carrying their improvised bombs. The trail took a turn into a wide canyon with a flat, sandy floor.

Rafiq called the Iraqis with the bombs to the front of the column. He placed his hand on the shoulder of the shorter, more confident bomb-maker, and with his other hand he pointed to a small pile of rocks three hundred meters away. "Place your device there with the PIR trigger facing to the east." His palm floated to the arm of the thin Iraqi. Even in the dimness, Hashem could see the sheen of sweat gleaming on the man's forehead. "You place your device by that outcropping, with the detector facing west." The man's eyes followed Rafiq's finger to a spot a hundred meters closer to them.

It took the two men a half hour to set up the IEDs on the improvised road. Meanwhile, one of the Hezbollah men disappeared and returned driving an older-model American Humvee.

Rafiq's smile was a slash of white in the darkness. "A training aid courtesy of our Syrian friends."

Hashem took a step closer to the idling vehicle. The top was scarred from shrapnel and the doors were missing. It was obvious the truck had been pieced together from bombed-out units. He grunted in satisfaction.

"I am impressed, Rafiq," he said, loudly enough for all the men to hear. "My country's money is well spent."

"Now for the fireworks, Colonel," Rafiq replied. He called to the Hezbollah man driving the Humvee, and Hashem watched as the man pushed a piece of wood through the open space on the steering wheel. The driver braced one end on the dash and snugged the other against the seat cushions before putting the vehicle in gear. He put a second brace against the gas pedal and accelerated down the track toward the IEDs. When he was 150 meters from the first bomb, he jumped from the vehicle and lay flat on the ground.

Rafiq handed a pair of night vision binoculars to Hashem and raised another pair to his eyes. Together, they watched as the Humvee coasted past the first IED.

Nothing happened.

Rafiq grunted as if he had been punched, and Hashem could hear his brother's teeth grind together.

The Humvee continued along the track toward the second IED. Hashem squinted through the greenish night vision sight at the tiny bump next to the pile of stones.

A flash of light filled his field of view, followed by a shock wave that nearly knocked him down. Hashem's ears rang, but he could dimly hear the Iraqis cheering behind him. Their celebration grew louder as his hearing returned.

"A great victory, brother," he said to Rafiq.

"Not a great victory, Colonel. A failure." His voice was tight with rage. He approached the group of Iraqis, who shrank back until the tall thin one was standing alone. Rafiq poked him in the chest. "You. Go fix your IED. We will run the test again."

"Sir, that is not recommended," the explosives engineer interrupted. "The IED will have been destabilized by the other blast. The PIR might be damaged . . ." The man's voice trailed off as Rafiq turned on him.

Rafiq cocked his head as if he were speaking to a small child or a pet. When he spoke, his voice was silky. "Would you like to join him?" The Iranian engineer gulped and took a step back. He tried to catch Hashem's eye, but Hashem ignored him.

The Iraqi's hands shook as he clasped them in front of his chest. "Please, sir. I promise I will do better next time—"

"This is your next time, you stupid fuck. Move."

The man staggered slightly as he left the group, but some amount of resolve seemed to have returned. Rafiq watched him through the binoculars until he was certain the man was going to complete the task. He motioned to one of his Hezbollah men. "If that idiot actually manages to disarm the bomb, kill him." He turned to the explosives engineer. "He failed your course, Professor. Teach them better."

He waved his arm for the group to head back to the vehicles. There was a stirring among the Iraqis, but a word from the Hezbollah man quieted them.

Just before they arrived at the Range Rover, they heard the explosion, muffled by distance and the twisting canyons.

Hashem settled against the soft leather cushions of the Range Rover. Rafiq climbed into the seat beside him, and sat very still.

"I'm sorry you had to see that, brother. I failed you."

"Picking the right man is a tricky business, Rafiq. The Iraqi was a liability—you did the right thing. The rest of them will work that much harder." He paused. "And you will get my full support to expand your operation in Iraq. Whatever you need, just ask."

Rafiq bowed his head. "I will not let you down, Colonel."

"There is one more thing, my brother," Hashem said.

"Name it."

Hashem slid a slim mobile phone from his pocket. He pressed the phone into Rafiq's palm and covered it with his own hands.

"Keep this phone with you at all times, Rafiq. I may have a special assignment for you . . . a task that can only be entrusted to a member of the family."

CHAPTER 6

The briefing room was packed.

Brendan swore to himself. All the briefings were crowded now, ever since the surge troops had started arriving last month, but this was worse than normal. He picked up a briefing packet and stood near the back of the room between an Australian Army captain and a Royal Air Force major. *Like the friggin' United Nations around here.* He gave a brusque nod as they brushed elbows.

The cover page told him the CIA briefing today was for the commander of CJSOTF-Arabian Peninsula. Brendan searched the front of the room for General TJ Haskins, an Army one-star who had been running the Combined Joint Special Ops Task Force for the last four months. The general's icy blue eyes were fixed on the empty podium, his face set in a scowl.

Brendan checked his watch. One minute past the hour. His eyes flicked over to Haskins. If there was one thing the general hated it was tardiness, and he usually made his feelings known in colorful terms. Most of these briefings were painfully dull; this one might prove entertaining.

He checked the podium to see who was briefing today. The CIA guys tended to keep to themselves, but after four months in country and dozens of briefings, you got to know them by reputation. Brendan suppressed a smile; there must be an issue with the projector. Two backsides were facing the audience, one covered in BDUs and the other—wider and softer in appearance—in civilian clothes.

"Lieutenant Mason, we're three minutes behind schedule. What seems to be the problem?" said General Haskins in a voice that could scratch glass. Chuckles went around the room. Haskins silenced them with a glare.

The uniformed ass became a red-faced head with a blond crewcut. "Sir, we're still having connection issues with the microphone. I'll look into another conference room and we can reschedule—"

"The hell you will! I'm not about to waste another second. Tell your CIA friend to use his big-boy voice and project to the back of the room. Do I make myself clear?"

"Yes, sir," the staffer replied. He bent over the still-kneeling form of the chubby CIA analyst and spoke to him urgently. There was a loud crack as the microphone was disconnected and both men stood up.

Brendan caught his breath. The CIA analyst was Don Riley.

His former plebe made a vain attempt to tuck his shirttail back into his pants. His belly bulged over his belt and strained against the buttons of his dress shirt. Don's face was red despite the frigid air blasting through the room, and he wiped sweat from his forehead with a bandanna handkerchief that he pulled from his hip pocket.

"Good afternoon. My name is Donald Riley—"

"Louder," someone called from the back of the room.

Don's voice strained as he pushed up the volume. "My name is Donald Riley, and I'd like to brief you on a terrorist cell we've been tracking for a few months now."

The room fell silent as Don put up the first slide, a bomb crater at least twenty meters across. Twisted metal, bits of trash, and body parts littered the churned-up earth.

"Amiril, earlier this month. One hundred and fifty-six dead."

The slide shifted, showing another bomb scene.

"Earlier this week, truck bombing in Kirkuk. Eighty-six people killed."

The room was silent except for the whirr of the air conditioning.

"What do these two events have in common?"

The next slide showed an Iranian ayatollah—Brendan couldn't remember which one—and Don's voice was drowned out by the coughing of the RAF officer next to him.

"We have solid intelligence that Iran, working with Lebanese Hezbollah, is providing materiel and funds to a select Shia militia. The bombings in the north at Kirkuk and Amiril were test cases of the militia, a way to try out their latest tactics using newer and more powerful bombs."

"Tell us something we don't already know, G-man," someone said in a stage whisper. A ripple of laughter ran around the room.

The general ripped off his glasses and tossed them on the briefing book. He rubbed his eyes for a long moment. Brendan held his breath. Haskin's reputation as a hard-ass was well known, and it looked like Don was about to get a face full of one-star justice.

Haskins adjusted his spectacles on the table so they were square with the edge of the briefing book and laced his finger together. He squinted at Don. "Son, is this your first briefing?"

"Yes, sir."

The room grew tense, and everyone leaned forward. Brendan closed his eyes.

"Just get in country?"

"Yes, sir, I arrived this morning."

"Where's the regular briefer?"

Don gulped. "Sick, sir."

"So your boss has the shits, the microphone dies on you, and you get me as your first briefing?"

"Yes, sir."

Brendan cracked open an eyelid.

General Haskins offered Don a grim smile. "You must have really pissed off someone in a former life, Riley. Here's what I want you to do. Our motto here is Find, Fix, and Finish. I want you to find me some bad guys, fix eyes on them, and I'll go finish them. Now fast-forward through the history lesson and give me some actionable intelligence—something I can raid, someone I can kill, some fucking building I can blow up that gets me incrementally closer to ending this fucking war. Can you do that for me, son?"

Don nodded. He fast-forwarded through a dozen slides or so, stopping on the grainy image from a Predator drone camera. It showed three buildings arranged inside a high-walled compound. He stepped back and lit the first building with his laser pointer. Don drew in a deep breath and spoke in a loud voice.

"This is a known terrorist cell near the town of Kalar, a few kilometers from the Sirwan River and just over the border from Iran." The next slide showed a map with Kalar highlighted and the Iran–Iraq border painted in red. "The cell consists of approximately ten members and has been under regular surveillance for the past month. Normally, they are quiet, more bark than bite, but two weeks ago that started to change."

He shifted to a thermal imagery shot. The number of bodies in the buildings had more than doubled. The next series of slides showed truck deliveries and men off-loading boxes and weapons. Don hit his stride as he rattled off details about the site.

"We have solid HUMINT that this cell is receiving Iranian arms shipments and technical support. We believe this is the right time to raid this site and capture as many as possible for interrogation."

"Now we're talking, Riley," Haskins said, nodding. "Captain, what's your take?"

Captain Andrews leaned back in his chair and pursed his lips at the screen. As Naval Special Warfare Task Group Commander, his SEALs would lead the raid to take down the insurgents. "I need minimum three hours to prep the raid, sir. Eight would be better."

"You've got four hours." Haskins twisted in his seat. "Colonel James," he said to the senior Army intelligence officer. "I want eyes on this site full time. Make sure we know everything they know. Report any change in patterns to Captain Andrews's team immediately." He raised his voice. "Where's my RAF rep?"

The man next to Brendan piped up with a sharp, "Here, sir."

Haskin's eyes swept past Brendan, landing on the Royal Air Force major next to him. "Your team has close air support on this operation?"

"Affirmative, sir."

The general nodded and looked around the room. "Alright, people, our CIA friends have given us what we need, so let's lock it down and sweep these bastards up. I want to see full mission briefs by 1800." The general stood, signifying the end of the meeting.

The mass of men began to move toward Brendan's position near the exit. He angled for the wall and fought against the tide of uniformed bodies toward Don.

When he arrived at the front of the room, Haskins was still talking with Don. Don saw Brendan emerge from the crowd and a look of shock crossed his face. The general must have noted it, because he turned toward Brendan.

Brendan felt his face grow hot. "I'm sorry, sir. I didn't mean to interrupt. Mr. Riley and I know each other . . ."

Haskins's eyes drifted down to Brendan's name badge. "Really, McHugh? How do you know a CIA analyst?"

"He was my plebe, sir. At the Academy."

The general's eyebrows went up, and his skeptical gaze swept over Don's out-of-shape physique. "I suppose that's a story for another time." He held out his hand to Don. "Good briefing, Riley. Rough start, but you got the hang of it. Welcome to the war, son."

Don wiped his palm on his pants before accepting the general's hand. "Thank you, sir," he said, coloring slightly. Brendan stood aside to let the general pass and they were alone in the empty room.

"You're the last person I expected to see here, Don," Brendan began. "How did you—" He stopped when Don looked down at the floor, blinking his eyes.

When he finally spoke, his voice was husky. "It wasn't my fault, Bren. I swear it. It was at the end of youngster year," he said, using Academy slang for his sophomore year. "I got sick—really sick. Abdominal stuff, you know, and before I knew it I was medically NPQ'd." Brendan winced at the term for being found "not physically qualified" to continue in the United States Navy.

"It was the worst thing that could have happened to me, and I— I was so ashamed. All I wanted to do was serve my country, and for six months, I couldn't be more than five minutes from a toilet. It was awful. I just went home and lived like a hermit. Then, one day, the CIA knocked on my front door. Remember at the end of my plebe year I helped Professor Klaus write that paper on organic cryptology? You know, encoding messages in DNA?"

Brendan had no idea what Don was talking about, but he nodded his head anyway.

"Well, somebody at the CIA read it and they called me up. The fucking CIA, Bren! They offered me a full scholarship to MIT. I got my health together and finished in two years. Now I work as an analyst in the National Counterproliferation Center in DC. Pretty cool, huh?" Don was smiling now. This was the Don he remembered. Brendan punched him lightly in the arm. "Good for you, Riley. You were a shitty plebe anyway. This new gig suits you."

"Yeah, I guess I was. If it hadn't been for you and Liz I never would have made it through plebe year. How's Liz, by the way? Is she here, too?"

It was Brendan's turn to look at the floor. "I don't know. I haven't talked to Liz since the grad party at Marjorie's."

When they went their separate ways after graduation, rather than remind himself how much he missed her, it seemed easier to just not talk to Liz. Then the not talking became a habit, and pretty soon Brendan was too embarrassed to call her. At first, Marjorie pestered him to call Liz, but after a while even she stopped.

"Really?" Don's eyebrows were raised. "After I got kicked out of the Academy, I was too ashamed to keep in touch with anyone, even Marjorie, but I figured you two would always be together."

Brendan shook his head. "Well, you figured wrong, buddy." It was strange how talking to Don made him suddenly want to call Liz, like their conversation had triggered some strange need to reconnect with his once best friend. He wondered what she was doing right now.

Brendan's phone buzzed in his pocket. He pulled it out and saw it was his task unit commander, Lieutenant Commander Radek. "This is Lieutenant McHugh, sir," he answered.

"Brendan, I need you back at home base on the double. You're on the mission tonight."

CHAPTER 7

The walls of the compound glowed an eerie, pale green through the lens of Brendan's night vision goggles. His earpiece crackled and Radek's voice said: "Five minutes to go. McHugh's team will breach the wall."

Brendan dialed the volume up a touch. When things got hot, he wanted to make sure he could hear Radek over the background noise.

He squirmed deeper into the dirt. The land around him was rock, sand, and a few scrubby trees—not much cover. Even though the sun had gone down hours ago, the ground beneath him was still warm, and the gentle desert breeze did nothing to cool him off.

The only sign of life was a lone dog barking from a cluster of houses a few hundred yards away. The entire area was without power tonight, thanks to US control of the power grid in this part of Iraq. These people rarely had more than a few hours of electricity a day anyway, so no one would think anything amiss. Some of the houses, including the one in front of him, surely had generators, but fuel was too valuable to waste on electricity and lights would only attract unwanted visitors.

Radek's whisper floated in his ear as his OIC acknowledged their air support: two RAF Tornados were somewhere up in the moonless sky, each with enough ordnance to level the compound in front of them many times over. They also had a Quick Reaction Force of an additional sixteen SEALs on fifteen-minute standby.

Brendan waited for the final call to engage from CJSOTF. Before that, Radek would get a final sitrep from the intel team. In the situation room back in the Green Zone, there would be live feed from the on-station Reaper UAV up on the big screen. The drones were piloted out of air-conditioned secure trailers on Creech Air Force Base, half a world away in Nevada.

"Standby for final head count," Radek's voice whispered in Brendan's ear. Brendan tensed and pictured the compound in his head. "We have a total of nine, I repeat nine, hostiles in two locations. Two are in the main house on the second floor, six in the east building, probably a bunkhouse. IR indicates the lone guard just went to take a leak. Be advised we want live captures, if possible.

"McHugh's team will breach the wall and take the main house, my team has the bunkhouse. McHugh, you are cleared to place the charges."

Brendan keyed his microphone. "Roger, team leader." His hands automatically checked his weapons: M4A1, the Sig Sauer P226 on his hip, the Bowie knife strapped to his calf. He shifted his torso inside his Kevlar vest as he came up on one knee and signaled to his team. The men moved as a unit over the next hundred meters, crouching low, the only sound the whisper of sand under their boots. Three men remained at the recover point to provide covering fire, while the rest continued to the wall. Two men placed charges eight feet apart, working quickly to outline a makeshift doorway. They retreated to their rally point.

"Charges in place, team leader," Brendan whispered into his mike.

"Blow it."

"Fire in the hole." Brendan nodded to his demolition expert and put his face in the dirt to save his night vision. The trigger man punched the remote, radio-frequency trigger.

The muffled explosion, like someone had slammed a door, rang through the night air. His team was on their feet before the echo had even faded, racing through a rain of concrete and cinder block chunks.

The first few seconds were the most critical of any raid—those few moments when the targets were roused from sleep by the noise, stunned, unsure whether the sound was real or part of a dream. Before any lights were turned on or weapons found in the dark. Those first few seconds made all the difference between a high body count and a successful raid.

Brendan's team burst through the cloud of dust that filled the gap in the compound wall and made a sharp left toward the two-story house. The first two men in the team hit the wall on either side of the door, while the third man shot through the lock and kicked the door open. The first two tossed in flash-bangs, and the glass on the windows next to them blew out as the concussion grenades went off. Weapons raised, they entered the room and fanned out.

"Clear!"

Brendan rushed in with two more men behind him. The sharp smell of the expended grenade lodged in his nostrils. He dimly heard more flash-bangs being detonated from the direction of the bunkhouse, followed by sharp bursts of automatic weapons fire.

The first team took the back room on the ground floor, while Brendan's team took the stairs to the second floor. The muscle memory of "kill house" tactics took over. As the first man, Brendan stood by the door as the rest of his team stacked in tight single file behind him. He kicked open the flimsy door. The flash-bang was in his hand and through the door before he even formed the thought in his head. He closed his eyes.

Bang.

Eyes open, weapon up, through the door. Scan.

Two targets registered in his senses. The first held a handgun.

Brendan released two shots to the man's chest and a third to the head.

Shift.

The second man raised his arms.

Calls of "Clear!" sounded from his left and right as the rest of the team swept the room.

"Take him down," Brendan shouted back. The other two SEALs rushed at the target while Brendan kept his rifle trained on him. They forced the man to his knees, and Brendan heard the sound of zip ties being tightened. The pair heaved their prisoner to his feet and patted him down. One let out a low whistle as they pulled out a long knife from a sheath in the small of the man's back. In the ghostly green of the night-vision goggles, the handle glowed a brilliant white. The SEAL handed Brendan the knife, a Zippo lighter, and a half-used pack of Marlboros from the man's breast pocket before marching him to the door. The captive's jaw quivered as the SEALs forced him to step over his comrade's corpse.

The assault team met in the dirt yard formed between the three buildings and the wall. One of the SEALs had found a generator and energized the lights. The team who had raided the bunkhouse frog-walked their prisoners into a line and forced them to their knees. In the harsh illumination of the floodlights, the prisoners looked confused and a little frightened, their hair matted with sleep and their dirty beards bent into all sorts of odd shapes.

Brendan saw that most of them were his age, maybe even younger.

All except the man he had taken down in the upstairs bedroom. He was old enough to be Brendan's father. Their commander? Brendan studied him in the white glare of the spotlights.

Whereas most of the captives stared at the ground or exchanged furtive glances with one another, this man returned Brendan's gaze without fear. His dark eyes, icy with confidence, were set in a thin, handsome face. Despite having been roused from bed, he looked fresh and alert, and his short-cropped hair, shot with gray at the temples, was neatly trimmed around his ears. A few days' worth of stubble coated his chin. Unlike the others, he was dressed in tan trousers and shirt, and his breast pocket was still undone from when the SEAL had removed his pack of cigarettes.

There was something else, the way the man wore his clothes . . . like a uniform. This guy was military, Brendan was sure of it.

Brendan weighed the knife in his hand. Then he stepped forward and slid the cigarettes back into the man's shirt pocket.

"Thank you," the man said, in perfect English.

Brendan's thoughts were interrupted by Radek. "McHugh, what's your status?"

Brendan turned away from the prisoner. "Two hostiles in the upstairs bedroom. I took one out, this one surrendered. He was carrying this." He hefted the blade in his hand. The slight curve of the handle seemed to mold to his palm.

Radek let out a low whistle. "Wow, dibs on that, McHugh. That is a beautiful we—"

"I don't think so, Commander," the prisoner said.

Radek's eyebrows went up, and Brendan said, smiling, "Oh, and he speaks English really good, too."

"Well," the man replied.

"What?" Radek asked.

"He speaks English really *well*, not really *good*. 'Well' is an adverb that modifies the verb 'speak,' while 'good' is an adjective which can only be used to modify a noun." The man gave them a smug smile. "May I have a cigarette, please, Commander?"

"I don't fucking believe this," Radek said. "I'm getting fucking grammar lessons on my own fucking language from an Iraqi in the middle of the fucking Iraq desert."

The sound of the UH-60 Black Hawk helo landing outside the compound made conversation difficult for the next few minutes. A wave of dust rolled through the breach in the wall, followed by the Sensitive Site Exploitation Team, whose job it was to strip the compound of anything that might be useful: cell phones, laptops, maps, papers, anything that wasn't nailed down.

Radek held up three fingers to the team lead to indicate he needed three body bags. The man nodded and spoke into a handheld radio. Radek raised his voice: "Alright, let's get bags over their heads and get them loaded on the Black Hawk. I—"

"I won't be going anywhere, Commander." The older prisoner's icy voice cut through the background noise and made Radek pause. Brendan saw his OIC ball up a fist, and for a moment, Brendan thought Radek might punch their captive. He took another step closer to the kneeling man.

"Bag this guy, McHugh. And if he says another word, gag him."

"That would not be a wise move, Commander." The man smiled at Brendan. "Lieutenant, could you please retrieve my passport from my bedside table upstairs? I think we can clear this up quickly and I can be on my way."

Radek's eyes narrowed, then he gave Brendan a tight nod. "Take one of the EOD guys with you, Bren. I don't want any surprises."

Radek needn't have bothered; the drawer was half-open already, the Iranian diplomatic passport in full view. Brendan realized the man must have been reaching for it when the raid started. The dark maroon cover was worn, and the gold letters faded, but Brendan could make out the title: Islamic Republic of IRAN. On the inside of the back cover was the inscription, "the holder of the passport is not entitled to travel to occupied Palestine," which Brendan knew meant Israel. He flipped to the inside cover. The man's unsmiling picture was there, along with his diplomatic clearance. Alizera Mogadaham was his name.

He beckoned to one of the techs who was taking pictures of the room. He placed the passport on the nightstand, open to the picture page, and laid the knife next to it. "Get some pictures of these things," he said, "and see if you can get a couple of shots of the older guy in the courtyard—without being too obvious about it." Normally, they didn't photograph their captives until processing in the Green Zone, but he wanted to make sure they got something.

Brendan collected the photographed items and returned to the dusty courtyard. All the other prisoners were gone and the Iranian was on his feet, his hands still bound behind his back. His eyes lit up when he saw Brendan return with the passport in his hand.

"Lieutenant McHugh," he said with a thin smile. "You found it. Excellent."

Somehow, the fact that this man knew his name made Brendan pause. He handed the passport to Radek, and his OIC's lips pursed as he studied the document. Radek gave a brief nod to the SEAL standing by to take the Iranian to the helo. "Cut him loose." He keyed his mike. "Black Hawk, you are cleared to fly. Our final passenger has opted to stay behind."

Brendan heard the reply in his earpiece. "Roger. Black Hawk, out."

The rotor tempo increased, and another wave of dust rolled through the wall breach. Silence fell over the courtyard as the helo lifted away.

Radek snapped the passport shut and handed it to the Iranian, along with his lighter. "Well, Mr. Mogadaham, it looks like this is your lucky day. Mind if I ask how you came to be here in the first place?"

The Iranian took his time tapping out a cigarette. He slid the crushed red and white Marlboro pack back into his breast pocket and rebuttoned the flap. He made a great show of straightening out the bent cigarette and lighting it with his Zippo. The flame from his lighter flashed in his eyes. He took a deep drag on the cigarette and held the smoke in his lungs for a long moment.

"Yes, I do mind, Commander." He exhaled as he spoke, a wreath of smoke obscuring his face.

Radek stared at him through the smoke. "I see. Well, you're free to go, sir."

The Iranian turned to Brendan. "Lieutenant McHugh, my knife, please."

Brendan started. He had forgotten he still had the weapon. He extracted the knife from a cargo pocket in his pants and flipped it around to hand it over hilt first. The perfectly balanced blade moved as if it had a will of its own.

"It's a beautiful piece, sir. Is the handle ivory?"

The man nodded through another cloud of smoke. "Yes, ivory. It's been with me a long time." He accepted the blade and it disappeared behind his back. He crushed the cigarette beneath his shoe. "A very long time."

Mr. Alizera Mogadaham, Iranian diplomat, made a stiff bow to Brendan and Radek.

"Gentlemen, I believe the American saying is: 'it's been real.'"

He brushed between Brendan and Radek, stepped carefully over the remains of the breached wall, and disappeared into the darkness.

CHAPTER 8

Tehran, Iran
15 September 2007 – 1330 local

Hashem left the sound on the TV muted. He couldn't bear to listen to Al Jazeera's never-ending rant about how the American troop surge and the Sunni Awakening were carrying the day, pushing back the militias in Iraq, including *his* Shiite militias.

His fingers itched for another cigarette, but he only had two left, and he would need them after the meeting with Aban. He thought about calling his driver—his new driver, he reminded himself—to fetch another pack. He sighed. He never realized how much he missed Delir until the man was gone.

Hashem blushed when he thought of that night in Iraq. How could he have been so stupid as to let himself get captured by the Americans? They had his picture now, and anonymity was an intelligence operative's best friend. The false name would throw them off the scent for a while, but he was now "in the system," as the

Americans would say. Eventually, they would find out his real identity.

He looked at his watch and cursed. Aban was making him wait. He extracted the second-to-last cigarette from the pack and sparked his lighter. Drawing deeply, he let the smoke fill his lungs, calming him.

Hashem called out sharply and the door snapped open. His new driver stepped into the room. Thick muscles rippled under his suit and his shaved head merged into his shoulders, eliminating the need for a neck. "Sir?" he said, coming to attention.

He waved the package of Marlboros. "Find me more of these."

The man's brow knitted together. "Yes, sir. Where do you get them?"

Hashem waved his hand and blew a stream of smoke toward him. "Figure it out." The door snapped shut.

Strong, loyal, and with the creativity of a teacup.

He sparked the lighter again, a gift from Delir. How many years ago? He couldn't even remember now. He recalled how the man used to smile secretly every time Hashem lit a cigarette. Every single time.

Delir—even his name meant "brave." That night in Iraq he had seen Hashem reaching for his knife, and he had drawn the American SEAL's fire. The American, McHugh, was twenty-six? Maybe twenty-seven? Not a single gray hair in his stubbly beard, and he had gunned down loyal Delir in less than two seconds.

He stared sightlessly at the TV and clutched the lighter in his palm. The picture showed a US soldier handing out candy to a child in Iraq. Candy. They were going to win this war with fucking chocolate.

"Brother? Am I interrupting?"

Hashem whirled around, his hand instinctively going to the small of his back.

Aban stood in the doorway, his hands folded across his stomach, eyebrows arched. Awaiting the ritual.

Hashem dropped to one knee, head bowed. "Forgive me, Eminence. I—I was lost in thought."

Aban let him kneel longer than normal, and when he bid him rise it was more command than encouragement. The traditional kiss on each cheek was cold, formal.

Hashem poured fresh cups of tea for both of them and they sat down.

Aban gestured at the TV. "So this is where we are. The Americans are winning in Iraq with their surge and the Israelis attack a peaceful nuclear reactor with impunity. This is what we pay you for?"

Hashem's jaw tightened. Aban was referring to Operation Orchard, the Israeli attack on a Syrian nuclear installation. Whatever one wanted to say about the Israelis, they did not lack for balls. A pinpoint air strike into a neighboring hostile country, with not a single casualty . . . breathtakingly bold. And their operational control was equally impressive. Hashem's network had not even felt a tremor of suspicion about the raid before it happened.

"Disappointing" was all Hashem managed to say.

"Disappointing?" Aban snorted as he adjusted the robes of his office over his growing belly. Hashem's holy man brother was getting fatter. Aban waved his hand at the cup of tea. "A cup of cold tea is disappointing. An enemy strike against our friendly neighbors is . . . is . . . deeply concerning." His look indicated he was not satisfied with that description either.

Aban's jowly face quivered as he frowned at his brother. "I am worried, Hashem. Worried that we, too, underestimate our enemies. Even you, my cautious brother, were captured by them! How?"

Hashem felt his face reddening. "It was"—he almost used the word *disappointing* again, but stopped himself—"unfortunate. An unfortunate confluence of events. They could not have known I was there, and my diplomatic credentials freed me immediately."

"And your dead driver?"

Hashem felt a prickle of rage at the way his brother needled him about the death of a good man. His fingers found the table leg and he gripped it until the muscles of his forearm ached. "Collateral damage," he said, as evenly as possible. "The Americans shoot first and ask questions later."

Aban harrumphed. "Tell me about your trip to Syria."

Hashem almost sighed out loud. Finally, something positive he could talk about with his brother. He forced a smile as he briefed Aban on the details of Rafiq's explosives training for Iraqi Shia militia.

Aban pursed his lips. "Tell me about this Rafiq. Can he be trusted?"

Hashem shrugged. "He's my brother, half brother—"

"Bastard half brother by a Lebanese whore," Aban interrupted him.

Hashem paused, then continued carefully. "He is illegitimate, that is true, but I found him to be loyal to our cause, and very capable."

The truth was more complicated. He and Aban shared the same mother. Aban's father had died when he was just a child, and his mother remarried a Lebanese mining expert who had been lured to Iran by the oil-rich Shah. Tamir Aboud had been good to Aban, legally adopting him and paying for an expensive Western education—in mining science, of course.

Hashem had been born within a year of his mother's remarriage, growing up in the heyday of the Shah's power. He'd adored his older brother and his father. Hashem wanted nothing more in life than to become a mining expert and travel the world with them discovering oil deposits and gold mines.

His world came apart when the Shah fell. Their wealth evaporated overnight, their place in society went into free-fall, and his father began spending more and more time out of the country. One day they received a telegram that his father was dead. Heart attack, that was what his mother said, but he knew from the way she acted there was more to it than that. He managed to get a look at the telegram and wrote down the name and address of the woman who sent it.

Tamir's body never even came back to Iran. He was buried in Lebanon. Aban and his mother changed their surnames back to Rahmani—Aban's father. When Hashem asked why, they changed the subject.

Hashem kept the slip of paper with the mysterious woman's name for many years, along with his favorite photograph of his brother, his father, and himself on a prospecting expedition, the same trip where they'd found the cave. Even today, he could recall every detail of that excursion, how they had laughed and sweated and walked and talked together for three glorious weeks. He never wanted that trip to end.

It wasn't until Hashem had entered Iranian intelligence, well after his time as a draftee in the War against Iraq that lasted most of the '80s, that he decided to find out more about the woman. It was a simple search, really, something he could have done years ago. Finally, with shaking fingers he dialed her number one night.

"Hello?" The woman's voice was soft and low, almost musical.

"Hello, may I speak with Jamila?"

"Speaking."

Hashem almost hung up. What should he say? He cleared his throat.

"Tamir Aboud was my father. My name is Hashem."

There was a long pause on the other end of the line. "Does your mother or brother know you are calling me?"

"No. Who are you?"

Another lengthy pause. The phone line crackled, and Hashem thought they might have been disconnected.

"Hello," he said. "Are you there?"

"I'm here. What do you want from me?"

"You knew my father?"

She laughed. "How old are you, Hashem?"

"Twenty-three."

"Old enough, I suppose," she said. "I was your father's lover. And I was with him when he died."

Hashem sucked in a breath. It all made sense now—the name changes, the lack of a funeral, everything.

"I see," was all he could think to say.

"Do you know about your brother—half brother, I mean?"

I have another brother? "No," he said in a whisper.

"His name is Rafiq, and he's eight. I was pregnant when your father died. He never saw his Lebanese son."

Now it was Hashem's turn to take a lengthy pause. "Is he a good boy?" he asked finally.

The woman laughed. "That is a question your father would have asked, Hashem. And, yes, he is a good boy. You should meet him."

Hashem cleared his throat. "Perhaps it is time we considered a back-up plan, brother."

Aban sipped his tea. "Meaning?"

"The Israeli strike on Syria is only the beginning. The Americans are regaining lost ground in Iraq and their political rhetoric is turning against us again. If they choose to take action against our nuclear program, it would be good to have options for a counterattack."

"What do you have in mind?"

"I want to share our secret cache with Hezbollah—but only with Rafiq. Hold some of our power in reserve for a secret strike."

Aban slurped his tea. "You can trust this bastard?"

"The circumstances of his birth are not his fault, Aban. He is a good man, a loyal man."

"But is he strong, Hashem? Does he have the iron will necessary to make hard choices?"

Hashem thought of Rafiq sending the Iraqi militiaman back to defuse his own bomb. "I am sure of it, brother."

CHAPTER 9

The waters of the Persian Gulf lapped gently against the pilings of the dock.

Rafiq breathed through his mouth to avoid the stink of the waterfront, a nasty blend of dead fish, human sewage, and rotting seaweed. The edges of the moon were fuzzy from the humidity in the air. He eyed the ship tied up next to them on the pier.

A breakbulk freighter was what Hashem had called it, meaning the vessel carried cargo that wasn't loaded in standard shipping containers. Rafiq guessed the vessel was 150 feet long, with a white, winged bridge that stood like a giant cross over the cluttered deck. In the shadows under the prow of the ship he could make out the name painted on the hull: *Lumba*. Hashem had said it was the Malay word for "dolphin."

This is where I'll spend the next three months of my life.

Rafiq kept his face still, but inside his mind churned. He was a rising star in Hezbollah. They needed him, he needed them—it was a symbiotic relationship that suited him just fine.

It was his Hezbollah brothers who had taken a lost, fatherless fourteen-year-old boy and taught him how to belong, gave him something to believe in. He often wondered about the depth of his religious belief. He said the words, he made the required motions, but what he really loved—what he really believed in—was the violence. The planning, the watching, the execution of the raid, the way the shock waves from the explosions would tickle his flesh, the way the AK-47 kicked in his hands when bullets sang out . . . it was better than any woman he'd ever had.

That was why he chose Hezbollah. He adjusted his trousers, glad for the poor lighting of the dock. Just the thought of his last raid made him hard.

"Rafiq?" Hashem said, his tone impatient. "Shall we have a look at the hold area?"

"Of course, brother."

Brother—the word still sounded foreign on his tongue.

Rafiq had seen his half brother more in the last year than in the twenty years prior. He could still recall his first meeting with Hashem: he, an awkward and lonely boy of ten, and Hashem, a young man with the bearing and uniform of an Iranian military officer. This was before he'd met his Hezbollah brothers, before he'd found a home in Lebanon. He'd hung on to Hashem's every word, wanting this strange young man to like him.

Hashem had spoken to Rafiq's mother first, and he came full of brotherly wisdom. Stay in school, be a good boy. The meeting was awkward for both of them on so many levels that it was almost too painful to recall.

That all changed after the Hezbollah attack on Khobar Towers in

Saudi Arabia. Rafiq was only sixteen at the time, but his role in the attack was an important one. In the intervening years, Hashem had secured a place in the Iranian Quds Force, and Rafiq had entrenched himself in Hezbollah. His small but crucial role in Khobar Towers had put him back on Hashem's radar.

Their second meeting went very differently. Hashem showed up in civilian clothes, his quiet confidence filling the room along with the smoke from his ever-present Marlboros. There was no visit to Rafiq's mother this time; Hashem came to see his brother only.

"I understand you had a hand in Khobar," Hashem said, firing up a cigarette, his eyes never leaving Rafiq's. He tapped out another and extended the pack toward Rafiq, who shook his head. Hashem did not offer to stop smoking.

"I did my part," Rafiq replied with a smug smile.

"You did." Hashem nodded and blew a stream of smoke at the ceiling. "We see an excellent future for you."

Rafiq noted that his brother remained vague about the parameters of the future. He inclined his head. "I am happy to serve our cause in any way I can."

"I'm glad to hear that, brother."

Brother. That was the first time Hashem had ever addressed him that way, and Rafiq felt as if a great hand was squeezing his chest. He coughed to cover up the sudden rush of emotion. "I will do my duty."

"Good." Hashem ground out the cigarette in the overflowing ashtray. "I want you to go to America."

The air rushed out of Rafiq's lungs. "America? Why? What can I do there?" The warm glow after being called "brother" became a hot pulse of anger.

Hashem reached behind his back and laid a knife on the white tablecloth. The detailing on the blade caught the light, making the metal seem to move, and the ivory handle glowed. "Because you have skill, Rafiq. You are a weapon in our fight against the West, but you are a small knife in this fight. With the right training, you can become a sword—perhaps the finest, deadliest weapon this world has ever seen." Hashem's eyes grew bright and he carved the air with his hands as he spun out his analogy. Rafiq suspected this was simply an intelligence officer tactic, designed to boost his ego, but because it was Hashem, Rafiq allowed it to work.

"So you will send me to New York? Or Washington, DC? So I can scout out our next target?" Rafiq asked.

Hashem shook his head. He tapped out another cigarette, and held it between his thumb and forefinger as he pointed it at Rafiq. "No, you will stay as far away from any of those cities as possible. You will live in their heartland, the Midwest, and you will go to university. I have selected a small liberal arts college, a place where the elite all over the world send their children. These are future congressmen and diplomats. I want you to know them, know how they think, how they talk, how they act. I want you to become one of them."

Rafiq got to his feet and paced the room. "No. What you ask is too much. Four years? How can I leave my home for that long?"

"It will be more like five years."

"Five, then! Even worse."

Hashem stood, his cigarette still unlit between his fingers. "Brother, please sit." He drew both of them fresh cups of tea and sat back across from Rafiq. "The Americans would say you are a big fish in a small pond, a light that shines brightly against weaker flames. You could be the greatest fighter in a generation, but you need to complete your training."

"Maybe I could go next year—" Rafiq began.

"No!" Hashem said, slapping his hand on the table. "It must be now, before you come under suspicion from the Americans. With this last operation . . ." He shook his head. "It must be now."

Rafiq was quiet, sipping his tea to buy time. The logic of his brother's plan was unassailable. Even he had felt it, had seen the hesitation of the older fighters when he spoke, their lack of understanding about how their actions would look on the world stage. His brother had seen the same thing, Rafiq was sure of it. He swallowed hard and nodded at Hashem. "I will do it."

"Good." Hashem fired up his cigarette in celebration. He laid a briefcase on the table and snapped the lid open. He drew out a large envelope and slid it across the table to Rafiq. "You have been accepted to Carleton College in Minnesota, USA. In this package you will find everything you need: passport, money, bank account details, everything."

Rafiq flipped open the cover of the worn Canadian passport. His picture stared back at him, along with his new name: Ralf Faber. He looked up at Hashem. "What is my course of study?"

Hashem smiled. "International relations."

"Rafiq, please, we must hurry."

Hashem's hand appeared on his elbow, guiding him toward the steep gangplank that connected the deck of the ship to the pier. The steel rang hollow under his feet and he stubbed his toe on the inch-high treads that ran across the path.

The captain, a short Malay with more gums than teeth in his smile, scrambled ahead of them. He wore a holed tank top and cutoff shorts, and thick yellow toenails poked out from worn sandals. He turned when they reached the deck.

"This way, boss," he called with another gummy grin. His jaws worked rhythmically on a wad of something and he spat over the side of the ship.

Rafiq stepped onto the deck of the *Lumba*. Even with it tied to the pier, he felt a tremble beneath his feet, as if the floor was moving. His stomach quivered.

Three months . . .

"This way, this way. You come, you come." The little captain hopped between open spots on the deck, while Rafiq and Hashem picked their way along with more care. They had discussed the option of using a large container ship to transport their cargo across the ocean, but the threat of detection from a radiation monitor in a large port was too high. No, they needed anonymity of the kind afforded them by one of the thousands of smaller, ancient breakbulk freighters that plied the seas running odd lots of loose, or "broken," cargo between ports too small to handle the mega container ships.

"Come, come," the Malay captain called again. He passed through the dim outline of a door and shot down a steep staircase with the agility of a monkey coming down a tree. The captain placed his hands on the bright steel rails that bracketed the narrow steps and, lifting his feet, slid to the bottom. He grinned up at them. "You try."

Hashem went down the steps first, his feet ringing on the steel treads. Rafiq hesitated at the top. A thick smell drifted up to him, a fog of diesel fuel, fetid seawater, and unwashed bodies. He swallowed hard before following Hashem down into the hold.

The staircase, or "ladder," as the crew called it, made three hairpin turns before they reached the bottom, the smell intensifying at each level. The little captain waited at the base of the steps with Hashem. He spat into the space behind the stairs.

"I show you the lock room," he said, moving away again in his bandy-legged gait. They conversed in English, the only language the three of them had in common, although Rafiq had his doubts about the captain's real grasp of the language.

They moved forward in the ship—at least, Rafiq thought it was forward; it was hard to tell when they were belowdecks. The passageway was not even large enough for two men to pass shoulder to shoulder, and the steel walls seemed to close in about him as they walked deeper into the ship. He could hear a faint clanking of metal on metal overhead, like some distant Morse code.

The hallway dead-ended at a massive watertight door with a large wheel in the center. The captain moved a long handle and spun the wheel, then pulled the heavy door open and latched it on a hook in the wall. He entered the room, flipping on a light switch. A lone bulb in a protective cage against the ceiling cast a harsh light on the space, a cube of metal walls, maybe fifteen feet across. Save a foot-square ventilation grating and an ancient black telephone hanging on the wall, there was nothing else in the space.

"This is perfect," Hashem said. He pointed to the door. "Lockable from the inside, one entrance in or out."

Rafiq said nothing. He was feeling claustrophobic just looking into the room, and he could only imagine how the space heaved when this tiny boat was at sea . . .

Three months.

Hashem turned to the captain. "Perfect. We need to have an armed man in this space at all times. Understand?"

The captain's eyes narrowed in his nut-brown face. "Armed? What this mean?"

Hashem made a pretend gun out of his thumb and forefinger. "Armed. Guns. Man with gun stay here all the time with our cargo."

The captain's greasy hair swung as he shook his head. "Not possible. Nobody down here at sea. Nobody allowed." His eyes stayed slitted and he gave Hashem a broad smile as he spoke. He spat on the deck in the room, leaving a blotch of moisture on the painted metal plates.

Rafiq closed his eyes. The man wanted more money—let Hashem handle that. He nodded to his brother and pointed up to indicate he was going topside. Hashem waved him away.

Even the horrible-smelling dockside air seemed fresh after the stench of the hold. Rafiq struggled to get his stomach under control as he made his way back to the pier.

Jamil and Farid, the pair guarding the cargo, might have been twins. They were squat and powerfully built, with thinning hair and full beards, and both held their AK-47s with an ease that spoke of long practice. He nodded to Jamil and received a grunt in return. Hashem had said to bring his best fighters. Unfortunately, fighting skills and personality rarely came in the same package. This would be a long couple of months.

The wooden box was about the size of a coffee table. It was heavy, but a pair of men could lift it if they needed to. He mentally measured the narrow end and decided it would fit through the watertight door of the special hold.

Hashem joined them, smiling and bouncing on the balls of his feet. He handed Rafiq a large triangular key on a braided lanyard. "It is done. Here is the only key to the special hold. The little bastard held me out for more money, but you and your men have access to the hold twenty-four hours a day." He unslung a leather bag from his shoulder and passed it to Rafiq. "There's money—I paid Sing Wat, the captain, half already, in dollars. He gets the rest when you reach your destination, and there's plenty for bribes . . . or entertainment for the men."

Hashem stepped aside to let the dock workers fix a sling onto the cargo. He and Rafiq watched as the wooden box swung high into the air, stabilized for a second, then moved over the deck and lowered into the hold.

Hashem lit a cigarette. In the light, it looked to Rafiq like his hands were shaking. His voice was low and urgent when he spoke again. "There is a new phone in the bag as well, and the codebook for our communications. I can't stress how important this mission is, brother. You hold our future in your hands."

"How long, Hashem?"

The tip of his brother's cigarette glowed a fierce orange, and he blew out a long stream of smoke before he answered. "Years. Maybe never, who knows. Our strength is our patience. When they think they've won, you will be there to light a fire the likes of which the world has not seen in many decades."

Rafiq kept his face very still so as not to betray the feelings that roiled his insides. Years . . . years of his life spent waiting, for what? He looked up at the deck of the ship where Captain Sing was waving to him. His stomach clenched.

But first he needed to make it through the next couple of months.

CHAPTER 10

Minneapolis, Minnesota
15 December 2007 – 0600 local

The hatch of the 1996 Subaru Outback wheezed open, the sound loud in the stillness of his parents' driveway. Brendan had driven this car in high school, and he remembered to push the hatch fully open so he didn't hit his head.

He set down the box of groceries, then wedged it in place with his duffel bag. Not much gear for a week at the cabin. He could remember the summers when he and his brother went to the cabin with his grandparents: the back would be packed to bursting, along with gear lashed to the top and a trailer or bike rack to boot.

A long time ago.

The visit to the cabin had been a spur-of-the-moment idea. Brendan was home on leave following his six-month deployment in Iraq. He'd made no plans in advance of coming stateside. He figured he'd connect with an old girlfriend or catch up with some Academy classmates.

The girlfriends had all moved on—a few were even married—and all the calls to people he knew went to voice mail. He knew he could go to work and just hang out, but that seemed lame.

After a week in his apartment in San Diego, Brendan McHugh faced facts: he was lonely. He bought a plane ticket home to Minneapolis to see his parents.

After two days at home, Brendan was no better off in the loneliness department. His folks knew better than to ask him about specific operations, so their desultory conversation about the war was limited to inane comments like, "Looks like the surge is working, huh?" His father had turned into an MSNBC junkie, and the endless parade of talking heads seemed like backup singers to every conversation.

Brendan decided he needed a vacation from his vacation. The idea came to him suddenly. His mother had made chicken divan for dinner, his favorite hotdish, and he was ignoring Brendan Sr.'s latest MSNBC-induced sermon on the state of global politics. Brendan looked up and saw the family reunion picture on the wall.

The picture was taken at his grandparents' cabin in Glen, Minnesota. He'd been nine, maybe ten, his brother a year younger. He could pick out their faces amid the gaggle of kids jumbled on either side of his seated grandparents. The adults were all standing in pairs, bunched into the field of view of the camera. Most were holding beers and sunburn painted their fair skin. In the background, next to the lake, he could make out a row of tents. His grandparents' cabin was tiny, barely able to sleep six if they rolled sleeping bags out on the floor.

"I'm going up to the cabin tomorrow morning," Brendan said, interrupting something his father was saying about Rachel Maddow.

His mother's brow wrinkled. "Are you sure that's a good idea, Brennie? No one's up there this time of year."

Brendan smiled at her. "I'll be fine, Mom." He didn't say

anything about her calling him Brennie. No one called him that anymore, except her. He knew she was worried about him. "I just want to get away for a few days."

"Well, if it's okay with your father, I guess it's okay with me."

Brendan suppressed a smile. He had his own key to the cabin and the property had been passed down to the family, not just his father, but he played along anyway.

"What d'you say, Dad? Okay with you if I head up the cabin for a few days?"

Brendan Sr. pursed his lips. "I don't see why not. Not sure what you're gonna do all by yourself . . . the lake might even be frozen over by now."

Brendan raised his plate toward his mother. "May I have some more, Mom?"

His mother beamed at him. "Of course." She heaped his plate with another helping of the chicken and broccoli mixture. "And you have a good time up there, Brennie."

Dawn wasn't even a smear on the horizon when he backed out of the driveway. Traffic this early was light and he made good time to I-35, the main corridor north out of Minneapolis. He set the cruise control and watched the sky lighten around him.

He loved winter skies. The lack of moisture in the air made the colors seem so delicate, almost pure. A pale pink preceded the sun this morning, and he breathed in a sigh. So different from the heavy reds of Iraq and the desert sun. All that was so very far away.

He'd expected to have dreams, nightmares, but nothing like that happened to him. He still felt normal, maybe a little disconnected from life as an American, but that was to be expected.

Rosen had talked to all of them before he sent them on leave. Use the time to decompress, he said, but don't spend too much time alone. Spend the time with your families. Reconnect.

Brendan laughed. Okay, maybe he wasn't quite normal.

The exit for Hinckley came up just as the sun was fully over the horizon. He disengaged the cruise control and eased off the highway. The sign for Tobie's loomed in front of him, and he pulled into the parking lot by habit as much as by choice.

He took a seat by the window, ordering a caramel roll and a coffee. The glazed roll was as big as his fist and covered with glistening nuts. The crowd in Tobie's was the breakfast-and-coffee set, with a few scattered business meetings. He watched them roll through: high school kids, businessmen in suits, soccer moms with kids in tow, a guy in hospital scrubs. Not a one of them gave a thought to the wars in Iraq and Afghanistan. Most of them probably didn't even know anyone who had served in either place.

When he first went to Iraq, he'd had a good feeling, like he was an anonymous superhero saving the world while the population slept. But now . . . now, it didn't feel so good anymore. His badge of service in Iraq was more like a membership to a special club. People clapped when uniformed servicemen walked through airports, and he'd even gotten upgraded on his flight back to Minneapolis, but no one took the time to *understand*. His SEALs and all the rest of the troops were out there changing the world.

Brendan just hoped they were making it better.

This is the kind of mental bullshit Rosie warned us about, he thought as he paid his check.

Brendan had made this drive so many times he'd forgotten the road numbers. He drove west out of Hinckley, then turned north for a time. Another west–north cycle, then Glen, Minnesota, appeared in his windshield.

The new Glen Store & Grill was a far cry from the old shed he used to bike to every afternoon with his brother. They rode over three miles of dirt road, much of it shaded by tall trees that met overhead, making it seem like they were riding through a tunnel. At the end of the ride were a cold Dr. Pepper and a handful of Swedish fish. The two were terrible if you ate them together, so he and his brother always drank their pops sitting on the front step of the store and saved the Swedish fish for the bike ride home. By the time they made it back to the cabin, the remaining fish would be a sticky mass of red jelly in his pocket. Brendan smiled at the memory.

"Can I help you, son?" The old man behind the counter didn't recognize Brendan. Mr. Anderson was his name.

Brendan shook his head and headed for the very modern drink cooler in the back of the store. He carried a carton of milk to the gleaming cash register. Mr. Anderson waited with a small paper bag of Swedish fish.

"Thought I didn't recognize you, Brendan McHugh?" the old man said with a smile.

Brendan felt himself choking up. He took a deep breath. "I—I didn't. Thank you. How much do I owe you for the milk?"

"Your money's no good here, son."

Brendan remembered that Mr. Anderson was a veteran. Vietnam? Korea? He studied the man. Vietnam, he decided.

"Thank you, sir."

"Don't you sir me, Brendan. I was an enlisted man. I worked for a living, you know."

Brendan laughed at the old joke.

The old man narrowed his eyes. "How are you doing, son? I mean, really. It's tough coming home after you've seen action . . . no one to talk to. I've been there."

Brendan experienced the same choking feeling again. "It's okay, Mr. Anderson. I just felt like I needed a few days away, you know?"

The lines on the old man's face stretched into a grin. "I know what you mean, son. I spent a lot of time in the woods up here when I first got back from 'Nam. It was the best medicine—for me, anyway. I hope you find the same peace I did." He grew suddenly shy. "Now how about a Dr. Pepper to go along with those Swedish fish? On the house, of course."

Brendan shook his head, but he ended up leaving the store with a can of Dr. Pepper anyway.

He took his time on the drive to his grandparent's cabin, letting the old Subaru coast along the dirt roads. The leaves were gone from the trees, and the bare branches overhead let patches of weak winter sunlight filter onto the road. Brendan turned at the crooked sign that read Sugar Lake. He smiled to himself. The sign was repainted every few years, but it had always been crooked for as long as Brendan could remember.

The driveway to their cabin was long, with wide turns that wound through the trees. He rolled down the window to hear the crunch of leaves under his tires. He stopped the car next to the porch he and his grandfather had built one summer and let the silence of the place settle over him. The mechanical *chunk* of the car door opening seemed foreign to such a natural setting.

Brendan walked to the lake edge and onto the dock. The shoreline was thick with ice, but the center of the lake was clear. His breath frosted the air in front of him, a tiny flicker of movement in an otherwise perfectly still setting.

He shook himself and started back to the car. The cabin was tiny: two small bedrooms, a kitchen, and a bathroom. The original structure had been a one-room log cabin, and he braced a knee against the horizontal logs that made up the face of the building as he unlocked the front door.

He spent the next hour getting settled: stowing groceries, splitting firewood and starting a fire, making up a bed. When he was finished, he sat on the porch and drank his Dr. Pepper. He checked his mobile phone. No signal. Not surprising. The phone companies promised better service out here for years, but nothing ever came of it.

Brendan grabbed his bag of Swedish fish and set off into the woods, heading for a rocky bluff that overlooked the lake. He walked slowly, chewing the candy and allowing the quiet to take him.

The trip to the cabin was just what he needed. It was time to do some thinking about his life, decide what he wanted. His service commitment would be up in another year and he hadn't given one thought to what was next. Stay in? Get out and get a job? One thing was sure: the loneliness of San Diego was not for him. He needed something more.

Like Don Riley. He'd known Don would eventually find his niche, and it looked like the CIA was the right place for him. A kid that smart would do well with the spooks. Don knew what he wanted out of life.

"What about me? What do I want out of life?" A startled squirrel chattered at him from a high branch.

Brendan finished the last of the Swedish fish and crushed the bag in his hand. He stepped out onto the bare rock bluff and threw out his arms. "Brendan McHugh!" he yelled, laughing as the sound echoed back to him from across the lake. He and his brother used to scream out their names before they jumped off the ledge into the lake below. He peered over the edge to the ice-crusted water.

He found his jumbled thoughts turning to Liz. He hadn't spoken to her since graduation. She'd left Marjorie's early the next morning without even saying goodbye, off to Quantico to become a Marine.

He hadn't called her. Call it pride, call it stubbornness. Whatever the reason, it seemed easier to just not try, and he'd let Liz slip out of his life.

Brendan pulled his phone from his pocket. Up this high, he had one bar of mobile signal. Just enough to make a call.

Maybe she was lonely, too. Maybe she was wondering what to do with her life. Maybe they could figure it out together . . .

He texted Don Riley. *Do u have Liz mobile?*

The squirrel he had disturbed earlier decided that Brendan's presence near his tree was an invasion of his privacy. It settled on a nearby branch and heaped chattering abuse down on his head.

The phone beeped. *Sure. 202-789-6578. Call her, Brendan.*

Brendan's fingers shook as he dialed the phone. It rang once . . . twice.

"Hello?" The male voice was a warm baritone, and it sounded like he had just been laughing.

Brendan's heart sank when he heard Liz's voice in the background saying, "Who is it?"

"Hello?" the male voice said again.

"Sorry. Wrong number."

CHAPTER 11

Fray Bentos, Uruguay
15 February 2008 — 0600 local

Rafiq leaned against the rail and breathed in the early morning air.

Jungle and river water. After the last three months, he almost missed the tang of sea salt in his nostrils. The muddy brown Uruguay River slid beneath the keel of the *Lumba*. The captain jabbered on the radio in a blend of broken English, Spanish, Portuguese, and Malay.

The ship heeled slightly as the captain made a broad turn around the final bend in the river, and the city of Fray Bentos came into sight. Rafiq studied the shoreline. This was as far as they could go with the ship; the river beyond was not deep enough to allow them to continue. They would meet their South American contact here, a man he knew only as Dean.

Rafiq had eventually gotten used to the never-ceasing motion of the ship, but it had taken about a week. A very long week. His hand went to the scar on his right bicep, a reminder of their encounter with the Somali pirates.

The first few days at sea found Rafiq barely able to stand, let alone take his turn guarding their cargo belowdecks. Just the thought of going back down into the hold made his stomach lurch.

So he slept, and slept. When the gonging noise sounded in his ears, Rafiq thought it was part of his dream. The ship's cook had given him a dose of some horrendous-tasting home remedy for seasickness, and ever since he'd been wrapped in a series of fantastic dreams, each wilder than the last.

The gonging sound was just part of the dream, he told himself. The part where a giant monkey beat on a drum in perfect time with high, ringing peals.

Then came the gunshots.

Rafiq's head snapped up. Gunshots were not part of his dream— they were real.

He staggered to his feet, the room wavering in his vision. He gripped the wall for support and peered out the window of his cabin. Blue sky, flat ocean, bright sun, no sign of anything amiss.

He leaned down to pick up his rifle. The gun had been sitting under an air conditioning vent and the cold metal chilled his clammy flesh. He slipped a Colt Commander into his belt at the small of his back, then eased the door open. The narrow passageway beyond was deserted, lit only by lights at knee level that shone down on the linoleum in glossy puddles.

Rafiq struggled to remember the layout of the ship. He'd spent almost the entire time since they'd left port passed out in his bunk. *Think, dammit.* He decided the bridge was to the right and one deck up from his current position. He moved down the hall, rifle at the ready. His feet seemed like they belonged to someone else, and his hands shook, not from fear, but from the seasickness. He gulped in the dense air, nearly gagging on the ever-present scent of diesel that seemed to pervade everything on this stupid ship.

He reached the ladder, and did a quick look upwards.

Clear. He crept up the metal rungs until his eyes were level with the deck above him.

He'd guessed correctly. The door ahead of him was labeled BRIDGE in bold letters, followed by AUTHORIZED PERSONNEL ONLY in three different languages.

Rafiq crept to the door and pressed his ear against the faux wood. A muffled exchange of broken English was going on in loud tones a few feet away.

"How many crew? How many?" a voice asked. High-pitched, borderline screaming, in English with a flat East African accent.

The captain was pretending he didn't understand, replying only in Malay, punctuated with the occasional, "No speak English, no speak!"

The interrogator seemed to be losing his patience. There was a smacking sound and the captain let out a wail. The man in charge barked out a few orders in a language that Rafiq didn't recognize.

He pictured a map in his mind and where the ship would be after—how many days had he been out of it? Two? Three? The answer bloomed in his mind.

Somalia. They were being hijacked by Somali pirates.

A mixture of rage and adrenaline coursed through him. The dull ache in his stomach went away, the feeling of deadness in his limbs evaporated, and the fogginess in his mind was pierced by a sharp white light. He stood up straight.

"*Psst.* Boss." Jamil's head poked up from the stairwell.

Rafiq crept closer to him.

"Five pirates. Three on the bridge, two searching the ship," Jamil whispered.

"The cargo is safe?"

Jamil's stoic face offered up a faint smile. "Farid's on watch."

Rafiq chewed his lip. "You take out the roamers—quietly. Then give me a distraction. I'll handle the bridge."

Jamil nodded and his head disappeared back down the ladder. The man was efficient, Rafiq had to give him that much. Within three minutes, Rafiq heard the rattle of muffled automatic weapons fire. It was a long blast, undisciplined. Jamil was putting on a show.

Cries of surprise came from the bridge as Rafiq shouldered open the flimsy door. The muzzle of his AK-47 found the first pirate, a rail-thin man with wild hair and a wisp of a goatee. One short blast and the man went down.

The Malay captain and his two mates were on their knees in front of the large round wheel they used to steer the ship. The man who stood over them looked up at Rafiq's entrance, his mouth open. Rafiq took two steps forward and smashed the butt of the rifle into the man's face. He collapsed to the deck.

Rafiq could sense the other pirate turning toward him, the man's weapon coming to bear. The pirate was a half-second ahead of Rafiq, so he dove to the floor behind the chart table. A stream of bullets ripped through the stack of charts, and strips of paper floated in the air like confetti.

Rafiq's ears rang as silence settled over the bridge. The Malay captain's hand reached across the space to grip Rafiq's arm. His lip was mashed into a pulp and he seemed to have even fewer teeth than before. "Bastard pirates. You kill! You kill them!"

Rafiq licked his lips and stroked the stock of his AK-47.

"You come out now. I'll not hurt you! We just want to leave," the remaining pirate called.

"Okay, I'm coming out. Unarmed." Rafiq stood, his arms raised.

The pirate was no more than a boy, really. His hair was cropped close to his head and he didn't even have a beard. He held the AK-47 in an awkward manner, halfway between his shoulder and his hip, but the muzzle was aimed at Rafiq.

"He's my father. Let me leave with him and we'll be gone."

"You speak English well, boy."

"I've been to school."

"Why are you doing this?"

The muzzle of the boy's weapon wavered. "My father owes a debt to a warlord. He's paying it off with ransom money."

Rafiq kept his eyes on the boy's face, but he saw the shadows shift on the wing of the bridge. "Tough way to make a living."

The boy swallowed hard, and the muzzle of the rifle drooped a little more. He opened his mouth to reply, but he never got the words out—his face exploded in a mass of red that painted the bridge. When the boy's body fell, Jamil stood behind him, grinning at Rafiq.

"Nooo!" The scream came from behind him.

Rafiq sensed rather than saw the flash of a knife deep in his peripheral vision on his right side. He brought his arm up to block the cut and felt the blade bite deep into the flesh of his bicep. He clamped his hand down on the hilt of the blade so the man could not get another cut. When Rafiq head-butted him, his forehead sank into the mushy wetness of an already-broken nose. The man fell back to the floor, crying.

Rafiq pulled the knife out and clamped his hand over the cut. It was deep, but his arm still worked. His flesh would heal; his pride, not so much. He could feel Jamil's disapproving eyes on him. Rafiq should have killed the man while he'd had the chance. Dead men don't fight back.

The captain stood and began kicking the pirate, his sandaled feet making wet smacking sounds against the man's flesh. Rafiq pulled him back and motioned for Jamil to take the radio from the man. They needed to make sure they took care of the pirates' boat. No loose ends.

Rafiq knelt down next to the lead pirate. "Listen to me. I don't want any more killing. Call your boat in, and I'll set you free."

The man looked up at him, his eyes streaming with tears, his nose a squashed mass of red blood and snot. The eyes registered comprehension, hope. "You let me go?"

Rafiq nodded and handed him the radio. The Malay captain screeched, but Rafiq pressed him back against the chart table. He palmed the handgun from his belt and pressed the muzzle against the captain's stringy neck. "You will stay out of this, Captain. You'll be paid for your cooperation."

The captain's yellow eyes grew wide. He nodded and his shoulder relaxed in Rafiq's grip.

Rafiq turned back to the Somali and offered him a hand up. The man stood slowly. He was older than Rafiq had first thought, his head covered with thinning gray nap and his face lined with wrinkles. He handed the radio to the pirate. "Make the call."

The man walked out to the port wing of the bridge, stepping over the body of the first pirate Rafiq had shot. Jamil covered his movements with his rifle. Rafiq could hear the Somali talking on the radio. He waved his arm, and the radio squawked in reply. "They come," he said, reentering the bridge.

He limped to the far side of the room where the body of his son lay. He looked at Rafiq. "I take him with me?"

Rafiq shrugged and motioned for the two Malay crewmen to carry the body down to the main deck. The men grumbled, but did as they were told.

The Somali pirates' transportation came along the port side of the *Lumba*. Rafiq had ordered the captain to go dead in the water, and the freighter rocked gently in the light swell. The motion didn't bother Rafiq. His stomach rumbled with hunger.

But first he needed to conclude this business.

The pirate boat was a large open craft, some sort of fishing vessel, Rafiq guessed, with an immense motor attached to the back. One of the Malay deckhands threw a rope ladder over the side as the boat bumped against the hull. The outboard motor idled into a slow burble.

The pirate leader stopped at the rope ladder. "I need some help to get my son's body into the boat."

Rafiq stepped forward. "Allow me, sir." He gripped the boy's shirt in his hand and heaved the body over the side. It made a splash as it hit the water.

The pirate's eyes widened. "You said you would let me go."

"No, I said I would set you free." Rafiq kicked the pirate in the chest and the man fell over the side. Rafiq turned to Jamil. "Take care of the boat. I'm hungry."

Jamil leaned over the railing, spraying the pirate's boat with bullets, ripping holes in the hull. The pilot slumped to the floor of the boat, bloody water washing over his ankles. The boat began to drift away as it slowly filled with seawater, the outboard engine chortling in a low rumble. Jamil loaded the grenade launcher on his weapon.

It took three grenades to sink the pirate boat, but it was good practice for Jamil.

The Malay captain whistled to get Rafiq's attention, then pointed at the furthest dock. Rafiq nodded, and lifted his hand to shade his eyes. A few dock hands lounged along the pier, dark-skinned men dressed in ratty T-shirts, shorts, and flip-flops.

A smaller boat was docked at the extreme end of the pier. This craft looked more like a motorized yacht with a long, sleek hull and a broad fantail. Unlike the cluttered deck of the *Lumba*, this power yacht appeared clean and professional. Rafiq spied a man in a white shirt and shorts making his way across the deck, carrying a tray.

The door to the cabin opened and a woman stepped out. She plucked a pair of sunglasses from a mass of dark hair and covered her eyes as she watched the freighter approach the pier.

The men of the *Lumba* sprang into action around Rafiq. For days, they had spoken of nothing but women and sex. When the ship had sailed past Buenos Aires, the little Malay captain had a near riot on his hands when he told his men they were not stopping. Rafiq had quelled the issue with a ten percent bonus for the crew, but the tension was still there. These were men ready for shore leave.

The lines went across to the pier and the ship was snugged to the dock in no time at all. The crew of the *Lumba* was already lined up, ready to go ashore. The Malay captain screamed down at them from the bridge, but the men ignored him.

The brow made a loud clank as the crane dropped it against the gunwale. The two men closest to it secured it with chains, but no one rushed down the gangway. Instead, they stepped back to allow a woman to board the ship, the same woman Rafiq had seen on the deck of the pleasure craft.

The crew looked at her with barely disguised lust in their eyes. The one closest to her sniffed the air as she walked by and licked his lips. If she noticed his behavior, she didn't show it.

She was dressed in faded blue jeans that hugged her slim hips and disappeared into a pair of worn cowboy boots. A white muslin blouse, open at the neck, was tucked loosely into her jeans, and Rafiq caught a glimpse of white lace in the plunging neckline. He felt a tug in his groin. Maybe the crewmen weren't the only ones in need of some release.

The woman picked her way across the deck with easy movements, aware the eyes of all the men were on her. It took Rafiq a second to realize she was approaching him.

She stopped in front of Rafiq, a ghost of a smile on her lips. She pushed her sunglasses up into her dark hair. Her smoky gray eyes crinkled at the corners as her lips widened into a smile.

"You must be Rafiq." Her voice was low and husky, and he felt his breath catch in his throat. She put out her hand.

"I'm Dean."

CHAPTER 12

Green Zone, Baghdad, Iraq
03 July 2009 – 0730 local

Liz watched the UH-60 Black Hawk settle to the ground in a cloud of dust. She pulled her shirt away from her sweaty back. Even this early in the morning, the Baghdad heat was already stifling. Between the dust and the heat, she probably looked a mess—but she was only stopping in the Green Zone for a day, and she had to see him.

The door of the helo rolled open and a group of SEALs jumped to the ground. They guided out three prisoners, hooded with their hands zip-tied behind their backs. Liz squinted at the SEAL team. They all looked the same, like dusty, well-armed cavemen with scraggly beards and dark sunglasses. The column moved in her direction.

"Alright, gentlemen, let's get our guests to their new accommodations," called the lead man. Liz's heart skipped a beat. That was Brendan's voice.

All of a sudden surprising him didn't seem like a good idea. They hadn't talked in what, six years? And her idea of a reunion was to show up in a war zone looking like something the cat dragged in. Her hand went to her hair, brushing off the fine layer of dust she knew was all over her head and tucking the loose strands behind her ear.

He moved with the quick steps of an athlete; his booted feet seemed to barely touch the ground. SEALs were allowed to customize their battle gear, so he was dressed in a combination of REI and military issue: cargo pants, a bullet-resistant Kevlar vest with trauma plate over a skin-tight Under Armour shirt, kneepads, fingerless gloves, and his beloved Ray-Bans. Dust frosted his curly dark hair and beard.

"Liz?" The line of SEALs and their prisoners stopped behind him. He pushed his glasses up his forehead and squinted in the early morning sun. "What are you doing here?"

His blue eyes met hers and she felt the breath leave her lungs in a rush. That was a great question; one she should have had a ready answer to. She tried to say something, but her voice seemed to be on hiatus. She stepped forward and gave him a hug. His shoulders were knotty with muscle beneath her hands.

"Hi!" she choked out.

He didn't say anything, but the embrace was longer and closer than she had planned. There were people all around them, for God's sake. She twisted away and stepped back, taking a deep, shaky breath. Brendan was staring at her chest.

"Sorry, I got you all dirty."

When she looked down, stripes of dust from his uniform crisscrossed her dark blue polo.

"Skipper?" called one of the SEALs, a grin forming under his shaggy blond beard. "Maybe we can play the dating game later?"

Brendan started and dropped his sunglasses back over his eyes. "Right." He sharpened his tone. "All right, people. Let's move." He stepped back and waved the line forward.

One of the prisoners, the large one in the middle, leaned his hood close to his comrade and whispered. The other man laughed. Liz looked up sharply; they were speaking in Farsi.

The SEAL with the blond beard punched the big prisoner in the lower back. "No talking! *Oskot!*"

"Gonzo, that's enough! Get them inside now." Brendan stepped close to Liz and touched her forearm. She shivered in response. "I have to go. Can I see you tonight? Cafeteria at 1800?"

Liz still didn't trust her voice, so she just nodded. Brendan flashed a grin and trotted away. Liz looked down to the ruts she had worn in the dirt from shifting her feet back and forth.

She closed her eyes and blew out a deep breath.

Liz decided to wear her engagement ring to her dinner with Brendan. A two-carat, square-cut diamond in a platinum setting, it felt ostentatious when she wore it stateside. Here it felt like the worst kind of bling. *I'm engaged. He needs to know that.*

She slid into a booth a half hour early and sipped a soda to calm her nerves. She fiddled with the ring. The truth was that she hated her engagement ring. She'd begged James to get something smaller, more tasteful, something more like *her*. He'd just laughed in that irritating, charming way he had and said, "Nothing's too good for my Elizabeth." She'd always preferred Liz. That had taken some getting used to as well.

When she looked back, their engagement seemed fated. Liz had known James for as long as she could remember. His family owned the house across the street and their parents traveled in the same social circles in the Los Angeles Iranian community. They were both caboose children who'd been born in the US and James grew up like a brother to her. Well, maybe not a brother—James was the first boy she'd ever kissed.

They grew apart in high school and completely lost touch when she went to the Academy, but they'd reconnected when Liz was home on leave a few years ago. Her service commitment was ending and she wondered what she wanted to do with her life. James stepped in at exactly the right time. This was a man she could share her life with, a man who understood her as a person, as a woman.

After a perfect long weekend at a Laguna Beach resort, he'd popped the question and put this enormous engagement ring on her finger. There was no reason to say no.

"Lizzie."

She looked up and bit her lip. Brendan's skin was flushed and clean from a recent shower, his hair still damp. Before she realized what she was doing, she had jumped out of the booth and wrapped her arms around his neck. He smelled six ways to wonderful and she could feel the hard muscles of his back beneath the thin material of his shirt.

Brendan gave a quick hug, then whispered in her ear. "Hey, we're being watched." Liz looked up to see a whole room full of faces turned in their direction.

"Sorry," she said, sliding back into the booth, her face burning. "It's good to see you, Bren."

Brendan took the seat across from her. "Likewise." He gestured at the ring. "That's quite a rock. Who's the lucky guy?"

She covered the ring with her free hand. "His name is James, and he is a lucky guy."

"No argument here." Brendan's blue eyes seemed to have gone a little cold. "In fact, I think maybe I talked to him once."

Liz raised an eyebrow.

A flush of red crept up Brendan's neck. "It's a little embarrassing. I called you around Christmastime two years ago, and a guy answered the phone. I heard you in the background . . . you sounded happy. So I hung up."

Liz took a sip of soda. James had proposed to her that Christmas in Laguna.

"That would have been James. You'd like him, Bren." She went back to her drink, desperate for a change of topic. "What about you? Anyone special in your life?"

"I thought you'd never ask." Brendan reached into his breast pocket and pulled out a picture.

Liz felt her jaw tighten, but she kept a smile on her face. *He had her picture right there, just waiting for me to ask about her.*

Brendan slid the photograph across the table. The girl in the picture had long auburn hair and stunning green eyes. A row of perfect white teeth caught the edge of her lip, adding zing to her sultry smile. The girl wore a bikini and the picture looked to have been taken poolside. Liz flipped it over. *To my one and only, Love, Amy.* The letter "y" in her name was in the shape of a heart.

"Wow," Liz said. "She looks like a model."

Brendan laughed. "She is. Swimsuits, mostly. Amy's hoping to get into *Sports Illustrated* this coming season."

Liz bit back a snide comment about bimbos and slid the picture back across the table. "Well, are there any wedding bells in your future?"

Brendan colored again. "We'll see . . . Amy's kinda high maintenance and she's not much for commitment." He gestured to her shirt with the FBI logo. "FBI? What happened to the Marines?"

Liz almost let out a sigh of relief. Finally, a safe topic. "Well, I did my five years and then decided to try my luck elsewhere. FBI is hot on language specialists, so I applied, was accepted, finished at Quantico—again!—and they transferred me here immediately."

Brendan wrinkled his brow. "Farsi, right? I didn't realize you were that good."

She nodded. "I'm leaving in the morning for Basra, translating Iranian communications and interrogations. Based on what I heard this morning, I don't even need to leave the Green Zone."

"I don't follow."

"The prisoners you brought in. They were speaking Farsi."

Brendan stared at her. "Are you serious?"

"You didn't know?"

"They acted strange from the moment we picked them up. During the firefight, as soon as we got the upper hand, they just gave up. That never happens. The insurgents usually fight to the death. And then when we cuffed them, they settled right down. Almost no talking, like they were trained to stay silent." Brendan stood up. "This could be big. Let's go talk to these guys."

They made the walk to the detention center in silence, moving through pools of light cast by the streetlamps. Even with the sun down, it was like an oven outside. Liz watched Brendan from the corner of her eye.

The doors of the detention center were in sight when Brendan spoke again.

"I've missed you, Liz," he said softly.

She caught his hand in the darkness between two pools of light. "I missed you, too." She felt him grip her fingers, and she realized she was shaking. In that split second, she was sure he was going to pull her into his arms and kiss her . . . and she was okay with that.

Their intertwined fingers moved and her ring sparkled in the night, the way only a two-carat diamond in a glittering platinum setting can sparkle.

The flash seemed to bring Brendan back to his senses. "I'm sorry. I shouldn't have . . ." He strode forward and yanked open the door to the detention center for her. He was breathing heavily and avoided her eyes.

It's okay, she wanted to say, but instead she stayed quiet and walked into the building.

Sergeant Dixon, a skinny black kid with a Texas accent, was manning the duty desk.

Brendan smiled at him. "Hi, Sergeant, I'm looking for access to three prisoners who were processed in this morning by my SEAL team. Name's McHugh."

Dixon checked his records and shook his head. "Sorry, Lieutenant, just missed them. We released them to the Iraqis about an hour ago."

Brendan swore under his breath. As part of the cooperative agreement between the US and Iraqi governments, any detainees not deemed "high value" by the Americans were turned over to the Iraqis.

"What about tape?" Liz interrupted.

"Pardon, ma'am?"

"Did you record them in their cell?"

"Yes, ma'am, that's standard protocol. You can listen to it during normal working hours—"

"I leave for Basra in the morning, Sergeant. How 'bout we listen to them tonight?" Liz flashed her badge that gave her access to the intel files.

With a minimal amount of grumbling, Sergeant Dixon connected them to the intel team leader, who called up the recording of the prisoner cells. He even let them use his office, where Liz and Brendan crowded in front of his laptop to watch the video. The room was dark, only the glow from the laptop on their faces.

On the screen, three men sat on the cell floor, one against each wall, silent. The audio made a loud hiss that filled the tiny office.

Liz's shoulder barely touched Brendan's and she did her best to focus on the screen. "I'm going to fast-forward to see if they ever move close enough to talk." The figures on the screen made minute jerking motions and the time stamp in the lower right corner raced by. Finally, the large one got to his feet, crossed the room, and settled next to one of his cellmates. The remaining man scooted across the floor until all three were huddled together.

Liz stopped the fast-forward and notched the audio up to its highest setting. She closed her eyes in concentration, and tucked her hair behind her ears. The foreign voices, in scratchy whispers, filled the room.

"One of them lost a weapon," she said. "A knife." She screwed up her face and pouted her lips. "No . . . it's a code name. Maybe a new operation or a weapons system?"

She opened her eyes and sat up straight. On the screen, the three men retreated to their own walls again. "That's it. Look, I need to write this up."

Brendan got the hint. "I think I'm going to turn in," he said, standing up.

"It was great to see you, Bren." She stood. Because of the desk in the cramped office, it seemed like they were unnaturally close together and his blue eyes blazed in the dimness.

Brendan reached out and brushed his hand against her cheek. "Bye, Lizzie. I wish you the very best."

Then he was gone.

CHAPTER 13

Don Riley huffed his way up the last steps to the third floor. One more to go. The stairs were adjacent to the bank of elevators, and he longingly eyed the wide silver doors.

No. New Year's resolution. More exercise. Good for me. Christ, he was even panting in his thoughts.

He could feel the sweat sticking to the underarms of his T-shirt, and he knew his face was probably bright red now, but he attacked the next set of steps with something that approached vigor. When he was out of sight of the elevators, he took a quick sniff of his right armpit. Nothing too rank. Yet.

He pulled his way up the last step, slapped his badge against the card reader, and punched in his personal code. The light on the reader shifted from red to green and the door made a chunking sound as the magnetic lock released.

Don did a quick check that his dress shirt was still tucked in after the exertion of climbing four flights of steps, then straightened his tie. He wasn't sure why he bothered. Most of the analysts at NCPC didn't wear ties, or even dress shirts half the time.

NCPC was founded by President George W. Bush in 2005 as a way to counter the threats caused by chemical, biological, radiological, and nuclear weapons—commonly known as weapons of mass destruction, or WMDs. After the scathing findings by the 9/11 Commission, Congress and the Bush administration agreed on the most far-reaching reforms to the US Intelligence Community that had happened since World War Two. The Intelligence Reform and Terrorism Prevention Act of December 2004 established the Office of the Director of National Intelligence, and also created a number of specialized agencies. The NCPC was one of these new organizations, overseen directly by the new Director of National Intelligence. As bureaucracies so often did, the agency split into seven "kingdoms," known in Washington-speak as "directorates." Don was in the WMD - Security Directorate.

Like almost everyone in the building, Don was assigned, or detailed, from his home agency to the NCPC. In theory, this built personal connections between agencies, but teamwork was really based on the leadership of the Deputy Director for each directorate, one of the few permanent employees of the NCPC. If you had a DD who was confident in the system, and capable, the personal connection concept worked well. If you had Don's DD as your manager, it didn't.

He did his best to pass Clem's office as quickly as possible. Not fast enough.

"Riley! Get in here." Clem's voice stopped him in his tracks. He turned and took a step into the open doorway.

The first impression of Clem Reggins was always a good one. Tanned, with biceps that bulged out of his shirtsleeves and pecs rippling under his shirt, his icy blue eyes and short blond hair screamed "all-American boy." And that impression was a fraud. The Clem Reggins that Don knew was the worst kind of narrow-minded, power-grubbing bureaucrat. Worse than that, the man was a bully.

"Running a little late this morning, Riley?" Clem's voice was a touch higher than one might expect in a man of his physique.

Probably the steroids, you sick fuck. I hope your nuts shrink to the size of soybeans. "Traffic, Clem . . . you know."

Clem came out from behind his desk and stretched so that Don could admire his magnificent arms. He stared pointedly at Don's belly straining against his belt. "Not me. I hit the gym before work. No traffic at 0430, Riley. You should try it." He struck another pose.

"Get out of here, Riley. Half the day's gone already. Oh, and remember, no more of those stupid RFIs. We don't need them to do our job."

Don opened his mouth to protest, but decided against it.

An RFI was bureaucratic talk for a request for information. Basically, if an NCPC analyst wanted more information on a topic, he could query another agency using an RFI. All RFIs for his department had to be signed by Clem, and in his boss's steroid-addled worldview, asking for help was a sign of weakness. It irked Don even more that he was officially a CIA employee on loan to NCPC. If he wanted a piece of intelligence from the CIA—his home agency—he needed to write an RFI, which was then promptly denied by his boss.

So much for interdepartmental cooperation.

Don sighed and backed away from Clem's muscle show.

His desk was the normal junkyard of paper. For all his tech background, Don preferred paper copies when he really wanted to dig into a topic. His normal mode of operation was to scan the message traffic and then print off the ones he wanted to read in detail. And he never threw anything away. If he printed it off, it meant his brain had picked up a connection somewhere, even if he didn't know the reason right then. The idea just needed time to marinate.

His message queue was the typical Monday-morning train wreck. Hundreds of unread items in bold letters waited for him in his secure email inbox. He pulled a warm Diet Coke from his bottom drawer, cracked it open, and took a long sip. The acidic taste cleansed his palate of Clem's cologne.

Don slouched in his chair and opened the first message, a follow-up from a Baghdad car bomb. He scanned it and moved the message to trash. His mind slipped into neutral as he chewed through the messages one by one, hitting his stride. He finished the first Diet Coke and retrieved another without stopping reading.

He reached the end of a summary report about jihadi activity and scanned the footnotes. FBI Special Agent Elizabeth Soroush was mentioned as the author of a referenced report. Liz was in Iraq? He clicked on the link.

Liz's original report was short, only a page in length. Basically, it reported that three suspected jihadis had been picked up in a raid and processed in the Green Zone. During a review of the detention footage, Liz had noticed the detainees were speaking in Farsi. Attempts to question the men further were not possible, as they had already been turned over to the Iraqi government and subsequently "lost in the system." Don snorted.

Lost, my ass—they bribed their way out of Iraqi jail. Or they were simply released to the Iranian authorities. As the US began to make noises about leaving Iraq, it was obvious to Don that the Shia-dominated Iraqi government was already paying a certain amount of fealty to their powerful Shia neighbor to the east.

But what held his attention was Liz's summary of their conversation.

Prisoner 1: What about the blade?
Prisoner 2: [*unintelligible*]—take care of it.

Prisoner 1: Fuck him. He got taken once, too.

Prisoner 2: I'll let you tell him.

Don stared at the screen for a long moment, then hit PRINT. He took the long walk to the printing station—Clem had denied his request for a personal printer, too—and stared at the page all the way back to his desk.

Liz had concluded that the detainees were of Iranian origin, and the reference to "the blade" was most likely a code name for a new weapon they were planning to use against the coalition forces.

Don stared at the paper, the buzz of curiosity tingling in his brain. He was onto something here; he could taste it. He fired up his connection to the Joint Worldwide Intelligence Communications System, or JWICS—the US government's top-secret Internet—and started a search around the term *blade*, adding in some parameters to focus on Iranian origins. It always gave Don a chuckle that the most-used search engine inside the most secure intelligence network in the world was also the most popular search engine in the civilian world: Google.

Multiple hits came back. Some about various ancient weapons, some about the latest knives being bought and sold for use by foreign militaries. The analyst who had written the report obviously had a thing for ancient weaponry. Don read through the description of the curved ivory handle and ancient blade, then clicked on the link for the picture of the weapon.

He nearly dropped his soda.

He'd seen this knife before. In Iraq. The Iranian diplomat that Brendan had picked up back in 2007 had been carrying it.

Using his CIA login, he called up the data from the raid. Clem would have a kitten if he found out Don had bypassed the RFI process—which he wouldn't approve in the first place—but Don could feel that he was on the verge of a breakthrough. There was a connection between Liz's report and that raid. Somewhere in this puzzle was the magic link he needed to make all the pieces fit together. He just needed to keep looking.

He scanned through the folder. They'd uncovered a major weapons cache, including the source of the more sophisticated EFPs that were just showing up in the region. The explosives were of Iranian origin and the technology impressive, especially for local militia. These guys obviously had advanced training.

He pulled up the digital photos from the raid, tapping the cursor until he found the one he was looking for. The knife was in someone's flat palm. It had a curved white handle and a short arced blade, wrought with filigree designs. The next picture showed a crushed pack of Marlboros and a silver Zippo lighter.

He scanned the text of the after-action report from Brendan. The Iranian diplomat's bodyguard had been killed in the raid. How important did you have to be to rate your own bodyguard?

Don pulled up the picture page of the Iranian diplomat's passport next to the photo of the ivory-handled knife and focused on the man's face. A classic face, with a noble nose, steady dark eyes, and thin lips set in a cruel smile.

Alizera Mogadaham, who are you?

He flipped back to the text from Liz's report. *What about the blade?* That was what the Farsi-speaking prisoner had asked.

The puzzle pieces in Don's mind snapped together: They weren't talking about a weapons system, they were talking about a *person*.

And now Don had his picture.

CHAPTER 14

Somewhere in the Zagros Mountains, south of Gerash, Iran
06 June 2010 – 0200 local

Hashem paused the Range Rover on the top of the rise and flashed
the headlights three times, leaving them off after the final flash.

He stared at his watch, letting the second hand sweep around the
face twice. Two flashes poked out of the darkness.

The sign for all clear.

Hashem turned his lights back on and put the car in drive. The
chains he dragged behind the Rover to obliterate his tracks in the
sand rattled gently as he pulled forward. Satellite imagery of the area
was unlikely, but one could never be too careful.

It amazed him how much these desert drives relaxed him. He
barely glanced at the GPS monitor on the dashboard. When he first
began to make the treks into the desert, he'd always taken a security
detail of two or three. Then it was just Delir—he paused at the
memory of his driver. Now he preferred to make the drive alone.

He'd come to the secret cave so many times over the years he could find his way even in the dark. But it was good to have a backup plan. He smiled to himself. He could hear his brother's voice in his head: "Always the cautious one, brother."

And his trademark response: "The cautious ones keep their heads, Aban."

He descended down a steep rock slope onto a flat valley floor, the last stretch of road before he reached the cave. Hashem shifted in his seat to ease the tightness in his back. There was a shorter path into the secret base, one that stayed to the lowland flat stretches and was used for bringing in supplies or heavy equipment. His security forces normally kept it blocked with heavy boulders to discourage unwanted visitors. He could have had them unblock the access road, but it was a point of pride with Hashem to follow the same security protocols he demanded of his men.

He kept his speed low, giving his men plenty of time to scan his vehicle for heat signatures, verifying he was alone. Hashem always felt a rush of nostalgia when he pulled into the entrance of the cave. The delicate hood of rock extended out over the sand, blocking the stars from his view.

When he and Aban and their father had first found this cave, it had looked to them like just another of the hundreds of ancient lava tubes littering the area, extending back into the mountain ten or twenty meters until deadending in a blank wall. But this one kept going. The three of them had gotten out their headlamps and crawled on their hands and knees the last ten meters—Hashem remembered fearing they would crawl into a nest of snakes—until the cave expanded into a vast cavern. They'd shouted and called into the darkness, and Aban lit a flare.

The cave was a vast complex of linked caverns that extended three hundred meters in either direction, with a source of fresh water and links to the outside world for fresh air.

Hashem parked the vehicle in front of the gunmetal gray steel doors that covered the entrance now. The blackout screen lowered behind the Rover, shutting out the dim desertscape in his rearview mirror. He closed his eyes, trying to preserve that memory for a few more seconds. It had all been perfect then, the three of them exploring the natural beauty of this underground wonderland.

It had all gone so wrong after that.

The light from the opening doors reddened his closed eyelids. He opened his eyes and put the Rover in drive.

His father and brother would not recognize the cave today. Gone was the warren of caverns, replaced by a floor hewn smooth by the chisels of his stonemasons. Pillars of steel sprouted out of the bedrock and lined the walls in weak areas. Over the course of three years, Hashem had brought in over two hundred immigrant laborers— Bangladeshis, Pakistanis, North Africans, wherever he could find desperate men who would work without asking questions.

They never returned to their families, of course. The next of kin did receive a handsome stipend from an anonymous donor, but their loved one never came home. Eventually, the men figured it out, and a few tried to escape. Three even made it to the open desert, but Hashem's men assured him they would never survive the harsh environment to reach civilization. But most never complained. It amazed Hashem how many men simply accepted their fate.

A golf cart and driver waited next to where Hashem parked his Rover. He returned the salute, dropped his duffel bag in the cargo space, and slid across the vinyl seat. The driver pulled off immediately, racing around the perimeter of the cavern. They paused at the barracks, where Hashem changed from civilian clothes to a dark blue jumpsuit, the uniform of his operation. The only adornment to the uniform was a belt which held a radiation monitor.

He splashed water on his face and closed his eyes again. His room, barely the size of his walk-in closet in Tehran, consisted of a bed, a desk, a washstand, and a small prayer rug on the floor, but it felt more like home than any house he'd ever owned.

He dried his face and rejoined the driver on the golf cart. "Take me to Yusef."

Yusef Kharmanian looked up from the video screen as Hashem entered his workbay. Wild locks of unruly black hair and a thick black beard framed his face.

It had taken Hashem a long time to adjust to Yusef's eyes. One solid black pupil stared at him intently, burning with passion. The other eye wandered as he spoke, first seeing Hashem's shoes, then over his shoulder, then the ceiling. Hashem smiled at Yusef; after nearly three years, the wandering eye didn't bother him anymore.

"What present did you bring me on this trip, Colonel?" The young man's voice was surprisingly soft, and he had a lopsided smile to match his uneven eyes.

Yusef was perhaps his greatest find of the entire program. When he'd come across the boy at the age of eighteen, he'd already graduated from the University of Tehran with a double major in aerospace engineering and astrophysics. His passion was missiles. He watched videos of test flights constantly, dissecting the details of the flights and sending long missives to flight engineers in other countries telling them how to correct their failures.

His parents had been killed in a car accident a few months prior to their meeting and Yusef had become a complete recluse, living in his university lab. Convincing him to join Hashem's cause was easy: a state-of-the-art lab, freedom to build missiles to his heart's content, and complete seclusion from the outside world.

Yusef didn't realize he would never leave the secret cave alive, but Hashem would deal with that issue when it came up.

The "present" comment was their own private joke. Before Hashem had moved Yusef to the cave, he'd had the scientist draw up a shopping list of all the possible components and tools he might need. On each visit to the cave, Hashem always tried to bring some item from the list for his missile engineer. Behind the glass walls, Hashem could see the rows of machining equipment and 3-D printers.

Building a missile inventory had been surprisingly easy. Over the years, he'd put on the payroll a small group of quality assurance engineers who worked at Iranian missile factories. Using falsified documents, the QA engineers would pull Hashem's shopping list items off the assembly line for quality control. Invariably, the parts never made it back into inventory. Labeled as "Substandard, destroy," they eventually found their way into Yusef's secret lab.

Given the length of time that had passed, the Iranian missile models would occasionally change as new updates came available, but that mattered little to Yusef. He took the parts and, using his machine shop, was able to modify or fabricate new replacements. He often gave Hashem revised engineering drawings to pass along to the Iranian government missile development teams; Hashem destroyed them.

Yusef rose, jittery with anticipation for his mentor to see his work. "Show me, Yusef. Show me your babies," Hashem said.

Yusef's wild locks swayed from side to side as he made his way through the lab to a cleanroom airlock. The two men donned white coats, hairnets, and covers for their mouths and beards. With all his bushy facial hair tucked away, Yusef looked like his face was surrounded by puffy clouds.

The three missile guidance sections lay gleaming white in the harsh theater lights of the cleanroom. The solid rocket boosters were housed in a separate part of the cave. About the size of a phone booth, the open guidance section was packed with electronics. Yusef pointed out various new components in an excited voice. Hashem let the words flow over him. He only cared that they flew where he programmed them, and he knew Yusef was as good as his word.

His eyes strayed to the next workbench over—the warhead section. The missile shells lay open and empty. "What is Valerie's progress?" he interrupted Yusef.

Yusef blinked at him, his lazy eye making a slow survey of the room to Hashem's right. He shrugged. "You'll have to talk to the Russian about that," he said.

The Russian. Yusef never used Valerie's name.

"Good work, Yusef. Very good work."

Yusef beamed from behind his facial coverings, his eye swiveling momentarily forward.

Hashem left the cleanroom, stripping off the sterile robe and dropping it into a basket for cleaning and reuse. He'd dismissed his driver, so he walked the fifty meters to Valerie's lab.

The overhead gantries made shadows across his path as he passed the booster section of a missile. He shook his head. Stealing something the size of a tractor trailer was no easy task. He'd finally managed to pay off the general manager of the facility where they tested the boosters. The man had falsified the testing of one booster and sold it to Hashem's man. The plan had worked—barely—but he'd ended up needing to have the general manager replaced with a more compliant choice when he went back to him for a second unit. These operations took time.

He pushed open the doors to Valerie's lab, spying the man's gray head hunched over his workbench. Valerie looked up at Hashem's entrance and gave him a sad half-smile as he rose to meet him. Sad was the only adjective to describe Valerie. The bear of a man approached Hashem with a shambling gait, his belly straining against the belt on his uniform. He folded the Iranian into his massive arms, holding him so tightly that Hashem could hear the slow thud of the man's heart in his chest. Even his heartbeat sounded mournful.

"Colonel," he rumbled. "How good to see you."

Not that Valerie didn't have much to be sad about. Hashem had first met Valerie Aminev in Chechnya in 1994. Even then, in his late thirties, the man had made a name for himself as a nuclear weapons specialist. Of course, in those days, he was primarily concerned with dismantling them.

Hashem spied the 8 × 10 picture on Valerie's desk. Raisa, his late wife, a smiling raven-haired beauty, and a Chechen Muslim of the minority Shia sect. Hashem had heard the story of Valerie's love life dozens of times: the whirlwind romance, his conversion from Russian Orthodox to Islam, their beautiful children—Hashem's eyes shifted to the photograph of the twins—and the slaughter of all three while Valerie attended a nuclear physics symposium in Japan when the Second Chechen War began in 1999.

When Hashem sought to recruit his Russian friend to his special team years later, he'd been shocked at the change in the man. Once a dark-haired, friendly giant whose booming laugh filled the room, Valerie had gone completely gray and silent. Only two things kept him going: vodka and hate. Hashem, despite his personal disapproval of alcohol, kept the vodka coming to Valerie by the case, and over the years, he carefully stoked the hatred for his own ends. The Russian's hate had no direction, he simply hated the world that had taken his family from him.

"My friend," Hashem said, pushing back from Valerie's food-stained uniform. He smelled of stale vodka and sweat. "Give me some good news."

Valerie's half-smile spread slowly—another joke between Hashem and his team. When he'd first shown the Iraqi nuclear weapons to Valerie, the man had snorted angrily, called them "nuclear firecrackers." For a long moment, Hashem's stomach had dropped, until the Russian took another long pull of his vodka and said, "But I can make them better."

And he'd been as good as his word. Hashem had learned more

from Valerie about nuclear weapons than he'd cared to admit. The Iraqi weapons had been gun-type warheads, essentially a gun barrel that fired two subcritical masses of low-purity, weapons-grade plutonium at each other to cause a nuclear detonation. They were crude, but would have been effective in a small area.

Valerie had painstakingly harvested the material from the three Iraqi bombs and refashioned them into spherical warheads, increasing the yield tenfold and repackaging them for Yusef's missiles. Delivered accurately and detonated at the right altitude, each warhead could now destroy an area kilometers in diameter, not to mention the nuclear fallout which would devastate a much larger area.

Valerie held Hashem by both shoulders, and his half-smile grew fractionally wider. "Come, I have much to show you."

He led Hashem to a window at the back of his lab. On three metal tables inside the cleanroom laid three boxes, each the size of a filing cabinet drawer. The covers were removed, exposing a ball the size of a large melon, and covered with wires that led to a series of circuit boards.

Hashem's breath fogged the glass as he leaned in. "They're finished?" he said.

Valerie nodded gravely.

Hashem squinted at the nearest device. A small metal tag was glued to the base of the unit, next to the explosive sphere. The tag looked hand drawn. "What is that?" he asked, pointing to the label.

Valerie pursed his lips. "I've named each of the bombs after my family, Colonel. That one is Raisa, that's Tanya, and Little Valerie." Tears seeped out of his eyes, and were lost in the gray nest of his beard. Hashem wondered how much he'd had to drink already tonight.

He gripped Valerie's arm. "Your vengeance will come, my friend. I promise."

The Russian nodded, the tears flowing freely now. "When, Colonel? When?"

When. That was a good question. He had one completely functional nuclear missile now, but the launchers were the one thing he could not steal from the Iranian weapons program. It had been nearly two years since he'd ordered three mobile launchers from the North Korean agent, Pak Myong-rok—and paid cash up front.

Everything depended on Pak now. Without those launchers, his missiles were no more than giant paperweights. The thought made his stomach churn. He forced a smile.

"Soon, Valerie. Soon."

CHAPTER 15

Going to Sine's Irish Pub the night before the election had been a mistake.

Don scanned the packed bar from his high-top table. Already he'd had to fend off three guys who wanted to take the empty chair opposite him. He flagged the waitress down.

"I'll have another. Harp," he said, holding up his empty glass. She eyeballed the empty chair and the standing-room-only bar. "And I'll have a grasshopper for my friend."

Don had only a vague idea what a grasshopper was, and no idea if Liz would drink one, but at least the waitress would know he was meeting someone. She raised her eyebrows in a "whatever" expression and pushed back into the crowd.

Sine's was the place for happy hour on Pentagon Row. People from all over the government circle migrated here for drinks after work, and no small amount of deals were done over beers at Sine's.

But not tonight. It was all about the election tonight. The Republicans smelled blood in the water and the Democrats were already making apologies for "off-year election" results. The TV over the bar had the sound muted—not that Don could have heard it over the din—and was showing a graphic of election issues: jobs, economy, healthcare, the list went on. Afghanistan was number ten and Iraq wasn't even on the list. The surge was over, troops were coming home, and the public had moved on. Out of sight, out of mind.

Don wished she would get back with that beer. This afternoon's briefing had been a complete disaster. With the off-year election looming, the only thing less interesting than Iraq to the Washington establishment was Iran, and his briefing had been on the Iranian nuclear threat. The admiral had sent his aide and the CIA guy hadn't even shown up. Not that he'd had that much to tell them anyway. The Iranians certainly had the wherewithal to go into the nuclear weapons business, he just didn't have any evidence that they actually were doing it.

He spied Liz in the crowd. She was jumping, trying to see over the taller people as she looked for him. Don half-stood on the rungs of his chair and waved to her with both hands.

Liz squeezed between two fat lobbyist-looking guys fawning over a middle-aged man who looked vaguely familiar, like Don had seen him on TV before. She hugged him fiercely, and Don felt her powerful shoulders under his hands.

Liz had matured since he'd seen her last. Her dark hair was longer, and pulled back into a silver barrette at the nape of her neck. Her features had sharpened into a square jaw and defined cheekbones that set off her dark eyes and the slight hook of her nose. She wore a dark blue suit that flattered her blocky frame.

The waitress arrived with his drinks. Her eyebrows went up again when she saw Liz was there. "One Harp." She dropped the beer in front of Don. "And for the lady," she said, placing the martini glass filled with green liquid on Liz's side of the table. "That'll be fifteen."

Don dropped a twenty on her tray. "Keep the change."

Liz waited until the waitress moved away before she leaned across the table. "What is this?" she asked.

Don flushed. "It's a grasshopper. I thought you might like it . . ."

Liz leaned all the way over and planted a kiss on his cheek. "It's perfect, Don. Thank you. It's been awhile since a man bought me a drink."

He knew she was just saying that, but it felt good all the same. The lobbyists noticed the kiss and Don sat up straighter in his chair, sucking in his gut a little.

"What do you mean?" he asked, pointing to her engagement ring, a two-carat beauty in a platinum setting. "I thought you were engaged."

Liz held out her hand, staring at the ring for a long moment. "Oh, I am. James is a dear. Our families have known each other since we were kids." Her voice trailed off.

"How long have you been engaged, Liz?"

Her brow knit together, and she pursed her lips. "Three years and change, I guess."

"What's he like?"

"He's a great guy. A dentist, maxillofacial surgeon, actually. He just got back from a trip to South America where he fixed cleft palates for indigenous people. He's a great guy."

"So when's the wedding?"

Liz blew out her breath and took sip of her drink. "It's complicated, Don. James's work keeps him busy and my deployment and training at Quantico keeps us apart." She brightened and sat up. "Oh, but I have news. I'm getting transferred to LA when my training's done. I got a slot at the JTTF. James went to school there and has lots of friends. It's perfect for us."

"Joint Terrorism Task Force, huh? I thought maybe you'd go for something in the Midwest, maybe Minneapolis . . . that's where Brendan's from, you know."

Liz avoided his eyes as she sipped her drink. "Have you heard from Bren lately?"

Don leaned forward. "Liz, what's stopping you two? You were perfect together at the Academy and then it all just fell apart." He paused when he saw Liz's eyes start to fill up with tears—he'd never seen Liz cry before. He held up his hands. "Look, it's none of my business, but you two should—"

"Riley!" The voice that cut him off made Don want to scream. Clem Reggins slammed his drink down on their table, spilling a little in the process. He positioned his arms on the high-top so his tanned biceps curved at just the right angle. He leered at Liz. "Are you going to introduce me, Riley?"

The only thing worse than Clem Reggins was a drunk Clem Reggins, and he seemed well on his way to drunkdom already. Clem snagged the waitress's arm as she passed by. "I'll have another Jack and Diet Coke—make sure it's Diet, babe—and whatever these two are having." He pulled a wad of bills from his pocket and peeled off a twenty. He dropped it on her tray. "If you make it back before I finish this one, there's more where that came from." He watched the waitress's ass as she plunged back into the crowd.

He turned back to Don and Liz. "Where were we? Oh, yeah, Riley was going to introduce me to this lovely lady." He raised his eyebrows at Don, and winked at him with the eye that Liz couldn't see.

Don gritted his teeth. "Liz, this is Clem Reggins, my boss at NCPC. Clem, Liz, an old friend."

Liz extended her hand. "Nice to meet you, Clem."

Clem gripped her fingers and flexed his pecs at Liz. He bent over to kiss her hand. Liz tried to extract her hand but Clem hung on.

Don felt the table shift as Liz's foot kicked out. Clem's eyes bugged out for a second, and he released Liz's hand.

She covered her mouth. "Oh, I am so sorry. Was that you?"

Clem's jaw was set as he breathed through the pain. "No problem. Coulda happened to anyone."

Don hid his laugh by downing the rest of his beer.

Clem clenched his drink in his hand and took a long sip. "So, did Riley tell you about his shitty afternoon? What a shit storm of a briefing, am I right, Riley? Nobody gives a flying fuck about Iranian nukes anymore. And when you started in on the legend of the rogue nukes, I thought the admiral's aide was going to puke right on the table. Whatever possessed you to bring that up?"

Clem's tirade was cut short by the arrival of the waitress. She dropped another beer in front of Don, a replacement grasshopper for Liz, and another Jack and Coke for Clem.

"This is Diet, right?" The waitress nodded, lingering at the table for the promised tip.

"I only drink Diet," Clem continued. He flexed his arms at her. "This body is a temple."

"I can see that," the waitress replied. "And it looks like I replaced the temple drink before your last one was gone. You said there was more . . ."

Clem pulled the wad of bills from his pocket and peeled off another twenty. "Here ya go." He held onto the bill as she tried to grab it. "But it's gonna cost you."

The waitress let go. "What?"

"Your number." Clem winked at Don. "You give me your digits and I'll give you the twenty."

"Yeah, I think I'll pass." The waitress walked away, leaving their empty glasses on the table.

Clem turned back to them with a laugh. "That line usually works for me. What a bitch." He spied someone across the room. "Excuse me, Riley and Lisa. I believe I have a date with destiny." His bodybuilder frame seemed loosely jointed as he pushed away from the table and into the crowd.

Liz looked at Don with wide eyes. "That's your boss?"

Don nodded.

"Holy shit."

Don nodded again. "*Shit* being the operative word."

Liz shook her head, and raised her glass. "To the good guys. That was not one of them."

Don clinked his glass with hers and drank deeply. He cleared his throat, intending to get back to the topic of Brendan, but Liz was too quick for him.

"So what was all that talk about rogue nukes?" she asked.

Don laughed and shook his head. "It's just something I can't seem to let go of."

"Tell me."

Don knew she was just avoiding the obvious conversation, but what the heck, it might be good to talk to someone else about it. He leaned across the table and dropped his voice.

"You remember all the press about WMDs before the Iraq War?"

Liz nodded.

"We were sure Saddam Hussein had nukes," Don continued, "and there was a good reason for it. We know he bought centrifuges from the Soviet Union in the '70s and was producing weapons-grade material at Osirak, before it was destroyed by the Israelis in '81. He had the material, he had the scientists, he had the time—but we never found anything."

Liz took a sip of her drink and raised her eyebrows. "Well, finish the story. Where did they go?"

Don laughed. "If I knew that, I wouldn't be working for that asshole." He jerked his thumb in the direction Clem had gone.

"Okay, where do you *think* they went?"

Don glanced around the bar. No one was looking at them, and the two beers already in his belly gave him a confident feeling. "Iran."

Liz sat back. "Iran? I don't get it—didn't Iran and Iraq fight a war in the '80s?"

Don nodded. "Yeah, but they also have a history of working together. In the First Gulf War, when Saddam Hussein's air force was getting pounded by coalition forces, he flew every single plane to Iran for *safekeeping*." Don made air quotes with his fingers. "And the Iranians kept 'em all. War reparations, they called it."

Liz gave a low whistle. "You're really into this, Don. Okay, keep going. How does this link to the mystery nukes?"

Don blushed. "Well, my theory is that Saddam did the same thing with his nukes. He gave them to Iran for safekeeping. Unfortunately, he's dead, his sons are dead, and anyone who might have known about the program or the exchange is either dead or not talking."

"So you gave up on the trail?"

Don laughed. "Liz, you have no idea what DC is like. If you even mention Iraq and WMDs in the same sentence, anybody who's anybody will run from the room. It's a toxic subject. Guys who were there when it all went down tell me that for the first year in Iraq, that's all anyone did was look for WMDs, anything to justify the invasion. But when they didn't find them, it became the topic no one wanted to touch."

"Except you."

Don touched his mug to the edge of her martini glass. "Except me."

CHAPTER 16

Hashem smoked his cigarette with fingers that trembled ever so slightly.

He'd noticed the tremor starting a few weeks ago, but had ignored it. Overwork, that was it. He hadn't had a decent night's sleep in months. He stabbed at the muted TV with the stub of his Marlboro before he ground it out in the ashtray and lit another.

Arab Spring. The name sounded more like a feminine hygiene product than an act of political treason.

And yet, it had spread like a virus through the region. First Tunisia, then Oman, Yemen, Syria, and Egypt. Egypt! With a long-standing dictator and an established military in his pocket, even that country had fallen in the protests.

It was no small wonder his brother had called this meeting. The Iranian secret police was on fire with rumors of a similar uprising in

Iran. The ayatollahs were worried—and they should be.

The door snapped open and Aban swept in. His bodyguard scanned the room and left after depositing an aluminum briefcase next to Aban's chair.

Hashem started to take a knee before his brother, but Aban waved him upright and drew him into a fierce hug. "Please, brother. We have much to discuss today. Much to discuss." He flopped down in the waiting chair, and closed his eyes.

For a moment, Hashem saw shades of his brother as a much younger man, before Aban had assumed the role of a religious leader. The young man who would stay up late with his adoring younger brother talking of his worldwide travel, the girls he had met, and rocks, always geology.

Aban opened his eyes and the moment was gone. His eyes blazed with fury, and the dark circles under them told Hashem his brother hadn't been sleeping any better than he.

Aban hoisted the briefcase onto the table, pushing aside the ashtray and Hashem's tea mug. Hashem noted the silver case was a larger model than usual: twice as deep, by his estimation. Aban snapped the locks open and pushed up the lid. The briefcase was completely full of American hundred-dollar bills, banded together in neat stacks. Hashem ran his hand over the money.

"Twice the usual amount, brother. I—we—are worried, very worried about the rapid changes in the region. Our normal channels of influence are failing us. We need"—his mouth moved as he searched for the word—"more creative methods of influence."

Hashem nodded. "The geology project is progressing nicely, brother," he began, using their code name for the secret cavern installation. "We have two complete units now and the third should be done by next—"

Aban's face clouded. "Stop fucking around in that cave, Hashem! Look at the world around you!" The door opened a crack and Aban waved at it. The door closed.

He stabbed his finger at the television. Al Jazeera was showing a protest in Damascus, Syria. Police in riot gear waded into a crowd, blood painted the street. The news crawler was giving stats on the American troop withdrawal from Iraq.

"Look at it!" Aban's face was flushed, and his voice cracked. "The Americans are leaving Iraq, walking away after eight years, leaving a Shia government in place. What an opportunity for our country! And what do our politicians do? They sit on their hands and worry about Israel and the United States taking action against us.

"This is our time." He was reaching a preaching cadence, and he beat his breast in a dramatic gesture. "In Syria, are we sure Assad will carry the day?" He gestured at the TV again. "The news media portrays him as a butcher, but he's *our* butcher. We need to support him."

"But the Israelis—" Hashem began.

"The Israelis," Aban spat back at him. He slapped his hand on the briefcase. "Use your head, brother. It is time for some misdirection. Give the Israelis something to think about other than our nuclear *aspirations*." They both knew the Iranian program was a joke, that Hashem's cache of former Iraqi weapons in the desert was years ahead of anything the official Iranian program had yet produced. Would ever produce, if the pro-Western collaborators inside the Iranian government got their way.

The truth was that the Israeli covert actions targeted against individual scientists and the US-led economic sanctions had all but doomed the official Iranian nuclear program. Worse yet, the effectiveness of US–Israeli actions had encouraged the moderates in Iranian politics. The latest name being floated for President was Hassan Rouhani, but with elections still two years away, anything could happen. At least Rouhani would behave like an adult instead of Ahmadinejad, that petulant child who now held the presidency.

The man seemed determined to bring down the wrath of America and Israel on Iran with his constant, irrational diatribes and empty threats.

Hashem took his time lighting another cigarette. He offered one to his brother, who bit his lip, then nodded and pulled one from the pack. Hashem lit Aban's cigarette with his silver Zippo. They smoked in silence for a few moments. Hashem had another moment of déjà vu: it was Aban who had introduced him to Marlboros. He'd started smoking that brand exclusively as a way to emulate his older brother. He smiled to himself. Maybe now the shoe was on the other foot.

Hashem blew a stream of blue smoke at the ceiling. "Let's take these problems one at a time, brother. First Syria. We've been sending them arms via official channels for weeks now. Bashar needs to handle this on his own. It's the only way for him to keep power long-term. If he begins to fail, I will encourage our Hezbollah friends to join the fight against the rebels."

"Why not get them involved now?" Aban asked.

Hashem pointed with his chin at the television. "As long as this is kept within Syria, the other nations will stay out—including the US and Israel. The moment outside parties get involved, it will expand beyond the borders of Syria. That means international intervention, or maybe something even worse: a Sunni uprising."

Privately, Hashem worried about Bashar's ability to put down this insurrection on his own. This never would have happened if his older brother, Maher, was in power. The truth was, Bashar al-Assad was an idiot, a Western-educated pansy without the backbone to rule a nation the way it needed to be done. Maher's death in a car accident was a stroke of bad luck for Iran.

Hashem lit another Marlboro, noting that he only had two left in the package and hoping his brother did not want another. He cleared this throat.

"In Israel, our best option is Hamas. With some cash infusion, we can ramp up their rocket bomb manufacturing capability. Let them poke Netanyahu with their little needles"—Hashem had no illusion that the homemade Hamas rockets would actually cause any real damage in Israel— "and Bibi will fly into his trademark overblown response. Let the international community harass him for a while."

The Israelis, especially Netanyahu, were often their own worst enemy. Their ranting on the American talk shows actually lost them support, but when they acted behind the scenes . . . Hashem shivered. The American president Teddy Roosevelt had it right: "Speak softly and carry a big stick." If Netanyahu ever learned that lesson, the Iranians were in real trouble.

"And that brings us to Iraq." Hashem crushed out his cigarette and resisted the urge to get another from the pack. Aban stubbed his smoke out at the same time, waiting for his brother to speak.

"I will handle Iraq myself," Hashem said. "Maliki has done well to remove the Americans from his country, and he will need support to keep a pure Shia hold on power."

Hashem marveled at Maliki's bold step of refusing to sign the Status of Forces Agreement, causing the Americans to withdraw wholesale from the country. Still, he wondered if that might not be a mistake in the long run. Bold moves were rarely without backlash, and already the Kurds in the north, and especially the Sunni extremists, were angry at the Maliki regime.

Aban nodded. "That is the most important thing—to keep Iraq in the hands of the Shia majority." He stared at Hashem for a long moment.

"I was upset when I arrived today. I snapped at you, Hashem." Aban folded his hands and made a half-bow in his brother's direction.

"Please, update me on our geology project."

CHAPTER 17

Green Zone, Iraq
Thanksgiving Day, 2011

Brendan slammed the weights back onto the rack, making a clanking sound that echoed throughout the mostly empty gym.

The extra space from the troop drawdown in Iraq had seemed great at first: less people in the gym, shorter chow lines, more selection at the PX. But Brendan and his platoon were some of the last naval personnel left. His SEAL Team would be the last Naval Special Warfare Squadron deployed to Iraq in this war.

The combat ops against insurgent groups had ended weeks ago, and now all he had to look forward to was mind-numbing admin. The squadron would redeploy back to San Diego in a few weeks—in time for Christmas, hopefully—but before that they had to complete their own weight in paperwork, or the computer equivalent.

His phone rang. Commander Roesing, his CO. Brendan groaned, sure he was about to get saddled with some new survey or inventory assignment that needed to be done ASAP.

"McHugh here, sir," he answered, doing his best to wring all the whining out of his tone.

"Brendan, I need to see you in my office ASAP." There it was again: ASAP, the favorite word of military bureaucracy.

"I'll be there in five, sir."

He jogged out of the gym to the barracks. The Baghdad heat scarcely bothered him anymore as he passed from the gym to his quarters. He pulled on BDUs over his gym clothes, laced up a pair of combat boots, and snatched his cap off the hook by the door. Four minutes and sixteen seconds after the phone call ended he was outside Commander Roesing's door.

He knocked on the jamb. "You wanted to see me, skipper?"

Roesing looked up and pushed a pair of reading glasses up onto his forehead. He pinched the bridge of his nose. "Come in, Brendan. I've got a beauty for you." He waved to the chair in front of his desk. "Are you tired of paperwork yet? I'll be glad when we get out of this goddamned place and back in the good ol' US of A."

Brendan took a seat and nodded. "What's the job, sir?" Visions of another raid danced in his head. Finally, something to break up the monotony.

"I need you to take a couple of guys and help out State with security for the ambassador this afternoon."

Brendan did his best to keep his face still. The State Department had their own diplomatic security team, so the SEALs would be backup at best.

Roesing read his face. "They've stopped using private security contractors. Too much controversy."

War was good business for a certain breed of ex-military entrepreneurs. Private security companies had made millions from the war in Iraq. Brendan didn't blame the guys who went the way of the mercenary—he'd heard the pay was fabulous—but some contractors had gotten reputations as "shoot first, ask questions later" outfits. Deserved or not, once a company was labeled as an outlaw by the media, politics was driving the bus. Some tried to rebrand themselves by changing their company name. Apparently, State wasn't buying it.

Brendan chose his words carefully. "I'm sure we can help them, sir."

"That's the spirit, Lieutenant. The RSO is expecting you. Go make the ambassador safe."

Brendan swung back through the barracks and tapped three SEALs to join him at the State Department briefing.

The US Embassy seemed like a palace after the sparseness of the military barracks. The entire Green Zone fit into a point of land formed by a huge bend in the Tigris River, and the Embassy occupied the best spot in the Zone. The massive hundred-acre facility overlooked the river from a high bluff. Brendan and his men fast-walked down a hallway where one entire wall consisted of floor-to-ceiling windows. On the far bank of the river, the city of Baghdad seemed to stretch on forever.

The Regional Security Officer was a dark-skinned man in his early thirties with a touch of gray on his temples. "Lieutenant McHugh, I'm John Davis—call me JD." When he smiled, the skin around his brown eyes crinkled. "Thanks for helping out on short notice. I guess you heard we're not using private security anymore. Just as well, I'd rather have you guys any day of the week."

"Glad to help, sir."

Davis wasted no time on further formalities. "We're under some time pressure here, gentlemen. There's an emergency meeting at the MOJ this afternoon that the ambassador needs to attend—"

"This afternoon?" Brendan interrupted. "You need us as escorts to the Ministry of Justice today?"

"1800," Davis replied.

Brendan checked his watch. That was three hours from now. "Alright, JD, you're going to owe me one . . ."

Davis grinned and passed out a map with the convoy route. Thirty minutes later, Brendan and his men were back in the barracks. Brendan quickly tapped four more SEALs, bringing his team to eight, and assembled them in the conference room. He had the mission outlined in his head and ran the briefing as a checklist: route, positions on the detail, comms, ammo load-out, backup air support, and of course, medical support and an exfil plan if the shit hit the fan.

By the time he was done, they had less than an hour to be ready. He glanced at his watch; it was after six o'clock in the morning in San Diego, just enough time to call Amy and wish her a Happy Thanksgiving before she left for her mother's place.

He hustled back to the barracks and found an empty office with an Internet connection. A few seconds later, he had his Skype account up and had called Amy's connection. After six long rings, she answered.

"Happy Thanksgiving, baby!" he said.

Her hair was a mess and her makeup smudged around her eyes. She was wearing one of his old T-shirts and no bra. "Brendan, do you know what time it is?" she replied in an irritable tone.

"Yeah, sorry, I just wanted to talk to you before I left on a mission." Mentioning "mission" usually sweetened her mood.

She rubbed her face with both hands. "I have such a hangover, Bren. I was out with Roger last night."

Roger was Amy's agent, the one who'd promised her the cover of *Sports Illustrated*. Brendan felt his jaw tighten; he did not like how Roger looked at his girlfriend.

"I hope you had a good time," he said stiffly.

"It would be better if you were here," she said.

That was more like it. Brendan gave her a wicked smile. "Oh, really? What would you do if I were there right now?"

He was interrupted by a knock at the door. Petty Officer Gonzalez, in full battle dress, peered through the glass. Brendan held up a finger.

"Look, Amy, I need to go—"

"You just called and woke me up and now you're hanging up on me?" She pouted. "Why even bother to call at all?"

"I'm sorry, I'm in the middle of—"

"Wait, I need you to take care of the autopay on the water bill. Your credit card's about to expire and they called twice now."

Brendan gritted his teeth. She was living in his apartment, couldn't she deal with the water bill? "I'll do it as soon as I get a chance."

"You need to do it *today*. They called twice already and I'm leaving tomorrow for a photo shoot."

Gonzalez rapped on the glass again. Brendan held up his index finger again.

"Okay, go into my filing cabinet. There's an envelope in the very last folder that has the password for my accounts at USAA. The credit card info is in there—"

"So you want *me* to pay *your* water bill? Really?"

"If you want it done today, you need to do it yourself. I'm sorry, Amy. I need to go now." He hit the red icon to end the call. "Love you, too," he muttered to himself.

Brendan blew out a long breath and motioned for Gonzalez to enter.

"Doesn't sound like your lady is much of a morning person, sir."

"Gonzo, there are times when my lady is not much of a person."

His team rolled up to the Embassy in two Humvees at exactly 1740. Brendan rode in the lead vehicle passenger seat. He tugged at his body armor to move it a fraction of an inch to the left and rapped on the trauma plate that covered the center of his chest.

Convoy duty was his least favorite activity. On a raid or any other ground op, at least he had the ability to move, to respond to a threat. With convoy duty, you were a sitting duck for any insurgent attack. Sure, the up-armored Humvee they were riding in offered some level of protection, but it also kept them contained, bunched up, a target.

The ambassador's unmarked, armored car idled in the parking lot bracketed fore and aft by two State Department Diplomatic Security vehicles. The door to the lead vehicle opened and Davis stepped out. He wore dark sunglasses and body armor and was packing an M4 carbine and a 9mm Sig Sauer in a hip holster. His mouth was set in a firm line that was all business, the easy smile from earlier gone for now.

"Lieutenant," he said with a nod. "We're on channel five. Stand by for a comms check."

Brendan listened to his team call in, then ordered his team to shift to their backup channel. He adjusted his earpiece, and nodded to Davis. "Test sat, sir. We're ready whenever you are."

Davis checked his watch. "Just waiting on the bossman, Lieutenant."

The door to the Embassy opened and the ambassador strode into the hot Baghdad sun flanked by two bodyguards. Brendan caught a glimpse of a tall, spare figure with neatly trimmed gray hair, clad in a dark blue suit, and then the door to the ambassador's car slammed shut.

Davis's voice crackled in Brendan's ear. "Alright, gentlemen. We have our package. Just like we rehearsed it. Let's move!"

The heavy gates separating the embassy from the rest of the Green Zone opened and the barriers designed to stop car bombers retracted down into the earth. Davis's lead car roared out through the gate, closely followed by the ambassador's car and the other State security vehicles. Brendan's team took up stations on either side of the ambassador's car.

The distance they had to travel was ridiculously short, maybe a kilometer as the crow flies, but probably triple that once they factored in the ground traffic. Once they left the embassy compound—even in the Green Zone—the ambassador became a target for insurgents.

The scenery flashed by Brendan's window. Davis's voice, calm and flat, filtered into his ear. "I'm seeing a suspicious object up ahead. Shifting to secondary route."

The lead car cornered sharply to the right, and the convoy followed without question. They were headed directly west now, into the sun. Brendan squinted. This was not good. His hand tightened on his HKM4, and he fingered the seat belt release. If something went down, he wanted to be mobile as fast as possible.

Another corner and the stone facade of the Iraqi Ministry of Justice building came into view. They roared into the courtyard, Brendan's vehicle bumping over a curb along the way. He and his men piled out of their vehicles, forming a standard two-layer security detail around the ambassador: State Department men on the inside, SEALs on the perimeter. Brendan's men faced outward, weapons at chest height pointed down, eyes roving the buildings and landscape around them.

Brendan had flown over the MOJ building many times, but he had never seen it close-up. From the air, the curved walkway formed the shape of a question mark, and it served as a common landmark for Black Hawk helo pilots.

But today was not a time for sightseeing. The team hustled the ambassador up the curved walk.

When the detail reached the front doors, the heavy doors swung open. Thinking the Iraqis were expecting them, Davis hustled his team into the doorway—straight into an exiting group.

On the front right of the outer layer of security, Brendan came face to face with a man dressed in a dark blue, double-breasted suit that fitted his thin frame like a uniform. He had close-cropped black hair, shot with gray, and a neatly trimmed mustache. Brendan caught a whiff of cigarette smoke. The man raised the dark glasses covering his eyes.

Brendan froze.

The icy dark eyes showed a flicker of recognition. "Pardon me, Lieutenant McHugh." His voice was soft as he stepped to one side.

The momentum of the ambassador's security detail swept them forward, and Brendan rushed to resume his post. They reached the meeting room and posted a security detail outside the door.

Davis pulled Brendan aside. Snatching his sunglasses off his face, he leaned into Brendan and lowered his voice. "What the fuck happened back there, Lieutenant? You lost it for a second."

Brendan's mind raced. The man had known his name. His mind latched onto the smell of the cigarette smoke. The Iranian with the diplomatic passport.

"Well?"

"Sorry, JD, I need to make a phone call."

CHAPTER 18

Königstedt Manor, Finland
22 February 2012 – 1000 local

"The Minnesota Wild is a good team, yes?"

Don looked away from the frozen river flashing by his car window, and focused on the words of the driver. The man had introduced himself twice . . . what the hell was his name?

Jaakko. Yes, that was it, Jaakko.

"Pardon, Jaakko?"

The US embassy driver's pale blue eyes locked onto Don's in the rearview mirror. The edges squinched together as he smiled. "The Minnesota Wild is good team, yes?" He said it with a little lilt at the end and he pronounced the *w* as a soft *v*.

Don racked his brain. The Minnesota Wild . . . football? No. Basketball? No. Ice hockey. That was it.

"Oh, the Wild," Don replied. "Yes, very good ice hockey team. Very good."

The car made a little twist on the ice-covered road as Jaakko tossed a glance over his shoulder, all smiling white teeth and pale blond hair. "Yes. Very good. Who's your favorite player?"

Don pursed his lips as if he were thinking, but he doubted he could name even one ice hockey player, much less one from Minnesota. "It's hard to say," Don said, hoping Jaakko would take the conversation and run with it.

"Mine is Mikael Granlund," Jaakko said immediately. "Great player, one of the best Finnish players in many years. He will play for the Wild next season." He said the last bit with eyebrows raised, looking back at Don, as if that was a statement that Don might want to discuss. Don chewed his lip like he might be considering it, then shrugged his shoulders. The car rounded a bend in the road and their destination came into view.

Königstedt Manor. Don knew this building, and the Finnish government, had a long history of direct involvement in international diplomacy. On numerous occasions during the Cold War, Königstedt Manor had served as a secret meeting place for US and Soviet negotiating teams, away from the prying eyes of the news media.

When the US and Iran sought a location for a low-level exploratory meeting on nuclear talks, Königstedt came up immediately as an option. Both nations had embassies in the country, and Finland in February served as a natural deterrent from incidental contact with the news media.

Don's official role was one of technical support on the subject of nuclear nonproliferation verification. His status with the CIA was to be kept a secret. Don felt a little thrill at the thought of being an undercover agent, but his CIA supervisor had quashed those ideas.

"You're there to listen, Riley, nothing more. You take notes, you watch people, you answer technical questions about nuclear shit, and that's it." Andrea was a dumpy woman in her mid-fifties, with reddish-gray hair and a tired face. "Your status as CIA is not why you're going, you're there as a technical advisor." She pushed a stray curl away from her face and leaned toward him. "Clear?"

Don bit his tongue so as not to ask her if he could carry a weapon.

Jaakko drove the car slowly past the front of the house, pointing out the wide stone steps leading up to a columned portico that reminded Don vaguely of the White House. Thick bushes, the branches bare in the snow, lined the steps. "You should see this place in the summertime," Jaakko said. He kissed his fingertips like an Italian. "Perfect."

He pulled the car to the rear of the building and scrambled out to open his passenger's door. The packed snow crunched beneath Don's dress shoes, and he shivered in the open air. Jaakko deposited his roller bag next to him, offering a short bow. "It was good to meet you, Donald."

"You as well, Jaakko." Don dug into his pocket for some change, but the Finn waved his hands.

"Go Wild," he said with a laugh as he drove away.

A thin woman, iron-gray hair pulled back in a severe bun, met him inside the door. "Mr. Riley," she said in English, consulting a clipboard. "Welcome to Königstedt." Her handshake was dry and firm. "I am Mrs. Juntilla." She turned on her heel and, without waiting for Don, walked away.

"The meetings have started," she said over her shoulder. "I will show you a place to freshen up and then take you to the conference room." She walked like she talked, in short, clipped steps. Don had to race to keep up with her.

Mrs. Juntilla led him to a room that looked like something out of a European travel brochure. A four-poster bed, laden with heavy quilts and pillows, dominated the space. He tossed his bag on the bed and zipped it open, extracting a shaving kit.

The bathroom was equally extravagant, with marble double vanities, a huge freestanding tub, and a glass enclosure with multiple showerheads lining the wall. He looked longingly at the shower but decided that would take too long. He stripped to the waist and ran a sinkful of hot water to wash his face and shave.

The face that stared back at him in the mirror was tired, but there was a gleam of excitement in his red-rimmed eyes. He grinned at his reflection. Finally, his chance to make a difference in the real world.

Refreshed, he followed Mrs. Juntilla through the wide halls lined with oil paintings and fresh flowers, his repacked roller bag clicking along behind him. She paused at the end of the hallway, outside a set of double doors that extended up at least nine feet. She rapped on the door with her knuckles, then pushed into the room.

"Excuse me, gentlemen," she said. "Mr. Riley has arrived."

The room must have been a ballroom at some point in its history. The ceilings were at least twenty feet high and finished with ornate plaster castings. The walls were a pale yellow, warmed by the sunshine streaming in through the French doors that lined the wall. Outside, Don could see a wide veranda and the frozen Vantaa River beyond.

For the meeting, an area rug covered the beautiful honey-colored parquet floor, and two rows of tables faced each other separated by about six feet. All of the chairs, twelve on each side, were occupied—except for one. Don dropped his computer bag and stood behind his chair. He felt his face grow hot as he faced the room. "Good morning—afternoon, I mean, everyone. Sorry to interrupt. Flight delays . . ." He let his voice trail off.

No one said anything, so he sat down.

The meeting continued. Don pulled out his laptop and waited as it booted up. He scanned the opposite side of the table, trying to commit the names and faces to memory. He'd read the dossiers on most of them, and they were your typical bureaucrats: low-level career paper-pushers.

The third man along the row of Iranians was an unexpected

member of the delegation. Don read the paper nametag on the table in front of him: Reza Sanjabi. The man's laptop—the only one in the row of Iranians—was closed, and he took sparse notes on a yellow legal pad. Don did not remember seeing this man's dossier.

He looked to be in his late forties, with a pudgy, clean-shaven face and large hooked nose. The man seemed to sense he was being watched. His liquid brown eyes met Don's, and he offered a slight smile and a quick nod before breaking eye contact.

Don stared down at his computer screen, and tried to find the spot in the agreement they were discussing.

The day passed with mind-numbing slowness. Don now saw why no one else had volunteered to come to the meeting. The negotiators described this as a "trust-building meeting," a gathering where they talked about how they might talk about an agreement. They'd spent a good portion of the afternoon on one paragraph of the potential draft document and the word *nuclear* had not even been used in any of the text so far. Don felt a headache building.

After a break to freshen up, the attendees gathered back in the ballroom for cocktails before dinner. Don quickly realized that the entire US team had worked together before. They acted professionally toward Don, but they also made it clear he was not welcome for anything other than work matters. He got a Jameson at the bar and moved to the French doors overlooking the darkened river.

In the brightly lit room behind him reflected in the darkened glass, the diplomats were arranged in small groups according to their rank. A figure broke off from one of the nearby groups and approached Don.

"Hello," he said in flawless English. "My name is Reza." He had a trace of a British accent.

Don turned and shook his hand. His palm was soft, but the

handshake firm. The man's molten brown eyes seemed to look right through Don. "It is a pleasure to make your acquaintance, Donald." He made a broad gesture to the room. "This is a remarkable place, is it not?"

Don nodded. He could see that a few members of the US delegation had noticed he was speaking with Reza. "Yes, I understand this building has quite a history as a location where the seeds of peace have been planted."

Reza smiled. "I have heard that." With his drink hand, he motioned at the chandelier, a monstrous affair of crystal and gold. "Magnificent."

"And this location . . ." Reza turned to face the darkened glass. "Such natural beauty."

Don followed his lead and faced the glass, away from the rest of the room.

Reza spoke softly. "It must be a sight in the spring, when the snows melt and new life blooms."

Don's reflection nodded.

"Not unlike countries," Reza said. "They come through a winter of hardship, and new leadership creates new growth, new alliances . . . even peace where before it was not possible."

Don could see the head of the US delegation glancing in his direction. He looked like he might be about to come over.

"New leadership can make all the difference," Don said.

"We have such a leader in Hassan Rouhani," Reza replied. He was watching the gathering behind them in the glass, and seemed to sense they were about to be interrupted.

Don knew Rouhani's name, but consensus in the US was that his chances in the election were slim.

"Mr. Sanjabi, is it? I don't believe I've had the pleasure." The head of the US delegation held out his hand. "Richard Welker."

"Mr. Welker, the pleasure is mine," Reza replied in a warm tone.

"I was just remarking to Mr. Riley about the beauty of this place."

"Yes." Welker's tone said he didn't think much of the beauty of Finland in winter or Donald Riley. "I suppose if you enjoy snow and cold, it's fine. Why don't I introduce you to the rest of the US delegation and freshen that drink for you?"

"Of course, that is very kind of you," Reza replied. He turned to Don, extending his hand. "Mr. Riley, it was a pleasure to make your acquaintance. Please enjoy your stay in Finland, and I hope you see this beautiful country in the bloom of spring."

His hand closed around Don's, and Don felt something press between his ring finger and middle finger.

A slip of paper.

He curled his fingers around the paper and thrust his hand in his pocket.

He tilted his glass in Reza's direction and smiled. "To spring," he said, and drank off the last of the Jameson.

CHAPTER 19

Estancia Refugio Seguro, Argentina
13 June 2012 – 2200 local

Rafiq could see Javier's face illuminated briefly as he lit his cigar. The flame jumped erratically as the old man puffed on the Cuban, his features hazy in the smoke.

In the orange glow, Rafiq could make out Javier's neatly trimmed goatee, his square jawline and hooded eyes. He wore his hair long, like the locals, gathered at the nape of his neck in a ponytail. On any other man, the ponytail might seem pretentious, but on Javier it looked distinguished.

It was the perfect disguise, Rafiq realized, and the perfect trap. The same trap he was walking into.

Javier. That wasn't his real name, of course; it was the name he chose when he came to Argentina in 1983, shortly after the bombing of the US Marine barracks in Beirut. Javier's part had been large enough that he was sent to South America for a cooling-off period.

That was thirty years ago, and Javier was still in Argentina.

Thirty years . . .

As Javier told the story, he'd met Consuela, the only daughter of a wealthy rancher, during his first week in the country. There were various versions of the story—some involving Consuela riding up on a pure white stallion, others in which he helped her across the street, and even one where they met at a costume ball and kissed at midnight—but they all ended the same way: Javier married Consuela, became a wealthy landowner, and never went back to his homeland.

I've been here four years, Rafiq thought. Is this how I will spend the rest of my days, drinking wine and smoking cigars in the dark? He reminded himself again that he was performing a sacred duty for his brother, a task that only he could perform.

That excuse was wearing thin on his conscience.

In truth, Javier's role in the Tri-Border Region did more for the cause of Islamic freedom than anything he might accomplish in the Middle East. In addition to the safekeeping of Rafiq and his "cargo"—that was how they referred to Rafiq's mysterious charge—he provided a steady stream of funds for Hezbollah as well as the occasional recruit from the local Lebanese diaspora.

Rafiq kept his own name but otherwise maintained a low profile. The Tri-Border Region was well known for Hezbollah operations, and the lack of presence by the Israelis and the Americans still surprised Rafiq. He knew it was due to men like Javier, Lebanese immigrants who had grown up in the community and knew who to pay, and when, and how much. He supposed the odd overlapping of Brazilian, Argentinean, and Paraguayan responsibilities in the area allowed the authorities to defer to local control—or no control.

Not that there weren't mistakes. Only three months ago, a group of Hezbollah brothers had arrived in the area. They'd committed an unauthorized attack on Israel and were seeking safety from the wide net of Mossad. Javier and the rest had welcomed them with open arms.

But the men were young, restless, and stupid. Within a few weeks of their arrival, they were caught planning an attack on a local Jewish community center. Javier had enlisted Rafiq's help to deal with the situation.

There were now five unmarked mounds of earth in the *pampas* one hundred kilometers south of Javier's ranch. The role Javier played in the area, and the funds sent from this place to support operations back home, were far more important than the lives of five young men with more zeal than common sense. Their families would be well cared for.

"Are you going to let an old man smoke alone?" Javier's voice was rich and suave, exactly as one might expect a wealthy rancher to sound.

"Throw me the lighter, old man."

Javier laughed as he lobbed the silver lighter across the veranda. His laugh was gentle, like a grandfather's laugh, or the father Rafiq had never known.

Even in the poor light, Rafiq caught the lighter one-handed. He smiled to himself as he snipped the cigar end and sparked a flame. He'd worked hard to stay in shape, to keep the edge on his combat skills. He insisted on daily hand-to-hand sessions with his men and brought in locals as sparring partners. He'd even tried his hand at Gracie-style jiu-jitsu, a Brazilian invention, but he preferred not having to fight on his back all the time.

He stared at the glowing tip of his cigar. Still, four years was a long time. How much longer would he have to wait to return to the real fighting?

Rafiq checked his watch, the glowing face of the timepiece telling him he had another hour before his monthly check-in with Hashem. Even the watch had been a gift. A Rolex, no less, a present from

Nadine on his thirtieth birthday. Paid for with Javier's money.

"How's the cargo?" Javier asked him in a lazy voice. He heard the man take a sip of wine, and the clink of the glass as he rested it back on the end table.

Rafiq laughed out loud in spite of himself.

It was their private joke. When Rafiq had first arrived at Estancia Refugio Seguro, he'd overseen the placement of Hashem's special cargo in the deepest wine cellar of the plantation, a dry cave with heavy iron bars, an ancient lock, and oaken wine racks. At Rafiq's request, Javier had added a secret compartment complete with steel door, cypher lock, and state-of-the-art security system.

During the entire time the secret bunker was being constructed, the "cargo," as Rafiq referred to the crate, was under constant guard by Rafiq and his men. Rafiq always checked on the night watch before he turned in—with Nadine to keep him company. Within weeks they were lovers, a state of affairs he felt sure Javier would frown on. One night, after months of sneaking away late at night to "check on the cargo" with Nadine, Javier called to Rafiq as he crossed the veranda.

It had been a night much like this one, with the old man smoking and drinking his wine in the dark. Rafiq had squirmed and shifted his feet like a schoolboy who'd been caught stealing from the local drugstore.

"Why do you always check the cargo late at night, Rafiq?" Javier asked.

Rafiq tried to read the voice, closing his eyes to concentrate on the old man's tone. "It's my duty," he said finally.

"Hmmm."

Rafiq tensed.

"Maybe you should think about checking the cargo in the comfort of your own bedroom. I don't like Dean out late at night."

Nadine had appeared at the entrance to the veranda at that point, her face a pale glimmer in the gloom. "Papa, stop it," she said with a low laugh. The huskiness in her voice made Rafiq's breath catch in his throat. She glided across the flagstones and grasped his hand, pulling him gently back into the house. "And I don't like being called 'cargo,' Papa," she said over her shoulder.

The old man's laugh chased them through the dark halls.

Rafiq checked his watch again. Thirty minutes until his call with Hashem.

Tonight was the night. Tonight, he would tell Hashem that he had to come home to Lebanon. He had been away too long, away from the fight, wasting his life in this . . . paradise.

As if on cue, Nadine appeared in the doorway.

"What are you two doing out here? Smoking your nasty cigars and telling lies about me?" she said.

"Deanie, my dear, come give your poor old papa a kiss." The old man's voice was drowsy.

In her flowing white nightdress, she looked like a dark angel crossing the veranda. Rafiq heard her plant a kiss on her father's forehead and a slight clink as she took away his wineglass and the bottle.

"You look so like my Consuela, Deanie. So beautiful . . ." Javier mumbled.

"Yes, Papa." She crossed to Rafiq and, after depositing the glassware on the table, slid into his lap. He felt himself respond as her backside nestled into his groin. Nadine ran her hands over his hair, pushing her satin-clad breast against his cheek. Her nipple, erect beneath the material, rubbed against his lip. He nipped at her and she pulled away, teasing him.

Across the room, Javier let out a loud snore.

"Come to bed," she whispered in Rafiq's ear. Her breath was

warm against his neck and full of promise.

Rafiq's eyes dropped to the glowing face of his Rolex. Twelve minutes.

"I need to—"

"Shhh." She put a finger to his lips and shifted her body so she straddled him in the chair. Rafiq dropped his cigar to the stone floor in a shower of sparks. She ground herself against him, and Rafiq stifled a moan. He slid his hands down her sides until they rested on the small of her back. In front of his face, her breasts trembled under the satiny material.

"No," he said, more roughly than he intended. He pushed her off him. "I need to get ready for a phone call. Now."

Nadine shivered in the night air, wrapping her arms across her chest. "I'm sorry. I thought—"

"No, I'm sorry, Nadine," Rafiq whispered, drawing her close. "I shouldn't have started anything. I—I have to go now."

Nadine kissed his cheek. "Brush your teeth before you come to bed," she said with a low laugh. "I'm not making love to an ashtray."

Rafiq hurried to the office, feeling strangely guilty at having let Nadine down, and at the same time angry with himself for this feeling of tenderness. He was a warrior, fighting a battle that required his full attention. Nadine was a distraction—a distraction he needed to get away from.

Tonight's the night. Tonight I tell Hashem I am coming home.

He locked the study door and booted up the computer. The Windows theme music echoed loudly in Javier's study as he logged into his phantom email account.

The room was comfortable, rich with mementoes of Javier's life as a ranch owner. Rafiq settled into the deep leather armchair and cursed the slowness of the computer. He wished now he'd brought his cigar with him.

He opened the Deleted Files section of his email and searched for the spam message that had been sent to him at exactly noon on the fifth of the month. It showed a link to a XXX porn site, which Rafiq clicked.

A plain text chatroom with a five-minute countdown clock in the lower corner filled the screen. Hashem was already logged in.

By the time they had completed the prearranged script to verify their identities, there were less than four minutes remaining.

How is our package? Hashem wrote. Even in this secure environment, they spoke in vague terms.

No change, Rafiq typed back. *How much longer must I stay here?*

Hashem took a long time to respond. *As long as it takes. Be patient.*

Rafiq wanted to scream. It had been four years! His fingers shook as he typed.

I need an end date.

Another long pause. Was Hashem deliberately running out the clock to avoid the conversation?

Your mission is to be the hidden sword, the blade of death they never see coming. Be patient.

The countdown clock was less than a minute now.

I need to get out!

I have faith in your strength. WE have faith in your strength. You will not let us down.

The screen went black as the timer ran down to zero. The program automatically erased his web session and wiped his deleted files clean.

It had been like this every month for the last four years. Is the cargo safe? Stay in place. When would it end?

Rafiq shut down the computer, and switched off the desk lamp. He eased back into the soft leather of the chair, letting his eyes adjust to the dimness. The only sound in the quiet of the ranch house was his own breathing.

You have a good life here.

The thought came to him unbidden, and the truth of it hurt. He liked his life—no, he *loved* his life here on the ranch. But he could not shake the thought that if he didn't leave now, in thirty years he'd be like Javier, getting drunk every night, missing the only woman he'd ever loved.

Nadine.

Rafiq stood and crossed the room with swift strides. He flung open the door to the study and almost ran down the hall to their bedroom, unbuttoning his shirt as he went.

Nadine had left the curtains open when she'd gone to bed and moonlight lit the room in stark black and white. He dropped his shirt in the doorway and stepped out of his shoes as he moved to the bed. He unbuckled his belt and yanked down his trousers and underwear together. His sex swung heavy and free as he slid between the sheets.

She'd left her nightgown on the chair, and he ran his hand down her naked back, stopping to caress, then kiss, the small of her back. She rolled her hips toward him and he rubbed himself against her spine.

"Ohhh." She let out a soft moan as she slid her hand down his belly.

Rafiq's hand cupped her breast. He used his chin to push aside her hair and nuzzle her neck, nipping at the soft skin of her throat. She was breathing heavily now, her nipples hard under his fingers. He lay Nadine on her back and mounted her, letting out a sigh as he slid deep into her silky wetness. Her feet locked behind his hips and her hands grasped his buttocks as she pulled him deeper into her, her back arching with the effort.

Together they found a rhythm, and her breathing grew sharp with lust. The skin of Rafiq's sides went slick with sweat under her grasping hands as he held himself back, waiting for the magic moment when her body told him she was ready.

He thrust again, felt her hips spasm around him, and he let himself go . . .

He woke to the feel of Nadine's hands stroking his face. She traced his jaw lightly, running her fingers across his lips. She faced him, propped on her side, one hand under her head, the other caressing his face. Her naked breast lay a few inches from his lips, and Rafiq teased her nipple with his tongue.

"Do you love me?" she asked.

Rafiq could make out her face in the shadows, her eyes glimmering large in the light of the moon. In all the time they'd been together, he'd never said he loved her, and she'd never asked.

"Do you love me?" she said again, her tone insistent.

"Yes," Rafiq said, surprising even himself. But it was true, he did love her. This whole crazy night had done nothing but reinforce that to him.

He slid closer so his face was only inches from hers. She was taking quick, sharp breaths, as if she were still in the throes of their lovemaking and her eyes were glassy bright in the darkness.

"Yes," he said again. "I love you."

"Marry me. I don't care if you have to go away. I'll do whatever you need me to do, be whatever you need me to be. But, marry me. Please."

CHAPTER 20

Captain Rick Baxter pushed the rim of the ball cap up and swiped his forehead with his wrist, careful not to let any of the paint stripper touch his skin. The stuff stung bare skin like the dickens. He really wanted to rub his eyes, but settled with blinking them a few times in rapid succession.

"I didn't agree to no break, *sir*," came a rumbling wheeze from behind him.

Rick smiled at the extra emphasis on *sir*. "And I don't recall volunteering for this gig, Master Chief."

The rumble turned into a laugh, followed by a sucking sound as he drew on his pipe. The old man appeared at Rick's elbow. He gestured at the yacht with the chewed stem of his pipe. "She's lookin' good, skipper. Shapin' up nicely, she is."

Rick stood to his full height and stripped off the rubber gloves he was wearing. The old man barely reached his shoulder. He'd known Master Chief O'Brien for almost thirty years, ever since he'd started at Annapolis. As a green, newly minted ensign from the Naval Academy, O'Brien had even been there to get Rick's first salute, and the special silver dollar that went along with it. It seemed like the Master Chief had appeared somewhere in every sea tour Rick had done in his career. The old man was retired now, but he worked in the shipyard at the Naval Station across from the Academy. Rick had made a point of looking up the old codger when his work brought him to Annapolis.

He smiled down at the weathered face. He'd looked like that for as long as Rick could remember, so old that one of the wise-asses onboard his first ship had nicknamed him "The Ancient Mariner." Rick shook his head. Say what they might, the old man had more energy than any sailor half his age and twice the experience. Oh, and he managed to flout every naval regulation on smoking.

The pipe stem still pointed at the hull, and O'Brien's bushy gray eyebrows arched at Rick. "Are we havin' a senior moment, *sir*? I believe I asked you a question."

Rick laughed. "You're right, Master Chief, she's a beauty. She'll be just perfect."

The ship was a beauty, a forty-four-foot yacht he'd managed to wrangle from the Naval Academy sailing fleet. She was an old-style racer, a little wider in the beam and with a heavier keel than the latest models, and therefore a touch slower, but for his project, she was perfect. He touched the hole where they'd be placing the hidden hydrophone and stepped around the fuel cells that would power all the electronics he planned to cram into the hull.

The fuel cells had just arrived this morning, and they were even better than he'd hoped. The latest DARPA could offer him, the two blocks were the size of car batteries but could power a small apartment building for a week. Each.

He smiled to himself. This was going to work. All he needed to do was to get this ship through refit, find a crew, and get it to sea. Then they'd see what kind of intel he could bring in. He tightened the arms of the coveralls tied around his waist. Finishing the refit was the key. This morning, he'd even stripped off his uniform shirt and donned a pair of coveralls to help out.

He checked his watch: 1045. He needed to get ready for lunch with Vice Admiral Jake Abrahamson, the Naval Academy Superintendent, in a few minutes. Keeping close ties with the institution on the other side of the Severn River was key to his plan: the Naval Academy sailing team fleet was the perfect way to launder the sales of any future yacht purchases he'd need for his fleet of surveillance boats.

Jake Abrahamson knew what side his budget bread was buttered on. Rick's plan—if it worked—was a boon to the activities funding for the rest of his term at the Academy. Jake was a shrewd operator, and he stayed close as Rick pitched his yacht surveillance project up the intelligence community chain of command. He'd been present when Rick secured about half of the "black" funding needed for the refit of the boat that stood before him now.

Rick tugged the coveralls higher on his waist. "Alright, Master Chief, let's see how much of this we can get done before I have to break for lunch with the Supe."

Master Chief O'Brien muttered something into his pipe about officers and working half-days, but Rick's attention was drawn to a figure running in their direction. Lieutenant Michelle Malveaux puffed to a halt in front of Rick. The collar of her working khakis was rimmed with sweat and her face was beet red. Master Chief O'Brien's bushy eyebrows angled toward her heaving bosom.

"Sir," she gasped. "They're on their way."

Rick frowned. "The Supe's early? We were on for noon—"

"It's not just Admiral Abrahamson, sir, he's got two others with him: OPNAV N2/N6 and the CO of ONI. I got a call from the Supe's secretary, they're on their way now."

Rick swore under his breath. An ambush? Abrahamson was an experienced bureaucracy guerrilla, maybe he was the culprit. He knew Rear Admiral Cork, the head of the Office of Naval Intelligence. Cork was the one who'd given them the funding for the refit, and he seemed supportive, but Rick was not good at the Beltway shuffle. Maybe giving him half funding and letting him fail was Cork's way of telling him no without saying it.

He took a deep breath. "Alright, Michelle, let's get lunch moved up and staged in the conference room. I'm going to need the latest program overview and funding proposal—the one I used at ONI— up on the projector. Lots of Diet Cokes, that's the only thing the Supe drinks and he likes 'em nice and cold." Malveaux nodded once and hustled off.

Rick turned to O'Brien. "Master Chief, I need—"

"One inspection coming right up, skipper." The old man stuffed his pipe into his pocket.

Rick took his time walking back to the office. He had fifteen, maybe twenty minutes if traffic was bad; no sense in getting all sweaty, and he needed to think this through.

Maybe he'd judged Abrahamson and Cork too harshly. Maybe this was OPNAV's doing. Vice Admiral Jack Daugherty had gotten his third star and the OPNAV N2/N6 job about six months ago, about the same time Rick had met with Cork for his program funding. Daugherty had a reputation as a no-nonsense kind of guy with a big job to do—maybe an impossible job.

Working for the Secretaries of the Navy and Defense, Daugherty was charged with merging all the information-related fields of the US Navy into a single Information Dominance Corps, or IDC. The very size of the task made Rick's head hurt. Cryptology, meteorology, computer networking, oceanography—any data stream now fell under his purview. Daugherty was the test case for the rest of the services. If he succeeded, they would all go the same route.

Rick reached his office and stripped off the coveralls, leaving them in a heap on the bathroom floor. He splashed water on his face and inspected his reflection in the mirror. He could use a haircut, but no time for that now. He automatically reached for the shaving cream and lathered his face, still thinking through the problem.

So he had a go-getter admiral with a huge job and little margin for error. His budget was probably underfunded and he was being picked apart by the Washington bureaucrats, so he needed money and a winning program that gave him new data streams for the IDC.

Rick dried his face and settled his uniform shirt over his shoulders. He pulled a tight tuck on his khaki uniform shirt and aligned the seam of the shirt with his belt buckle.

He opened the door from his office into the conference room just as the three men were being led in by Malveaux. Rick surveyed the scene. Abrahamson had a hangdog look on his face and shot Rick a glance that said "I'm sorry." Rear Admiral Cork's lips were pressed together in a thin line of white flesh, but the rest of his face was flushed. Clearly a man who was holding his tongue. From the looks of the two men that he knew, Rick guessed the car ride across the river had been less than pleasant.

Vice Admiral Jack Daugherty looked young for a three-star, closer to Rick's age than either of the other two men. His close-cropped brown hair was only lightly peppered with gray, and the chest of his uniform shirt was a wall of ribbons over the round OPNAV emblem that covered his breast pocket.

Rick stuck out his hand to Daugherty. "Rick Baxter, Admiral. It's a pleasure to meet you, sir." Normally, this was the part in the conversation where the senior officer took the meeting formality down a notch with something like, "Call me Jack."

The eyes that met Rick's were blue, steely, and cold. "Likewise,

Captain." He took the seat at the head of the table. Rick hastily shook hands with Cork and Abrahamson, receiving another apologetic look from the Supe, before he made his way to the front of the room. While the projector warmed up, Lieutenant Malveaux placed a tray of sandwiches on the table and a silver tureen filled with ice and Diet Cokes. The Supe pulled a soda from the pile.

Daugherty waved at the sandwiches. "Captain, I'm not here for the food, I'm here to defund your silly sailboat project. You have fifteen minutes to convince me why I shouldn't."

Abrahamson did not open the soda. The silver can sweated onto the table.

Rick gulped. This was worse than he'd thought, the man had already made up his mind. He flashed up a cross-section of the Naval Academy yawl, the cabin packed with electronics.

"The program is tentatively called 'Feisty Minnow' and is modeled after the Soviet AGI program from the Cold War, when the Soviets disguised surveillance boats as fishing vessels and stationed them outside ports such as—"

"I'm familiar with the Soviet AGI program, Captain. Move on."

"Yes, sir, I'm sure you are, but there's a big difference here. The Soviets made no attempt to hide the fact that their AGIs were surveillance vessels. The ships had every radio antennae known to man on them, and some didn't even have fishing gear. We've taken the opposite approach. The provenance of every boat is clean and crewed with a mix of sexes posing as rich dilettantes. All of the electronics and the antennae are hidden." He showed schematics and 3-D mockups of the cabin with electronics stowed and then opened.

Daugherty chewed his lip. Rick took that as a good sign.

"Through the use of fuel cells, the latest DARPA is willing to allow us to use, we were able to reclaim the space normally used for fuel tanks as additional space for electronics—"

"What about data streams?" the admiral interrupted him again.

"What can you give me that I can't get elsewhere?"

Rick pulled up the slide that showed the signal-gathering capability. The admiral made a note in his steno book. "I can send your office a copy of these slides, sir," Rick said.

Daugherty stared at the screen for a second and nodded absently. "Continue, Captain."

Rick flashed the slide with the world map showing red dots were he planned to place the surveillance fleet. "As a private yacht, we'll be able to penetrate a number of ports where any type of naval-flagged vessel could not normally enter, or would be under constant surveillance if they did. We have plans for a direct uplink back to DC so we can make best use of the intel on a real-time basis." Rick let his gaze slide toward Rear Admiral Cork, but the man who had already funded the first ship in the program stared at the table and said nothing.

"How much?" Daugherty said.

Rick drew in a deep breath. "Well, sir, it depends on a lot of factors. We're hoping to partner with the Naval Academy to use some of their older yawls—"

"Don't bullshit with me, Captain. How much is the line item in my black budget?"

Daugherty's eyes had narrowed to slits and Rick gritted his teeth. He fast-forwarded through the budget buildup slides to the final tally.

The admiral let out a hiss. "No fucking way, Captain." He turned to Cork. "You funded a pilot of this bullshit scheme, Steve? There's some useful intel, I'll grant you, but where do you think we'll find the money?"

Cork's voice was tight. "It's a good program, Admiral, and it gives us stuff we can't get anywhere else—"

"Why don't we take a tour?" said Abrahamson in a bright tone. "Rick's got the first boat on blocks out in the yard and the interior's roughed out for the electronics. You should see the first article, Jack. It'll help you see what we're trying to accomplish."

Rick stared at the Supe. What the hell was he doing? The ship they were working on was no more than a shell; there was nothing to see at all. Malveaux, a look of panic in her eyes, slipped out the door to alert O'Brien.

Daugherty checked his watch, then stood. "Alright, Jake, we still have a little time. If you think it'll make a difference, I'll give you another few minutes."

Rick led the way out of the conference room and into the yard. The sweltering humidity of an Annapolis summer enveloped the group, and Rick sweated under his uniform shirt. He wondered to himself whether the admiral would at least let him finish the pilot boat or pull all funding immediately. They rounded the final corner before they reached the boat. With a quick scan, he could see that O'Brien had done a nice job cleaning up the work site. The old man stood at some semblance of attention next to the hull, his pipe nowhere in sight. Rick nodded at the master chief and turned to face the tour group.

"This is the vessel, Admiral. She's not much to look at yet, but as you can see . . ."

He did not have Daugherty's attention. The admiral was looking past Rick. Rick turned around to find O'Brien saluting.

Admiral Daugherty had stopped in his tracks. "Master Chief? Is that really you?" He snapped a quick salute, then strode forward and grabbed O'Brien's hand. The sternness had drained away from his face, and he smiled broadly. "How long has it been, Master Chief?"

"Long time, Admiral. You've done well for yourself, sir, if you don't mind me saying so. I always knew you'd make flag."

Daugherty blushed. "It's all because of you, Master Chief."

Rick cleared his throat. "Admiral—"

Master Chief O'Brien spoke up. "Sorry to interrupt, *sir*. Do you mind if I give the admiral the tour of our project? It'll give us some time to catch up."

The Superintendent answered for Rick. "I'm sure that would be fine, Master Chief. We'll meet you back in the conference room. Take your time."

Rick stared at Abrahamson, who smiled and gave him a slow wink.

CHAPTER 21

Königstedt Manor, Helsinki, Finland
31 August 2013 – 0900 local

Don put his television on mute and turned to the open window overlooking the Vantaa River.

The waterway glistened in the morning sunshine, and a pair of kayaks zipped by. Even though it was only late August, the leaves of the trees that lined the far riverbank had already begun to turn colors. Don shivered when he thought about what this place would look like in only a few weeks.

He blew out his breath. This trip was stacking up to be a complete waste of time. He threw a glance back at the television, where CNN was rerunning Netanyahu's 2012 speech to the United Nations for the hundredth time. The schoolboy quality of his "redline" rhetoric and the ridiculous poster of a cartoon bomb made for good banter on the punditry circuit, but neither accomplished anything in the real world.

Don knew the Israelis had both the capability and the willpower to strike Iran if they felt cornered, but in the US, it was a different story. The public was done with war in the Middle East; "war-weary" was the new Capitol Hill buzzword. Iraq was finally over—at least as far as the US population was concerned—and it was time to start getting out of Afghanistan as well.

The silent TV screen divided, Netanyahu on one side and Obama on the other. The irony of it made Don grimace. It seemed that one man was doing all he could to avoid a war and the other doing all he could to get into one.

And now this last-minute meeting with Iran to screw up his three-day weekend. It had always been on the schedule as a possible event, but it was also expected to be canceled. There were formal P5+1 negotiations planned in Geneva less than six weeks away, and everyone expected the new Rouhani administration to make a statement there about their plans for the nuclear talks.

This was only a working group meeting, and Rouhani had been in office less than three weeks. The man was probably still learning where the bathrooms were located. The P5 members, or the permanent members of the United Nations Security Council—namely the UK, US, China, Russia, and France—were joined by Germany—the +1—to make up the official negotiating team for the Iranian nuclear talks. The Finnish meetings were true working sessions, staffed by a core group of third-level technical experts tasked with hammering out pre-meeting language and rules. The tier-one negotiating team ignored these meetings as nothing more than bureaucratic grunt work.

The gathering today was expected to be even more sparse than usual. With the end of summer in the northern hemisphere, the US Labor Day holiday, and the expected reset from Iran in October, everyone had expected this meeting to be canceled. Even the most hardcore staffers were deserting the meeting like rats fleeing a sinking ship.

Not that Don hadn't tried. He'd put in for leave, which was promptly denied by Clem with a bullshit "outta my hands, buddy" excuse. Don thought about going to his CIA supervisor, but he finally decided to take the trip. His stomach rumbled, and he belched gently into his fist. Minor food poisoning from the meal aboard the plane was just the icing on the cake for what looked like a total fucking waste of his weekend.

He glanced at his watch. Time to get ready. With one last longing look out the window, he snatched his tie off the bed and faced the mirror.

The French doors of the ballroom were open, filling the room with fresh air and the warm scents of late summer. Birdcalls filtered in from outside.

The tables were arranged as before, two rows facing each other. Of the dozen seats on either side, only about two-thirds of the places had name tags. Don wondered if he had enough time before the meeting started to call the airline about getting an early flight home.

The US delegation leader was there with a few of his cronies. He nodded to Don but didn't bother to come over to say hello. They'd found out he was CIA and that made him persona non grata to the career bureaucrats.

Don claimed his assigned seat on the far end of the table—they always put him on the end, as far away from the action as possible. He filled a coffee cup from the urn and wandered out onto the veranda. The sun seemed like a pale imitation of the sunshine in Washington, DC, but he closed his eyes anyway and angled his face upwards. His stomach burbled and he suppressed another burp.

"May I interrupt you, Donald?"

Don turned to find Reza Sanjabi, the Iranian diplomat he'd met during the winter meeting.

"Reza, what a pleasant surprise. I didn't know you were coming this time." Don held out his hand.

Reza took a quick look over his shoulder back at the meeting room. "I think you will find many surprises at this meeting, Donald." He hesitated, taking another look around them. "I need you to listen very carefully. I work for President Rouhani in a . . . special capacity. I see that his wishes are fulfilled in the real world. Do you understand what I am saying, Donald?"

Don nodded. Reza worked for MISIRI, the Iranian equivalent of the CIA. He'd suspected as much after their last meeting, but this was confirmation.

Reza gave him a tight smile before continuing. "My new president wishes that today's meeting be the start of a new page in the Iranian nuclear negotiations. I am here to make sure that happens . . . and I hope you will join me. There are entrenched interests on all sides who are very concerned about maintaining the status quo. President Rouhani means to overcome these special interests, but he cannot do it alone. I believe your own president faces similar challenges."

Reza's liquid brown eyes stared at him with intensity. Don swallowed hard.

"I believe I can trust you, Donald Riley," Reza said. "Can I trust you?"

"Of course." Don realized his coffee cup was trembling in his grip. He wrapped his other hand around it and pressed it back against his chest.

"In our last meeting I gave you a way to contact me," Reza said.

Don nodded again. The number had been untraceable, probably a cut-out number.

"Do not hesitate to reach out to me, Donald. Our interests are aligned." He pressed his hand against Don's forearm and gave him a quick smile. "Now, I believe we should go inside. The show is about to begin." He strode away.

Don reentered the ballroom and took his seat at the end of the table, his mind racing. He needed to excuse himself as soon as possible and report this contact with Reza. Surely the Iranian knew he would report it; he was probably counting on it.

The double doors to the ballroom opened and the Iranian delegation filed in as a group. The first dozen took the seats at the table and the next twelve carried chairs with them that they set up as a second row. Reza, seated in the back row, adjusted his chair so that he could make eye contact with Don.

The entire front row of the Iranian delegation was new faces. They removed the old name tags from the table, replacing them with new ones. The Iranian delegation leader was a spare man with a gleaming bald pate and a pair of intelligent eyes that reminded Don of a hawk. His name tag said Dr. Ali Zhargami, in English and Farsi.

Richard Welker, the paunchy leader of the US delegation, swept his eyes down the row of Iranians and licked his lips. "I believe we may have different expectations for this meeting, sir. Perhaps we should adjourn so I can consult with my team."

Zhargami responded in a reedy voice. "It is not this meeting that concerns us, Mr. Welker. My team and I are here to ensure that the meeting that will take place in Geneva in less than six weeks is no less than a stunning success." He paused, and placed his hands flat on the table in front of him before he continued.

"President Rouhani has an ambitious agenda. One of his top concerns is ending this ridiculous feud with the western nations. It causes unnecessary hardship to the Iranian people and cripples our economy. The Iranian nuclear agenda is peaceful in nature." Welker opened his mouth, but Zhargami held up his hand. "Please, let me finish, sir."

Welker pressed his lips together and sat back in his chair. The man on Welker's right scribbled something on a pad and pushed it in front of the delegation leader. Welker glanced at it and nodded.

Zhargami waited patiently until he had Welker's attention again.

"As I was saying, the Iranian nuclear agenda is peaceful in nature, and we are prepared to allow IAEA visits to confirm this fact."

Don raised his eyebrows; the International Atomic Energy Agency visits were thorough and invasive. That was a major concession right up front.

"We will be making some changes in our delegation to ensure the October negotiation takes the right direction. Effective immediately, the leader of the Iranian negotiating team will be Foreign Minister Javid Zarif."

Welker sputtered. "You're replacing your lead negotiator six weeks before an international negotiation? That's preposterous! We will need to reschedule the event and prepare a new—"

"There will be no rescheduling, Mr. Welker. I am sure you will find the new Foreign Minister amenable to making progress on this process. Which brings me to my next point: the timetable for an agreement."

Welker's forehead wrinkled. "We said we wanted to have a preliminary agreement in place by the end of 2015. You want to push it out even further?"

Zhargami smiled without showing any teeth. "Sir, you have not been listening to me. President Rouhani has an agenda of progress, speed, and action. We wish to have a negotiation framework agreement in place by the end of this year that will allow the P5+1 nations and my country to reach a final settlement."

Welker gaped. "*This* year? You want a negotiating framework deal signed by the end of 2013?"

A gasp rippled down the US delegation table. Welker shook his head. "That's impossible. No way do we have enough time to reach an agreement in three months. Our two sides have been talking for *years*, sir. An agreement in less than three months? I expect you to be serious." Welker folded his arms. Several delegation members imitated Welker's closed position.

Zhargami didn't flinch. "Mr. Welker, I assure you that we are serious. It is true that our two sides have been talking for years, and where has that gotten us? President Rouhani is a man of action. He expects to have the framework agreement by year-end and a final deal in 2014. I intend to make sure he gets both of them."

Welker sat forward in his chair. He picked up the printed agenda and packet of documents that were the topic of today's discussion and dropped it to the table with a slapping sound. "And where do you propose we start, sir? By your own admission, this agenda—this meeting—is wasted."

The Iranian delegation leader shook his head. "This meeting is only wasted, Mr. Welker, if you allow it to be so." He nodded to a young woman on the end of the second row. She loaded her arms with a sheaf of folders and hurried to the US delegation side of the room. She deposited a folder in front of each person.

Welker opened his folder and scanned its contents. He pursed his lips, but his forehead was still set in a frown.

"Ladies and gentlemen," Zhargami said, when all the delegates had open folders in front of them. "I propose a new agenda for this meeting, one that will meet our goal of having a signed framework agreement in place by the end of 2013." His eyes came to rest on Welker's scowling face. "Mr. Welker, you are skeptical and I understand why."

His smile broadened. "I only ask that you listen."

CHAPTER 22

South China Sea, 100 miles north of Palau Matak, Indonesia
10 September 2013 – 0310 local

Captain Kim Hang-son had to piss. Again.

The North Korean merchant ship captain closed his eyes and listened to the engines. Sometimes focusing on something else for a few minutes made him forget the sharp pain in his bladder. Lately, he was getting up two or three times a night to take a leak. There must be something wrong with him, but trying to see a doctor back home was almost impossible. Maybe when they got to Iran he could see one.

He shifted in his bunk and the pain in his bladder increased. With a curse, he sat up and put on his glasses so he could see the clock on the wall: 0312. He stumbled to the head and relieved himself, letting out a little sigh as the urine dribbled out of his body and the pressure in his groin eased.

The captain sat on the edge of his bunk. Back to bed or check on the bridge crew? They would never expect to see him this early . . . just the way to keep his crew on their toes.

Captain Kim was one of the most experienced merchant ship captains in the North Korean fleet—and one of the most discreet. His ship, the *Be Gae Bong*, had carried all manner of cargo in its day, but with his large open hold area and onboard crane capability, his specialty was big machinery. Like the Transporter Erector Launchers (TELs) he had in his hold.

At fifteen meters long, the combination truck–mobile launcher package was the latest model—it still had the factory paperwork affixed to the windshield to prove it. But that was the only normal aspect of this shipment. For starters, there were only three units. His hold had room for at least six, but his buyer had insisted he only carry these three.

Then there was the port. Bandar Lengeh? Who delivered to Bandar Lengeh? They would transit right by Bandar Abbas, the largest seaport in Iran, to get to Lengeh. The little port had nothing but camels and sand to keep a man happy. Again, the buyer had insisted. And finally, the secrecy. Captain Kim was used to being discreet, but this job took discretion to a whole new level. He was actually running short of crew just because the buyer had objected to bringing on new crew members before they left port. He'd finally agreed to let him add one new mess cook.

Kim groused to himself as he pushed his legs into his trousers. The buyer was obviously well connected in the North Korean government; he could at least have taken the central committee member's son off the ship. The boy was an idiot.

At least the job paid well, and the buyer had insisted he supply all the required end-user certificates and official stamps. He even paid extra to do so. The resulting forgeries were fine work, but why pay to do your own fake documents?

Kim shrugged as he snapped on the light over his sink. More money for him. He splashed water on his face and pressed the heels of his hands over his eyes to suppress the redness. He ran a palm over his chin. Maybe he should shave. He decided to wait until after breakfast.

The bridge was quiet as he slipped through the door and closed it softly behind him. The heavy watertight doors on the bridge wings were open and he breathed deeply of the moist sea air. Five bridge stations were manned: a helmsman, a radar operator, a lookout on each bridge wing, and a watch officer. The view outside the windows was nothing but a pitch-black sea underneath a carpet of stars. Directly in front of him, the watch officer nodded over a chart. Kim pressed his lips together as he cleared his throat loudly.

The man snapped to attention. Without turning around, he said in a loud voice, "Captain on the bridge!" One by one, the other watch standers parroted back, "Captain on the bridge, aye."

All except the radar operator. His shadowy form remained slumped over the round screen, bathed in a soft green glow.

The watch officer roared out, "Radar operator, acknowledge."

Nothing.

"Seaman Park! Acknowledge." The watch officer's voice slid up an octave to near hysteria.

The ghostly green lump that was Seaman Park gave a start and sat up. He turned in the watch officer's direction and saw the captain. His gulp was audible in the stillness of the bridge. "Aye, sir! I—"

The portside lookout burst onto the bridge. His eyes were owlish and his voice cracked. "Captain! We're being boarded!"

Captain Kim ran to the bridge wing, where the lookout pointed with a shaking finger. Three men, no more than shapes in the darkness, ran along the open lower deck. Kim used the door frame to vault back into the bridge. Even in the dark, he knew every knob, fixture, and piece of equipment on this bridge. "Sound the emergency alarm," he said to the watch officer as he reached for the VHF radio handset.

He mashed down the transmit button. "Any ship in sound of my voice, this is Democratic People's Republic of Korea ship *Be Gae Bong*, located at—" He moved to the GPS display and read off the latitude and longitude of their position. "We have been boarded by pirates. Request immediate assistance from any warship near our position. I repeat, we have been boarded. Request immediate assistance."

"Captain, should I open the weapons locker?" The watch officer's face was pinched with fear and his voice shook.

Kim pulled the key to the weapons locker from around his neck and threw it to the watch officer. The man fumbled the catch, and it fell to the floor with a clink.

He needn't have bothered. The lookouts ran into the bridge. "They're here!" they screamed in unison.

Automatic gunfire sounded outside on the wing and everyone on the bridge dropped to the floor. Two men rushed in from either side and someone turned on the overhead lights, flooding the space with harsh fluorescent illumination.

The pirates wore tattered shorts and T-shirts, with dirty sandals on their feet. Bandanas covered the lower halves of their faces and black face paint was smeared across their foreheads. They screamed at Kim's crew in what he recognized as Tagalog. Kim's heart sank. Filipino pirates were notorious for not taking prisoners. He should have armed his men, at least given them a fighting chance.

The leader was a short, powerfully muscled man armed with a rifle and a very large knife strapped across his chest. He looked over the cowering crew. His eyes fastened on Kim.

He took two quick steps forward and hauled Captain Kim to his feet. Gripping the North Korean's shirt front, he slammed the man against the wall next to the radar station. "You Captain," he said in accented English.

Kim thought about pretending he didn't understand English.

The man's eyes narrowed, and the grip on his shirt front tightened. The pirate pointed the muzzle of his rifle at the watch officer, who shrieked in fear.

"I am captain," Kim said.

"Good." The pirate released his shirt. He picked up the ship's PA system handset and handed it to Kim. "Tell the crew meet in galley. No tricks. I find any loose . . ." He drew his finger across his throat.

"Will they be safe?" Kim asked.

The pirate shrugged. "I find any loose, I kill them."

Kim's gaze dropped to the radar screen and stifled a gasp. A large green blip glowed on the screen. He checked the range setting on the instrument. Twenty-five miles. An object that size could be a tanker, but it could also be a warship. It was maybe twenty miles away—just over the horizon—and closing toward them. The lights of the ship would be visible soon from the bridge. He needed to get the pirates off the bridge now.

Kim stood in front of the radar screen and accepted the microphone from the pirate leader. He pressed the button on the handset. "All crew, this is the captain," he said in Korean. "Report to the mess deck. No one will be harmed if we do as we're told. Report to the mess deck immediately."

One of the other pirates watched him closely, giving Kim the feeling the man had understood him. Using the muzzle of his rifle, the pirate motioned for Kim to join his crew huddled by the door. As he replaced the PA handset, Kim reached down and switched off the power to the radar.

The green blip faded from the screen.

The captain and his bridge team were hustled onto the mess deck where the rest of the crew was already waiting. The pirate leader poked Captain Kim with his rifle muzzle. "Crew all here, Captain?"

Kim did a quick head count and nodded.

"Good. In there. Now." He motioned toward the dry stores area.

The space was just large enough to hold all twenty of his crew members. The pirate leader pushed the last North Korean into the room. "Two guards outside. No problems." The designated guards raised their weapons.

The pirate leader snapped off the light and slammed the door shut.

Kim felt the ship turning. Toward the mysterious blip on the radar.

Please, let it be a warship. Please.

The man next to him shifted out of the way and someone else took his place. "Captain?" It was his first mate. Kim grunted.

"You miscounted. We're missing Lee."

Kim cursed to himself. He'd forgotten about the mess cook they'd brought on just before leaving port. He hadn't even seen the kid once since they'd left North Korea.

The ship steadied on its new course.

Please let it be a warship.

CHAPTER 23

USS *Chung-Hoon* (DDG 93), South China Sea
10 September 2013 – 0430 local

The Arleigh Burke–class destroyer ran silent and dark through the humid night. Two RHIBs hung over the water on davits, rocking gently.

"Standby, sir," the chief petty officer operating the winch said to Brendan.

"Very well, Chief." Brendan adjusted his bulletproof vest and took a deep breath to still the butterflies that always crept up on him before a mission.

The sailor on the sound-powered phones acknowledged an order and said to the chief, "From the bridge. Launch both boats."

"Launch both boats, aye." The chief's smile was visible in the night. "Happy hunting, sir. Go get some bad guys." He activated the winch and Brendan's team dropped toward the dark water. The SEALs fore and aft unclipped the lines, and the driver gunned the engine.

"Boat one away," Brendan said into his mike.

"Boat two away," came the reply.

"On me, Starkie," Brendan said, switching to the secure channel.

"Aye, sir."

The RHIBs, rigid hulled inflatable boats, rocketed across the water at thirty knots, blowing humid wind in Brendan's face. They overtook the North Korean ship quickly. The merchant vessel was well lit and he could make out the name on the fantail: BE GAE BONG. He wondered what that meant in English.

Their attack plan was to come at the ship from behind and launch the assault from both sides. When they were about a hundred yards out, Brendan keyed his mike. "Break and engage, Team Bravo."

"Break and engage, Bravo, aye." The boat behind them slewed to the right and made for the starboard side of the North Korean freighter. Brendan's team took the port side. The driver cut the engine to half-speed when they passed the fantail.

"Standby for boarding," Brendan called. The other two SEALs stood in the centerline of the RHIB. They rapidly extended long telescoping poles with rope ladders affixed to the ends.

"Now," Brendan said.

The driver threw the engine into reverse, and the SEALs raised their poles up the side of the freighter. Brendan heard a quiet thud as the rubber-coated hooks on the end of the rope ladder made contact with the railing. The man nearest to him disappeared up the side of the ship, Brendan close on his heels. As he threw an arm over the railing, he found himself looking right into the face of one of the pirates.

The man pulled his bandana down, revealing a wide grin. "Little slow, sir. Bravo's already all onboard."

"Bite me, Martinez," Brendan replied. "We're all secure?"

"Tighter than my little sister on prom night, sir. I've got them locked in the dry storage area with the lights out. They pretty much shit themselves when we showed up."

Brendan nodded and changed the channel on his radio. "Control, this is Alpha. Ship secure. Commencing phase two."

"Acknowledged." The reply had a tiny bit of distortion that came with secure satellite comms.

The SEALs from his boat had already pulled up two black Pelican cases and were standing by. They followed Martinez through the nearest watertight door. Brendan tried to keep a sense of direction, but he always found it difficult to do onboard ship. Martinez slid down yet another ladder and hauled open a steel hatch.

"Your patient awaits, gentlemen," he said in a mocking tone.

Three TELs were lashed to the steel deck of the hold under the glare of floodlights. The vehicles were about forty-five feet long and at least twelve feet high. The launchers stood empty, just giant curved rails the size of a waterpark slide, waiting for a missile—maybe even a nuclear-tipped one.

His two men ran to the front of the nearest vehicle and climbed on top of the cab. Brendan passed them the Pelican cases. "You're on the clock, guys," he said, setting his watch to fifteen minutes.

He could hear one of the men knocking on the top of the vehicle, looking for the hollow space the intel guys told them was there between the cab and the engine compartment. The body of the TEL was made of some kind of composite material that Brendan supposed was designed to reduce the radar signature of the vehicle. Somehow, the intel geeks had figured out there was a void between the two compartments which would be ideal for their purposes.

The sound of power tools echoed in the hold. The second team arrived with cameras and began to document all aspects of the TELs.

The men on top of the first launcher called down to Brendan. "Boss, we're ready to close her up."

Brendan hoisted himself to the top of the vehicle. They had opened a hole about as big as his hand. One of the SEALs shined his flashlight into the hole. The sensor was glued to the wall of the void, as close to the top as possible. Below it, a battery pack was glued in place. "Run the self-test yet?"

The SEAL nodded. "Self-test sat, sir. Ready for the sat comm check."

Brendan keyed his mike. "Control, Alpha. Standby for sat comm check."

"Ready," came the reply.

The SEAL slipped the dip switch into the up position. A green light on the sensor glowed once, then went out.

A full minute went by before Brendan got a response from the radio. "Test sat. Standing by for nuclear detector check."

"Let's do it," Brendan said to the second SEAL.

The man blew out his breath. "If I end up being sterile from carrying this shit around, I'm gonna sue the Navy." He pulled a small lead tube out of the case and stepped back to the launcher rails. "About here?"

Brendan nodded. The SEAL snapped open the lid of the tube and counted: "One-Mississippi, two-Mississippi, three-Mississippi." He snapped the lid shut and hurriedly replaced the lead tube in the case.

Brendan tapped his foot and keyed the mike to make sure it was still working.

"Nuclear detector test sat."

"Alright, let's close it up," Brendan said. He checked his watch. "We're a minute behind schedule, so let's get a move on."

"You can't rush art, sir," one of the SEALs muttered. He fitted the piece they'd cut out of the truck body back into place and glued it. Then he filled the gap with quick-drying epoxy resin and dried it with a heat gun. The second man was standing by with a Dremel sanding tool. He smoothed out the epoxied piece, stopping to put his face next to the cab and look for any remaining ridges in the light.

The SEAL with the sander sat back. "That's good. Give it a quick paint job, Ricky."

While his partner was completing the sanding job, Ricky had been matching paint colors. He made one final adjustment to the blend and, after a few quick passes with the wand, stepped back to survey his work.

"I knew my time at Maaco would come in handy someday," he said.

Brendan jumped to the deck. "Alright, gents, let's move," he called to both teams. "Everyone topside in five for the big finale. Petty Officer Rickson, you're on cleanup detail."

"Aye, sir," Ricky replied over the whine of a tiny vacuum cleaner. His job was to sweep the area to make sure they hadn't left anything behind from the operation.

Brendan waited for Ricky at the door. The SEAL held up a trash bag and flipped Brendan a mock salute. "All trash present and accounted for, sir."

Brendan ignored him and keyed his mike. "Control, this is Alpha. Phase Two complete. Ready for Three." Brendan snapped off the light switch, plunging the room into darkness.

By the time Brendan reached topside, he could hear the helo coming toward them. It hovered over the deck for about a minute before swinging out over the water and releasing a torrent of live fire into the sea next to the ship.

Brendan found Martinez in the group of pirates. "You're sure they can hear this down there?"

Martinez smiled. "Oh, yeah, they can hear it." He pulled his bandana up over his mouth and nose.

Brendan keyed his mike. "Alright, Alpha and Bravo teams, let's go Hollywood on this piece of shit."

The pirate teams and the SEAL teams ran to their staging posts on the ship. Live fire echoed throughout the superstructure as the "good guys" put on a show of gunning down the pirates. He listened to the "pirates" scream in mock death.

Brendan mentally checked off the bursts of fire. "Alright, let's paint the crime scenes and get back on the main deck so we can release our guests."

He gave a thumbs-up to the petty officer who had been in charge of the shooting on the main deck. The man unscrewed a Nalgene bottle filled with blood and painted the bulkhead where he had "killed" one of the pirates. If the North Koreans ever tested the blood, they would find it was human—compliments of a US Navy hospital blood bank.

Brendan looked past the petty officer to a watertight door that stood ajar. His heart stopped. A face looked back at him, a thin, pinched face with almond-shaped eyes and a gaping mouth in need of dental work.

The North Korean saw Brendan at the same time. The face disappeared into the ship.

Brendan charged after him, hitting his mike as he did so. "Martinez, we have a runner. I'm on the main deck."

Ahead of him, the man spun around a post and slid down a steep stairwell without touching any steps. Brendan raced after him, cursing in a steady stream.

The fleeing man entered a long passageway, lit infrequently from lights set in the base of the wall. He was throwing terrified looks over his shoulder, and Brendan could hear him breathing in high-pitched, ragged gasps. He reached the end of the hall, his hand out for the door handle. Brendan put on a burst of speed and launched through the air.

He crashed into the man, smashing him flat against the door. *It's a kid,* Brendan realized as he grabbed the skinny shoulders and slammed him facedown onto the deck. He put his knee on the boy's back and gripped his chin. If he snapped the kid's neck, no one would question it on a mission like this.

But he couldn't.

He yelled into his radio. "Martinez, get down here. Third deck. Forward. Port side."

Brendan flipped the boy over so he was facing up. The kid held up his hands in front of his face. He was crying and snot ran out of his nose. He was maybe fifteen years old and small for his age at that. Brendan eased his knee off the boy's chest so the kid could breathe.

"You speak English?" Brendan demanded.

The terrified blank look in the boy's eyes told him the answer was no.

Martinez came thundering up the hallway. Brendan glared up at him. "You told me this fucking ship was secure! Now I find this kid roaming around. Who knows what he saw."

"Are you gonna waste him, sir?"

Brendan got to his feet, leaving the crying boy on the deck. "No, I'm not going to waste him. Get me a set of zip ties, we're taking him with us."

Out of the corner of his eye he saw the kid move, and Martinez started to yell. Then a white-hot stab of pain ran through his right knee. He looked down and saw the handle of a knife protruding from the back of his leg. Brendan moved the joint and felt the point of the knife scrape against the inside of his kneecap.

Martinez let loose a burst from his AK-47 and a wet slapping sound hit the floor behind Brendan.

Brendan leaned against the bulkhead and slid to the ground, keeping his right leg out straight. His ears rang from the gunfire. His vision tunneled inward to blackness.

CHAPTER 24

Bandar Lengeh, Iran
02 November 2013 – 0330 local

Hashem lit another cigarette even as he crushed the last one under his heel. In the glare of the pier lights, he could see the bullet holes in the bulkheads of the *Be Gae Bong*.

How could this have happened? Pirates operating that far out in the South China Sea? It was rare, but not unheard of. Still, as an intelligence officer, it made the hair stand up on the back of his neck.

The merchant ship had pulled alongside the pier more than fifteen minutes ago and the dock crew was still fussing with the lines on the massive white-painted bollards. The men moved at a snail's pace, clearly not accustomed to working this late at night.

Hashem made a rolling motion with his index finger to Mansour, the head of his security detail. His team was outfitted as working men, in dirty green coveralls, and as their foreman he wore an open-necked polo shirt and trousers. He wished for a breast pocket to stow his cigarettes.

Mansour drew the crew leader of the dock workers aside and was reaching into his pocket. Hashem smiled. Mansour had learned that greed is a better motivator than fear. The pace of work on the dock increased, and within minutes the crane lowered the gangway into place. Hashem crossed before they had even disconnected the crane hoist lines.

The North Korean ship captain met him on the main deck, a short, thin man with a shaggy gray crew cut and black-framed glasses. The man bowed and extended his hand. "You must be—"

"Not here," Hashem answered curtly. "Inside."

The captain's smile vanished and he nodded. That was the one thing Hashem liked about working with North Koreans: they understood how to obey orders.

He followed the captain's painfully thin shoulders into the superstructure of the ship and up three flights of steep steps. The man's cabin was about the size of Hashem's walk-in closet at home, with a narrow bunk, a fold-down desk, a washbasin, and a picture of the Great Successor. Hashem looked from the pudgy jowls of Kim Jong-un to the skin stretched sharply over the captain's jawline, and he shook his head.

The captain offered Hashem the only chair and sat on the edge of his bunk.

"Tell me," Hashem said, in English. "Everything."

The captain spoke in passable English, describing the pirate attack. Hashem interrupted him immediately and demanded to see the chart. The captain scurried from the room and returned with a dog-eared nautical chart. Hashem drew out a tablet and compared the latest intelligence reports with the captain's information.

He grimaced. The location was a bit beyond the operating area for pirates in that region, but not improbable. "How did they board your ship?"

The captain squirmed. "They boarded from the stern, where the lookouts could not see them," he said finally.

Hashem frowned. "What about radar? Did you have radar operating?"

The captain nodded.

"Well?" Hashem said. "Why didn't you see them?"

"The radar operator was asleep on watch." The captain hung his head.

"Asleep? Are you serious? What did you do to him?"

The captain squirmed again. "He is the son of a central committee chairman . . . there is nothing I can do."

Hashem lit a cigarette. "Show me where you were confined."

The captain led him to the galley and the dry stores area. Hashem tested the strength of the door. "How long were you held?"

The captain shrugged. The pirates had taken their wristwatches. "Maybe two hours," he said.

"And then what happened?"

"We heard helicopters, then the sounds of gunfire—heavy caliber—then small arms fire on board. After about twenty minutes, we were freed by the Americans, Navy SEALs." The captain extended his arms and flexed his muscles as he recalled them. "They were taking body bags off and two of the pirates were in handcuffs. And one SEAL was injured. He was in a stretcher being lifted off by the helicopter."

Hashem flicked his cigarette into a nearby sink and tapped another out of the package. The captain was clearly infatuated by the Americans, and even worse than that, he believed every word of what he was telling Hashem.

"And all of your men were accounted for?"

The captain shook his head. "We lost one. A mess cook, just a boy. I didn't even realize he was missing until after we were locked up."

"Dead?"

"The pirates killed him. That's what the Americans said. We stopped in Singapore to ship his body home. It delayed us almost two weeks."

"And the Americans, they looked at your manifest?"

The captain puffed out his chest. "My documents are the best. Your buyer made sure of that. The stupid Americans matched the manifest to the cargo and left."

"Did they do anything else?"

Captain Kim shrugged. "They took pictures."

"Nothing else?" Hashem pressed him. "Were they alone with the cargo for even a few minutes?"

The captain shook his head emphatically. "Absolutely not!"

Hashem's phone rang. "Cargo on the dock?" he said into the receiver.

"Yes, sir."

"We'll be right down."

Hashem smoked in silence as the captain shifted from foot to foot. His hand touched the knife at the small of his back. His years of experience told him the captain was telling the truth. Using more forceful measures would only cause the North Korean to try to tell him what he thought Hashem wanted to hear, and it would take a long time. Even as he sat staring at the captain, the Americans might have a satellite overhead taking photos of his newly acquired TELs, the final piece in his decade-long plan to bring nuclear strike capability to his beloved Iran.

No, the captain was telling the truth. This had been a pirate attack.

The crane hoist lines were just lifting away from the third TEL on the pier. Glistening black in the harsh glare of the overhead lights, the units looked deadly. Hashem smiled to himself when he thought about how they would look with his missiles loaded onto them.

Mansour met him at the base of the gangway. "We've been over all three and found nothing that could be a transmitter. We're fueling the trucks now. We'll be ready to leave in another fifteen minutes." He handed Hashem a small briefcase, and then hesitated. "Should I hand out the GPS units, sir?"

Hashem pursed his lips. The GPS units were programmed to guide them to the bunker location—or he could store the launchers locally and do a more thorough search, maybe one with x-ray capability. But then he would have to move the TELs again, increasing his exposure to the American satellites.

Captain Kim seemed to understand that Hashem was making a significant decision. His eyes grew wary and he stepped back, away from the gangway.

Hashem smiled suddenly and handed the briefcase to the North Korean. "For your trouble, Captain Kim. I want you to leave this port as soon as possible, but make sure you get the bullet holes in your ship repaired before you return to North Korea. Have a safe trip home."

The captain accepted the case with trembling hands. "Thank you, sir."

Hashem nodded as he tapped out another Marlboro. His lighter flared up, and he focused on the glowing tip of the cigarette.

"Hand out the GPS units, Mansour. I will ride with you."

⤙✕⤚

CIA Headquarters, Langley, Virginia
01 November 2013 – 1900 local

Victor Warren fingered the bump under his chin. It felt to him like the start of another pimple. He pressed down hard on the little bump until it hurt. He'd read somewhere that the pressure would suppress the swelling and prevent a pimple from forming. Probably one of the old *Cosmo* magazines that Gloria had left stacked next to the toilet when she moved out. She'd be back.

He heard the door to the command center open behind him and saw the square of light reflected in his computer screen. Victor sneaked a glance behind him. They didn't often get visitors down here in the bowels of the CIA on a Friday night unless there was something going on.

The visitor was a naval officer, a rangy black guy with his broad back facing Victor. When he turned, Victor caught a glimpse of a sizeable patch of medals on the front of his service dress blues, and the four gold stripes of a captain.

Victor sat up straighter in his seat and adjusted his headset. Maybe this shift wouldn't be boring after all.

The officer and his shift supervisor were taking a long time conferring. They broke off as the supervisor put up a time-lapsed satellite feed on the big screen. Victor's eyebrows went up when he saw it was Iran. Now *this* was getting interesting. They were discussing a beat-up merchant ship that had docked next to the pier. Victor called up a tab on his screen and typed in the lat-long: Bandar Lengeh, Iran. He ran his eyes over the port details. Small port on the Persian Gulf. Nothing unusual about the port or the ship.

He flicked his eyes up to the big screen again, where the supe had thrown up some new images. Holy shit! TELs! Even he could tell they were North Korean models.

"Warren," the supe called.

"Yes, sir."

"We're going to do an activation sequence on one of the devices for the captain here."

Victor twisted around in his chair. "I'm ready whenever you are, sir."

The officer snagged a chair from one of the vacant stations and rolled it over to Victor's desk. The man had a square face that looked deadly serious until he smiled. He put his elbows on his knees and leaned forward, holding a single sheet of paper. His hands were huge, with scarred knuckles.

"How ya doin', son?"

"Fine, sir. How about yourself?"

"Ask me after we see if this friggin' thing works or not," he growled. "We went to a lot of trouble to get it in place."

Victor tried not to show the surprise he felt. They had a tracking beacon on a North Korean TEL that was being off-loaded in Iran? He cursed the fact that he couldn't talk about his job outside of work. Gloria would definitely take him back if he could talk about this kind of shit.

Victor called up a sensor activation screen. "Standing by, sir."

"Alrighty then. Let's do this. Xray, Delta, Xray, Seven, Niner, Papa, Romeo, Xray."

Victor repeated the letters as he typed them in, then again reading them off the screen. The captain confirmed, and Victor toggled the box that said ACTIVATE.

The status changed from INACTIVE to STANDING BY with three dots that ran on and on.

"How long does this take?" the officer asked.

"Well, sir, these are low-energy signals and are very sensitive to shielding, so it might not pick up on the first pass. I've seen it take only a few minutes or a few hours." He hesitated. "Or not at all."

The captain made a face.

Victor switched screens to the satellite map. "We've got a bird coming over the horizon in a few minutes that has a good angle of attack. If they're still in the clear, I'm sure we'll see your sensor, sir."

The officer fidgeted next to him, folding and unfolding the paper.

The sensor status went to ACTIVE.

"Supe, we're live on the captain's sensor," Victor called out. "Getting parameters now."

"Acknowledged."

"We're okay?" The officer crowded next to Victor's chair.

"I'll tell you in a minute, sir. Just as soon as the sensor tells me." Victor's fingers flew over the keyboard. He called out again. "Supe, sensor is active, and location correlates with the satellite feed. Programmed for hourly location pings, battery at ninety-nine percent, no radiological emissions present."

A nuke detector! If only Gloria could see me now.

"Acknowledged, Warren."

Victor turned to the captain. "Is that what you were looking for, sir?"

The smile said it all. "That's perfect," he said. "How does this thing work?"

Victor turned in his chair. "The sensor puts out a low-energy ping that can be picked up by any friendly satellite in range. It's a simple binary string on a header. That piggybacks on any available comm signal, then the NSA strips it off in processing and it comes to us. I'll warn you, this is not real-time comms. The sensor sends out a signal once an hour, but it has no idea if it's connecting or not. It might take us another hour to get the signal from processing. If the launcher is stored in a big metal hangar or underground, you may not get a signal at all."

The captain blew out a long breath. "Okay, I guess that's all I need for now."

"Warren, let's put that new sensor on the watch list."

"Yes, supe." Victor made the necessary adjustments. Adding the sensor to the watch list meant that all locational data would be collated daily and released to a preset distribution list. He looked up at the officer. "I assume you want to be added to the distribution list for this sensor, sir? I'm going to need your name."

"Baxter, Richard," the officer replied. "But you can call me Rick."

Victor looked up the name in the database. He clicked the check box with a flourish. "You're all set, Rick. If this puppy activates, you'll be one of the first to know."

Victor settled in for a long shift after Baxter left. He periodically toggled back to check on the new sensor. The TEL was on the move, heading north for two hours, then due west into the desert.

CHAPTER 25

Walter Reed National Military Medical Center, Washington, DC
04 November 2013 – 1100 local

"I'm sorry, sir. Are you telling me that you gave this person access to your personal information, or that she stole the information?" The woman's voice had a professional tone, but underneath Brendan could almost hear her saying, *You fucking idiot.*

"It's complicated," he said.

"Which part, sir? If she stole from you, you need to contact the police. If you want to remove her from an account, then you need to contact your bank and get them to remove her from the account. We're just a credit agency, sir, we just report the data."

You fucking idiot, Brendan finished for her.

He pressed his free palm against his eye socket. "Can you just make a note that I called, please?" he said, trying to keep the whining tone out of his voice. "Any new credit cards that get opened in my name are not mine. Please."

Computer keys clicked as she typed. "Are you pressing charges against this woman, sir?"

"No—yes. I don't know, I haven't decided yet." He pressed his palm harder into his face. "I'm still in the hospital right now and I'm on the other side of the country . . . it's complicated."

"Well, I do hope you get better soon, sir. Is there anything else I can do for you today?"

"Uh, no, I guess not—"

"Wonderful, if you could take a short survey after this call to tell us about your experience with—"

Brendan slammed the hospital phone down, one of those hard plastic desk jobs with the coiled cord attached. His financial life was so fucked right now he couldn't even get a goddamned cell phone.

He clenched his eyes shut, afraid that he might actually cry.

How could Amy do this to him? He was her "one and only"— she actually used to call him that, her one and only. She even signed her emails to him with O&O, their own private joke.

And she was gone. Not only was she gone, but she had left his life a financial wreck in the wake of her departure. Brendan was afraid to even think about the list: Car—repossessed. Apartment overlooking Imperial Beach—evicted. Bank accounts—overdrawn. Credit cards—maxed out. She'd even opened new ones in his name and maxed those out, too.

And she was gone.

But that wasn't even the worst part. He was pretty sure he still loved her. Five-foot-ten, auburn hair, green eyes, and a body that just would not quit, Amy had it all. Okay, maybe he didn't love her, but he still missed her. If she walked through the hospital door right now, he'd take her back despite all the damage she'd done to his life.

You are a fucking idiot, McHugh.

Brendan shifted in the bed, wincing when he jostled his knee. The heavily bandaged joint was suspended in the traction device over his bed. He was now a veteran of three knee operations, performed by the ortho docs at Walter Reed. They'd considered trying the first operation at Balboa, in San Diego, but his CO had insisted they send him to Walter Reed. The orthopedic surgeons here had the most experience putting kids from Iraq and Afghanistan back together, and his skipper wanted only the best surgeons working on Brendan's knee.

He needed all the help he could get. The knife the North Korean kid had stabbed him with was a rusty piece of shit that he'd apparently used to gut fish. To say it was crawling with bacteria was an understatement; the little knife was like a direct bacterial injection into his leg.

After the first operation, the infection got so bad the doctor had wanted to take the leg off above the knee. Brendan remembered the whispered argument next to his bed between his CO and the doctor—or maybe he'd dreamed it? Who knew; he was completely out of it by that point, his head swimming in fever from the infection. It was all a foggy half-memory.

The second operation was what the doctors called "stabilization." They had talked about cutting out the dead tissue and laying down a base of healthy material to build on. Brendan only half listened. What was he going to do, not have the surgery?

His mother came to visit between the second and third operations. She was the one who asked about Amy. Brendan hadn't fully realized the extent of his girlfriend's destruction at that point, and he'd laughed off her absence with a "you know Amy" comment.

Mom was full of Minneapolis family gossip and talk about his father's heart condition, but by the end of the third day, Brendan was ready for her to go home.

And then operation number three, the one where they put his knee all back together again, just like Humpty Dumpty. The third operation was the easiest of the three and the doctors were all smiles afterwards, which Brendan took to be a good sign.

A knock at the door interrupted his thoughts.

Dr. Rob Bearon stood in the doorway—*filled the doorway* was a more apt description. He was a huge man who the nurses called "Bear" behind his back. He had short, thick brown hair, a dense, close-cropped beard of the same color, and squinty eyes.

"Lieutenant McHugh," he boomed, "how we doing this fine morning, sir?"

Despite his foul mood, Brendan smiled. It was impossible not to smile with Dr. Bear. But his smile faded when he saw that the doctor had company with him.

Rear Admiral Steve "Wiz" Wizniewski was a top dog at the Washington office of US Special Operations Command, or SOCOM, and well known in the SEAL community. He had been CO of BUD/S, Basic Underwater Demolition/SEAL school, when Brendan went through the Program. He could still recall Wiz doing PT with the SEAL candidates half his age—and kicking their asses. Wiz had even pinned on Brendan's Trident—the "Budweiser," as the SEAL warfare pin was called—after he'd passed both Underwater Demolition and SEAL training.

Wiz crossed the room in two strides and gripped Brendan's hand. "Good to see you, Brendan. It's been a long time."

"Yes, sir." Brendan tried not to choke. Wiz's grip said it all: he's here to let me go. A dark cloud settled over his head as he half-listened to the Bear's explanation.

The big man had amazingly gentle hands. He lowered the traction line and removed the bandage like he was unwrapping a historical treasure. Brendan's knee was a greenish-purple lump of cuts and stitches. It didn't even look like a knee.

"The injury occurred from the rear of the joint, piercing the hamstring and cutting all the way through to the patella." Brendan gritted his teeth when he thought about the feeling of the knifepoint scraping the inside of his kneecap. Bear took out his pen and pointed to the lumpy right side of the knee.

"The early infection was extensive and resulted in bone loss and tissue decay on this side of the joint. We were able to regrow a section of hamstring using some newer tissue regeneration techniques, and we spliced that new material into the existing hamstring." He squinted at Brendan. "Physical therapy will not be pleasant, I'm afraid. The new material will need to be stretched into shape slowly—and painfully—but it will work if you stick with it. We tried an experimental bone matrix process to encourage bone regrowth. That was partially successful. We also grafted a metal plate into the left side to stabilize the joint."

"Alright, doc, let's cut to the chase," Wiz said. "What's the prognosis?"

Bear rewrapped the bandage around Brendan's knee before he answered. "Well, the lieutenant won't be running any marathons, but with hard work and lots of PT, he'll probably be able to manage an easy 10K."

Brendan looked up, feeling a smile grow on his face. "So I'm going to get cleared for duty again?"

Dr. Bearon held up his hands. "Whoa, cowboy, that's not what I said. Brendan, you're lucky you can walk, much less run—you almost lost your leg, remember? I said you would be able to use the knee again, that's all."

Brendan gave the admiral a hard look. "So you're here to put the icing on the cake, sir?"

Wiz's face softened. "Look, Brendan, you know the rules as well as anyone. You can't be on the active roster with a bum knee. It's not fair to the rest of the team. You know that."

Brendan nodded, not trusting himself to say anything. He gritted his teeth so that his chin wouldn't tremble.

Wizniewski continued. "I've been on the phone with the community manager, as well as Admiral McRaven down at SOCOM HQ in

Tampa. Yes, we're going to have to let you go, but the Navy has lots of options out there, Brendan. Some of them might surprise you."

"Supply corps, sir?" Brendan said, trying to keep the bitter edge out of his voice. He failed. "C'mon, sir. You know me. How long would I last as a pencil pusher?"

Wizniewski glanced at his watch and stood up. "Brendan, do you trust me?"

Brendan swallowed and nodded his head. His voice failed him again.

"The doc says he's going to release you next week. You've got some medical leave coming to you and the holidays are right around the corner. Take the time, clear your head, and don't do anything stupid—like resign your commission."

He put out his hand. His Naval Academy class ring gleamed in the light. Brendan shook his hand. Wiz's grip was cool, dry, reassuring. "Something will come up, Brendan. And sooner than you think. Trust me."

"Yes, sir. Thank you."

Brendan stared out the window for a long time. Lunch came and he left the tray untouched. They came back to get the tray, and he ignored them.

His girlfriend, his career, his money, his car—it was all shit. His entire life was shit.

He tried to will himself to call the next company on his list and just could not screw up the gumption to let one more credit agency lady explain to him why he was a fucking idiot. He laughed bitterly, a sharp bark in the quiet room. *O&O, my ass.*

There was a soft knock at the door. A tall black man stood in the entrance, close-cropped hair with a touch of gray at the temples. He had a tentative smile on his face.

"Lieutenant McHugh?"

"Yes." Brendan eyed the man. He had a lean build and was dressed in khakis and a blue dress shirt open at the neck. He extended his hand.

"Rick Baxter, Lieutenant."

"Brendan, call me Brendan."

"Brendan, then." Baxter put his hand on a chair. "May I?"

Brendan shrugged. "Suit yourself, Rick. I've got nothing but time." Even as he said it, Brendan could feel the bitterness in his own voice, like acid on his tongue.

Baxter lowered himself into the chair and scooted close to the bedside. "I was in the neighborhood and thought I'd stop by, Brendan. I run a small office over at ONI. We've got a few guys from your community in our group, all solid guys. I'm putting together a new team and your name came up as a candidate."

Brendan sat up in bed. ONI was Office of Naval Intelligence. But there was more than that; Baxter's voice seemed so familiar.

"Me? What kind of team, Rick?"

Baxter laughed. "All in good time, Lieutenant, all in good time. For now, I just wanted to stop by and say thank you."

"I'm not following."

Baxter's eyes dropped to Brendan's knee. "What you did out there, it paid off for us. It was worth it."

Brendan scowled. Somehow, he knew that voice. His mind struggled to place it through all the pain meds he'd received over the past weeks.

Baxter stood up abruptly. "Well, I think maybe I've overstayed my welcome here, Brendan. Tell you what. You think about our conversation, and when you can walk on your own two feet, call me and we'll have lunch."

Baxter pulled a card from his breast pocket and laid it facedown on the bedside table. Then he shook Brendan's hand, replaced the chair where he'd found it, and walked out the door. The whole visit had taken less than five minutes.

Where did he know that voice from? Brendan picked up the card. It was plain white stock with two lines of heavy black text: Rick Baxter and a phone number with a DC area code.

CHAPTER 26

Hashem shifted in his seat. More than anything else in the world, he wanted a cigarette. The pack of Marlboros in the breast pocket of his jacket breathed up a little scent of tobacco every time he moved. He sniffed at it and closed his eyes.

The speaker at the front of the room changed again, but it was the same tired drone of bureaucracy they'd already heard ten times. Everyone felt the need to speak, but no one felt the need to listen. This was why Hashem stayed as far away from politics as possible, these never-ending meetings where everyone said the same thing and no one agreed with anyone else.

For a body called the Expediency Council, they were anything but. They were supposed to be the appointed group that arbitrated legislative disputes between the elected Majlis, the Iranian Parliament, and the appointed twelve-member Council of

Guardians, which consisted of a mix of clerics and legal scholars.

Somehow, Aban managed to hold seats on both the Expediency Council and the Council of Guardians—a rare feat. And Aban had asked him to attend this meeting.

Their mutual problem was the bill recently passed by the Majlis, which cut funding to the Quds Force. Moreover, it cut funds in a very specific way that impacted Hashem's off-the-books desert operation.

Under the Ahmadinejad administration, Hashem reflected, he'd really had an easy time of it. The cost to run his operation was surprisingly reasonable. He'd used the cash from Aban to construct their desert hideaway and most of the equipment was acquired via bureaucratic sleight of hand. The only real ongoing costs were operating expenses for food, fuel, and salaries. These he covered via a fictitious line item within the Quds budget called the "Department of Water Security," a squad of special agents whose sole job was to protect the nation's water reserves. What bureaucrat would argue with water security?

But they had. Since President Rouhani had entered office less than six months ago, sweeping legislative changes were on the move. The new Rouhani-backed budget made dramatic cuts to the Quds Force, some of them surprisingly specific in nature. The changes included dismantling a number of programs, among them the Department of Water Security. The specificity of the cuts made Hashem smell a rat.

It had taken him four weeks to find the rat himself. And he was sitting two rows ahead of Hashem right now.

He studied the back of the man's head. The dossier in his briefcase told him the man's name was Reza Sanjabi. The attached photos made him look entirely ordinary: medium height, medium build, tending toward softness in the middle, neatly trimmed dark hair, and a clean-shaven jaw. Not handsome, not ugly, just average.

The best ones always are, Hashem thought.

He knew Reza was a spy working for Rouhani, but where did he come from? The man seemed to have materialized out of thin air. Not from within Quds, that was clear; there was no possible way a secret organization could have established itself within Quds without his knowledge.

Then where? And why was he here now?

The Expediency Council had finished debate on the funding bill for the cuts to Quds. Aban wore a grim smile. Hashem knew that look well: his brother had won, but at a cost that was dear to him.

The double doors at the back of the room opened, letting the sounds from the hallway enter the meeting room. The cleric chairing the Expediency Council rose to his feet, but instead of calling for order, he raised his hands and clasped them together. He had a broad smile on his face.

"Welcome, Mr. President," he called, his voice booming over the PA system. "Thank you for accepting my invitation."

Hashem caught a glimpse of Aban before the crowd of incoming people—reporters, security detail, staffers—blocked his view of the front of the room. Aban's face was slack with shock, and his fingers gripped the white cloth covering the table.

President Rouhani knew how to make a politician's entrance, reaching around his security men to grasp the hands of well-wishers, taking his time to get to the front of the room. He made it to where the Council was seated in a semicircle, and his security team held back anyone from proceeding further.

Hashem watched Rouhani cross the open space and walk behind the raised dais, shaking hands with the Council members as he went, until he reached the center podium. The Chairman clasped Rouhani's outstretched hand with both of his and beamed up at his new President.

"I object!"

Aban's voice thundered through the hall, dampening the noise level as all eyes turned in his direction. Aban was on his feet and had pulled the microphone out of its stand on the table before him.

"I object," he said again, with a little more control this time.

The Chairman leaned forward so he could look down the row of seated Council members. "On what grounds, sir, do you object?"

"Bringing an outside speaker to the Expediency Council meeting is highly irregular. The President was not on the agenda."

"Point taken," the Chairman replied. "The scheduled agenda for this meeting of the Expediency Council has been completed. I vote to conclude this meeting. Do I have a second?"

"Seconded," Aban cried.

The Chairman rapped the podium with his gavel. "This meeting is adjourned. Any Council members who wish to leave are excused." He turned to Rouhani. "Our President has agreed to hold an unscheduled press conference here today. Anyone who wishes to stay may do so."

No one in the room moved.

Aban's face had gone purple with rage, and his hands shook as he tried to replace the microphone in the table holder. He finally gave up and laid it on the white cloth.

Hashem leaned forward in his chair as Rouhani stepped up to the podium. This was actually the closest he'd ever been to the new President of Iran.

Rouhani wore the full robes of a cleric over his stocky frame. The hands that gripped the sides of the podium were square, with fingers on the short side and manicured nails. A lick of gray hair peeked playfully out from under his snow-white turban, and his carefully trimmed beard lent a slightly western flair to his clerical garb. Behind his wire-rimmed glasses, his gray eyes crinkled with friendliness.

"Good morning," he said, his even voice filling the quiet room. "And thank you, Mr. Chairman, for your kind invitation."

"When I was elected only a few short months ago, I promised to bring the great country of Iran back into the pantheon of world powers. The diplomatic effort my administration undertook has yielded a framework agreement—" Spontaneous applause broke out in the room, but Rouhani raised his hand. "Please. It is only a first step, merely an agreement to continue talking with the western powers about ending sanctions. An important first step, mind you, but still only the first step of a long journey." He paused to take a drink of water before continuing.

"Now we enter the most difficult part of the negotiation. Our nuclear program is for peaceful purposes, but we face a skeptical world order, a group of nations that seek proof of our peaceful intentions. And we will provide these skeptics with the proof they desire.

"But let us face facts: the Western sanctions have devastated our economy and our efforts to satisfy the western powers will cost money. My administration has announced a series of cuts in government programs, and redirected those funds toward the nuclear negotiation effort. These cuts are necessary to allow the great nation of Iran to rejoin the world community. I thank the Chairman and the Council for their valuable assistance in reconciling this critical legislation."

The applause filled the hall again and Rouhani allowed it to continue for a full minute before he waved them quiet. With his trademark grandfatherly smile, he offered to take questions from the reporters. Hashem saw Aban slip out the side entrance and hurried to join him.

His brother's face was white, and he gnawed at his thumbnail. Aban scanned the hallway. "Do you have a cigarette?" he asked.

Hashem partially tapped out two Marlboros and extended the pack to Aban. His brother snatched a cigarette, sucking greedily as Hashem held out the flame. He held the smoke in his lungs for a long moment before he let it out in a fierce blue stream.

"Brother, we're running out of time."

CHAPTER 27

Brendan hung up the phone and sat back in his chair. He crossed off the last line on his handwritten checklist.

He was free. Amy was out of his life.

It had taken him months, a lawyer he couldn't afford, paid with money he didn't have, to rid himself of that crazy bitch, but he'd done it. He'd gotten his identity back, shut down the false credit cards she'd opened in his name, and had his few remaining personal belongings shipped from San Diego back to Minneapolis, where they sat in his parents' garage.

He closed his eyes. He was thirty-two years old, broke, and living in his parents' basement. This was not how it was supposed to work out. He was a decorated Iraq war veteran—a Navy SEAL, for Christ's sake—and he was living in his parents' basement.

He could blame Amy, but deep down he knew he was just as

much to blame. When he did something, he went all in. He'd been in love with Amy, so why not give her power of attorney over his affairs while he was overseas? Why not put her on the lease to his apartment and give her all the passwords to his financial accounts? Sure, they weren't actually engaged, but he knew she loved him . . .

He looked down at the pages of scribbles and crossed out to-do lists on the yellow legal pad in his lap. That's why, Brendan, you fucking idiot. You just spent the last three months unfucking your life because you didn't think.

You blamed yourself when the Skype calls from Amy became more infrequent, and then stopped altogether. You ignored the emails from the bank and told yourself Amy would take care of it. You could have asked the CO's wife to check up on Amy, maybe even stop her, but you didn't want to cause any trouble. You were so sure you could work it out.

He threw the pad across the room, watching the pages flutter in a buzz of yellow. It slapped against the circa-1970s wood-paneled wall of the basement.

"Everything okay down there, Bren?" his mother called from the kitchen at the top of the stairs.

Brendan took a deep breath. "Fine, Mom." He hoisted himself out of the chair. "I'm going for a walk."

"Do you want some company, honey?"

"No, Mom, I'm fine." He threw an old overcoat over his sweats and pulled a watch cap over his ears. He put some weight on his knee, flexing the joint. All in all, the knee had healed better than he'd expected. He had most of his previous range of motion, and maybe half the pre-injury strength. He could walk with only the slightest limp, and even run on it for a few hundred yards at a time.

He pushed open the sliding door on the walk-out basement and stepped out into the snow. It had been a brutal winter, the snowiest in something like 150 years. The path he'd shoveled from the back patio around to the front of the house was more like a tunnel, with three feet of packed snow on either side.

When he reached the driveway, his mother opened the front door. "Can Champ come with you?"

Brendan smiled. "Sure, send him out." She opened the door wider to let the dog out. Champ, their ancient black Labrador retriever, huffed his way to Brendan, his leash folded in quarters and dangling from his mouth.

Brendan squatted to pet his friend, breathing through the pain of bending his knee. "Who's walking who here, boy? Huh?" The leash trick was something Brendan had taught Champ in his younger days. He used to love to run around Lake Harriet with the dog, and the city had a leash law. Brendan thought letting Champ hold his own leash was pretty clever.

Their running days were over—for both man and dog. Today's pace was a walk with occasional slow jogs, if they both felt up to it.

"Let's go, boy," he said, starting off.

It was one of those wonderful Minnesota winter days when the city experienced a midday "thaw." While the nighttime temps stayed below zero, the days would warm up to high-thirties or so, enough for the running paths to stay clear of snow and ice. For the locals, used to near-zero conditions, the temporary reprieve from freezing— even for a few hours—inspired bursts of outdoor activity. Some brave souls even wore shorts when they ran around the lakes.

"What do you say, Champ, wanna scope some chicks around Lake Harriet?"

In their prime, the running loop around Lake Harriet had been a favorite haunt for both of them. Brendan, a senior in high school and already accepted to the Naval Academy, had become a workout fiend. He ran with his shirt off most of the time, with his faithful sidekick Champ, then just a year-old Lab. That was the year he'd taught Champ the leash trick. Brendan laughed out loud.

"Look at us now, buddy." He reached down to scratch Champ's ears. "Couple of broken-down old men, aren't we?" Champ looked up at him and huffed noisily around the lead crammed in his jaws.

The sun was warm. By the time they reached the Harriet loop, Brendan had zipped open his overcoat. The sweat felt good, always a sure way to lift his spirits. It was lunchtime and the loop was crowded with runners. He watched one girl lope by in running tights that left nothing to the imagination, blond ponytail bouncing behind her. Brendan shook his head. In his younger days, he and Champ would have matched her stride for stride until she noticed his beautiful dog with the lead in his mouth and started a conversation.

Brendan tried to jog a few steps, but stopped when the pain spiked in his knee. His black mood closed in again. Those days were gone—long gone.

They neared the Lake Harriet Bandshell and Brendan got off the path. He guided Champ to the plaza behind the shell and found an open spot on the steps. Champ stretched out on the warm cement beside him. Although they looked out over the snow-covered lake, the sun was warm and the spot sheltered from the wind. Brendan took off his jacket and balled it behind his head as a pillow, letting the warmth of the sun seep into his body.

He needed to make some decisions soon. Rear Admiral Wizniewski had given him a staff job in DC for "as long as he wanted it," but Brendan knew Wiz was just being kind. He was finished as an operational SEAL, and there was no way he'd be able to handle being a desk jockey in the SEAL community. His pride wouldn't take it.

He could get out of the Navy, that was one option. There would even be some sort of disability for his knee injury. And do what? The only thing he'd ever wanted to do was be a SEAL, and now that was gone.

And then there was the mysterious Rick Baxter and his intel job.

Brendan had to admit it: when Baxter read him into the program a few weeks ago, he was impressed. But was it really for him?

At Baxter's invitation, he'd taken the DC metro out to Suitland, Maryland. The Office of Naval Intelligence building was part of the National Maritime Intelligence Center complex, just another of the myriad of alphabet-soup agencies that Brendan knew nothing about.

He processed through the security center and waited for Baxter to meet him. It was Brendan's first time back in uniform since his hospital stay. He was out of shape, and his service dress blues felt tight in all the wrong places. The knee brace he wore allowed him to walk, albeit slowly, but at least he didn't need crutches.

Baxter arrived in civilian clothes, but he wore the navy blue suit like a uniform, with a white shirt and a muted pattern tie with a perfect double Windsor knot. When he shook Brendan's hand, Baxter's brown eyes searched his face. "Good to see you, Brendan. How's the knee?"

"Fine, sir."

Baxter laughed, a deep belly laugh with lots of white teeth. "Alright, McHugh, let's get this straight. Inside this program, I'm Rick and you're Brendan. No 'sirs' allowed. Got it?"

Brendan smiled. "Sure, Rick."

They took a long walk through a cubicle farm, passing through two security checkpoints along the way. Just when Brendan's knee was hurting enough to ask for a break, they arrived at a conference room. Baxter gestured at a small refrigerator with a glass front, then busied himself with a laptop and projector. Brendan took a bottle of water from the fridge and sank into a chair, gritting his teeth as he bent his knee to a ninety-degree angle.

Baxter fired up the overhead projector. The image had the ONI seal and the title, Project Briefing: FEISTY MINNOW. Below that it said TOP SECRET, followed by a paragraph of legalese. Baxter cleared his throat.

"First things first," he said, opening up a manila folder. He slid a single sheet of paper across the table. "Before I can brief you into the program, I need you to sign this. Read it first—I mean it, this is not your ordinary nondisclosure form."

Brendan accepted the sheet and scanned it. Baxter was right, it was much more stringent than the typical NDAs Brendan was used to, but it basically came down to one thing: he could never, ever, under any circumstances, talk to anyone about the program. Ever.

His pen made a scratching sound in the quiet room as he signed the form. Baxter looked strangely relieved when Brendan passed the sheet back across the table.

Baxter stayed seated as he triggered the next slide. It was a world map with seven red dots sprinkled across it. Brendan scanned the locations: Eastern Med, Baltic Sea, Sea of Japan near North Korea, South China Sea, Caribbean, Indian Ocean, and the Med off North Africa.

"Intel is about collecting and analyzing information," Baxter began. "These are all places where we'd like to have more information than we're currently able to gather. SIGINT, ACINT, MASINT, IMINT—you name, we need it."

Brendan held up his hand. "Come again, Rick? I'm not sure I'm following all your INTs. I know SIGINT is signals intelligence, comms and stuff like that, but what are the others?"

Baxter gave another deep laugh. "Sorry, we're just like any other agency with our acronyms. ACINT is acoustics, and MASINT is measurement and signatures, which is a catchall term for everything else, like nuclear detectors—"

"It *was* you!" Brendan exclaimed. "The sensor we put on the North Korean TEL, when I got injured. You were on the other end of the line."

Baxter gave him a look full of meaning. "That program is outside the scope of this briefing, Brendan, but that type of operation could fall under my purview." He turned back toward the screen.

"Sorry," Brendan replied, blushing. "It's just that ever since we met, I felt like I knew you somehow."

"Continuing," Baxter said, without turning around. "These are all places where we would like to have more information to supply to our intelligence services, but lack ways to gather it. Naval ships and submarines are too obtrusive, and frankly most nations these days are just more aware of their EM footprint. The Chinese, for example, are pretty savvy. They simply shut down all comms when there is a US Navy ship within twenty miles of their coast." He smiled as he flipped to the next slide. "What we need is a less obvious way to gather information."

A picture of a sailing ship filled the screen. Brendan scanned the image. A forty-some-foot sloop, a real beauty, a more current model of the ones he'd sailed at the Academy.

"Operation Feisty Minnow will commission seven sailing vessels as clandestine intelligence-gathering platforms. The ships have been specially configured with the latest hardware, all of it hidden onboard. The crews are all trained intel officers, but they pose as rich people with money to burn and a passion for sailing."

Brendan sat back in his chair. "So they sail along the coast of these countries and gather intel along the way?"

Baxter nodded. "They're very careful to stay outside the twelve-mile boundary, in international waters, but yes, that's pretty much the idea."

"How does it work? For the crew, I mean."

"Well, you get a new identity, a cover story with a bank account, and a platinum credit card that never runs out of money."

Brendan whistled. "No expense reports? What's the downside?"

Baxter frowned. "Brendan, this is serious. If you're discovered, some of these countries won't give a rat's ass about international waters, and the chances of a Navy ship being able to intervene is nil.

You're on your own. Each ship in the Minnow fleet is equipped with an automatic scuttling system. If you're taken by a foreign power, there are no extract options and the US will deny all knowledge of your existence."

Brendan looked at the picture of the sailing ship for a long time. "And you want me to do what?"

"I want you to skipper one of these boats, probably the one in the IO. You'd have a crew of five, plus yourself, but four of them are likely going to be IT techs. They may know nothing about sailing. You and one other person are in charge of all sailing and navigation."

"How long is the cruise?"

Baxter shook his head. "You're not hearing me, Brendan. This is a *command*. Do you understand? You'd be the captain of a naval command. This will be your ship, your life, your responsibility, for the next three years."

Brendan sat back in his chair, for once forgetting about the throbbing of his knee. He wasn't sure what he'd expected from Baxter, but this was not it. A sailboat as an intelligence spy boat? His own command? What if he got captured? He'd be held as a spy. What did that even mean?

Baxter scratched at his jawline, his eyes scanning Brendan's face. "Look, I've laid a lot of information on you today. Think about it. This is a commitment every bit as serious as Special Operations, maybe even more so. It's not something to take lightly. You're due back in DC on March first, right?"

Brendan nodded.

"Think about it and call me when you get back in town."

The phone in Brendan's pocket buzzed, interrupting his reverie. He flipped open the clamshell of the prepaid mobile phone and shielded it from the sunlight. Very few people had this number.

He recognized Marjorie's home number.

"Marjorie?"

"Happy Valentine's Day! How's my favorite SEAL?"

Brendan gave a wry smile. "Still with a broken flipper. How'd you get this number?"

"Brendan, Don works for the CIA," she said in a serious tone. "He can get me anything I want." She paused. "Just kidding, I called your mother."

Brendan laughed. "Well, it's good to hear your voice anyway."

"How are you doing, honey?" Marjorie's tone took on a concerned note.

"I'm good, Marje. Really, I am."

"You're full of shit, Brendan. It's the middle of the day and you answered the phone like I just woke you up."

"Marjorie, I'm good."

"Uh-huh," she said. "When are you back in DC?"

"A week from Monday. My convalescent leave ends March first."

"Okay, I want you to come visit me when you get back. Come for dinner. I'll invite Liz and Don, if they're in town."

"Sure," Brendan said. He swallowed. "Is Liz still in DC?" He tried to keep his tone casual.

"Why don't you call her and find out?"

Brendan started to answer, but Marjorie cut him off. "Brendan, call her. It's Valentine's Day, for Pete's sake. Let her know you're thinking about her."

"Marje, she's married—"

"Call her. Now. Promise me."

Brendan took a deep breath. "Alright, I'll call her."

"Finally," Marjorie said. "And dinner, too. Let me know when you get settled in DC."

Brendan stared at the phone after the conversation ended. He punched in Liz's number, his finger hovering over the SEND button. He'd been able to dial the number from memory, from all the times he'd gotten to this point. But so far, he still hadn't worked up the courage to actually make the call.

He moved his finger to the DELETE button and watched the digits disappear one by one.

Brendan thumbed his way to the phone book. It contained only three numbers. He keyed down to the last name and hit SEND.

"Baxter."

"Hi, Rick, it's Brendan. I'm in."

CHAPTER 28

Rafiq latched the heavy steel door open and snapped on the light as he stepped into the vault.

The wooden crate sat in the center of the room. The cargo. His mission for the last seven years. A big wooden box.

He checked the temperature and humidity monitor on the wall and inspected the seals on the packaging. All secure. The same as they'd been every afternoon for the last seven years. Well, not every afternoon. He'd taken a one-week honeymoon with Nadine after their wedding, but even then they'd only gone to Buenos Aires, and he could have been back within a day at most.

Rafiq rested his hand on the dried wood. Some days he was tempted to just open it and have a look inside. According to Hashem, everything he needed to complete his mission was in the container. But he was not to open it unless directed by Hashem himself. They also had a failsafe protocol to follow if his brother failed to make their monthly check-in and the backup comms plans also failed.

He nodded to Farid and stepped out of the vault, then watched him lock the door and set the alarm. The man had aged in the last seven years—and not in a good way. Farid's crewcut was solid gray and he walked with a slight stoop. Rafiq had no doubt of the man's loyalty to him or their cause, but he feared there was some serious medical issue behind his sudden change in appearance. He frequently missed their daily workouts, and when he did attend, his performance was not up to par. Rafiq could not afford to have a sick man on his team.

Farid slid the wine rack in place to conceal the vault entrance. The wine cellar, built into a mountain, was cool and shadowy around them. They were at the deepest point in the cellar, the spot where Don Javier kept his private stash of vintages under lock and key. Farid closed the door to the wire cage and snapped the padlock shut.

"Tomorrow, boss?" Farid said. They spoke in Lebanese, their home dialect of Arabic. They always spoke in their native tongue when they performed their daily checks on the cargo. Otherwise, they had both become fluent in Spanish and spoke it with almost no accent. They sounded almost like locals.

Rafiq hardened his tone. "Did you see the doctor as I told you?"

Farid's form stiffened. He cleared his throat. "Yes, boss."

"And?"

"Cancer," he said. "Pancreatic cancer. Inoperable."

Rafiq slumped against the nearest wine rack. He had expected something more benign, maybe a vitamin deficiency or a virus. "I—I'm sorry," he said. "Have you told Juanita yet?"

Following Rafiq's marriage to Nadine, both Farid and his brother, Jamil, had married their longtime girlfriends. They lived in twin bungalows on the edge of the vineyard.

Farid's shadow shifted as he shook his head. "I wanted to tell you first. I'm still strong, Rafiq, I can do the mission—if it comes to that. But . . ."

"But?"

"The doctor says I have less than six months to live. He says the last few months could be very painful."

"Ah, my friend, I am so sorry." Rafiq embraced the man. He could feel how the flesh had melted off Farid's frame. He should have seen it sooner. "Tell Juanita tonight—and tell your brother. We will take care of your family, you know that."

Farid nodded, wiping his eyes. "But the mission—"

"I will handle the mission, Farid. Spend the time you have left with your family."

Rafiq turned on his heel and walked quickly to the front of the wine cellar, welcoming the afternoon sunlight. He shivered to himself.

"Papa!"

The boy running at him full tilt had a headful of dark curls and his mother's eyes. Rafiq caught the child in both hands and tossed him into the air. The boy wrapped his arms tightly around Rafiq's neck when he landed back in his father's grasp. His grip was getting stronger every day; it amazed Rafiq how quickly the boy developed new skills. His curly hair pressed against Rafiq's face, and he breathed in the scent of his son.

His son. The idea still took his breath away. Before Nadine, he'd never even considered becoming a father. Now he was married with two children.

"I wanted to go into the wine cellar to meet you and Uncle Farid, but Mama said I had to wait outside," the boy said. He pulled back to study his father's face. His gaze was thoughtful, warm, just like his mother's.

"And she's right," Rafiq replied. He poked the boy in the stomach. "But I'm free now."

Little Javier wriggled out of his arms to the ground. He gripped his father's hand and began to pull him toward the path to the stables. "Mama is waiting with Consie at the stables."

Rafiq pretended to resist, but staggered forward when Javi redoubled his effort. "You're too strong for me, son." He shook the boy's hand free and sprinted ahead. "I'm going to reach Mama first!"

He threw a look over his shoulder. Javi's nearly three-year-old legs churned as he ran after his father, a determined look on his face. They rounded the bend and the stables came into sight. Rafiq slowed to let his son catch up.

Nadine turned to greet them, little Consuela in her arms. If anything, motherhood had made Nadine even more beautiful. It had given more curves to her athletic figure and added heft to her bosom—both of which Rafiq found very sexy—but it was more than that. He finally decided it was in her face: she glowed when she looked at her children, as if she couldn't believe she had created these little beings from her own body.

Javi put on a burst of speed and passed Rafiq, tagging his mother's thigh with a loud smack of his hand. "I won, Papa. I won."

Rafiq came to a halt in front of Nadine. "You're right, Javi, you won."

Nadine kissed him, then pinched his earlobe between her teeth. "You'll get your consolation prize later, Papa," she whispered with a wicked smile.

"You can help me take the sting out of losing," he whispered back, snatching a kiss from his wife and then planting one on the sleeping baby's head.

"Can I ride now? Can I?" Javi pleaded.

Rafiq nodded to the ranch hand in the doorway. The man disappeared into the stable, returning a few minutes later leading a midnight-black pony fitted with a child's saddle. He stopped the animal in front of Javi. The boy held a sugar cube on his open palm and the pony eagerly snapped it up. Javi giggled. "It tickles."

The stable hand helped the boy into the saddle and handed him the reins, but kept a firm grip on the pony's bridle until they were safely inside the paddock. Javi whooped as he dug his heels into the pony's flanks. The beast broke into a canter.

Nadine handed the baby to Rafiq and stepped up onto the fence rails, calling out encouragement to her son in Spanish. Rafiq bit his tongue. He was still not completely comfortable with large animals, and certainly not with his three-year-old son riding a horse by himself. Nadine often laughed at his discomfort and called him a *chico de ciudad*, a city boy.

Little Consuela stirred when she was handed over, then settled back to sleep, her lips pursed as she suckled an imaginary breast. In contrast to Javi, Consuela seemed more like her father. Fairer of skin, with deep, watchful eyes. Unlike her tornado of a brother, the baby almost never cried.

Rafiq let the moment settle on him. His beautiful wife, eyes flashing, long, dark hair whipping around her face as she shouted out to her son. Javi, riding as if he'd been born in a saddle, let out a laugh of pure joy as he urged the pony faster. Consuela reached out and gripped the pocket of his shirt—

"Boss." A hand touched his arm.

Rafiq turned around. Jamil was panting. "There's been news," he said. "News about . . . home." He handed Rafiq a smartphone.

He had the web browser open to Al Jazeera, and a story about ISIS. Rafiq bristled. The so-called Islamic State fighters, nothing but a shell for Sunni extremists, were in the news all the time now. He and his men often lamented the fact that they were in South America when the real fight was back in Lebanon with their Hezbollah brothers. Rafiq always reinforced the necessity of their mission for Hashem, but deep inside even he sometimes wondered if what they were doing was worth it.

"Read the article, Boss," Jamil urged. His face was gray with worry.

Rafiq scanned the news story. He was about to flick the text up when his thumb froze over the screen.

ISIS forces attacked the small Lebanese village of Arsal, near the Syrian border, this morning. Initial reports are that the town was decimated by the Sunni extremists...

Rafiq handed the baby to Nadine and ran for the house.

His chest was heaving with effort and sweat darkened the neckline of his shirt when he reached the study. He slammed the door shut and locked it behind him. His hands shook so badly it took him three tries to get the wall safe open. He flipped to the back of the codebook, where there was a list of email addresses next to a column of code words.

He booted up the computer, cursing the deliberate slowness of Microsoft Windows. Finally he was able to open his email. He typed in the email address from the codebook and put in a few lines of meaningless text in the body of the email. None of that mattered. He went back to the header and typed the phrase "sunrise service" in the subject line.

He hit send.

Rafiq gripped the edge of the desk. *Don't make assumptions. She'll be alright. She has to be alright.*

In his mind he could see the streets of Arsal, his boyhood home. The cafe on the corner, the elementary school down the street, the park across the road where he was allowed to play by himself as his mother watched him from their second-story apartment. The same apartment where she still lived.

The computer gave off a soft ping and the bold letters of a new email showed up at the top of his inbox. The header said "undeliverable message." He opened the message and scrolled past the meaningless text to the link at the bottom of the screen.

The link took him to a one-time-use chatroom, with a countdown timer in the lower right corner. The space was active for only five minutes, then it would be wiped off both computers.

He watched the cursor blink at the top of the blank screen.

Are you there? he typed.

Two agonizing minutes went by.

Yes.

I know about the situation at home.

I'm sorry for your loss.

So it's true, she's gone?

Yes. I confirmed this just two hours ago.

I must go back.

Absolutely not. Remain in place.

Rafiq looked at the timer. Less than a minute remained.

I need to make funeral arrangements.

I will take care of it. You must stay.

Fifteen seconds.

Rafiq clenched his teeth together so hard he heard ringing in his ears. *I understand,* he typed.

The timer ran to zero and the screen closed automatically. The computer rebooted itself and ran a program to remove all traces of the chatroom event.

But he didn't understand. Seven years he had done what his brother—half brother, he reminded himself—had asked of him. Without question. Now his own mother, his true flesh and blood, was dead, and his half brother expected him to sit on his ass in South America drinking wine and riding horses while his boyhood home was attacked by the Sunnis.

He reached into the drawer and pulled out the last letter he had received from her. It was dated three months ago. Their communications were sporadic, mostly letters hand-delivered through the Lebanese Arab network. He leafed through the spidery handwriting to the last page. His mother had always been an artist. He had sent her a snapshot of her grandchildren, and she had reproduced the picture in pencil for him, just as she used to draw Rafiq when he was young.

He traced the outline of the drawing with his finger. The anger and the grief settled in his chest, making it hard to breathe. Hot tears stung his eyes.

There was a knock at the study door. Rafiq took a deep breath to compose himself. He stored the codebook in the safe before he opened the door to the study. Jamil and Farid stood in the hall, worry written on their faces.

"It's true," he said.

The brothers exchanged glances. They were from the same village as Rafiq. He knew what they were about to ask him.

"I'm sorry," he said. The brothers' eyes fell to the floor. "Only one of you may return home to make arrangements." The twins looked up, surprised. Rafiq smiled to himself. Fuck his half brother and his stupid mission. Hashem had told him *he* was not allowed to return to Arsal. He said nothing about the brothers.

"I will go," Farid said. It was clear that the twins had already decided this in advance.

Rafiq nodded, and he embraced each man before they left.

Nadine waited for him in the hallway. Her face was white and drawn, making her dark eyes look even larger.

"My love," she said, opening her arms. "I am so sorry."

Rafiq buried his face in her shoulder and cried.

CHAPTER 29

Brendan held his breath as the mast lifted free of the *Arrogant*.

The crane operator halted the lift when another gust of November wind whipped in off the Chesapeake Bay. The shipyard worker tending the line leaned back to counter the force of the stiff breeze. The mast steadied.

Slowly, moving inches at a time, they landed the butt end of the mast into the customized holder and lowered the top end down into a waiting cradle.

Brendan expelled a long breath.

"You and me both, sir," said the man to his left. Chief Petty Officer Timothy Scott, aka Scottie, rubbed his hands together. In the military, with a name like Scott, you were invariably connected to the iconic *Star Trek* character. He affected a Scottish accent. "I'll have a wee look inside tonight, sir, and see what's the problem with the blasted receiver."

"Scottie," Brendan replied, "we've talked about this. No 'sirs' around here."

Scottie blushed. "Sorry, skipper—Brendan—won't happen again. Old habits, you know."

"I know, Scottie. Don't I know it." It was true. Although he still retained his commission as a naval officer and had even been promoted to Lieutenant Commander, the idea of forgoing naval etiquette had hit him harder than he'd expected. The fact that the Naval Academy was visible across the windswept Severn didn't make it any easier. So many memories, some of them even military.

He shifted the conversation back to work topics. "I just hope you can fix this thing. Having to order a new mast will completely screw up our schedule."

They watched the long mast being driven away slowly toward the secure hangar. The fifty-four-foot *Arrogant*—she would be the largest of the Minnow fleet—looked strangely small and denuded without the pole towering over her deck.

The mast was probably one of the most advanced pieces of electronic surveillance equipment in the world. Built into the aluminum structure was a host of receivers designed to pluck any electronic transmission out of the air. Without a functional mast, the *Arrogant* was basically just another sailboat full of millions of dollars of worthless electronics.

"Don't worry, Brendan," Scottie assured him. "If anyone can fix her, it's me. She'll be good as new by Monday morning. This will not impact our date with the IO."

Brendan took comfort in the fact that Scottie's assurance had a basis in fact. As part of the Feisty Minnow program, Baxter had insisted that at least one crew member personally build each piece of specialty equipment. Scottie was their mast expert. He'd spent six months at Raytheon and at Fort Meade building and testing two masts. In fact, Scottie's new design was so good the other sailboats in the secret fleet would be refitted with the new mast as soon as Baxter found the budget for it.

Brendan checked his watch. Another fifteen minutes and he needed to leave to change before dinner at Marjorie's. The thought of seeing Liz again—and Don, he reminded himself, Don would be there, too—made him excited and nervous at the same time.

Easy, Tiger. She's a married woman now.

He brought himself back to the moment. Time to check in with Rick. He pulled out his phone and thumbed through the speed dial until he found the number.

"Baxter."

"Hi, Rick. It's Brendan. I wanted to let you know we had to pull the mast again. The high-band receiver is still acting funky. Scottie says he's sure he can fix it this weekend and have it replaced on Monday."

"Hmmm. Well, if anyone can fix it, it's Scottie. You're lucky to have him."

"You can say that again," Brendan replied. He hesitated. "What about the rest of the crew? How's that looking?"

Recruiting for Brendan's team had been slow. Besides Scottie, they had only one other tech to run the specialized equipment, and time was running out. The *Arrogant* and her crew were scheduled to deploy to the Indian Ocean—the IO—in March. Brendan mentally ran through the list of major items that needed to be fixed between now and then, and that didn't even include shakedown cruises and live testing of the receivers before they left. He shivered. Sailing the Chesapeake in January and February was not for the faint of heart.

Baxter made a snorting noise. "I'll get you candidates as soon as I have them, Brendan. If you didn't keep rejecting them, you'd have a full crew by now."

Brendan held his tongue. Their IO deployment was planned for eighteen months, and he wanted to make damn sure he was bringing on a crew that wouldn't kill each other during that time. Baxter thought he was being too picky.

"Anyway," Baxter continued, "I'm sending another over on Monday. Ex-Navy gal turned analyst, USNA Class of 2007. Name's Magdalena Ambrose. Smart as a whip and she's done embedded tours in Afghanistan and Iraq, too. Might fit the bill."

Brendan's hopes rose. The double combination of Naval Academy graduate and field experience gave him confidence that Magdalena—he hoped she went by Maggie, because her full name was a mouthful—would work out.

"I hope so, Rick. I'm getting worried about the schedule." Getting electronics experts who didn't *look* like electronics experts was a major part of the job description. If they were supposed to be rich dilettantes, they needed to look and act the part.

"Son, that's why you get paid the big bucks—so you can worry about the schedule and I can go home early on Friday night. Speaking of which, don't you have a date tonight?"

Brendan sputtered. "What? How did you know about that? And, anyway, it's not a date. It's a couple of Academy friends having an early Thanksgiving dinner—"

"I don't know, Brendan. Master Chief says she's hot."

"She might be, but she's also *married*."

Baxter's voice took on a teasing tone. "C'mon, Brendan, a woman has a right to change her mind."

"Not this woman, Rick. Once she does something, it's for good. I had my chance a long time ago, and I blew it. End of story."

"Well, have a good time, all the same." Baxter laughed.

Brendan ended the call, gritting his teeth. The Master Chief had found out about Liz when Don visited one afternoon in the summer. Now all the old man wanted to talk about was Brendan's "Navy gurl," as he called her.

The teasing had gotten out of hand; he needed to talk to the

Master Chief about it. He hurried to his locker to get his coat. When he opened the door, a white bottle of Old Spice aftershave sat on the top shelf.

A deep gravelly laugh came from behind him. "I figured you needed to call out the big guns for your date tonight with your Navy gurl, sir. So I got you a little present."

Brendan whirled around to face the Master Chief. A wide smile wreathed the old man's face. He reached out to pat Brendan's arm. "Just joshin' you, sir. Have a good time tonight with your friend." He walked out the door with his peculiar rolling gait, leaving Brendan somewhere between speechless and touched.

Traffic on the bridge was heavy heading back into Annapolis. He cut off Route 450 and made his way onto the back roads, passing the back gate of the Naval Academy and setting off another round of nostalgia.

He maneuvered into the narrow streets of old town and found a lucky parking spot on the street. Brendan took the stairs two at a time up to his apartment, feeling the twinge in his knee as he did so. The joint had healed enough that he could run now, but like the ortho doctor had said, his knee had nowhere near the same strength as before.

The apartment was the size of a closet and cost more than he could afford, but he liked living in the old town section of Annapolis. He took a quick shower in the tiny stall and burrowed into his closet for some fresh clothes. After a few trips to the mirror, he settled on a pair of khakis, a crisp white shirt, and a blue blazer. Pretty much what a Navy guy would wear when out of uniform. *Screw it, it's just dinner.*

He jogged to the end of the street and picked up a bouquet of flowers for Marjorie. The traffic was just as heavy going back over the bridge, and he arrived a few minutes late. A new BMW was already parked in Marjorie's driveway. Don must have gotten a new car; Liz would be driving a rental.

The walk to the front door brought back more memories of being a midshipman—and his June Week mistake with Liz. He shook his head. He'd be glad when they finally deployed and he could move on with his life. By hanging around the Academy and all its memories, he was turning into a maudlin loser.

He paused at the front door. In the old days, he would have just walked in and called out to Marjorie, but that was a long time ago. The rules had changed.

Just as he reached for the brass knocker, the door opened.

✺

Liz took a long sip of her Chardonnay. She put the glass down. *Go easy, you need a clear head, girl.*

She noticed Marjorie was watching her, her eyebrows raised expectantly.

"I'm sorry, Marjorie. I spaced out for a moment. What were you saying?"

Marjorie smiled at her. "He'll be here soon. You know Bren, always a few minutes late. It's a wonder that boy made it through Plebe Year at the Academy."

Liz colored. "I'm not—I wasn't—it will be nice to see him again." She took another sip of wine. They'd helped each other make it through Plebe Year. They'd just been friends then, of course, but theirs had been a partnership, the kind of partnership that should have lasted—if only she'd given it a fighting chance.

She looked down at her left hand. The engagement ring and matching wedding band sparkled up at her. Her conscience prickled, and she covered the rings with her other hand.

James was kind, attentive, a good partner. Sure, he worked too much, but what successful person building his career these days didn't work too much? She didn't even need to work and she worked too much. Besides, their extended separations actually helped their

217

marriage by letting her see his good qualities anew each time they reconnected.

But for all James's many good qualities, he lacked the one she needed the most: Liz did not love him.

What is wrong with me?

Liz took another sip of wine. The sound of a car crunching down the gravel drive got her attention, and her heart gave a little jump.

"Why don't you get the door, Liz?" Marjorie's silver-gray hair gleamed as she jerked her chin toward the front of the house. She smiled. "Just remember, it might be Don."

Liz stepped into the front hall and smoothed her skirt over her thighs. She'd selected this outfit carefully: a plum-colored pencil skirt that hugged her in all the right places and a creamy silk blouse, open at the neck, that did wonderful things for the olive tone of her skin.

She could hear him on the porch, waiting. She took a deep breath and pulled the door open.

His dark hair was still wet from a recent shower, his face leaner than the last time she'd seen him.

"Bren . . . hi," she said. Her voice sounded breathy to her ears, as if she was gasping for air.

Brendan was having his own troubles. She felt his eyes sweep over her and he swallowed hard. He pointed over his shoulder at the BMW. "The car . . . I thought . . . Don."

Liz gave an embarrassed laugh. "Yeah, even though the FBI rents me a car for work, James—my husband—insists that I drive a BMW when I travel for more than a day or two. He's like that." She winced as she said it. Why bring up James in the first sentence?

"Come here, you big lug. Give me a hug." She stepped into him, burying her face into his shoulder. The scent of him took her back to a simpler time, a time when she'd felt more in control, happier. His arms circled her, completing the feeling. "I've missed you," she whispered.

Brendan didn't say anything. Behind her, the phone rang and she used that as an opportunity to break their embrace.

Liz stepped away and snatched the flowers from his grip. "I'll put these in water."

She took time in the laundry room to compose herself before she reentered the kitchen.

"Don called," Marjorie announced. "He says he'll be late and to start without him." She nodded to the stack of plates and silverware on the counter. "Would you and Bren set the table for me, please?"

Brendan seemed anxious to keep the table between them while they laid out plates and silverware. Then Marjorie called out for him to carve the turkey and Liz to carry the food in. She poured the wine while he carved the bird, and before she knew it, they were seated for dinner and Brendan had not said another word to her.

Marjorie sat at the head of the table, flanked by Liz and Brendan. Brendan raised his glass toward Mark's picture on the wall. "To absent friends," he said, with a catch in his voice. They all took a sip of wine.

Marjorie wiped her eyes. "I'm sorry," she said. "I still miss him so . . ." She took a deep breath and sat up in her chair. "But enough of that—Liz, tell me about the FBI."

"Well, I'm with JTTF in LA—"

"English, please. I'm a civilian, Liz," Marjorie cautioned.

Liz laughed. "Okay, JTTF is the Joint Terrorism Task Force. We lead a multiagency group in charge of responding to any sort of terrorism threat. I—we—took the assignment because of James's work." She looked at Brendan. "My husband's a maxillofacial surgeon at Cedars-Sinai in LA. He travels a lot, so we don't get much time together."

"Anyway," she continued, "I'm just glad I was in DC for this little shindig, Marje. James is in South America for the next month, so this is my Thanksgiving."

Marjorie looked over at Brendan. "And what about you, Bren? How's the knee?"

"Good enough for government work, I guess," Brendan said. "I'm over at the naval station, refitting sailboats for the Academy sailing team."

Liz shot him a meaningful look. "Nice work if you can get it, I guess." She didn't believe for a moment that a decorated SEAL was a Program Manager for refitting sailboats, but she knew better than to ask.

Liz took another sip of wine and relaxed, letting the sound of Marjorie's voice flow over her as she told a Mark story, one they'd heard a hundred times before. Brendan laughed at the expected punchline, a deep belly laugh. With a pang, Liz realized she didn't laugh much anymore.

"Liz?"

She jolted in her seat. "I'm sorry. What?"

Marjorie smiled at her. "I'm going to clear the table. How about you take Brendan into the study and pour some drinks, please?"

She stood up. "Can I help you clear, Marje?"

Marjorie was already stacking plates. "No, I insist. You two kids run along and I'll be in with coffee and pie in a minute. Have a Baileys ready for me."

Liz followed Brendan into the study. She could detect a familiar scent in the air, like a lost memory. "Are you wearing Old Spice?" she asked.

Brendan blushed and gave a nervous chuckle. "It was a gift from a friend at work. He swears it's the only way to get women."

Liz turned on the gas fireplace and took a seat on the sofa. "Is that what you want, Bren? To get women?"

Brendan set a shot of Baileys on the side bar for Marjorie. "Can I get you something?" he asked.

"How about an answer to my question?" The words came out

more sharply than she'd intended, causing Brendan to look over. She softened her tone. "Why didn't you come to the wedding, Brendan? I sent you an invite, but it came back marked 'return to sender.'"

Brendan busied himself at the bar. "I was deployed, I think."

"I checked. You were in the States. That really hurt me, Bren."

He looked at the fireplace, refusing to meet her gaze. The flickering light played across his features, casting his eyes in shadow.

She patted the cushion next to her. "Come over here, Bren. Please."

The leather on the sofa creaked when he sat, the sound loud in the small room.

Liz's heart thundered in her ears as she slid a few inches closer to him. "Why did we let it get so difficult, Bren?" she whispered. "We were good for each other, and then we just walked away . . ."

Her hand was a fraction of an inch from his, so close she could feel the heat from his fingers. One twitch of his hand and he would be touching her.

"*We* just walked away, Liz?" His hand moved away. She almost reached out and grabbed his fingers. "It was what *you* wanted, remember? 'You're a SEAL, I'm a Marine, we're going different places . . . and we're not going to get there together.' I believe those were your exact words, right?"

Liz sat back as if she'd been slapped. "I meant—"

"I know *exactly* what you meant, Liz. And you got *exactly* what you wanted—"

"I don't love him, Bren," Liz interrupted.

"What does that mean?"

She slid her left hand under her thigh to hide the rings. The enormous stone seemed to bite into her flesh. "James. He's a good man, and he's good to me . . . but I don't love him."

"So you're getting a divorce?"

The question stopped Liz cold. What was she going to do? The thought of hurting James just because she was broken inside didn't seem right. "I—I don't know. I thought since you were through with Amy, maybe we could—"

"You don't know anything about my relationship with Amy." His voice was hard, with a bitter edge. "We've spent a grand total of three hours together in the last decade. People change, Liz."

"It's all my fault. I know that now," she said in a small voice. "I just hoped we could start over."

"Liz, I'm your friend, I'll always be your friend, but I am not about to break up a marriage."

Her phone, sitting on the cushion between them, rang. The soft light illuminated his face from below. She kept her eyes locked on him, afraid that if she wavered for even a second, he would be gone. The phone rang again. She knew from the ringtone that it was James.

"Are you going to get that?"

Liz's eyes went blurry with tears. She snatched the phone off the sofa and stood to face the fireplace.

"Hi, honey," she said in as bright a tone as she could manage. "I'm right in the middle of dinner here. Could I call you back in an hour?"

"No problem, sweetie. Talk to you later. Have fun." James hung up.

Brendan was gone, she could feel it. Liz leaned both hands against the mantelpiece and let the flames dissolve in tears.

CHAPTER 30

The Iranians were telling the truth.

Don sat back in his chair and surveyed the stacks of reports arranged in neat piles around him. The master spreadsheet on his laptop accounted for every gram of fissile material that had ever been bought, refined, enriched, or disposed of by the Islamic Republic of Iran. The IAEA had been through every Iranian nuclear facility and verified anything that was verifiable by measurement.

The bottom line was that the Iranians were telling the truth: their program was for peaceful nuclear power generation. Yes, there had been some additional enrichment of material—significant enrichment, in fact, up into the early 2000s—but the Iranians had come clean about that, too. It seemed all the recent posturing in Congress and in Israel, all the dire warnings about the threat of a nuclear Iran, had been pointless.

He switched screens on his laptop to where his report was in draft form. He'd long gotten over the fact that his work ended up on the President's desk, but this one seemed like a moment in history to Don.

In a way, it was. Since the Iranian nuclear negotiations had been extended in November 2014, his report might be the proof the President needed to bless the pending P5+1 deal with the Iranians. A "green light" assessment would not play well with the hawks in Congress or in the DOD. Heck, most of the CIA was against dealing with the Iranians—but this was one instance where Don was grateful for Clem. True, the guy was an asshole, but in this case, he was Don's asshole and had been offering the needed cover from those who wanted to influence the outcome of Don's report.

It had been Clem's idea to put Don—and all his data—into a secure conference room, complete with his own printer and supply of Diet Cokes. The large table gave him the chance to spread out all the various reports and charts so he could cross-reference them easily. He couldn't imagine doing this project back in his tiny cube.

He turned back to the report, updating the Executive Summary with his findings, then moving to the detailed final section where he inserted his Excel tables. In the final analysis, he was able to account for every known transaction of raw material and each enrichment step, within an acceptable margin of error.

But what about unknown transactions?

Don's eyes drifted to the thick file on the floor beside his chair. While all the other folders in the room were stiff and new, with gleaming classification stickers, this one was weathered with age and overstuffed. The faded Top Secret sticker was partially torn. Across the body of the folder, he'd written ROGUE in block letters with a black marker.

That's what Don had taken to calling it, the Rogue File—his explanation of what had happened to Saddam Hussein's nuclear weapons. He was tempted to add a section to his report on the possibility that Saddam might have moved nukes to Iran in the days before Operation Iraqi Freedom. A footnote, maybe? Anything to let these people know that there was another potential threat out there.

He shook his head. Apart from being career suicide, this would guarantee that his report would be filed in the deepest, darkest hole the intelligence community could find. No, if he wanted to make a claim like that, he needed hard proof.

Don pushed the laptop back and dropped the file in front of him. It made a satisfying thud on the conference room table. He flipped open the cover and found himself staring at the 8×10 photo of the Blade, aka Alizera Mogadaham, most certainly a false name. While they didn't know his real identity, they were familiar with his handiwork. Don placed the picture to one side and looked at the next one: a Persian knife, called a *pesh-kabz*. He studied the wicked edge of the curved blade and the ivory handle worn satiny smooth with use.

The Blade had surfaced during the eight-year-long Iran–Iraq War. They knew he was a Quds officer, and his specialty was interrogations—using a knife. Don had seen pictures of a few of his suspected victims and they turned his stomach. Even experienced case officers chose to look away. By the end of the war, Don was told, even the threat of bringing in the Blade for an interrogation was enough to garner useful intel from an Iraqi victim.

The faked Iranian diplomatic passport photo was the only known picture of him. Whatever he'd done after the Iran–Iraq War, he'd kept a low profile. Using facial recognition matching, they'd been able to tentatively place him in Helsinki in June 2005 for reasons unknown, and Brendan had run across the Blade in Iraq twice: once during the 2007 raid and again at the Iraqi MOJ in November 2011. As far as they knew, that was the extent of the agent's travel outside of Iran. The CIA had classified him as a low-level operative, not worth spending resources on at this time.

Don studied the sharp jawline, the noble nose, and the dark eyes devoid of expression. It was a handsome face, but the deadness in the eyes made him seem unfriendly. He recalled Brendan's description of the man, his love of Marlboro cigarettes, and the beautiful knife he carried. Not a lot to go on: a handsome Middle Eastern–looking guy with unfriendly eyes, who likes to smoke and carries a knife. He sighed as he restacked the contents of the folder. He closed the cover and rested his hand on it for a moment.

The act of looking at the Rogue File was oddly comforting, like visiting an old friend. Someday, the puzzle pieces in his mind would snap together and it would all make sense. He was sure of it.

He dropped the file to the floor and pulled his laptop back in front of him. For now, he had a report to finish for the President of the United States.

CHAPTER 31

"It's happening again!"

Dot's excited voice filtered up from the cabin. Brendan grunted in reply, loud enough for her to hear him. She'd been analyzing the Israeli signal for the last two hours and was over the moon about it, claiming this was "major SIG" material—whatever that meant.

He uncrossed and recrossed his ankles, keeping his attention on the spectacular sunset off the starboard beam. The weather in the eastern Med had been nothing short of phenomenal: a steady light breeze to keep the sails full, but not enough force to disturb the electronics in the mast.

Brendan dropped his gaze to his knees and looked away immediately. His left knee, perfectly smooth tanned skin, contrasted with his right, which was a mess of lumps and twisted scars that would never tan over. The more his tan deepened, the more his damaged limb stood out.

"They shut down." Dot's head appeared in the cabin entrance. She gripped the rails and vaulted herself up the stairs, landing on the deck with a thud. A wide smile creased her narrow face and a few strands of frizzy gray-blonde hair escaped the messy bun at the nape of her neck. Dorothy "Dot" Pendergrass looked like a mild-mannered geek—which she was—but Brendan knew firsthand that she was more than able to take care of herself in any situation. During their work-up phase for deployment, Brendan had insisted they all take a self-defense refresher. He'd chosen Dot as his partner and had ended up face-first on the mat in an armlock before he even knew what hit him. She finally shared with the team that she was a third-degree black belt in aikido. More than a little embarrassing for a SEAL, and a good reminder that looks could be deceiving.

Dot's wiry frame quivered with excitement as she sat on the gunwale, blocking his view of the sunset. "It was spectacular! We didn't even know the Israelis had that kind of low-energy phased array radar. This has major SIG written all over it." Her voice was thin, and she had a habit of halting her speech in odd places, as if the words were getting stuck between her brain and her mouth. "These sailboats are pure genius, Brendan. Genius."

Brendan had his doubts that the Israelis would share her enthusiasm, but he had to admit their trip through the Med proved the premise of the Feisty Minnow intel-gathering program. The working theory that Baxter had sold to ONI was that all countries, friend, foe, or anyone in between, held back on their use of specialized comms and other electronic signatures when US Navy vessels were in the vicinity. But would the same restrictions apply when they thought a pleasure craft was off their coast? Apparently not, from the material they had gathered just from sailing down the southern Med coastline. From Gibraltar, they'd been able to capture signals from Spain, Morocco, Algeria, Tunisia, Libya, Egypt, Jordan, and of course Israel, all of which were sent back to NSA for processing.

That was when Brendan first heard the term *major SIG*, a subjective grade given to field data that "connected the dots" for the analysts. In this case, the signal was a new Israeli capability that showed the US ally had been very busy developing their own sensors—and not sharing their progress with their American friends.

Tomorrow they'd enter the Suez Canal and head for the Indian Ocean, where the real work would begin. He stood and hauled down the flag of the Maldives from the jack staff. For security reasons, the boat was registered in the Maldives, but it still bothered him not to have the stars and stripes flying over his command.

He grinned at Dot. "What do you say, Dot? Major SIG or not? I have a reputation as a spy boat captain to uphold here."

"Give me another hour and I'll let you know." She stood abruptly and disappeared down into the cabin. Brendan shook his head. That was Dot for you: the Energizer Bunny of signals intelligence. Baxter had told him she was the best at what she did, and Brendan believed him.

"More coffee, skipper?"

The voice that floated up from the cabin was the polar opposite of Dot. Whereas Dot was all chaotic energy and abrupt conversations, Gabrielle Marchese lived her life slowly, as if she meant to linger over the enjoyment of every moment. She extended a half-full mug to Brendan, allowing her fingers to linger on his wrist when he accepted the cup. Her touch was deliberate—and electric. Gabby waved her hands for him to move his legs so that she could sit down.

She settled into the bench seat, turning to face him. Gabby was a beautiful girl, there was no doubt about that. Her soft, languorous speech betrayed her New Orleans origins, and in the light of the dying sunset her impossibly large brown eyes were fastened on him. Tendrils of dark hair framed her face, the rest cascading over the caramel-colored skin of her shoulders.

"Penny for your thoughts, skipper," she said softly.

Oh, and she'd made it very clear that she was willing to sleep with him, so there was that. He mentally listed the reasons why this was a bad idea: she was nearly ten years younger than him, it was bad for crew morale, he would get fired, she reminded him of Liz . . .

The last one stopped him. He'd never really thought about it in those terms before, but it was true: Gabby was a softer, sultrier version of Liz.

Gabby, a civilian, had been a replacement for the Intelligence Specialist who had been diagnosed with jaundice a week before their departure. Due to her last-minute arrival on the boat, she'd only been on two shakedown cruises before they'd left Annapolis, and had been seasick both times—really seasick. But she'd gutted it out and followed through on every single duty assigned, even managing to cook a fabulous jambalaya in heavy seas. Eventually, her seasickness receded.

She kicked him playfully, and Brendan shifted his legs out of range. "Any of those biscuits left from dinner?" he asked.

"Sure." When she got to her feet, her sundress clung to her hips. Underneath the thin material, he could see the outline of the bikini she'd worn topside that afternoon. Brendan caught his breath. Many more afternoons like that and his resolve about not sleeping with Gabby would be worn paper-thin.

To put his mind on more appropriate matters, Brendan checked his heading and made a minor adjustment to the mainsail. He laughed to himself. It was the kind of adjustment that he'd always teased Liz about on the sailing team, the kind of niggling change you made just to have something to do. He wondered what she thought of him after his sudden departure from Marjorie's house after Thanksgiving dinner. It had certainly seemed like she was sending him signals—but she was married, for God's sake.

Brendan gritted his teeth. He was better than that. Even if he did have feelings for Liz, she'd made a commitment to another man, and he wasn't going to be the cause of a breakup.

The clock chimed eight times, the cheery tones ringing in the night air. The handsome brass chronometer, mounted next to the ladder in the cabin, had been a ship-christening gift from Baxter.

Scottie's tousled head poked up from the cabin. "You ready, skipper?"

"C'mon up, Scottie. I'll sit a minute more, but you can take the watch."

Scottie scrambled up the steps, and made his way forward for a pre-watch inspection. Even though they were undercover and flying the flag of a foreign country, they were still a US naval vessel, and Brendan insisted they run watches according to Navy traditions.

He was pretty sure that Scottie and Maggie, the other analyst besides Dot, were sleeping together. Brendan didn't actually have any evidence, just a feeling. Besides, was it really against regs? Scottie was in the Navy, but Maggie was a civilian now, a GS-11. He sighed. Add crew fraternization policy to the long list of things he should have asked Baxter about before they'd left on deployment.

As if on cue, Gabby's sleek form glided up the stairs, shadowy in the darkness. She held out a plate, a disc of ghostly white in the dark. "One biscuit, sir. Buttered just the way you like it." Her hand grazed his knee as she leaned over, and he felt his breath quicken.

"Can I get you anything else?"

CHAPTER 32

Estancia Refugio Seguro, Argentina
08 June 2015 – 1120 local

Through a gap in the drawn drapes, Rafiq could see a blindingly white slice of Argentinean winter sunshine. The gloom of the sickroom unnerved him, reminding him of Farid's painful last weeks battling pancreatic cancer.

He shifted in his chair, breaking the silence with a creak of wood and leather. The nurse reprimanded him with her eyes. Rafiq ignored her.

Javier lay in the hospital bed, his face the color of the bedsheets. His eyes flickered and Rafiq realized the old man was awake, watching him. His fingers beckoned to Rafiq to come closer. The nurse stood and wiped a line of spittle from his chin. Javier whispered to her.

"Pardon?" she replied in Spanish.

"Leave us," he said in a louder voice.

The nurse looked from Javier to Rafiq, opening her mouth to protest. Rafiq met her gaze, and she hurried to the door.

Javier patted the bed next to him; Rafiq sat and took the old man's hand in his own.

"Do you know what today is?" Javier wheezed.

Rafiq shook his head.

"I asked Consuela to marry me, forty years ago today." He paused for breath. The oxygen line under his nose had slipped down, and Rafiq adjusted it. "Today is the day I see her again."

"Papa," Rafiq said. It still amazed him how normal it felt to call this man his father. "Papa, don't talk like that."

Javier shook his head. "It is my choice. I want it this way. Today is the day." He paused again for breath. "Open the drapes, my son. I want to see the mountains again."

Rafiq rose and pulled the cord to open the heavy window coverings. Sunlight flooded the room, making both of them squint. Rafiq started to close them again.

"Leave it!" Javier called, with a cough. His hand found the controls for his bed and he raised his head up. He patted the bedside again.

For a long time, the two of them sat staring out the window. The ranch house was built on a bluff overlooking the hillside vineyard and a long valley. Mountains loomed in the distance, dappled by the shadows of clouds and dusted with snow.

"Nadine was an accident, you know," Javier said. "We were told we could never have children . . . my Consuela lit so many candles in church I was afraid she would burn the place down!" He laughed, a deep, phlegmy burble in his chest.

The old man's decline tore at Rafiq's heart. Only a few months ago, he'd been a healthy, hearty soul drinking his red wine and smoking cigars in the dark of the nighttime veranda. Now he was a pasty imitation of Javier, an abomination. Rafiq was glad today was the day and his adopted father would leave this world on his own terms.

Javier lifted his hand toward the window then let it fall back to the bedding. "This, my daughter, my life's work, everything I have, I leave to you, my son. My *estancia* is now yours."

Rafiq said nothing. They had reviewed Javier's will and the ranch finances together. He was a rich man.

"Your cargo," Javier said finally. "What are your plans?"

Rafiq avoided his eyes. "It's been more than seven years, Papa. If they were going to activate me, it would have happened by now."

Javier was having none of it. He struggled to sit up higher, beckoning Rafiq to put another pillow behind his back so he could see him eye to eye. "No," the old man said, when he had caught his breath. "They will call. They always call. You must tell them, son. You must walk away now. Give them a fortune, but walk away. For the sake of your family."

His hand latched onto Rafiq's forearm with a surprisingly strong grip. "Promise me," he whispered.

Rafiq met his gaze and held it. He nodded. "I promise."

Javier smiled and lay back against the pillows. "*Gracias.*"

A light knock at the door interrupted them, and the nurse peeked into the room. Javier waved at her to enter. "Bring in my grandchildren," he called out in a loud voice.

Little Javi burst into the room in a flurry of energy, rushing to his namesake's bedside. Rafiq stopped him before he leaped onto the bed. The old man reached out and buried his withered hand in the boy's mass of dark curls. "So much like your mother, Javi. How is the riding coming?"

Javi babbled on about his latest exploit on horseback, but the old man's attention was drawn to the doorway. Nadine entered, stooped over so that Consie could hold her hand as she toddled into the room. The baby let go of her mother's fingers and made the last few steps to the bed on her own. The old man's face lit up. "Oh, how I wish your mother could see these two, Deanie. She would be so proud."

The expression on Nadine's face sucked the breath out of Rafiq's lungs. The strain of her father's sudden illness had taken a toll on his beautiful wife. Her face had thinned and paled, sharpening her cheekbones and enlarging her dark eyes. A line of silver hair sprouted from her right temple, trailing down over her shoulder. Rafiq knew she had bought hair dye to hide it, but the package had lain in their bathroom cabinet for over a month, unopened.

Her eyes were dry. *She knows,* Rafiq thought. *She knows today is the day.*

Nadine's arms trembled as she picked up Consie. "Children, it's time to say goodbye to *Tito* now." Her voice broke when she said the Spanish word for grandfather, and the baby turned sharply to study her mother's face. Nadine placed her lips on Consie's forehead and held them there until she had regained some control.

Javier leaned over so Javi could place a kiss on his cheek. The old man fluffed the boy's dark curls. "You grow up to be as good a man as your father, understand, boy?"

Javi stopped short at the tone in his grandfather's voice, then nodded. He looked up at Rafiq. "Can I ride Storm past Tito's window?" Rafiq nodded automatically and the boy sped out of the room.

Nadine leaned in so Javier could reach his granddaughter. The little girl placed one palm on either cheek and studied the old man's face, her smooth brow wrinkling with concentration. Javier smiled at her. "You have wise eyes, little one. Just like your grandmother."

"Pa—pa," replied Consie.

"Give Tito a kiss, Consie," Nadine whispered.

The toddler wrapped her chubby arms around the old man's whiskered neck and planted a kiss on his cheek. Rafiq's vision went blurry for a few seconds. When he regained control of his emotions,

Nadine had placed Consie in the care of the nurse and shooed the woman from the room.

Nadine stripped away the oxygen line from his nostrils and removed the other monitors from her father's body. The machines beeped in protest, so she turned them off and pushed them roughly against the wall. Then she curled up next to her father on the bed. Rafiq sat on the other side, taking the old man's hand in his own.

For a long time, the three of them just sat there, staring out the wide picture window. The sun painted the mountains in tones of gold and rippled across the grassy valley. Javi, seated astride his beloved Storm, burst into view. The boy was crouched close to the horse's neck, his face almost in the animal's mane, as he urged him faster across the yard.

"He rides almost as well as you did at that age, Deanie."

Out of the corner of his eye, Rafiq saw Nadine nod. "Better."

Rafiq was not much of a horseman, but he loved to watch his talented son ride. The boy swung the animal around for another pass in front of his grandfather's window. Rafiq looked over at Javier to say something and stopped.

The old man's gray eyes were fastened on the window, but all the life had gone out of them. Nadine, still curled up against her father's shoulder, met Rafiq's gaze. Her dry eyes held a haunted look.

Rafiq squeezed the cooling flesh of Javier's hand. "I promise," he whispered.

There were two funerals for Javier.

The first was at sunrise on the third day following his death, in the small chapel near the ranch. Fog clung to the gray stones of the old church and the interior was cold and damp. The priest, a gray-haired man, said mass in a plain cassock, the unfamiliar Spanish words rolling over Rafiq like a meditation. Javier had converted to Catholicism at the request of his beloved Consuela, and yet his whole life had been spent funneling money and support to the Muslim organization Hezbollah in his homeland. His entire existence was a carefully balanced commitment to two diametrically opposed causes.

How did you do it, old man?

Consie fussed in the pew next to him. Rafiq shifted the girl onto his lap, where she snuggled against his chest and went to sleep. He kissed the back of her head. His promise to Javier burned in his ears.

Despite the hour, the building was full to bursting with plainly dressed ranch hands, vineyard workers, and local shopkeepers. Rafiq was shocked at the turnout and touched by the sincerity of the people as he shook their hands following the mass. Nadine stood at his side, veiled in black but hauntingly beautiful at the same time.

The second mass, held at the Basilica in Ciudad Del Este, was for the elite—and they turned out in force. Mayors, politicians, police chiefs, military officers, anyone who was anyone from as far away as Buenos Aires was there, all saying the same thing to Rafiq: Whatever you need, just ask.

And then they were alone, just he and Nadine, in the massive ranch house. The children were with their nanny and the servants had all been given the night off.

They sat on the veranda as darkness fell, until the black of Nadine's dress made her body disappear and all he could see of his wife was the pale moon of her face.

"Are you forgetting something?" she asked.

"What?"

"The cargo. You haven't checked on the cargo today."

Rafiq reached for her in the dark.

"Not today."

CHAPTER 33

Liz sliced the packing tape on the last box.

Finally! Her favorite Chemex coffeepot was at the top of the box, swaddled in bubble wrap. She looked at the side of the box; the label said "books." She let out a snort. So much for the government move.

She added the empty box to the pile by the door that needed to be flattened and taken downstairs to the recycling bin. Liz carefully placed the coffeepot on the counter next to the sink, amid the sea of cups and plates she had yet to put away. It occurred to her that James had always done the organizing whenever they moved . . . and he wasn't here this time. She looked around the cluttered counters; this was all her responsibility now.

Be careful what you wish for, girl. It might come true.

She hadn't really fallen out of love, she was just never really in love with James in the first place. She cared for him—that was the truth—but it was more like the way you cared for your brother.

Liz had begun looking into a transfer over six months ago, before she'd even decided she was leaving James. Almost as if she was creating an excuse to leave him. Her personnel officer had shown her some great assignments—Hawaii, Florida, DC—but she chose Minneapolis.

When she'd finally told James, he was . . . well, he was James. Kind, understanding, gentle, rational. And all of a sudden she was the one who was crying and emotional and all the things she wasn't.

He'd held her in that way he had, with just the right amount of tightness around her shoulders, and she fit her face into the crook of his neck. At that moment, she knew she was leaving him for good. Not because he wasn't right for her, but because he was too good for her. He deserved better than she was able to give him—than she'd ever be able to give him.

Liz left that night. She just threw a pile of clothes in a suitcase and drove until the sky grew light in the east and she could barely keep her eyes open. She pulled into a rest stop in Utah and slept for a few hours, then she drove some more.

She made it to Minneapolis on the morning of the second day, a Sunday. The city sweltered under a summer sun and the humidity clung to her skin when she left the car. The sign said Lake Calhoun, and a fair number of early morning runners were out on the paved trail around the lake. Somewhere on the car trip she'd switched into shorts and a T-shirt. She rooted through the trunk until she found a pair of running shoes and laced them on her feet.

The coffee and hot dog she'd gotten from a gas station in Iowa a few hours ago made a solid lump in her stomach, but she ignored it. As she found her pace among the runners, her breathing evened out and she broke into a free sweat.

The trail was paved, flat and fast. Liz ran hard, letting the grime of the last day's ride in the car slicken on her skin. The trail split, and she followed the arrow that pointed to Lake Harriet.

When Liz returned to her BMW an hour later, she was drenched in sweat, had a stitch in her side, and was happier than she'd been in months.

She pulled a toiletry kit and a fresh change of light clothes from the trunk and headed across the street to a storefront labeled Calhoun Beach Athletic Club. The AC raised gooseflesh on her arms as she approached the desk. The kid behind the desk stood up, a smile on his face.

"Good morning, may I see your membership, please?'

Liz realized she looked like a wreck. "Good morning . . ." She focused on his nametag. "Aaron. I'm new in town and was hoping to use your shower."

Aaron colored. "Sorry, ma'am, this is a members-only club—"

"Who can I talk to about getting a membership?"

Aaron glanced at the clock. "They don't get in for another hour on Sundays, ma'am."

Liz put out her hand. "I'm Liz, Aaron, and I'd like to buy a membership here—the most expensive membership you offer—but I need a shower first. I need one now. Can you help me out?"

"Well, if you're a prospective member, I could give you a guest pass . . ."

"Now we're talking, Aaron."

Just as the run around Lake Calhoun had been somehow cleansing for her spirit, the shower did the same for her body. She let the warm water cascade over her as she scrubbed her skin clean—clean of her failed marriage, clean of the two-day drive, clean of the sweat from her run. Liz dressed in a light cotton blouse, a short print skirt, and sandals. As she stood in front of the mirror brushing her hair, her wedding ring glinted in the reflection. It was a plain gold band, the one she'd insisted that James give her. His plan had been a diamond-encrusted affair to match her massive engagement ring, but she'd put her foot down. Liz only wore two pieces of jewelry on her fingers: her Academy ring and the plain gold band.

She slipped off the wedding ring and left it in her toiletry kit.

On the walk back through the lobby, she noticed a bulletin board with a FOR RENT posting. Two-bedroom apartment, top floor, view of Lake Calhoun.

"What's the address here, Aaron?"

Aaron had been eyeing her legs behind the desk and he gave a start when she called his name.

"Umm . . . 2750 Lake Street."

Liz tapped the advertisement. "So this apartment is the top floor of this building?"

Aaron nodded. Liz pulled the page off the bulletin board. Aaron opened his mouth to stop her, but she held up a hand. "Relax, Aaron, it's off the market. I just rented it."

Liz sighed as she pulled a bottle of Chardonnay out of the fridge. At least she had wineglasses now. She hunted through the mess of kitchen items until she found the one she wanted and rinsed it out before filling it with wine.

Glass in hand, she stepped onto the balcony and sank into a chair. After the arid atmosphere of LA, the steamy heat of a Minneapolis summer felt luxurious on her skin. White triangles of sails dotted the lake and the shores were crowded with families, couples, lovers . . . everyone seemed to have someone this holiday evening.

She sipped the wine, letting the crisp sweetness linger on her tongue. *Everyone but me, that is.*

Maybe she'd go sailing tomorrow. That would be something to occupy her time. She hadn't been on the water since the Academy— had it been that long? A smile curled her lips when she thought about

Mark and Don. And Brendan.

Brendan . . . what was he doing now? That whole job at the naval station in Annapolis—what a joke! It had to be some sort of classified project, but he really was working on a sailboat, so that didn't add up either. And now, according to Don, he was deployed somewhere.

She should have called him after the dinner at Marjorie's. Just having him that close again made her realize what she'd given up, how badly she'd messed up her life—and James's. If her husband hadn't called at that moment, who knows what she would have done.

What was the saying? The truth shall set you free . . .

That night at Marjorie's was the first time she'd ever said the truth out loud: James was a good man, but she didn't love him.

Brendan had every right to be disgusted with her. She'd created this mess in the first place, and she knew she should respect his unwillingness to get involved with a married woman.

She stilled her thoughts and put her feet up on the balcony railing. *I'm here, Bren. And I won't make the same mistake twice.*

CHAPTER 34

Zagros Mountains, south of Gerash, Iran
15 October 2015 – 0200 local

It was a perfect desert night, with only a sliver of crescent moon, just enough to allow him to find his way without headlights.

Aban sat in the passenger seat of the Range Rover, his bearded face lit a ghostly green by the instrument panel. His brother was dressed in civilian clothes for this trip, an added precaution to avoid curious eyes.

Hashem had always thought of his older brother as a stout man, but one who carried his weight with authority. But in civilian clothes, Aban looked dumpy, and much older. Hashem noted the slump in his shoulders, the haggardness behind the bushy gray beard of his office. The look in his eyes spoke of tiredness and something else . . . resignation?

For months, Aban had led the fight against Rouhani and the forces of moderation, the path leading the country away from the old ways. Now in the last weeks before the election, Aban's posture told Hashem that his brother feared the outcome of the coming election.

For a few years, Aban had been able to stem the tide of change that simmered under the surface of public sentiment for the last decade. The so-called Arab Spring had perversely worked in the favor of the old guard—the Iranian people saw Egypt, Libya, Syria, and others rise up and throw out the established leaders, then promptly fall into chaos. They didn't want chaos, but they also didn't want the unyielding rule of the ayatollahs.

Rouhani's moderate faction sought to occupy the narrow breach between these two poles. With one foot in the camp of the Supreme Leader and one with the reformers, Hassan Rouhani navigated a narrow path of goodness that promised to restore Iran's place in the world order and get rid of the sanctions that had brought the Iranian economy to its knees.

Reform, but not too much reform. That was the implicit promise.

From the slums of south Tehran to the moneyed estates of the rich in northern Tehran, the fiery rhetoric of the old guard fell on deaf ears. Rouhani was winning, and Aban knew it.

So he was here with his brother in the middle of the night to inspect the alternative.

Rouhani may have popular support, but the public was a fickle beast. They expected results quickly, and didn't care to hear about the grinding machinery of international politics. Unless the sanctions were lifted—and quickly—Rouhani's power would bleed away like sand through his fingers.

Rouhani needed a nuclear deal with the West. He knew it, Aban knew it, the Supreme Leader knew it. This was where the news got really bad for Aban. Israel, the staunchest enemy of Iran, the dissenting voice against any compromise with Iran, was showing signs of conciliation.

And so Aban was here in the desert in the middle of the night with his brother, the spy, to see what his chances were of persuading Israel—and the world—to resume their Iran-hating ways.

Hashem paused the Rover at the checkpoint and flashed his lights three times. Since his night vision was compromised anyway, he took the opportunity to fire up a cigarette. He took a deep drag and offered the open pack to his brother. Aban shook his head.

The all-clear lights poked out of the darkness and Hashem drove down the steep grade to the valley floor. When they reached the cave entrance, Hashem watched his brother out of the corner of his eye to see if he had any reaction to revisiting the place they had discovered so many years ago with their father. Aban's jowly face showed no sign of recognition.

The blackout screen dropped behind them and the steel doors slid open, flooding them with harsh fluorescent light. Aban's eyes flew open when he saw the interior of the cave.

"It is magnificent, Hashem," he whispered. Hashem parked the car and his security detail opened the doors for them.

Viewing his brother in civilian clothes in the light, Hashem felt a flash of embarrassment. In his clerical garb, he seemed solid, a pillar of strength. In working clothes, without a turban to hide the wispy strands of gray hair, he looked ordinary. A heavy belly swung like a counterbalance whenever he moved, and his limbs seemed stubby, like appendages on a beach ball. He looked up at Hashem. "Brother, this is a wonder. I had no idea."

Hashem inclined his head with a modest tilt, but inside he glowed. Praise from his older brother was a rare gift.

They boarded the golf cart. "Perhaps you would like to change?" Hashem said.

"Yes, yes. But I am eager to see the weapons before morning prayers."

Hashem breathed a sigh of relief as he guided the cart to his quarters. He carried Aban's bag to the spare room, pausing in the doorway. "It's not much—"

"Brother, it is wondrous what you have done here," Aban interrupted him, his face glowing. He rested his hand on the hewn rock wall, his fingers tracing a vein of white granite in the dark rock. For a moment, he seemed about to make a comment about geology. Aban smiled. "I'll be right back."

The Aban who joined him in the golf cart seemed a new man. In the short time they had been in the cave, he acted younger than Hashem had seen him in years. His snow-white turban hid the thin hair and spotted scalp, and the robes of his office armored the sagging belly. He hopped into the cart and slapped the dash. "Impress me, brother."

The first stop was the rockets. Aban was out of the cart before the vehicle even halted. He almost ran to where the long white boosters lay in their cradles, running his hands along the smooth metal sides. At one point, Hashem thought he might hug one of the rockets. When he turned to Hashem, his eyes were wet with tears. They continued the tour by inspecting the TELs, Aban practically babbling questions about the North Koreans and then interrupting himself to ask even more questions about how things worked.

They reached the lab, and Yusef made his way across the space warily, taking a knee in front of Aban. Yusef's lazy eye was practically doing circles in his head.

"Salaam, my son," Aban said softly. "You have done Allah's work here." When he touched Yusef's shoulder, the man flinched. Aban threw a questioning look at his brother.

"Yusef likes his solitude. He finds the company of others disturbs his work," Hashem said hastily.

Yusef got to his feet without meeting Aban's eyes and gestured toward the cleanroom, where the guidance systems were fully assembled. His black curls, even wilder than usual, bobbed as he swayed his body. He edged further and further from Aban until he was speaking to him from the other side of the room.

Hashem's jaw tightened; the man's antisocial tendencies were getting worse.

Aban ended the interview with a chop of his hand. Yusef, now on the other side of the room, jumped at the gesture. "Thank you— Yusef, is it? Your work is much appreciated."

He muttered to Hashem on the way out the door. "I hope he is a genius, Hashem, because he clearly has problems."

If possible, the interview with Valerie was worse. For starters, the big Russian, stinking of vodka, tried to hug Aban. They gathered at the window of the cleanroom where Valerie's alcohol-soaked breath fogged the glass as he spoke. The warheads lay on assembly tables, already packed inside their capsules, ready to be loaded onto the missiles.

Despite the chill of the room, Valerie's shirtfront was soaked in sweat. He stabbed a finger at the closest warhead, leaving a sweaty smudge on the glass. "That is for my beloved Raisa," he said. Then he began to cry, mumbling about Tanya and Little Valerie and how much he wanted to bomb the Israelis into oblivion.

Hashem intervened, guiding Valerie back to his desk and the half-empty vodka bottle. Aban's eyes were wide as saucers as his brother led him back to the cart. They stood for a moment next to the booster sections. Aban rested his hands on the cool white metal; the touch seemed to revive his previous good spirits.

Hashem spoke first. "They are more than they seem, brother. Both are geniuses in their fields . . . you have seen them at their worst tonight."

Aban nodded. "I trust your judgment. You know that neither of them can ever go back into society."

Hashem pursed his lips. He knew it, of course, but he had also grown fond of these two men. Their faults aside, they had given their lives and their talents to make this project successful. The thought of killing them gave him no joy.

"I will do what needs to be done."

Aban looked at his wristwatch. "May we walk outside before morning prayers, Hashem?"

Hashem watched his brother out of the corner of his eye as he drove to the cave entrance. The disturbing visits with Yusef and Valerie seemed forgotten, and his face had once again taken on a smiling, youthful look. They parked and exited the brightly lit cave through a personnel entrance, after passing through two blackout scrims.

The air of the desert night was chilly after the climate-controlled cave. The moon had set, but once his eyes adjusted, Hashem could see easily with only starlight.

"Do you remember when we found this cave, Aban? With Father?" Hashem said.

Aban grunted.

Hashem drew in a deep breath of the clean desert air, so unlike the dirty atmosphere of Tehran. For once, he didn't want a cigarette. "It's like we've come full circle. We found this place with Father, now we are using it to set our country back on the right path—"

"Stop with your sentimental blatherings about our father. He was an infidel, an adulterer, a man of loose morals. He worked for the Shah! And when the Shah fell, what did he do? Fled back to Lebanon and started another family, leaving us to fend for ourselves. This is the man you wish to remember? To honor?" Aban hawked and spat with ferocity on the sand before them.

A wave of loss welled up in Hashem, leaving a sour taste in the back of his throat. For a brief moment he longed for the brother who'd spoken with such passion about the discovery of this cave, and Hashem was glad for the darkness that hid the hot flush of shame on his face.

Aban drew a deep breath. "You have done well here, Hashem, very well. The next few months will be pivotal to our cause.

Rouhani's men will win the election, of that I have no doubt, but winning and governing are two different things. Men—even Rouhani's men—can be bought. I am confident we can control affairs internal to Iran, it is the outside world I am concerned about. America has its own elections within the next year. Think what a coup it would be for a presidential candidate to be able to claim he had removed Iran's nuclear weapons as a threat to the world."

He paused, his breath rasping heavily in the dark. "That is where you come in. Israel has always been the one foe we can depend on to derail any possible peace negotiation, but if that snake Rouhani can convince even Israel to talk peace, then we will need to act—and act decisively."

Hashem said nothing. He knew he should be glad to finally use the weapons he had spent so many years building, but the thought of ending this project made him sad. This cave, these men—as flawed as they were—were the closest thing to a family he'd ever had.

Aban turned back toward the cave.

"Come. Pray with me."

CHAPTER 35

Estate of Ayatollah Aban Rahmani, North Tehran
Day after Iranian Parliamentary Elections, December 2015 – 0600 local

Hashem directed his driver to pull to the side entrance of Aban's mansion. The opulence of his brother's home, the clash between the cleric and the man, always made Hashem uneasy.

Maryam, Aban's personal assistant, met him at the door. The dark eyes that peered up at him from under her headscarf were bloodshot and worried.

"Salaam, Maryam," Hashem said. "How is he?"

"Salaam, Hashem." She gripped his hand in both of hers. "Thank you for coming so quickly. He is in his study."

Whatever gains Aban thought he had made against Rouhani's forces over the last year had been swept aside in the previous day's elections. With a voter turnout of over seventy-five percent, the Moderation and Development Party, led by Rouhani, had devastated the conservative opposition in the Iranian Parliament. Al Jazeera was berserk with the news, holding up Iran as the model of peaceful, democratic change in the Middle East, even further bolstering Rouhani's reputation in the world and at home. They were already predicting progressive gains in the Assembly of Experts, and that election wouldn't happen until next March.

Hashem tapped on the heavy carved door of Aban's study before he let himself in. The room was thick with cigarette smoke and Hashem detected the sharp scent of whiskey. Aban sat in a leather armchair facing away from him, toward the window. The study overlooked the gardens of his home, and beyond that the skyline of Tehran. The first rays of the sun were lighting up the pall of pollution that hung over the city in beautiful tones of red and orange, hiding the ugliness and the poverty and the decrepitude that lay in that jungle of concrete buildings.

"Salaam, brother," Hashem said. He lit a cigarette, not because he wanted it, but because he needed something to do with his hands.

Aban swiveled the chair around slowly, using his bare toes on the hardwood floor. He was slumped so deeply into the rich leather that his bushy beard touched the belly that domed up under his T-shirt. Dressed only in his underwear, with his scrawny white legs poking out of voluminous boxers, he looked like a sad clown. In his hand, he gripped an empty crystal tumbler.

"Salaam, brother." His voice was wheezy and weak.

Hashem went back to the door and cracked it open. "Tea, Maryam. And a fresh robe."

When he turned around, Aban had turned on the flat-screen TV, and the fluorescent colors played off his white underwear. The set was already tuned to Al Jazeera, with the sound muted. An attractive woman, her mouth working silently, was sharing a split screen with the Iranian election results. A color graphic showed the new progressive majority in the Iranian Parliament.

"How could the Supreme Leader let this happen? What is the

Council of Guardians for if not to screen out the weak-minded before they run for office?" Aban seemed to be getting animated now. He sat up in his chair so the bulk of his belly slid down to rest on his thighs.

A gentle tap on the door told Hashem that Maryam had returned. He cracked the door open and forced a smile. "I'll get it, Maryam. Thank you." When she had gone, he rolled the cart into the room. The silver samovar glinted with neon highlights from the TV as Hashem drew two cups of tea and piled a saucer with sugar cubes. He placed the mug and the saucer on the low table in front of Aban.

"Come, brother, drink." He removed the crystal tumbler from his brother's hand and slid his chair closer to the steaming tea. Aban popped two cubes of sugar in his mouth and took a long sip of tea.

Hashem winced. His brother had always had a sweet tooth, even going so far as to hold sugar cubes in his teeth while he drank his tea when they were younger. He'd given up those excesses when he entered the clerical life. Hashem watched him put another pair of cubes in his mouth and suck down half a glass of tea.

The sugar seemed to revive Aban's spirits. He leaped out of his chair and began pacing the room, an old man, balding, in baggy underwear with knock-knees and horny toes. To Hashem, he looked like a troll in one of his grandmother's fairy tales from when he was a little boy.

"Aban," he said, holding out the robe that Maryam had brought. "Please."

Aban threw the robe over his shoulders and continued his pacing. "Rouhani thinks he's won, but he didn't count on us, did he?" He snapped his fingers for one of Hashem's cigarettes. Hashem lit two and handed one to him.

Aban paused and winked at his brother. "We're playing the long game, eh, Hashem? Let Rouhani play whore to the West, let him bring in his inspectors and kiss the asses of Western leaders on Al

Jazeera. All the while, we will have our own missiles safely tucked away in our desert bunker."

Hashem nodded along with his brother. "Iran will be a nuclear power, Aban, because of your leadership."

His brother stopped his pacing and held up his hand. "Hashem, my dear, you need to think bigger.

"*Iran* is not a nuclear power, *we* are a nuclear power."

CHAPTER 36

Königstedt Manor, Finland
18 February 2016 – 1030 local

Thin, watery sunshine lit the snow-covered Vantaa River outside the window. Don shivered as he watched the icy landscape.

"Not a very hospitable place in the winter months, eh?" Reza's voice, with its cultured English tones, held a hint of humor.

Don smiled back at him and made an exaggerated shivering motion with his shoulders. The prep meetings in Helsinki between the P5+1 and the Iranian team had gotten very friendly, almost clubby, with both sides taking their meals together and lots of offline discussions.

Iran had agreed to a permanent monitoring of their nuclear program, a critical stipulation to move to the final step of negotiating a nuclear deal—and lifting the sanctions on Iran. Don knew the elections in Iran in December had given President Rouhani a much better power base at home, but to hold onto those voters he needed to get the sanctions lifted permanently.

Another blast of icy wind rattled the window, making Don take a step back. Reza stayed in place, his face pensive. Without turning his head, he said in a low voice, "I need your help, Donald, with a rather large request."

Don noted how tightly Reza's hand gripped his cup of tea. "Certainly, Reza, I'll do whatever I can."

"I'm going for a smoke. Meet me outside in five minutes." He turned on his heel and walked out of the room.

Don swallowed hard. This was spy stuff, a clandestine meeting. His heart raced as he casually checked his watch, refilled his coffee cup, and mingled with his colleagues. He faked a laugh at a half-heard joke about Congress, then checked his watch.

A minute had gone by.

He forced himself to show interest in the other people in the gathering and sip his coffee slowly. At four minutes and thirty seconds, he excused himself and left the room.

The smoking area was set up fifty paces from the back entrance of the Manor, under a spread of birches. In the first few meetings at Königstedt, the manor had set up separate smoking areas for the Iranians and the other nations, but for this meeting they had combined them.

Reza was alone in the roped-off area, smoking a dark-colored cigarette as Don approached. He had his collar turned up against the cold. Don winced as a blast of wind shook the branches overhead, setting off a fierce rattling sound.

"Smoke?" Reza held out the pack of cigarettes.

Don started to refuse, but Reza kept the pack extended until Don took one. He sparked his lighter, shielding the flame from the wind with his hand. Don poked the cigarette into the fire and took a tentative puff. It tasted like what he imagined burnt camel dung might taste like.

Don forced a smile. "Smooth," he said, smothering a cough.

Reza licked his lips. The branches rattled again and he dropped his voice so low that Don had to step next to him to hear what he had to say.

"I want you to know that I carry a message directly from President Rouhani. I would like you to set up a meeting—a private meeting—with your ambassador. I will agree to whatever venue you choose, but please know that I can deliver this message only to the ambassador, and only in verbal form. If word of this proposal leaked out . . ." Reza shook his head.

Don bit his lip, and he involuntarily mirrored Reza as he brought the cigarette to his lips. "Can you tell me what it's about, Reza?"

The Iranian shook his head. "I'm sorry, Donald, I cannot. My message is for the ambassador only. Please, you must trust me, this is not a trick."

Don tapped his foot as another gust of wind shook the tangle of branches overhead. He saw Reza's eyes shift to a spot over his shoulder, and he could hear the crunch of snow as someone made their way across the courtyard. "Meet at the Sauna Seura on Lauttasaari tonight at seven PM," Don said in a rapid voice.

Reza nodded, then turned to greet his Iranian team member as the man entered the smoking area.

Don arrived at the Sauna Seura at half past six. He'd managed to get to Ambassador Evans in the afternoon and convinced him to take the meeting with Reza. The ambassador had nodded when he heard Don's choice of meeting place.

"Very cagey, Riley," he said. "I like it. I'll have my assistant reserve a private sauna and send my bug man down to make sure it's clean. Very smart." The ambassador paused and swept his eyes over Don. "You'll be there, of course."

Inside, Don did a double fist pump. *Damned straight!* But he settled for: "I think that would be best, sir."

He considered sending a sitrep back to Washington in the afternoon, but decided to let the ambassador handle the official communications. After all, he was in Finland in his capacity as a nuclear analyst, not as a CIA asset.

Ambassador Evans joined him in the locker room a few minutes later, taking a stall further down the row. He nodded to Don, but said nothing. The sauna had been reserved under a false Finnish name from 6PM to 9PM. One of the embassy staff had swept it for listening devices and was occupying the room now.

Don watched the ambassador out of the corner of his eye as he disrobed. The man was mid-fifties, with a thick mane of gray hair and piercing hazel eyes. He was also in pretty good shape for a guy his age. Don wrapped a towel around his own milky white belly and made his way to the showers.

The plan was for Don to enter the room first, then Reza, and the ambassador would follow along last. Don tried to keep his flat feet from slapping on the tiled floor as he made his way to sauna number six. They had chosen well: sauna six was at the end of the hall, with the door facing him, so there was no room adjacent to any wall. Very secure.

The door creaked as Don entered. The embassy security man, a short, muscled man in his mid-thirties, nodded to Don and left.

Don took a seat on the wooden plank and tried to relax. Saunas were not really his thing—all he got out of them was sweaty and uncomfortable—but he was pretty proud of his quick thinking about the location.

The door creaked again and Reza entered. Like Don, he had a towel wrapped around his waist and kept it on when he sat down. His plump form began to glisten with sweat almost immediately. "Good evening, Donald." His voice seemed taut with apprehension.

The door opened again to admit the ambassador. He entered the room like a Finn—with full frontal nudity. Don averted his eyes, but not before seeing the mat of gray hair that covered a manly chest.

"Good evening, gentlemen," he said, and waited for Don to make the introductions. Evans sat on the plank across from Reza and Don and breathed deeply of the hot air. He leaned forward to rest his elbows on his knees and spread his hands. "What can I do for you, sir?"

Reza fidgeted with his towel. "I carry a message directly from President Rouhani. It is intended for the highest levels of the US government—Secretary of State at a minimum, and hopefully the President himself."

Evans leaned back against the wall and crossed his arms, his legs splayed open. "I can't promise anything, Mr. Sanjabi, but I am here to listen."

Reza nodded. "I understand. In the event that your government chooses not to follow through on this proposal, we ask that you keep its existence private. The proposal could be very damaging to President Rouhani at home. We will, of course, deny its very existence if it should become public knowledge in an unfavorable way."

Evans rubbed his jawline. "I'm still listening."

Reza took a deep breath.

"My president understands the mistrust of the world toward Iran. He especially understands the mistrust of the Israelis. Our recent past, under previous administrations in the Islamic Republic, likely conveyed to Israel no sense of shared interest in a peaceful and prosperous region. The formation of an Islamic State, the group you call ISIS, reinforces the feeling that the Middle East is becoming less friendly toward Western ideals.

"President Rouhani would like to change this dynamic in a meaningful way. In American history, you often cite Nixon's visit to China as a turning point in history. My President believes that we—

Iran and the US—should engineer another historic event, one that will change the trajectory of the Middle East forever. President Rouhani would like to request that the upcoming nuclear negotiation in May be hosted in Tel Aviv, and that he be invited to meet with Prime Minister Netanyahu in Israel."

Ambassador Evans's arms had uncrossed and he leaned forward as Reza spoke. His mouth hung open.

"It's brilliant," he whispered.

"I assure you, President Rouhani's proposal is quite sincere," Reza said. "If the Prime Minister of Israel makes this offer, he will accept. Furthermore, he will ensure that the lion's share of the credit for this diplomatic coup go to Prime Minister Netanyahu. This is a chance for Israel to secure a legacy of peace that will change the course of history." Reza placed his hands on his knees and leaned forward. A drop of sweat fell from his nose.

"My President would like to emphasize the need for speed in this matter. The forces against this meeting—on both sides—are substantial. Our only hope of success is if we move quickly."

"What about security guarantees?" the ambassador asked.

Reza's face clouded, and his voice took on an air of exasperation. "My country has opened our nuclear facilities to multiple inspections, given you all of our data, including our transgressions. Have we not been as transparent as humanly possible? We do not possess nuclear weapons; this is a fact." Reza shot a glance at Don, who nodded.

"Now we offer to go to the home of our most vocal enemy to show the world we are sincere, and you ask for guarantees from us?" Reza spat out the last words. Then he sat up and adjusted the towel across his waist, seeming to remember himself.

"I'm sorry," he said. "My admiration for President Rouhani is exceeded only by my concern for his safety. The offer, Mr. Ambassador, is genuine. I ask that you treat it as such."

The ambassador pressed his lips together. "Thank you, Mr. Sanjabi, and please convey my gratitude to President Rouhani for his boldness and his sense of history. I will do my best to make his request a reality." He shook Reza's hand and left the room.

For a long time, the only sound in the room was the wheeze of the hot rocks that heated the atmosphere.

"Thank you, Donald."

"I hope it happens, Reza. It could change everything."

Reza stood. "Perhaps, but that is not our concern at the moment. I'm told the food here is quite good. Would you join me?"

They took cold showers and secured robes before wandering into the common area. Reza pointed to a pair of comfortable chairs set apart from the crowd. They settled into the seats and ordered some beer and light food.

Reza scooted his chair close to Don's and leaned across the gap between them. "You have seemed on the verge of wanting to ask me something for the last two days now. What is it, my friend?"

Don squirmed in his seat. The Rogue File plagued him again. Surely a man with Reza's connections could fill in some of the blanks. Maybe he knew about the Iraqi nuclear program. Maybe he knew about this strange man they called "The Blade."

He cleared his throat and paused as the waiter set their food down on the small table. "Well, now that you mention it, there is one thing I've been wondering . . ."

CHAPTER 37

Oval Office, Washington, DC
18 February 2016 – 2000 local

The President paused on the darkened portico outside the Oval Office.

He drew in a deep breath and held it for a moment. The February air in Washington, DC, was more damp than cold this evening, and fog clung to the lawn of the White House. There was a smell of snow in the air. The Secret Service agent behind him fidgeted. He nodded for the Marine to open the door.

The National Security Advisor and the Director of National Intelligence were waiting for him. They rose to their feet when he entered and he waved for them to sit. "Good evening, ladies. How long til SecDef joins us?"

"He's five minutes out, sir," replied Letitia Lowen, the DNI. "And we have State and Ambassador Evans from Helsinki on the line as well."

The President forced a smile at Tisch Lowen. "How's the new job, Tisch?"

DNI Lowen's appointment to replace James Clapper had been one of the few appointments he'd made that was not blocked by the Republicans in the Senate. That was not to say her hearing had been easy, but the fact that it had gone through at all was nothing short of a political miracle.

"We're settling in fine, sir. Shall I open the phone line?"

The Secretary of Defense rushed into the room and took a seat on the couch next to the DNI. The President accepted a cup of coffee from the steward just as the light on the speaker phone went from red to green. "How's your flight, Mr. Secretary?" he called.

The flat New England vowels crackled with an undercurrent of static as the Secretary of State answered: "Fine, sir. This must be some meeting to get you away from your family this evening." The room smiled. It was well known that the President preferred to spend his early evenings with his family.

The President let the polite laughter die down before he continued. "Ambassador Evans—Charlie—are you there?"

"Yes, sir. I'm here and I have Mr. Donald Riley with me. Riley is with the CIA and currently assigned to the NCPC. He's been acting as a nuclear expert for the planning meetings here in Helsinki."

The President wrinkled his brow. "Good evening, Mr. Riley. Are you the same Riley I see on all the Iranian nuclear assessment reports?"

Riley's voice came over the phone as a squeak. "Yes, sir."

"Alrighty then. Charlie, how about you explain why you've gathered us here."

In the measured sentences of a professional diplomat, Ambassador Evans described the meeting with Reza and the bones of the offer from Rouhani. The President had heard the report already, of course, but he wanted to see the reactions from the rest of the team. Charlie Evans, an accomplished international law expert, was not the kind of ambassador to bring him sketchy offers. The tone of his voice told him that Charlie thought the Iranians were sincere.

The president waited a beat after Ambassador Evans finished speaking before he asked, "And whose idea was it to meet in a sauna?"

"Mine, sir," came Riley's voice.

"Very culturally appropriate, Mr. Riley. What is the nature of your relationship with this Reza character?"

Riley's voice grew stronger. "I first met Mr. Sanjabi as part of the Iranian delegation for nuclear talks. He approached me and offered a private contact number in the event that we needed back-channel communications. We've since learned he is very close to President Rouhani, acting as a special projects officer. He has several times fed me information about upcoming events that have proven out. In short, sir, my recommendation is that we treat his offer as genuine."

The President nodded. "Thank you, Mr. Riley. Charlie, I know it's 3AM there. We're going to let you both go get some sleep. The Secretary will be in touch in the morning with our answer." He waited until the Helsinki connection was dead before he continued. "State, what are your thoughts?"

"It's bold, Mr. President, maybe even brilliant. Rouhani realizes his time is now. He's at the height of his power, and he needs to deliver something. If the Israelis get on board, nothing can stop this agreement from going through."

It *was* brilliant. Rouhani had anticipated the needs of all sides perfectly. The fly in the ointment for the US had always been Congress. Even if they managed to get a nuclear agreement hammered out, lifting the sanctions still required Congressional action, something that could take months, maybe longer. Less than a year ago, forty-seven Republicans had sent a letter to Iran in an attempt to derail the nuclear negotiations. The political gymnastics those unfortunate senators would have to put themselves through to go back on that position were unthinkable.

But throw Israel into the mix? Show Israel as a supporter of the Administration's nuclear deal? The Congress—both sides of the aisle, and both houses—would be tripping over themselves to stay aligned with the Israel lobby.

"So why would Bibi go for this deal?" the President asked. "What's in it for him?"

The National Security Advisor leaned in, her eyes gleaming. "I think that's really the genius of this plan, sir. With Ahmadinejad in power, the Israelis' hard line was justified. But Ahmadinejad is long gone. As Rouhani gets more moderate and wins support, Netanyahu sounds more shrill, more like a war-monger, more out of touch with the reality of the world around him. Look, the Iranians have agreed to every inspection, every questionnaire, everything we've asked of them. How much longer can Israel hold out without looking unreasonable?

"The Arab Spring has left the region in chaos. But what if the two largest players got together and created a peaceful agreement? If Rouhani's moderates control Iran, the funding for Hamas, Hezbollah, Assad in Syria—it all goes away. Bibi Netanyahu goes from the guy holding up red-line cartoons in the UN to the Israeli leader who brought peace to the Middle East. Think about *that* as your legacy."

The President blew out a long breath. "Defense, what are your thoughts?"

The Secretary cleared his throat. "I have to agree. As Israel goes, so goes Congress. Getting the nuclear deal signed, lifting sanctions, it all becomes doable if Israel is behind it."

"Tisch, your turn."

The DNI removed her glasses and tapped them against her knee as she spoke. "Mr. President, I think we have to assume the offer is genuine. Bold, yes, but genuine. Everything we know about Rouhani says he's going for real reform. My interpretation is that the boldness of the offer shows us how precarious his position is within the regime. He needs to show progress quickly to stay in power. He's weighed the odds and decided to go for broke."

"State?"

"I agree with what's already been said, but I would add one thing. There are many ways Rouhani could have made this offer to us, but he chose a low-level meeting in Helsinki between an analyst and his man. If we assume the offer is legitimate—and I think it is—that tells us two things: this Reza character is plugged into the very top of the Rouhani power structure, and our man Riley is our way in.

"Our best weapon now is speed. If the hard-liners find out about this, they will go ballistic—pardon the pun. Every day that goes by increases the chances that the opposition from either side will find out and kill this plan before it ever sees the light of day. We need to get Israel to make the offer as soon as possible."

The President sat back in his chair and steepled his hands in front of his face. His strained relationship with the Prime Minister of Israel was a much talked about aspect of his time in office. He straightened up suddenly.

"Thank you all. If you'll excuse me, I have a phone call to make."

CHAPTER 38

The news broke on Tuesday evening in Tehran, timed to lead the evening segments in the Middle East, and hit the morning talk shows in the US. It went without saying that it would dominate the news cycle all week and into the next weekend.

The Al Jazeera screen shifted into its breaking news montage, settling on an attractive female anchor. The screen above her right temple blazed with the headline: *Israel agrees to host Iran nuclear negotiations.*

Hashem choked on a mouthful of tea, then snatched up the remote and increased the volume:

Israeli Prime Minister Benjamin Netanyahu announced this afternoon that the upcoming Iran nuclear negotiations will be held in Tel Aviv on May 16. In a surprise move, the Israeli Prime Minister also extended an invitation to meet with Iranian President Rouhani as part of the talks.

She cut away to a clip of Netanyahu, a stern look on his blocky face as he stood behind a podium making his announcement.

Israel's bold gesture of confidence in the nuclear talks met with widespread affirmation from the world community—

Hashem's mobile phone rang. He answered it without taking his eyes off the TV screen.

"Hashem, please come quickly. It's your brother." Hashem could hear the tears in Maryam's voice.

"Is he okay?"

"He's very angry, throwing things, and now he's locked himself in his office again and refuses to answer the door. I—I don't know what to do."

"I'll be there as soon as I can." Hashem reached for his jacket with one hand and thumbed the speed dial on his phone for his driver with the other.

The car was waiting for him in the front portico of his apartment building. He slammed the door as he got in and tried Aban's personal mobile for the third time.

Once they left the gated grounds of the apartment, they merged with the crawl of evening rush hour. His driver inched along, jockeying for position in the stream of cars on Valiasr Avenue, the main artery running north to the rich suburbs.

The city of Tehran lay in a vast valley surrounded by mountains. During the winter, in a weather phenomenon known as temperature inversion, colder air would settle over the region, sealing the warmer polluted atmosphere into the valley like a lid on a pot. Usually the weather patterns changed by March, but winter had been slow to release its grip this year and a fog of car exhaust and smoke swirled around the vehicle.

Hashem continued to watch the news on his mobile as he periodically redialed Aban's phone. Still no answer.

As the news developed, things got worse. Rouhani, looking to all the world like a smiling grandfather, gladly accepted Israel's "generous offer." He made the statement from the meeting room of the Expediency Council, surrounded by his cronies. Hashem closed his eyes, hoping that his brother had not seen that added insult to his pride.

The P5+1 nations negotiating the Iranian nuclear deal issued a joint press release endorsing the new location for the meeting. With a broad smile, President Obama, flanked by his Secretaries of State and Defense, endorsed Israel's "bold move to stabilize a troubled region." Then he praised Rouhani's "visionary leadership to bring Iran back into the world community." Even Saudi Arabia and Jordan offered their endorsements.

Hashem clenched his eyes shut. It was a brilliant move, an end run by Rouhani around the entire Iranian hard-line establishment. Worse yet, the Iranian intelligence organizations, so wrapped up in their own fights about budgets and staffing, had missed it. Completely. The thought of all the money he'd spent on informants made him sick.

The car picked up speed as it entered the more exclusive neighborhoods and the road took a gentle slope upwards. If Aban had been angry about losing the election, he would be apoplectic over this turn of events.

The gate to Aban's estate opened as they rolled into his street. Maryam was waiting for him on the front steps. The air was cleaner at this end of the city, and held a hint of spring.

"Where is he?" Hashem asked.

Maryam led him to Aban's study. In the dim hallway, he knocked on the heavy wooden door. "Brother, it's me. Hashem. Open up, please."

No answer.

Maryam pressed a key into his hand and hurried down the hall. He could hear her weeping.

Hashem braced himself, recalling the drunken hovel he had seen the last time his brother encountered bad news. He turned the key in the lock and pushed the door open.

A fire burned brightly in the fireplace, and a huge stack of files and loose papers were piled next to the hearth. Aban was seated at his desk, a pair of heavy glasses halfway down his nose. He looked up at Hashem and smiled.

"Come in, Hashem. Come in and shut the door."

Hashem pushed the door closed and felt the heavy lock click into place. "Salaam, brother." He hesitated, then crossed the room to stand before the desk. "You've heard the news?"

Aban's smile broadened. He unfolded a wide sheet of paper and gestured for Hashem to come around the desk.

The paper was a map of the Middle East with Iran in the center. Aban tapped Tehran and then slid his finger to the west, stopping on Tel Aviv.

"He thinks he's so smart." Aban let out a bark of a laugh. "Rouhani makes his backroom deals with the West, sells out our country to the Great Satan and the whores of Israel. But this time he has gone too far, my brother, too far. Rouhani's arrogance will be his undoing—and our gain." He tapped his thick finger on Tel Aviv.

"This is your target, brother."

Aban's eyes glittered behind his glasses, and his face was flushed. Hashem swallowed hard. After all these years, he would have the chance to use the massive weapons he had built in his desert hideaway . . . but on his own President? The very thought tied his stomach in knots.

As if sensing his unease, Aban reached out and grasped Hashem's hand. "It's perfect. Rouhani has worked so hard to convince the world that Iran possesses no nuclear weapons that your strike will take them all by surprise. While Rouhani's stinking corpse burns alongside his Israeli friends, I will take control here." His grip tightened.

"Rouhani could not have done this without the blessing of the Supreme Leader. When Rouhani fails, the Supreme Leader's position with the Assembly will be badly compromised. While he struggles to contain the chaos, I will go on television and blame the Islamic State. I will be the voice of reason and stability in the crisis. And when I've rallied enough votes in the Assembly, I will be the new Supreme Leader of Iran."

Hashem felt the hammering of his own heart. It *was* perfect. Aban had thought of everything. All those years of waiting and planning were nearly over. Together, he and his brother would change the world.

He dropped to his knees before Aban, the rich cloth of his brother's robe blurred behind tears of joy. "I am your instrument, my brother."

Aban placed his hands on either side of Hashem's face. His grip was tender, almost fatherly, and he placed a kiss on Hashem's forehead.

"They have sown the seeds of their own destruction. Let us reap the harvest."

CHAPTER 39

Ben Gurion International, Tel Aviv, Israel
16 May 2016 — 1000 local

The Iranian state jet touched down at Ben Gurion and taxied slowly to a halt in front of the band of dignitaries gathered on the tarmac. As the engines wound down, the ground crew chocked the wheels of the plane and rolled airstairs into place while another team rolled out the red carpet to the bottom of the steps.

An official band started playing as the door of the plane opened and Prime Minister Netanyahu strode across the carpet to the base of the steps. He was alone, as was Rouhani when he exited the plane and made his way lightly down the airstairs.

That was how both men wanted it—they alone were taking responsibility for the course of events. No Americans, no Europeans, no other Gulf States, just these two heads of state setting a new course for the future.

The two men met at the bottom of the stairs and shook hands, both automatically turning toward the cameras and holding their pose. They exchanged a few words, and Netanyahu gave his counterpart a tight smile—or it might have been a grimace. Even the most adept of lip-readers were unable to make out the brief, historic exchange between these two heads of state whose countries had been mortal enemies since before their parents were even born.

Then they walked side by side down the red lane to separate waiting limousines. Tires squealed as the vehicles pulled away.

The whole affair took less than ten minutes.

～

Zagros Mountains, south of Gerash, Iran
16 May 2016 – 1011 Tel Aviv (1141 local)

Hashem felt the mobile phone buzz in his pocket and glanced at his watch.

Rouhani would be in Israel by now. Hashem could imagine him getting off the presidential airplane in the hot Israeli sun and shaking hands with that clown Netanyahu, putting his entire country to shame. He was about to throw away decades of effort in their fight against Israel, all for what? To please the West enough to lift their sanctions? The West needed their oil, all Iran had to do was wait them out.

He'd read the intelligence reports about the US fracking technology and their claims of oil fields in their own country, but he knew it was a trick. They'd be back, they needed Iran's oil. All his country needed to do was wait long enough.

The phone buzzed again and he drew it out of his pocket and flipped it open. The screen held only one word, an Arabic word from the Qu'ran.

Din. Judgment.

Hashem's hand shook as he snapped the phone shut. He turned to face his men. They were all gathered in a silent knot, all watching him. The TELs stood in a row, loaded, ready to roll out of the underground bunker into the bright sunshine and rain destruction down on their enemies. Yusef and Valerie stood apart from the men and from each other, like two arguing siblings, both watching him with bright eyes.

Hashem smiled at them all. "My brothers in arms, it is time. May Allah smile on our cause today."

A cheer went up, and the men rushed to their assigned places. The engines of the TEL vehicles rumbled to life, belching great clouds of black smoke into the closed space of the bunker. Hashem waved to the men manning the entry doors. The heavy steel doors parted, allowing bright sunshine and a hot desert wind to enter the bunker.

The first TEL rolled out the door, followed closely by the second and third. Hashem took his place in the golf cart, and slapped his driver on the arm. He and Yusef had been out into the valley the day before and marked the launch sites for the three TELs. The monster machines were already in their assigned places, with the stabilizing arms already lowering to the sandy earth.

Hashem raised his radio to his lips. "Yusef, radio check, over."

Yusef's voice came back immediately, crackling with excitement. "Radio check sat. We are starting to raise the first missile now, Colonel. Twenty minutes to launch."

Hashem glanced at his watch. It was 1040 in Tel Aviv now. Rouhani, the traitor, would be at the meeting site by now.

CIA Headquarters, Langley, Virginia
16 May 2016 – 1040 Tel Aviv (0340 local)

Victor Warren liked his new job on the graveyard shift. Not too many people around, just him and the watch officer—and she was pretty easy on the eyes. Not like Gloria, mind you, but a good substitute while he was between relationships. It seemed like he had been between relationships for a really long time. No matter, he was pretty sure Gloria would be coming back any day now.

Well, seventy-five percent sure.

"I'm going for a pee break. You want anything from the vending machine?" the watch officer asked him.

"Dr Pepper, if they have it. Thanks." He waited until he heard the secure door click shut behind her before he pulled a graphic novel from his bag. Technically, he was allowed to read on watch, but he always felt the WO's eyes boring into the back of his head when he did. The vending machine was all the way at the other side of the building; she'd be gone for at least fifteen minutes.

He'd just put his feet up when his panel beeped at him. Victor huffed as he leaned forward and clicked on the alarm.

He almost fell out of his chair as he scrambled to face the screen. He would look up the code—it was part of the verification procedure—but he knew this sensor. He'd been there when it was put into service.

He transferred the sensor's lat and long up onto the big screen, where it showed him the deserts of southern Iran. But the scary part was the flashing message beneath the location.

NUCLEAR SIGNATURE DETECTED

He scanned the information on his screen. The sensor was embedded in a North Korean TEL, in Iran. The Iranians had a nuke on a mobile launcher in their desert. His mind refused to process the information.

Where the fuck was the watch officer?

Victor's mouth was dry, and he was borderline hyperventilating. This was her job. He was supposed to read the screens, and she was supposed to make the calls. He read the contact profile. It said to call the CIA Emergency hotline, which he knew would go straight to the Director himself. In the middle of the night.

He looked back at the door. Where the fuck was she?

He struggled to think straight. Seconds counted in situations like this one. He needed to make the call. Now.

Victor dialed the assigned number. A sleep-numbed voice answered after two rings.

"Hello?"

"Sir, I have you secure." Victor tried to keep his voice from shaking.

"Confirmed secure. Go ahead."

"Sir, this is the monitoring office at headquarters. I just received an alert on a signal from southern Iran, indicating a sensor on a North Korean TEL."

The voice turned caustic. "Yes, we receive occasional alerts on that sensor; the Iranians have many North Korean–made TELs."

Shit! He'd left out the most important part!

"Sorry, sir, this sensor is showing a nuclear weapon in close proximity to the TEL."

"What?"

"Sir, this sensor—"

"I heard you. Contact the National Military Command Center at the Pentagon immediately. Give them every bit of information you have. I'll be there in twenty."

The line went dead.

The secure door to the room clicked open, and the watch officer walked in holding two cans of soda. She stopped when she saw his face. "What's the matter with you? You look like you're about to hurl."

Victor pointed at the screen.

Her face went slack. "Get the CIA Director on the line—"

"I already called him."

"Then get me NMCC."

Victor turned back to his screen. The pinger sent another signal. It was set to ping every sixty seconds once it had a nuclear signature. Victor's hand started to shake.

Had it really only been one minute?

Zagros Mountains, south of Gerash, Iran
16 May 2016 — 1100 Tel Aviv (1230 local)

The first missile was fully erect, white, glistening in the sun. The second and third missiles were slowly coming into position. Hashem, never a religious man, said a silent prayer for their success. His heart felt crushed by the rush of emotions that swirled in his chest, and he fought to keep a clear head.

He keyed his radio. "Yusef, what's your status?"

Yusef's response came back muffled. "Loading the final coordinates now for primary target. Spinning up the gyros. Five minutes to launch."

Primary target: Tel Aviv. Valerie had explained how the missiles were programmed to detonate five hundred meters above the ground, the optimum altitude for blast overpressure. The intense heat from the explosion would vaporize thousands on the ground—including their own President Rouhani—and the shock wave would flatten everything within a few kilometers. Over time, the fallout would drift with prevailing westerly winds across the Israeli landscape, laying waste to the rest of the country.

The second and third missiles would do the same to Haifa and Ashdod, completing the destruction of the Israeli state.

Hashem and Aban had discussed a nuclear response from either the US or Israel, but that was the genius of their plan. The Iranian head of state was in Israel, killed by the attack. Who would suspect the Iranians of killing their own leader? Aban's television broadcast would blame the Islamic State, and while the world dithered on what to do about ISIS, Aban would consolidate his support in the Assembly. From there, his men would take control of key government positions, the intelligence apparatus, and the military.

"Colonel, I'm ready." Hashem looked up to see Yusef trotting back to the bunker, where they would initiate the launch.

Hashem spoke into his radio. "All hands, clear the area. Launch in one minute!" Hashem jumped into the golf cart and pointed his driver back to the bunker. They stopped along the way to pick up Valerie. The big Russian's shirtfront was dark with sweat and his chest heaved with the effort of walking in the desert, but a huge smile creased his gray beard.

Everyone had gathered behind the table they'd set up for the launch. Three big red buttons with plastic covers over them sat on the table. Yusef had already seated himself and plugged in his laptop. His good eye, mostly hidden behind a mop of dark curls, looked up at Hashem. Yusef was shaking with excitement, and his lazy eye wandered to the right.

Hashem glanced at his watch: 1115 in Tel Aviv. The meeting would have started by now. Rouhani would probably be making his opening remarks.

"Begin the launch sequence on missile one," he said. Valerie sobbed behind him.

Yusef's voice cracked as he began the countdown: "Ten . . . nine . . ."

Schriever AFB, Colorado, Integrated Missile Defense, Operations Center watch floor
16 May 2016 – 1115 Tel Aviv (0215 local)

"Sir! We have a missile launch indication!"

The big screen on the wall changed to a map display of the Persian Gulf as the technician spoke.

"SBIRS detects a ground firing . . . seven seconds ago . . . heat bloom is classified as an Iranian Shahab-3 medium-range ballistic missile."

The general manning the watch center stood and slipped his headset on. "Let's cut the chatter, people. Work the problem. This is not a drill."

The Space-Based Infrared System, or SBIRS, fed a continuous stream of data to the onsite computers on the watch floor. His finger hovered over the button that would put him in instant contact with the NMCC. Just a few more seconds to figure out if this was an unannounced missile test or some idiot trying to start World War Three.

"SBIRS indicates a westerly heading, sir." The tech's voice rose an octave as he spoke. No way, even the Iranians weren't dumb enough to launch an unannounced missile test toward the west. There was only one target west of Iran worth firing on: Israel. If it was real, then NMCC would task the US Navy guided missile destroyer in the eastern Med to blow the frigging thing out of the sky.

The general swore and stabbed the button to NMCC. "This is Schriever, I have positive confirmation of a missile launch from southern Iran with a westerly heading—"

"Sir, it's gone."

He muted the connection with NMCC. "Say again!"

"The missile is gone and SBIRS shows a large explosion on the ground."

"Work the problem, people. Let's get satellite coverage of the area now."

He unmuted the connection to NMCC. "Standby."

＞＜

Zagros Mountains, south of Gerash, Iran
16 May 2016 — 1119 Tel Aviv (1249 local)

When the missile lifted off the launcher, Hashem thought his heart might burst. The men around him were sobbing openly, hugging each other, and a few had fallen to their knees.

Their ecstasy was short-lived. The missile rose above the immense cloud of dust and exhaust into the sky. When it had cleared the rim of the valley, it began to wobble. Yusef looked up from his laptop, his eyes wide behind his goggles. Over the din, Hashem saw him mouth the word *No!*

The wobble increased. The missile corkscrewed, then flipped end over end like an enormous Roman candle. Everyone hit the deck when the explosion bloomed over the far ridge.

Time seemed to stand still for Hashem. He hauled Yusef to his feet and ripped the goggles off his face. "What happened?" he screamed.

Yusef's chin quivered. With the red lines of the goggles still imprinted on his face and his dark curls hanging over his eyes, he looked like an unkempt child. "The gyros," he whispered. "It must be a bad gyro."

"What about the others? Can we launch them?"

Yusef shook his head. "They're all from the same batch—but I have more in the back. I can replace them."

"How long?"

"A day . . ."

A day? Could they hide for a day?

Hashem released Yusef. He turned to his men. "Get the missiles back in the bunker now! I want all traces of the launchers removed from the valley immediately. Move!"

Hashem took a deep breath.

He needed to contact Rafiq. Now.

National Military Command Center (NMCC), Pentagon, Washington, DC
16 May 2016 – 1121 Tel Aviv (0421 local)

Colonel Tom Anderson had drilled for an event like this all his twenty-two years in the US Air Force, but he'd never expected to actually deal with a nuclear launch from a hostile nation.

"Get me the latest from the Agency," he said in a loud voice that he hoped conveyed calm. His underarms were soaked, and he clenched his teeth from the strain.

He had confirmation from two distinct intel sources—the SBIRS bird and the CIA "sneaky" source—that the Iranians had just attempted a launch of a nuke against someone to their west. Israel, most likely.

But that made no sense; their president was in Tel Aviv right now at the nuclear treaty talks—he was watching it live on CNN, for Christ's sake.

ISIS? A coup? What the fuck was going on?

His first call should be the Secretary of Defense, but the Secretary was in Tel Aviv.

"Get me the White House," he called.

"President on the line, sir."

The colonel jerked the red handset out of its cradle. "Mr. President, Colonel Anderson, NMCC. We've just received an alert from STRATCOM of a missile launch in southern Iran, mountainous desert, sir. CIA has an alert from a sensor that indicates the missile may be armed with a nuclear warhead. The launch failed after about seven seconds and crashed in the vicinity. No nuclear detonation on impact."

The president sounded remarkably clearheaded for a man who had just been woken up in the middle of the night. "Thank you, Colonel. Do we have interceptors in the region on standby?"

"Yes, sir. The Navy BMD-capable destroyers *Ross* and *Benfold* are both in the region, eastern Med and Persian Gulf, respectively. No indications of further missile launches."

"I'll be in the Situation Room in five minutes. I'll call you back. In the meantime, get SecDef on the line, pull him out of the meeting in Tel Aviv if necessary. Find the Chairman and have him meet me in the Situation Room."

The line went dead.

CHAPTER 40

USS *Arrogant*, Gulf of Oman, off the coast of southern Iran
16 May 2016 – 1215 Tel Aviv (1415 local)

Brendan squinted at the flat horizon through his Ray-Bans. It was going to be another hot one. The breeze was enough for them to leave a gentle wake in the dark blue ocean. It had been a long week of nothing and now they were sailing south for some liberty in Oman.

This last week had melted into a haze of three meals a day and flat seas. He longed for some action, something to make him sit up in his seat. Failing that, he could use a long run on a sandy beach.

He heard Dot call out below and a muffled response. Sitting in the bright sunshine, the cabin below was a black hole to him. Scottie hurried up the ladder, and said to Brendan, "Dot needs you below, skipper. There's something going on out there." He gestured at the flat, sunshined sea.

Brendan dropped into the cool of the cabin and pushed his Ray-Bans up on his forehead. The wall of cabinets had been rolled out of the bulkhead to reveal a row of gleaming electronic workstations. Dot hunched over the center console.

"What's up, Doc?"

The joke usually elicited a smile, but this time her face stayed in a frown. Maggie, leaning over her shoulder, glanced up at him with a disgusted look.

"I'm not sure," Dot replied, "but I'm sure it's not good. Basically, the world has gone berserk. About ten minutes ago, every satellite we own has been retargeted over this area." She pointed to the screen at southern Iran, where they were.

"Every single piece of electronic gear in the region has been turned on. Fifth Fleet HQ in Bahrain just put the AOR on full alert, and the destroyer *Benfold* is repositioning close to the boundary of international territorial waters off the Iranian coast."

Brendan whistled. The Fifth Fleet Area of Responsibility included the Red Sea, the Persian Gulf, and the northwest Indian Ocean. "Okay, so what are the Iranians doing to provoke us?"

"That's just it, nothing. This is all us."

"Any chance this is an exercise?"

Dot shook her head. "I'm getting some secure traffic that's outside our crypto capability—tons of it. This is being directed from Washington." She looked up at him. "It looks like we're about to launch an attack."

Brendan puffed out his cheeks. "Get me Baxter on the horn."

It was a few minutes before Maggie passed him the red handset. Baxter's voice sounded alert, even though it was very early in the morning in DC.

"Sorry to wake you, sir, but it looks like we have a situation going on here that I'm not sure how to handle."

"Does it involve your neighbors to the north?"

"Well, that's the issue. As far as we can tell, it's just us directed at them."

The line hissed for a moment.

"Brendan, do you remember when we first spoke? That time in the South China Sea?"

Brendan glanced down at his knee. Even now, it was still misshapen and had ugly pink scar lines. "Yes, sir."

"You remember what you were doing?"

"Yes, sir."

"It just turned on."

～✕～

Situation Room, White House
16 May 2016 – 1220 Tel Aviv (0520 local)

The President looked around the table at the stony faces: Chief of Staff, National Security Advisor, Director of National Intelligence, and the Chairman of the Joint Chiefs, who was speaking.

"The immediate threat seems to have abated for now, Mr. President. The first launch that failed made them pull back into what we can only assume is a bunker inside that mountain." He had satellite photos up on the screen showing an empty basin, with the ground hastily raked over. "As near as we can tell, they have three TELs, including the one that's already launched. No idea if they have a missile to reload onto it."

"What are our options?"

The Chairman adjusted the folio in front of him. "If we want to strike immediately, there's Tomahawks and air power in the region. They're in a bunker, and it's probably reinforced, so there's no guarantee we'd actually get them with this approach." He stopped to clear his throat.

"My recommendation is to launch JSOC immediately. It will take them twelve hours to get on station and be in a position to

284

launch a raid. In the meantime, we put bombers in the air and have Tomahawks standing by in the event that they poke their heads out again. If by some chance they manage to get a missile launched, we have the *Benfold* in the Gulf and the *Ross* in the eastern Med, both of which are Ballistic Missile Defense–capable ships. Nothing will get through to Israel."

The Secretary of Defense's voice filtered through the phone. "I concur with that, Mr. President."

"Very well, JSOC is authorized to launch." The President turned to his Chief of Staff. "Schedule a briefing on this for later today." He gave a curt nod to the Chairman. "Thank you, General. I'll let you get to it."

As the Chairman departed, the President turned his attention to the DNI. His face was tight with anger. "Explain to me how the hell the Iranians got nukes and why we don't know about it. We've been negotiating with these guys for two years and every single intel report I've seen says they're clean."

"I can't explain the how, sir, everything about this stinks. They were launching on their own president, for God's sake. We have two working theories: one is that ISIS has managed to set up a missile base in southern Iran and is trying to draw the West into launching on their enemies; the second is that someone in Iran is trying to stage a coup and betting we *won't* launch on Iran."

"A rogue element in the Iranian power structure? With nukes?" The National Security Advisor sat back in her chair. "If that's the case, we have to assume Rouhani's power base is not as stable as we thought."

The DNI nodded. "The question is how to deal with it. We're damned if we do and damned if we don't."

The President leaned his elbows on the table and blew out a breath. "Here's what we're going to do. We're going to tell Rouhani what's happened and see what kind of reaction we get. Then Mr. Rouhani is going to go back in and negotiate his ass off with the

Israelis to get a nuclear treaty done. Meanwhile, we're going to take down this bunker and clean up whatever mess is in there." He looked around the table. "You know what we're *not* going to do?"

"Tell the Israelis?" Chief of Staff volunteered.

"Exactly."

～⌒～

Oval Office, White House
16 May 2016 – 1250 Tel Aviv (0550 local)

President Rouhani's square face filled the video screen. A faint smile curled his lips, relaxed, but wary.

"You are looking well, Mr. President," he said in English, his voice a rich baritone.

The US President studied the screen for another long moment before he spoke. "I apologize for this unscheduled interruption, sir, but there has been an incident that you need to know about."

"Oh?" Rouhani's brow contracted a fraction, but the smile stayed in place.

"Firstly, I want to assure you this is a secure connection. There is no one listening apart from the Secretaries of State and Defense on your end and the National Security Advisor on mine."

"I understand."

"Approximately ninety minutes ago, our satellites detected a missile launch in the Islamic Republic of Iran, in the southeast portion of the country. The launch came from a mobile launcher of North Korean manufacture and was an Iranian Shahab-3 missile. The missile crashed shortly after launch."

Rouhani drew in a sharp breath and opened his mouth to speak, but the President stopped him with a raised hand.

"Please, sir, let me finish. We know from corroborating sensors that the missile was outfitted with a nuclear warhead. The trajectory of the missile showed it was aimed at Tel Aviv."

Rouhani's mouth gaped open. He stared at the camera. "You are sure about this?" he said finally.

The President nodded. "We believe there are at least two more launchers, but they have been withdrawn into a bunker—for now. What do you know of this event, sir?"

Rouhani shook his head. He appeared shaken and a little frightened. "The political situation in Iran is . . . difficult, but this is beyond the pale. I can assure you, I did not authorize such an attack or even know of the existence of any nuclear weapons."

The president gave him a tight smile. "Your current location would seem to exonerate you, Mr. Rouhani."

"May I ask what you are going to do?"

Balls of brass. I like this guy.

"I have air- and sea-based assets in place that can be put into action, if needed. There is a military strike team en route to the Gulf now and they will be in position to launch an assault in the next twelve hours. Our preferred option would be to deal with this situation quietly."

Rouhani had regained some of his previous composure. "And, of course, you need my permission to launch a US military raid on the sovereign soil of the Islamic Republic of Iran."

The President nodded. "Naturally."

Rouhani's image was so still the President feared they'd lost the connection. Finally, the Iranian leader stirred. "Very well then, Mr. President, you have my authorization to launch the assault. Now if that is all—"

"It's not."

Rouhani's face went still again, and the President could see him gritting his teeth. "Yes?" he said in a tight voice.

"Let's be clear: we have a shared interest in the success of these talks. You need this agreement; I need this agreement. I suggest you return to the nuclear talks, Mr. President, and make it happen. We will go down in history together as the men who brought peace to the Middle East and Iran back into the world order."

Rouhani nodded.

The Lincoln Memorial, Washington, DC
16 May 2016 – 1300 Tel Aviv (0600 local)

Baxter sat on the edge of the park bench, watching the sky lighten behind the Washington Monument.

He checked his watch again. His source had told him Vice Admiral Daugherty, now retired and a senior director on the DNI staff, was a habitual runner: always the same route, always the same time, rain or shine. As long as he was in town, he ran in the morning. Every morning.

As if on cue, Baxter heard the rhythmic crunch of someone coming down the gravel path. He stood, suddenly wondering if this was a good idea after all.

Jack Daugherty's profile came into view around the bend. He moved at a good clip, chin up, arms pumping, breath coming in easy puffs. He saw Baxter and slowed to a stop a few feet away. He checked the device on his wrist and hit the pause button on his run timer before meeting Baxter's eyes.

"Baxter, right?"

Rick gave him a brisk nod. "Yes, sir. Sorry to ambush you like this, but there's a situation."

Daugherty glanced around them, then moved toward the edge of the Reflecting Pool. "I've been briefed. Is there something new?"

"No, sir, not new, but we have an asset in the region that you should know about."

Daugherty glanced at his heart rate monitor and his lips tightened. "Spit it out, Baxter. Why are you here?"

"The Feisty Minnow Program"—Baxter winced at how fanciful the name sounded in this circumstance—"has an asset in the Gulf. The skipper is a former SEAL, and the same guy who ran the raid that placed the sensor on the North Korean launcher."

Daugherty stopped fiddling with the device on his wrist. "You mean to tell me we have a guy who has actually touched these TELs before? And he's in the region now?"

Baxter nodded.

Daugherty reached behind his back and fished out a mobile phone. He thumbed the device, then raised it to his ear.

"Tisch? Good morning, it's Jack." He laughed. "Yeah, no rest for the wicked. Listen, can I get five minutes with you this morning? It's pertinent to our situation. Seven in the White House cafeteria?" He looked at his watch, then at Baxter. "Perfect. I'll be bringing someone with me."

He stabbed the face of the phone with his free finger to end the call. His eyes dropped to Baxter's shoes.

"Can you run in those?"

>✕<

USS *Arrogant*, Gulf of Oman
16 May 2016 – 1430 Tel Aviv (1630 local)

"Skipper, incoming call for you on the bat phone."

Brendan scrambled down into the cabin, and pushed his sunglasses up on his forehead before he took the red handset.

"McHugh here."

"Brendan, how'd you like some shore duty for a few days?" Baxter's voice crackled in the receiver.

"Um, that sounds good. What did you have in mind?"

"Sorry, buddy, I can't brief you on this line, but stand by for a helo extraction in the next few hours."

CHAPTER 41

North Tehran, Iran
16 May 2016 – 1600 local

When they reached the tony suburbs of north Tehran, Reza leaned over from the passenger seat and flipped off the siren and lights. The traffic had thinned enough that it was no longer necessary. Besides, when Iranian drivers saw two black armored SUVs in their rearview mirrors, they usually got out of the way.

They made the final turn and Reza could hear the team leader telling the second car to cover the back and side entrances. He called over his shoulder, "Remind them again. I will deal with Rahmani, your men secure the building. I want him alive. Do you understand?"

The team leader's black ball cap bobbed once, and the reminder went out over the secure channel.

"Boss," the driver grunted. Reza turned his attention forward again. The gate protecting the entrance to Ayatollah Rahmani's house was closed. "Shall I take it?"

Reza nodded.

The high gates slammed down on the hood of the car, but they proved to be more for decoration than security. With the elaborate ironwork partially blocking his view, the first car skidded to a halt before the front doors. The second vehicle raced past them, bound for the back entrances.

A short woman in a dark headdress stepped through the wide double doors of glass and wood. Her hands went to her hips, and her voice was fiery as she screamed at them, "What is the meaning of this? Do you know whose house this is?"

Reza had to push his door hard to get it past a piece of the gate blocking it. He stepped onto the crushed gravel of the drive and waved the other security men to enter the house. They rushed past her, leaving only the two of them on the wide flagstone landing.

"Where is he?" he asked, keeping his voice as even as possible. Inside, he was burning with rage that someone—a fellow Iranian, no less—would stoop to using a nuclear weapon against his own people. He wanted to reach out and throttle this woman, but he held his hands at his side and his voice calm.

Her gaze fell to the stone steps.

Reza grabbed her arm and shook her. She was no more than skin and bones, really, like a china doll. He pulled her toward him and used his free hand to grip her chin, forcing her to look up at him.

"Do you have any idea what he's done? Where is he?"

Her dark eyes were black with fear, but she didn't cry. "He's in his study," she said.

"Take me there."

She led him swiftly through the wide hallways of the house, past sculptures that cost more than his apartment and paintings that could feed a south Tehran slum for weeks. The carpet under his feet was deep and soft, and the smell of the midday meal still hung in the air. He could faintly hear the calls of the security men as they cleared the house, but his radio was silent. No one on the security team had found the Ayatollah yet.

At the end of the hall, she paused next to a heavy door of carved wood. Reza turned the knob. Locked. The woman fished a key from her robe and pressed it into his hand.

"Go," he whispered. Her feet made no sound on the thick carpet as she hurried away.

Reza slipped the key into the lock and swung the door open.

He might have walked into a television studio. Industrial lights on metal tripod stands lit a heavy wooden desk at the far end of the room, and two cameras on rolling platforms were aimed at the desk.

Two men were consulting a clipboard behind the cameras. They looked up sharply, their eyes cutting between Reza and the man seated behind the desk.

Ayatollah Rahmani looked the part of the holy man. With his stumpy legs and big belly hidden behind the desk, he was transformed into a bust of strength and vigor. The snow-white robe and turban glowed in the brightness, setting off the iron-gray beard framing his full face. He had discarded his glasses, but he still wore a paper collar to protect his robe from the heavy makeup on his face and neck. A third tech was balanced on a ladder in front of the camera, making last-minute adjustments to the lighting.

Reza's entrance halted the buzz of activity. He snapped his fingers at the three technicians. "Out," he said. "Close the door behind you." They ran from the room. The security team would take care of them.

Aban's bulk shifted behind the desk. "Don't get up," Reza took his time moving the ladder aside and drawing a chair up so that he could sit across from the holy man.

"What is the meaning of this intrusion?" Aban said, his gaze shifting to the muted television in the corner. Reza followed his eyes to Al Jazeera. The commentators were chattering about the nuclear talks in Tel Aviv, rerunning the footage of Rouhani descending from the plane and shaking Netanyahu's outstretched hand. Reza felt the rage quiver in his belly, and he pushed it down. He needed information now; retribution would come later.

"Your missile failed to launch."

Aban went pale under the heavy makeup, but he kept his confident smile in place. "I don't know what you are talking about."

"Your brother attempted to launch a nuclear missile at Tel Aviv earlier today. The missile failed on takeoff. The Americans detected it."

The ayatollah's eyes cut to the silent television. The commentator's lips moved happily.

"There won't be any announcement of the launch. The Americans contacted President Rouhani. We are cooperating with them."

The composed face beneath the snow-white turban twisted in rage. "He is cooperating with the Americans? Traitor! I knew it! This just goes to show—"

"We know your brother has more weapons, and we intend to take them from him."

"I don't know what you are talking about."

Reza stood. "I thought so. In that case, you are of no use to me. Aban Rahmani, you are under arrest for treason against the Islamic Republic of Iran—"

"Let's not be hasty, sir." Aban interrupted him. "Arrest?"

"Do you know what they do to holy men in prison, Aban?"

"How dare you address me like that. I am Ayatollah—"

Reza leaned across the desk and lowered his voice. "You are seconds away from being stripped and thrown into jail. A nice fat boy like you, a fallen holy man . . ." Reza kissed his fingertips. "They will *love* you."

The fat man began to sweat, his makeup streaking down his cheeks. "Perhaps we can make a deal? Maybe I have some . . . small bits of information I can offer. I don't generally associate with my brother—half brother, actually, he's only a half brother. But perhaps I can think of some information that may be useful to you in recovering the other weapons."

"How many are there?"

Aban's mask slipped for a second. "Two—I mean, I think there are two more."

Reza looked over his shoulder at the camera. "I have an idea, holy man. Let's make a movie." He unclipped the radio from his belt. "Send the cameraman in here."

Within a few minutes, Reza had the camera set up to make a single digital copy of his session with the ayatollah, then he dismissed the cameraman and locked the door behind him.

He stood before the desk. "Take off your robe," Reza said.

The ayatollah started to make a fuss, then stood and slipped the robe off his shoulders. The white T-shirt underneath showed his saggy breasts and stretched tight against the bulge of his belly.

"Turban off, too."

When Aban removed the covering from his head, long gray wisps of frizzy hair leaped off his scalp. Reza nodded. "Perfect." He swept everything off the desk into a jumbled heap on the floor and indicated that Aban should take his seat again. In the camera monitor, he looked like a homeless man. Reza fingered the record button.

"This is our deal, holy man. If you tell me the truth, you get to keep this wonderful house and all your servants. If you fail, you go to jail and eventually, after I ensure you've been raped enough, you get hanged. Understand?"

Reza hit the record button.

The interview lasted thirty minutes. Reza asked him questions about the nuclear weapons in his brother's possession, and how they were being kept. He hid his surprise when he heard they had originated in Iraq. The ayatollah went on at length about the size of the facility housing the weapons and how it was guarded, but Reza detected another note of slight hesitation when he was asked about the number of weapons.

Reza stopped the recording and withdrew the thumb drive from the camera. He would call Rouhani and upload the file to the Americans for their raid. Let them clean up this mess.

He resumed his seat across from the ayatollah. "Well done, holy man, except for one thing. You lied to me."

The ayatollah started to protest, but Reza held up his hand.

"This is your last chance: how many nuclear weapons are there?"

CHAPTER 42

The pilot's voice was loud in Brendan's headset. "Commander, that's where we're headed."

Brendan followed the direction of his finger and sucked in a breath. According to the map in his lap, this was a small island on the northern tip of Oman, a wildlife preserve with a tiny airstrip.

Not tonight. The island was lit brilliantly, and in the glare Brendan could make out at least a dozen military transport aircraft, and teams of men unloading helicopters and pallets of supplies.

The Seahawk helo banked sharply as the pilot received clearance to land on the far end of the teeming airfield.

This was Brendan's second helo of the day. Two hours after Baxter's cryptic message, the *Arrogant* had been contacted by an inbound helicopter from the USS *Ross*. After Baxter's call, they made best possible speed away from the Iranian coast, and the horizon was clear of any surface contacts.

As had been agreed, there were no radio comms. With a wave at his crew, Brendan hit the water wearing only shorts and a T-shirt. After he had put fifty yards between him and the boat, he stopped and waved his arm up toward the helo. A line with a horse collar lowered to the water, the wash from the helicopter's rotor whipping the water flat around him.

Brendan let the line touch the water before he reached for it. The static charge built up by the rotors could be deadly until the line was grounded. He slipped the collar over his head and under his armpits before waving up to the aircraft.

The crew chief in the helo had a dry flightsuit and combat boots waiting for him. Brendan pulled on a pair of headphones.

"Welcome aboard, sir," the pilot greeted him. "You'll find our accommodations are a bit less luxurious than what you're used to, but it's the best we can offer." He gestured to the sailboat, which was rapidly blending into the haze of the Persian Gulf.

Brendan flushed. "Oh, that; I'm a—"

"No need, sir." The pilot held up his hand. "I've been briefed that you're a rich American businessman with a burning need to get to Muscat, and we're happy to help." He flashed Brendan a smile.

Brendan nodded and spent the rest of short trip staring out the window as they sped over the waves. He hadn't been in a helo since . . . since the mission in the South China Sea. As if in sympathy, his knee twinged with pain.

The Seahawk landed with a flourish at the edge of the Muscat airfield. A lone figure waited for Brendan as he ran under the heavy downdraft. The tempo of the rotors increased as the helo took off again.

Brendan's ears rang in the silence, and he worked his jaws to clear them. The middle-aged man opposite him wore a muted print

Hawaiian shirt with khakis and loafers. A wide-brimmed straw hat completed the outfit. He extended his hand. "Artie Brindle. You must be Brendan."

Brendan shook the man's hand. It was a firm grip that seemed in contrast with the man's overall innocuous appearance. He saw his smile reflected in the man's dark glasses. "Brendan. Can you tell me what's going on, Artie?"

Artie offered him a thin smile. "Sorry, my young friend, I'm just the middle man. I'm here to get you some fresh clothes, a hot meal, and a ride to your next destination in…" He consulted his wristwatch. "Two hours."

He swept his arm toward a waiting car, a late model SUV. Brendan realized Artie was probably an NOC, a CIA case officer in nonofficial cover, used to handle local needs when the CIA needed to keep an arm's length. What the hell had Baxter gotten him into?

The next two hours passed in a blur as Artie took Brendan to a small apartment where he had a stack of clothes waiting and some takeout food. "Sorry about the pile. I wasn't sure about your size, so I just bought the rack."

Brendan had no idea where he was going, so he opted for comfort and layers. He selected a pair of jeans, ankle-high hiking boots, an Under Armour T-shirt topped by a Patagonia long-sleeved shirt, and a dark-colored form-fitting Northface jacket. After a quick shower, he joined Artie in the small sitting room and was surprised to see it was already dark outside.

"Eat up," Artie told him. "We leave in fifteen minutes."

They rode in silence back toward the airport, and Brendan noticed he stayed off the main roads. Finally, Artie parked on the edge of the airfield and shut off the headlights. Darkness fell around the vehicle, and the only light in the area came from a lone overhead light outside a distant hangar.

The whipping cadence of rotors sounded overhead and Brendan

could make out a darkened Black Hawk helo descending toward the ground in front of them. Artie stuck out his hand. His smile was a white slash in the darkness as he leaned close to Brendan and shouted, "They don't tell me much, but this thing looks serious. Good luck, sir."

A few seconds later, Brendan was in his second helicopter of the day and being handed another set of headphones.

The pilot flared the rotors and landed gently in the harsh glare of the military encampment.

"This one looks big-time, Commander," the pilot said before Brendan pulled the headset off and handed it back to the crew chief.

He dropped to the ground and ran across the sand toward a waiting figure, a Navy lieutenant, who popped him a smart salute before he extended his hand.

The roar of the helo faded, letting the officer drop his voice to a conversational tone. "I know you've got questions, Commander, but right now, my orders are to get you to the general."

"But—"

"The general does not like to be kept waiting, sir." He was half-jogging toward a small building on the edge of the makeshift airfield, surrounded by smaller inflatable tents.

Brendan had never seen one, but this had all the earmarks of a JSOC exercise. The Joint Special Operations Task Force was the US military's quick response team. Designed to be able to launch a full-scale raid anywhere on the planet within a few hours of Presidential notice, JSOC had come to public fame following the raid that killed Osama bin Laden. While most of the media attention went to SEAL Team Six, the JSOC force was also comprised of Army Rangers and Green Berets, as well as the full-scale military transport fleet needed to move an elite fighting force anywhere in the world at the drop of a hat.

A Chinook helo, the immense double rotors folded back for transport, was being unloaded from one of the massive C-17 cargo planes. A team of techs stood by ready to prep it for immediate flight.

The lieutenant held the door for him as they entered the small command center. In contrast to the organized chaos outside, the interior of the building was hushed. An Army colonel looked up from one of the waist-high tables and stabbed his finger across the room.

"You! McHugh!" He might have meant it as a question, but it came out like an order. He stalked over to Brendan, his deep-set eyes fierce.

Brendan swallowed. "Yes, sir."

"You're late. Boss wants to see you. Follow me." He turned on his heel and marched to a larger table at the far end of the room.

The colonel touched an older man on the arm. "He's here, sir."

Lieutenant General Dave Sitler looked more like a grandfather than the commanding officer of the most lethal strike force on the planet. He offered a warm smile as he clasped Brendan's hand in his massive paw. "Welcome to the party, McHugh."

He cocked his head. "You look a little confused. Do you know why you're here?"

"No, sir. I was extracted from my sailboat this afternoon and flown here—"

"Sailboat?" Sitler's laugh echoed. "Son, what you do on your free time is up to you, but we're here to lock down some loose nukes in Iran, and I'm told you are an expert on the launchers."

A light went on in Brendan's head. The TELs—the sensor must have detected a nuclear-tipped missile. "The sensor my team placed on the North Korean launcher detected a nuke? In Iran?"

"No flies on you, McHugh. You led that raid and your expertise could make all the difference right now."

"How can I help, sir?" Over the general's shoulder, he could see a flat screen showing what looked like an interrogation of a fat man sitting behind a desk and wearing only a T-shirt.

"Gear up. You're going with us."

Brendan's knee throbbed. "Sir, I—"

"No time, son. Looks to me like you walk fine, and we're not planning on putting you on point. You have first-hand knowledge of the target vehicles. We need to be absolutely certain these are the same TELs your team tagged before we turn them into piles of slag." Sitler nodded to the lieutenant. "Get him geared up. We leave in twenty."

Brendan's mind whirled as the lieutenant pulled him toward the door. Outside, the tempo had reached a fever pitch. A line of helos, rotors extended now, were being swarmed by technicians and flight crews doing preflight checks.

They entered the open door of a large tent where a team of men were gathered around a crude topographical display. No one looked up. Brendan recognized the concentration on their faces. These were SEALs prepping for an assault. This was a bad idea. He had no business being here. Not anymore.

Two men detached themselves from the group and approached Brendan. The first stuck out his hand. "Lieutenant Dave Ringler, call me Ringo." He gestured to the man trailing him. "Meet Petty Officer Jack Wiley—we call him Coyote. He's your babysitter, Commander. I understand you have operational experience—that's great, but I need your word that you'll do whatever Coyote says." He leveled his gaze at Brendan. "His job is to get you in and out in one piece and with no extra holes. *Capisce*, sir?"

Brendan nodded. He held out his hand to Coyote. The man's dark eyes glittered and it seemed to take a long time before he grasped Brendan's hand.

Ringo clapped Brendan on the shoulder. "Wonderful. I'll leave you two girls to get acquainted." He pointed to a stack of assault gear on the side of the tent. "You can gear up over there, sir. You need anything, ask Coyote. Best step on it, we're outta here in fifteen."

Brendan sorted through the gear for battle armor, knee pads, and a helmet, wishing all the time that he had his own gear. Coyote watched him silently, his dark eyes following Brendan's movement, his mouth pressed in a thin line. Brendan finally stopped what he was doing and faced the man. "Is there a problem, Petty Officer Wiley?" He pitched his voice low, so that the men at the table wouldn't hear him.

Coyote's head swiveled in the direction of the briefing, then back to Brendan. He stepped forward and reached for a strap on Brendan's body armor as if he was helping to adjust the fit.

"I know about you, sir." He nudged Brendan's injured leg with his knee. "I know how this happened. A stunt like that gets people hurt or killed. We will not be turning our backs on any prisoners today. Clear?"

He was so close Brendan could smell coffee on the man's breath. A hot flush crept up Brendan's neck, and he choked back a desire to smash his fist into Coyote's tight-lipped mouth. Over the man's shoulder, he could see Ringo watching them.

Brendan jerked his body armor away from Coyote.

"Crystal."

CHAPTER 43

Zagros Mountains, south of Gerash, Iran
17 May 2016 – 0430 local

Hashem chewed what was left of his fingernails as he watched Yusef and Valerie put the access panel back on the missile. In the end, it had all come down to quality control: the gyros they had stolen from the Iranian assembly line were defective, causing the failed launch. Hashem grimaced at the irony that the gyros, which he'd been able to steal because they "failed" quality inspection, actually had failed the quality inspection.

Yusef jumped down to the ground next to Hashem. Valerie followed, moving his ponderous bulk carefully as he stepped down from the top of the TEL. "It will work now. I guarantee it," Yusef said.

Hashem ignored him, directing his questions to Valerie. "How long before the third missile is ready?"

Valerie shrugged. "We know what we are looking for, so we can have it done before sunrise." His hand shook; Hashem knew he wanted a drink.

"Do it," Hashem barked at them. "And hurry!"

He looked at his watch, trying to think. Maybe the Americans had missed the failed launch. He was so used to thinking of their technology as being invincible. Even if they saw the launch, what would they do? Counterattack? Tell the Israelis? If the Israelis knew, they would have ended the nuclear talks immediately. According to Al Jazeera, which he was checking every half hour, the two sides had entered a marathon negotiating session with the goal of reaching an accord this very night.

Not if he had anything to say about it. He could feel his chest swelling with pride at the actions he was about to take on behalf of his brother and his country.

"Colonel!" The interrupting voice was insistent. "Colonel, sir."

Hashem broke out of his reverie with a jolt. "What?" He had gone so long without sleep he was starting to daydream.

The security guard held up his phone. "The check-ins are one minute overdue. I know it's only one minute but you said to—"

Hashem held up his hand to stop the man as he pulled his own phone from his pocket and shifted it to all-call. One of his first actions while they were building the bunker was to install a local cell network repeater so that he had perfect connectivity within the bunker and with the external security personnel.

"All stations, report."

No response. He frowned. Either the network had chosen this most inopportune moment to go down or . . . *they were being jammed.*

"Shut the outer doors! Do it now!" The uniformed soldier by the door slammed the lever down and the heavy gray doors began to move inward.

The ground outside the bunker erupted under the impact of

heavy-caliber gunfire. The soldier next to the door disappeared in a wave of shrapnel. One moment the security captain was speaking to him about check-ins, and the next he fell against Hashem, his body riddled with bloody puncture wounds.

Using the body as a shield, Hashem wriggled behind one of the massive tires on the TEL. The heavy-caliber bombardment ceased as suddenly as it had begun. The doors had stopped in their tracks halfway closed. Hashem cautiously peeked out from behind the now-deflated tire just in time to see two helicopters descend to the valley floor and unleash a barrage of machine gun fire directly into the cavern entrance.

The lights died out, dousing the cavernous space in darkness. Hashem pressed his back hard against the tire until the lug nuts, each as big as his fist, cut into his back. His breath came ragged and fast, loud in the darkness.

His eyes slowly adjusted to the gloom, his ears ringing in the silence. He risked another peek toward the entrance. The half-open doors framed a gray landscape of predawn desert and mountains. He could hear the beat of helicopter rotors outside. Two, maybe three. The next wave would be ground assault forces.

Hashem pushed himself up, a sharp pain lancing into his side. He had been hit after all. No matter, he would still be able to get away. No one knew these tunnels like he did. He just needed to get away from the entrance.

He took a step and nearly fainted from the pain.

The golf cart. It stood on the other side of the doors, pointed toward the depths of the cave. And lights, it had lights and a first aid kit. He just needed to get there.

Hashem steeled himself and ran for the cart. His legs felt weighted, as if he were running in thick mud. He tripped over something in the dark, crashing face-first into the floor. Something soft and wet—a body, or what was left of one. Hashem could taste the dirt in his mouth as he crawled the rest of the distance. His fingers found the running board of the golf cart; he pulled himself up. The vinyl seat, the plastic steering wheel. His fingers fumbled for the keys.

From the corner of his eye he sensed movement near the open doors, a shifting of shadows against the sharp edges of the steel frame. They would have night vision goggles on . . .

His fingers found the keys and he wrenched them into the ON position. There was an audible click, and he threw the switch to turn on the lights.

Two soldiers were framed in the intense beams of the headlights. They both dropped to the ground, flipping the night vision gear away from their eyes, their weapons sweeping in Hashem's direction, already firing.

Hashem dove for the safety of the rock wall.

Brendan was able to see the whole assault through the front windshield of the MH-47 Chinook. The AC-130 Spectre gunship started the high-altitude assault using 105mm rounds to soften the steel front doors. The gunship flew in a tight circle at 10,000 feet using infrared spotting to ensure hyper-accurate firing while the rest of the assault team moved into place. The Spectre's job was to hammer open the front doors for SEAL Team Six to gain entrance.

The assault force commander had already released the MH-6 helos. These Little Birds, sniper platforms for the 160th Special Operations Aviation Regiment (SOAR), swept over the surrounding terrain, clearing the remaining external guards off the hillsides.

The pounding from the AC-130 ended as abruptly as it began, and a pair of Little Birds armed with side-mounted mini-guns dropped to the valley floor, hosing down the entrance to the bunker with thousands of 7.62mm rounds.

The call for assault teams to land came at the same time, and

Brendan felt the Chinook drop rapidly toward the sand. His landing team was the last stick. He ran out the back of the idling helo close behind Coyote. He could feel every jolt in his injured knee, and the borrowed combat gear hung heavy and awkward on his frame.

Brendan's stick was a reserve combat force, so they hunkered down near the doors awaiting direction from the assault force commander. Kneeling behind Coyote, his side pressed against an enormous boulder, Brendan did his best to control his breathing. The assault force commander was a fellow Navy lieutenant commander, a SEAL within a year group of Brendan. *That could have been me.* He realized how much his life had changed in the last few years.

The squad leader's radio crackled. "All clear, all clear. All Tangos are dead except for two. Send in the retrieval team and the medics."

"That's us, gentlemen," the squad leader said. "On me." He jumped to his feet and double-timed it to the doors. As they approached, the interior lights came on, flooding the opening with light. The ground, the walls, and the gray steel doors were riddled with heavy-caliber holes the size of golf balls. Beyond a fifty-foot radius of destruction around the door, the ground was untouched.

The inside of the cavern was massive, with high arching ceilings and an orderly cluster of small buildings and straight-line roads stretching back into the depths of the space. Three TELs, one empty, two still carrying missiles, were parked inside the entrance, riddled with bullet holes.

The squad leader let out a low whistle. "Look at this place. Man, these guys were serious."

The assault force commander was waiting for them by the TELs. "McHugh," he said. "I need you to verify that these are the launchers you tagged."

Brendan nodded and climbed on top of the first TEL. He showed the petty officer where to cut into the composite material. The sound of the hand tool whirred until he had opened a large enough hole to let Brendan look inside.

The space was empty.

The petty officer jumped to the ground, and clambered up the second TEL. The cavity between the cab and the launcher was empty on this vehicle, too. Brendan's knee was on the verge of locking up, and he could feel Coyote's eyes on him as he climbed the final TEL. By the time he made it to the top, the petty officer had cut a square into the truck body.

"After you, sir," he said, punching the material free.

Brendan peered into the hole. The sensor he had placed there three years ago winked up at him. He flashed a thumbs-up sign to the raid commander. "We got something. Verifying now."

He pulled a small container of solvent from a pocket of his cargo pants and squirted it on the adhesive that held the sensor in place. After a few minutes of working the device back and forth, he managed to pull it off. He checked the lower right corner where he knew Martinez had scratched his initials. There it was: MM. To be sure, he punched in the unique verification code Baxter had given him. The green light on the device shifted to blinking yellow.

He looked down at the raid commander. "We're verified. This is the launcher."

"Roger that, McHugh. Thanks." He stepped away and spoke into his radio. "We have positive confirmation on the launcher. The retrieval teams are starting work now."

From his perch atop the TEL, Brendan had a good view of the whole cavern. It went back at least another few hundred yards, with structural steel in place to shore up areas where they had cleared out overhanging stone. He knew the plan was to use the daylight hours to ransack the cave for useful intel, then transport everything off site under cover of darkness tonight. Everything that remained would be destroyed.

A team hustled two stretchers toward the cave entrance. One of the patients was a younger man with a head full of heavy dark curls, the other an older man with a thin face and—

Brendan froze. He knew that face.

"Stop!" he yelled. "Stop those corpsmen!" He half slid, half fell off the TEL, landing on his bad knee. A bolt of pain lanced up his leg. He gripped the side of the truck and pulled himself to his feet, hobbling after the stretchers. "Wait!"

Outside, a thin line of orange defined the eastern horizon, and the air was cool and dry. A MH-47 Chinook, dual rotors idling, waited with its ramp down.

The medics were moving at a quick pace; their job was to get any injured off site before dawn, and they were running out of time.

"Wait!" Brendan screamed at their backs. He broke into a run.

Coyote streaked past him, catching the corpsmen on the ramp of the waiting helo. They were arguing when Brendan puffed up. He knelt next to the stretcher.

It was him. The Iranian diplomat, the man he had seen at the Iraqi Ministry of Justice, the man from Don's file. His dark eyes were open, and as Brendan's face came into view, they focused on him. A light of recognition dawned.

"You," he rasped. "Lieutenant McHugh. I know you."

Brendan nodded.

The man grimaced, a horrible show of tobacco-stained teeth and blood. He whispered something, but it was lost in the noise of the rotors.

"Sir, we need to get him out of here before first light," the corpsman shouted over the noise of the rotors, a note of irritation in his voice.

Brendan held up a hand. He leaned closer to the injured man until he could feel his hot breath against his ear. Even then, his voice was growing weaker.

"You think you've won . . . with your technology and your . . ." He coughed, a deep gurgle. The corpsman tried to push past Brendan, but Coyote held him back.

"We have won," Brendan replied, staring into the man's dark eyes.

The Iranian shook his head, his eyes swimming with the effort of staying conscious. A bluish pallor crept over his features. "No," he whispered in a strangled voice. "*Dozdi shomal.*"

His labored breathing stopped suddenly. The corpsman swore and shouldered Brendan out of the way.

Brendan let himself be pushed back. It didn't matter what the medic did—the Iranian was dead.

CHAPTER 44

The long-awaited press conference from Tel Aviv was a carefully orchestrated event. They had negotiated all the previous day, through the night, and into the next day. The people on the stage looked like it.

Prime Minister Netanyahu led off the press conference, his voice raspy with exhaustion, but with what might pass for a smile on his square features. He yielded the podium to the Iranian President, who took a moment to gather his notes before he looked into the cameras. The paper shuffle was an old trick of his, Reza knew, to project a sense of slight disorganization and build a tinge of empathy with his audience. When he looked up and smiled, he was wearing his best stern grandfather face.

"Today we have made an historic movement toward peace and stability in our region. If Israel and Iran—two supposedly mortal enemies—can agree on terms to make this region a safer place, then together we can achieve anything. My country has never desired nuclear weapons, and has never had nuclear weapons. Our nuclear aspirations have always been for peaceful purposes. This accord, which will be signed by all parties in Helsinki on Monday, September fifth, of this year, will prove to the world that Iran is a peaceful nation dedicated to the prosperity of our people."

The US Secretary of State represented the P5+1 nations. Of the three speakers, he looked the freshest, his long face split by a genuine smile. A smile of relief that his deception of the Israelis has not come to light, Reza thought. The Americans had taken a massive gamble that had paid off—so far. With the US elections only a few months away, the outgoing President needed a win, a big win, for his party. In one fell swoop, he could bring stability to the Middle East and set his Republican opposition back on their heels. With Israel on his side, the Congress would not dare cross him. It was a bulletproof plan—as long as Reza did his part.

Aban had given him little to work with. There was another weapon, he was sure of that much, and it had gone to Hezbollah, to a half brother that Aban had never met. All he had was a name: Rafiq Roshed. A quick search of the Iranian Hezbollah files yielded nothing. If Rafiq even existed, he was off the grid.

Reza considered the possibility that Aban was lying, trying to string him along with new information. For now, he kept the ayatollah under house arrest while he looked into this Rafiq character.

The secure phone on his desk buzzed and he picked it up. He listened for the three-tone signal and the green light that told him the line was secure. "Congratulations, Mr. President. A great victory, sir."

"One that was nearly undone by my own people," came the reply. The mellow, grandfatherly tones of the press conference were gone, replaced by a harsh sharpness.

Even on a secure line, they hesitated to speak openly. Rouhani paused as he chose his words carefully. "Our friends are in town now, and they picked up three packages, including the damaged one. They've been cleaning all day today, but should be out of the house in a few more hours. For good. Do we have any nosey neighbors back at home?"

Reza frowned and decided he meant any local backlash. "No, it's been quiet here at home. No problems."

"What about the traitor?"

Reza's eyes shot up; that was a pretty clear word for anyone listening. "I have him staying at home. No need to raise the ire of his followers."

The only response was a hiss on the line.

"Mr. President?"

"Leave him there. For now." He paused again. "Is that all the, uh, packages? Are there more?"

Reza didn't hesitate. Whatever happened, his job was to insulate his president from damaging information. "I have it under control, sir."

"Good. That's what I want to hear, Reza."

Oval Office
17 May 2016 – 1830 Tel Aviv (1130 local)

The President clicked off the TV and tossed the remote onto the coffee table. He leaned back in his chair. "Now *that* is what I call a good day's work."

Each of them—Chief of Staff, Chairman of the Joint Chiefs, DNI, and National Security Advisor—responded with some variation of an appreciative chuckle and a nod.

The President threw a glance at the Chairman. "How'd we do on the ground?"

"Very well, sir. JSOC took two minor casualties in the raid. All the hostiles were taken down and three nukes recovered. It was like a Johnny Cash 'One Piece at a Time' operation in there. They literally stole bits and pieces of missiles for the last ten years and cobbled together three birds. The launchers, which they couldn't steal, came from the North Koreans. We'll strip the site and incinerate what's left. Our team will be out of Iran by tomorrow morning."

"And the warheads?"

The DNI answered. "They've been heavily modified, but initial indications are that they originated from Iraq. As far as we can tell, Rouhani's clean."

The President let out a low whistle. "So, Saddam Hussein really did have weapons of mass destruction? Wow—there's a lot of people in this town who would like to have that little tidbit out in the public eye."

The Chief of Staff cracked a rare smile. "There's a lot of people that *used to be* in this town that would like that information public." He switched to a more serious tone. "As you might expect, peace in the Middle East is polling phenomenally well. Now all we have to do is get this accord signed before the election."

The President leaned forward. "Let's make sure we have a complete embargo on this information—every last bit of it. A leak about what has happened in the last twenty-four hours goes beyond national security. It's *world* security we're talking about here. A leak could set back peace in the Middle East by a century. Are we clear on this point?"

He looked at the solemn faces around the table. They all nodded back at him.

"Good work, everyone. Thank you." He stood, nodding to the

Chief of Staff to stay. He walked to the window and waited until he heard the door closing before he turned around.

"I'd like you to reach out to the Speaker and the Majority Leader. Invite them over for a drink. No cameras, no post-meeting interviews, just a drink."

"They're going to want to know more than that, sir."

The President paused to stare out the window.

"Tell them I want to talk about being on the right side of history."

CHAPTER 45

Rafiq flipped on the TV as he entered the darkened den. Nadine had left it tuned to ESPN.

He never understood his Argentinean wife's obsession with American football. He'd enjoyed the game when he'd attended college in the US, even attended a few games at the Minneapolis Metrodome to see the Minnesota Vikings play, but he'd dropped the game once he left the country.

Through the magic of satellite TV, Javier developed a passion for the game and passed the bug on to his only daughter. They were diehard Dallas Cowboys fans. Maybe that was the connection: they identified with the American cowboys.

Rafiq had objected to showing American football to their children, so Nadine sometimes sneaked into his study to watch ESPN. The channel was running a special on football stadiums, with an interviewer standing in front of an enormous peak of glass and stone with a sign over the wide entrance that said: "Home of the Vikings." As Rafiq watched, the camera shifted to an aerial shot, showing the new stadium rising from the Minneapolis buildings like the prow of a ship. The commentator said the building cost one billion dollars to build.

Rafiq huffed as he changed the channel to Al Jazeera. A billion dollars! For a building they would use less than ten times a year. The epitome of American wastefulness. The Al Jazeera talking heads were still chattering about Tel Aviv and the nuclear accord, now due to be signed in early September. He watched the news crawler for anything new, then shut the TV off again.

He fussed at the computer, anything to kill time. His email was empty except for one message. It had come in over three weeks ago, just before the Tel Aviv announcement. It looked like just another piece of spam, but he had a clean email address, protected from most spam sources. The anonymous sender of the email had forwarded him a link from one of Ayatollah Aban Rahmani's famous Friday sermons titled "The Brotherhood of Man." He'd watched the video at least ten times and it was exactly what it purported to be: a rather long-winded Friday sermon. His half brother spewed hatred and flecks of spittle as he denounced the forces of progressive thought in Iranian society.

And then there were the Farsi words written underneath the link. STOP TEL AVIV.

At least ten times over the past weeks, Rafiq had come to this email with every intention of deleting it, but he couldn't. It was a message from Hashem, he was sure of it. But why would he risk sending a message in the clear? Rafiq hoped against all hope that he would get an answer to that question in the next five minutes.

He consulted the codebook again and recomputed the math. Yes, it all checked out. Their next contact was at 0223. Exactly on time,

Rafiq opened the Tor software and initialized the five-minute chatroom protocol. A timer in the right corner started a countdown.

As the timer passed through four minutes, Rafiq fidgeted with the mouse to keep the screen active.

He stood at three minutes and paced, never taking his eyes off the blinking cursor.

Please, brother. Answer me.

He reseated himself at two minutes and let his eyes sweep around the rich furnishings of the room. All this was his, his to lose. His heartbeat seemed to match the pulsing cursor.

One minute.

At thirty seconds, he looked away, his jaw tight with anger. His brother had deserted him.

When the countdown timer ran to zero, the chatroom window closed automatically and a shredder program ran to erase all evidence of the interaction. Rafiq sat back in his chair, scarcely able to believe what had just happened. Hashem had missed the third and final communications window, which meant his brother was either dead or captured.

The clock on the mantelpiece sounded like a jackhammer in the stillness of the room as Rafiq's mind processed what that meant.

I've been activated.

Eight years he'd waited for this moment. Seven years cut off from his home and his people, and now it was here: the day he'd hoped would never come.

It's all up to me now.

His gaze fell on the picture of Nadine and the children that graced the corner of Javier's desk—*his* desk. His beautiful wife had the children on her lap. Javi was almost four now, a spitting image of his mother. Consie looked older than her precocious three years, and took after her father with his blue eyes and fair skin. She gave a thin knowing smile to the camera, as if she knew what Rafiq might be thinking when he looked at his daughter's image.

Rafiq tore his eyes away from the photo. While he'd waited for this day to come, he'd made a new home, a new family, created a world where people depended on him. And he'd made a promise to Don Javier on his deathbed.

The house creaked as if to remind him of his new responsibilities.

Rafiq stood abruptly and exited the room through the French doors. It was a warm autumn night, and he broke into a light sweat as he walked to the wine cellar. He should probably wake Jamil. He was his partner in this holy mission, whatever it was. No, he decided, he would do this alone. The mysterious cargo was his responsibility now.

He paused to unlock the main entrance of the wine cellar. As he stepped through the door, the smell of crushed grapes was overpowering. It had been the best harvest in decades and had taken them weeks to get the grapes in and processed. Rafiq walked quickly past the stainless steel vats deeper into the cellar, through the rows of barrels and racks of bottles to the very back of the cave. Here, only a single bulb burned in front of a gated alcove set behind a wire cage. Javier's private storage area.

The gate opened easily on greased hinges. Rafiq pushed the catch to let the last row of bottles swing forward, uncovering a steel door. He pulled the key from around his neck, unlocking the door. The wooden crate occupied the center of the room. He snatched the prybar from its hook on the wall, where they had left it so many years ago in preparation for this day.

The dry wood of the crate cracked when he pushed the flat end of the crowbar under one corner of the lid. He levered it up and a shower of splinters burst into the air. Sweat popped out on his brow, and his breath came sharp and fast as Rafiq worked the edge of the lid, frantic now to see what was inside the mystery box. The lid fell to the floor with a hollow thud.

A black plastic packing case filled the interior of the wooden box. Rafiq smashed the crowbar against the corners of the crate until the sides fell away, revealing the whole case. A clear plastic folder, affixed to the top of the case, held a single sheet of folded paper. Rafiq slid it out and opened it.

Brother—

If you are reading this, you have been called to action. I have failed and everything we believe in now rests on you. If I cannot give you specific direction, I trust you will use this power to strike against the enemies of our cause.

May Allah guide you—

Hashem

Rafiq's hands shook as he pulled at the clamps that held the lid of the case shut. They snapped like rifle shots in the enclosed space. The lid made a little sigh when he lifted it up, as if he were opening a tomb.

He stared down at the contents of the case through a swirl of emotions. Nadine's face, the voice of his mother calling him for dinner in Lebanon, Hashem's lean smile, the laughter of his children. The babble of images and sounds rose up in his consciousness until he slammed the lid back down and one image remained.

A lone email with the words: STOP TEL AVIV.

CHAPTER 46

Beirut, Lebanon
13 June 2016 – 1015 local

Reza bought an *International Herald Tribune* from a vendor at the Beirut–Rafic Hariri Airport. The headline above the fold was still all about the Iranian nuclear accord. He slapped the newspaper closed.

He could smell the sea through the open window of the cab, and he dragged in a deep breath. The smell of the ocean was the smell of better days for Reza, reminding him of family trips when he was a boy. Family trips before the Shah fell and the hard-liners took over. Family trips before Israel had invaded Lebanon in '82. Beirut had never really recovered from the shock of the invasion and the subsequent acts of violence that seemed to convulse the nation every few years. The rise of Hezbollah, literally the Party of God, funded by his own Iran, and now the Islamic State . . . when did it ever end?

They passed a bombed-out building that stood like a silent reminder.

Rouhani could make a difference; Reza believed that. He'd believed it strongly enough to steer his career in the intelligence community toward working for Rouhani. It had taken some time for the great man to trust him, to make sure he wasn't another undercover agent from the hard-liners trying to worm his way into Rouhani's inner circle. It had taken time, but it had been worth it. Hassan Rouhani would bring his country back into the world order, make their mighty Persian heritage mean something again, and Reza would be by his side.

Over the years, they'd developed a shorthand in their conversation. From a political perspective, there were things that his boss should never have knowledge of but needed to be taken care of all the same. Rouhani hadn't batted an eye when Reza told him he'd be gone for a few days, maybe a week. The great man smiled and nodded, and didn't ask a single question.

He didn't need to. They had trust.

His eyes fell on the newspaper again. Aban had been sketchy on details, but he'd claimed there was at least one more nuclear warhead from the Iraqi cache. Hashem, Aban claimed, had been the mastermind behind the effort to place the Iraqi Air Force in "safekeeping" with Iran in 1991, so it made sense he would run the same play again when Saddam was under pressure from the Coalition forces in 2003. Except this time, Hashem had done it secretly.

For all his talking, Aban had given him only one solid lead: Rafiq Roshed, a name and nothing more.

Thanks to Hashem's oversight, the MISIRI files on Rafiq were almost nonexistent, hence his visit to Beirut.

The cab stopped in the tourist area, and Reza paid off the driver. He strolled along the boulevard, admiring the famous Rouche Sea Rock in the blue Mediterranean Sea and checking his tail to ensure he wasn't being followed. After forty minutes, he sent a text and walked briskly toward the Mövenpick Hotel and Resort. He made his way toward the coffee shop and selected a table in the corner, ordering an espresso. He left the newspaper open on the small wrought iron table.

A man wandered into the coffee shop and took a table an arm's length away from Reza. His eyes lighted on the newspaper.

"Strange times we live in, don't you think?" Reza asked him.

The man took a moment to meet his eyes. "But stranger times are likely ahead of us."

"Salaam," Reza said. "Will you join me?"

Bilal Hamieh lowered his bulk into the chair opposite Reza. With his graying beard, unkempt hair, and sagging man-tits, he looked like a cab driver, but Reza had read his dossier. Now forty-five years old, he'd started as a street fighter in the campaigns against the Israeli occupation of his country when he was no more than a boy and had risen through the ranks with each successive campaign. Today, he ran the intelligence apparatus for Hezbollah. Not especially political, Hamieh was reputed to be the most powerful—and the most secretive—man in the Party of God. Reza regarded the sharp eyes that stared back at him from across the table. If anyone could help him, it was Hamieh.

Bilal leaned forward. "Would you like to meet here or take a walk?"

Reza scanned the room. Good sightlines to the hotel lobby and the pool, and he'd selected the meeting place at random, notifying Bilal only a few moments before by text. "I'm fine here."

Bilal shrugged. "As you wish. What can I do for Iranian *Ettela'at?*"

"I'm here unofficially today. For some off-the-books assistance."

"So I've heard." Bilal's eyes narrowed a fraction.

Reza leaned forward and dropped his voice. "I'm looking for Rafiq Roshed. It's urgent that I find him."

"Rafiq has not been part of our organization for many years." Bilal shifted in his seat, so the afternoon sun streamed into Reza's eyes.

"But you knew that. He fell in with an Iranian Quds agent and disappeared. What would Iranian intelligence want with a man the Iranians took from me ten years ago?"

"The Quds agent was his brother. Half brother," Reza corrected himself.

Bilal let out a huff. "That I did not know."

"And when he took Rafiq, he was not using him for official business of the Islamic Republic of Iran."

Bilal moved again so that he blocked the sunlight on Reza. "I see." His gaze fell on the newspaper headline. "A loose end?"

Reza locked eyes with Bilal. "Let's say that the new leadership in Iran would be very appreciative of your immediate, and discreet, cooperation."

Bilal's shoulders hunched into another shrug. "There's not much to tell. The boy was a bastard, grew up in Arsal to the north." He waved his hand at the far wall. "A natural-born fighter, and smart, too. Could have been a leader in Hezbollah. He was in the Khobar Towers operation. Then the Iranian showed up, and Rafiq was gone. I heard he was in the US somewhere."

Reza tried to control his breathing. "What about his mother? Can I talk to her?"

Bilal's face clouded. "Not anymore, thanks to the Islamic State." He spat out the name like a curse. "The ISIS dogs attacked across the border from Syria a few years ago. Arsal, famous for carpets and beautiful women, was flattened by these sons of whores as punishment for our fighting on the side of Assad against them. Rafiq's mother was killed in the raid. Mortar shell, right in her living room."

"Did he come home for his mother's funeral?"

Bilal shook his head. "We assumed he was dead. What kind of son doesn't come home for his mother's funeral?"

Reza sat back in his chair, deflated.

"There is one other possibility," Bilal rumbled.

Reza raised his eyebrows at the Lebanese spy.

"Two brothers disappeared at the same time as Rafiq. Twins. One of them did show up for the funerals. He stayed with his mother only a few days. The rumor is that he is living in South America."

"And he is with Rafiq?"

Bilal shrugged again. "Unclear, but maybe his mother would talk to you."

Reza drained his cup and stood.

"Perhaps a drive in the country?"

CHAPTER 47

Don looked at the caller ID on the trilling desk phone.

Clem. He rolled his eyes toward the ceiling. Why now?

"Riley."

"Donny boy. Top of the morning to you, son. It's your lucky day. Get your ass in my office, pronto."

Don stared at the dead handset and slowly shook his head. He took one more look at the nuclear verification procedures for the Iranian nuclear accord he was editing on his computer.

Clem bounced out of his chair when Don knocked on the doorjamb of his office. He waved Don to a seat, shut the office door, then leaned back against the front edge of his desk. He hugged his arms across his chest so that his biceps popped. Don ignored the muscle show.

"Comfy?" Clem said, then without waiting for an answer, thrust a sheaf of papers in Don's face. "Read. Sign."

Don took the papers and looked at the heading: Non-Disclosure Form. Okay, he'd signed these many times. He scanned the first few lines, and his eyebrows went up.

"I know, right?" Clem said. "Serious shit, eh?"

Don nodded. This was unlike any NDA he'd ever seen. Basically, it said he was about to be read into a program called Project Caveman and if he ever disclosed anything he'd be thrown into a deep, dark hole for the rest of his natural born life.

"Do you have any idea what this is about?"

Clem shook his head. "I can tell you that they asked for you by name—and I'm being told that it came from the top. The very top."

"They asked for me?"

"You. By name."

Don's heart rate went up a few notches as he signed the last page of the document and handed it back to Clem. "What now?"

"Well, we have you set up in the small conference room, the one with no windows." He chuckled. "If you want to take files in with you, show them to your manager first so they can be marked as preexisting."

"My manager? I thought you were my manager."

"Sad as I am to say it, Riley, I am not read into this deal. Go figure, huh? Who wouldn't want a piece of this?" Clem struck an Atlas pose.

Don cleared his throat. "Are we done here?"

Clem relaxed his pose and reseated himself behind his desk. "Sure."

"Riley?" he called, just as Don's hand touched the doorknob.

Don looked over his shoulder. Clem's face was set in a scowl.

"Be careful, man. This looks like some serious shit, ya know?"

Constance, with her dark hair pulled back into a severe bun and tortoiseshell glasses, reminded Don of a librarian. She gave him a tight smile when he showed up at the conference room door a few minutes later.

"Mr. Riley?" She stuck out her hand. No rings, no bracelets, no jewelry of any kind save a pair of small pearl earrings. "I'm your case officer."

"Don," he replied. In a dark blue pantsuit and cream-colored blouse, she could have been anywhere from late twenties to early forties.

"I prefer to keep a personal distance from my subjects," she said. "If it's okay with you, sir. I'll call you Mr. Riley."

"And I should call you . . ."

"Constance."

"Do you have a last name, Constance?"

"Yes. Please come in, Mr. Riley. We need to get started."

Don entered the conference room and took the seat she offered him. "What's all this about, Constance?"

She locked the door, then turned back to him with her ever-present tight smile. Constance slit the TOP SECRET seal on a banker's box and began unloading a stack of files, a laptop, and an overhead projector. She handed the laptop to Don. "This device is biometrically coded to you. Please use this laptop—and only this laptop—for all work on this project."

Don nodded and pushed open the lid. It booted up automatically and waited for his fingerprint. He pressed his index finger against the sensor. The screen snapped to a CIA seal with the title underneath: Project Caveman.

Constance was laying out a series of pictures on the table. Iranian Shahab-3 missiles, loaded on a North Korean–made mobile launcher. They looked to be in some sort of crude garage with a dirt floor. More pictures showed a wrecked missile, burned pieces strewn across a sandy crater.

The final picture showed a missile with the warhead access panel removed. Don sucked in a breath. It was a nuclear device. Crude by modern standards, but a nuclear device nonetheless.

Constance cleared her throat. "These pictures were taken in an uninhabited region of southern Iran on May seventeenth." She paused long enough for Don to look up at her. She was cute, and on the low end of the age scale, Don decided, probably his age. She offered him another smile without showing her teeth. "We have reason to believe these devices originated from the Iraqis."

Don's daydreaming came to a screeching halt. He looked back at the picture of the nuclear bomb. Constance leaned forward and locked eyes with Don.

"I need you to tell me everything you know—and everything you *think* you know—about the Iraqi nuclear program."

CHAPTER 48

Reza strolled into the packed German stein hall on the outskirts of Ciudad Del Este, known locally as CDE.

He wrinkled his nose at the smell of stale beer. Men and women jostled each other on benches set beside long wooden tables, producing a clamor that filled the high-ceilinged room. To his eye, the smallest serving size was a pitcher of beer and the locals seemed to be perfectly comfortable drinking from the huge mugs.

He pushed his way to the far end of the bar where the servers dropped off their orders and caught the eye of the man working behind the counter. Reza slid a piece of paper across the surface, avoiding the puddles of beer. The man, barely glancing at Reza, picked up the paper and submerged it into a vat of soapy water. He jerked his head toward the stairs behind him.

Reza took one more look at the crowded hall before he started up the steps. He wondered if the old woman who'd led him here had any idea the trouble her son had gotten himself into.

In the end, it was less of an interrogation than a trip down memory lane with the old woman.

She drifted in and out of reality, sometimes talking as if she were a little girl, sometimes in present day. It was Bilal, the Hezbollah head of intelligence, who made the difference. The big man, his bulk balanced atop a rough wooden stool, held the old woman's hand and spoke to her in the local dialect of local matters of people long dead and common acquaintances.

It was more than two hours before he managed to get her talking about her sons, the twins.

"They were good boys," she said. "Both of them. Soldiers, you know?" She looked up into Bilal's eyes.

"Good soldiers, Mother, good men," Bilal agreed in a soft voice. "Have you heard from them?"

The old woman shook her head. "No, they went away." She lowered her voice. "I'm not supposed to talk about it."

"Talk about what?"

"What they're doing. It's very important to the cause."

"It is very important," Bilal agreed. "Very." He patted her gnarled hand. "Are they in good health?"

The old woman shook her head. "No, my Farid had the cancer . . . He's dead now. Poor boy, and his poor family, too." She let go of Bilal's hand and dug into the table next to her bed, producing a worn photo of a thin man with a dark-haired woman and a baby. "I am a grandmother!" she said.

Maybe it was the shock of seeing the picture of the baby again, but the old woman lost touch with the present day for another hour. Reza's ass was numb from sitting on the uncomfortable chair in the darkened room, but Bilal seemed unaffected.

"Farid came home for the funeral," the old woman announced out of the blue.

Reza saw Bilal's shoulders tense. "What funeral, Mother?"

The old woman made a spitting motion on the ground. "After the Islamic State dogs ruined our town . . . so many were dead, so many funerals. But Farid came home. He came home to say goodbye to his mother."

"Did he tell you where he's been?"

The old woman shook her head sadly. "No, he said it's a secret. Every time Jamil calls me, he says the same thing."

Reza's heart skipped a beat. Call? Bilal leaned in closer to the old woman. "Does your other son call you, Mother? Is he a good boy?"

The old woman's eyes narrowed. "I'm not to say."

Bilal sat back. "That's as it should be, Mother. Have you spoken to him this week?"

"No, he only calls every other Wednesday night at eight o'clock. I just spoke with him last night."

Reza stopped breathing.

He'd had to wait another two weeks, but it was a simple task to trace the call to a cell tower in CDE.

Reza stopped at the top of the stairs and loosened the 9mm pistol at the small of his back. The landing was narrow and dimly lit, with the only way out back down the steps. A red light winked at him from the camera in the corner above his head.

He knocked three times. The door snapped halfway open and the muzzle of a gun was pointed at his face. Reza forced a smile, saying in his best Lebanese Arabic: "Beirut is alive with the spirit of forgiveness."

The man behind the gun stepped back to let him enter. "I do not know you."

"Bilal sent me."

The man's swarthy face cracked into a smile. "Ah, my favorite cousin, how is he?" he said, lowering the gun.

Reza allowed himself to relax. "Bilal is well. He sends his regards."

"Please, come in, come in," the man said. "May I get you some tea?"

"Tea in a beer hall?"

The man flopped into a leather armchair behind a wooden desk. "My cover, pretty good, eh? Who would think to look for a devout Muslim in a German beer hall?" he said with a laugh.

Reza laughed along with the man, leaning forward in his seat. He slipped the gun from behind his back and held it against his leg. "My friend, Bilal, told me to ask you a question. About Lena's hair—what color was it?"

The smile on the man's face slipped a notch. "Lovely Lena," he said. "Lovely, lovely Lena."

Reza felt cold metal poke him in the back of his head. He froze.

"Lena was my sister, and she was blonde as a Swede. She hated it, and when she was twelve, she dyed her hair black." The voice was cool and low, with an edge that made sweat break out under Reza's armpits.

"May I stand?" His dry tongue rasped against the roof of his mouth.

The muzzle pressed against the back of his head moved away, but he still felt the imprint on his scalp. He let his own gun drop to the floor as he stood and turned.

Walid Wehbe was not a tall man, and not thickly muscled, either. Still, his wiry frame oozed a certain deadly confidence that few would cross. His thin smile was more a baring of teeth than an offer of friendship as he extended his hand. Reza could feel every muscle and tendon in the steady grip.

Walid waved his pistol at the desk and his man, who had now risen. "My apologies for the pretense. My visitors usually have an agenda. And they're not usually Iranian." He narrowed his eyes at Reza. "The code phrase from Bilal is among our most protected, to be used only in an emergency. You must have some urgent business."

As he spoke, he slipped his gun back into his waistband and beckoned Reza to follow him. They made their way back down the stairs and out a back entrance. The smell of spoiled beer and rotting food was heavy in the air, and Reza tried to ignore the large rats that scattered from their path. Walid moved quickly; Reza had to trot to keep up.

Once away from the beer hall, he cut down toward the river where a speedboat waited. Walid leaped from the dock to the driver's seat in one bound, making the boat rock. Reza moved with more care, crabbing his way from the steady dock into the heaving boat. As soon as he was aboard, Walid cast off lines and pulled away into the dark.

Reza tried to stay calm, comforted by the fact that Walid had let him keep his gun. Still, the roaring engine, the smell of the river, the humid air, and his jet lag all combined to keep his head in a fog. He stared at Walid's spare frame, outlined by the soft glow of the dashboard lights, and offered a silent prayer that Bilal's influence extended to South America.

The speedboat slowed, making a sweeping turn into a small cove. Walid cut the engine and let the craft coast the last thirty feet toward the dock. When he was close, he tossed a rope to a waiting man. He leaped from the boat to the dock, calling in Spanish to the man. "Bring our guest to the house, Pablo."

Reza waited until Pablo had secured the speedboat before he stood. When Pablo reached down a hand to help him up to the dock, Reza's grip was lost in the man's huge mitts, and he felt himself almost lifted bodily out of the boat. Pablo was a short, stocky man with the features of a Paraguayan native and arms like Popeye. He grunted as he looked up into Reza's face, and jerked his head toward the end of the dock. Reza took a deep breath and followed him.

The unlit trail wound up the small hill to a low, modern-style ranch house. Pablo nodded to the man guarding the front door, whose eyes flicked over Reza, locking on the handgun behind his back. Reza's eyes fell to the submachine gun the guard was carrying.

The interior of the house was clean and modern, with well-lit rooms and tasteful paintings on the walls. Pablo pointed to the rug when he entered. Reza wiped his feet carefully, eliciting a satisfied grunt from the stocky man. Pablo deposited him in a living room, where a small fleet of leather armchairs were arranged around a massive low table that looked like a cross section of a tree trunk.

"Beautiful, isn't it?" Walid said from behind him. He had changed into a fresh shirt and loose-fitting trousers, and his feet were bare. "It's from a mahogany tree. It reminds me of a map." The irregular shape did look like a map of a continent. Walid handed him a cup of tea in a clear glass mug. Reza nodded his thanks. He could feel his strength ebbing away, the jet lag taking over.

Walid flopped into one of the chairs and crossed his legs. "Now, tell me why my cousin would send an Iranian intelligence agent all the way to South America, where you are so clearly out of your element, and give you one of our most secret personal codes."

Reza sat on the edge of a seat across from Walid, separated by the massive expanse of the tree trunk. He set the tea down on the table. Walid tossed him a coaster, which he placed under the hot mug.

"I am looking for this man." Reza pushed a picture of Rafiq across the table.

Walid's eyebrows shot up. "Rafiq? Why do you want him?"

"You know him?"

Walid laughed. "Everyone knows *of* Rafiq, very few *know* him. He owns one of the largest *estancias* in the area. He married into wealth and inherited everything when his father-in-law died."

Reza sucked in a breath. "You know where I can find him?"

"Depends on why you want him."

Reza licked his lips. "Rafiq was sent here under false pretenses. He is working for his half brother, an Iranian. He needs to be stopped."

Walid leaned forward in his seat. "You're asking for my help to raid one of my own? Why?"

Reza took a deep breath, and told him.

Walid leaned back in his chair when Reza had finished speaking. A ridge of muscle sharpened his jawline. "Rafiq is well protected on his ranch. Getting to him will not be easy. You'll need a team of at least a dozen men."

"How many men do you have here?"

Walid's face split into a wolfish grin. "A dozen."

CHAPTER 49

Off the coast of Perth, Australia
06 August 2016 — 0600 local

Brendan watched the sky pinken over the western coast of Australia. Port, finally.

The last ten weeks at sea had given him new respect for his surface warfare classmates from the Academy. Putting this many people in this small of an area for that long defined a whole new level of stress for Brendan. It seemed like even the smallest issue—watch schedules, dinner menu, cleaning rotations—blew up into a big deal. As skipper, it was his job to solve it, and he was tired of it.

Well, that's what leave is for. A few days and he'd be back in Minnesota and as far away from an ocean as one could get on the continental United States.

Still, the last mission to Iran proved to him that he belonged here, onboard his ship, not back with the SEALs. He knew he was a step behind his spec ops buddies now, not up to the task of jumping out of helos or assaulting targets. But here, here he was making a difference. Their trip from the Arabian Gulf down to Australia had been another success for the program. Who knew the Indonesians were using Russian-made Rezonans-N long-range air search radar? Dot guessed they'd installed it after the loss of Malaysian Airlines Flight 370 in March 2014. Thanks to the crew of the *Arrogant*, that piece of data was now in the hands of the intelligence guys to figure how and why it had happened.

Gabby poked her head up from the cabin. "Coffee, skipper?"

Brendan nodded. He checked the sails, which were tight under a brisk morning breeze. At this rate, they'd be in Perth before lunchtime.

Gabby handed him a steaming mug and took a seat next to him on the bench. Her dark curls were tousled and her eyes still puffy with sleep. A gull rode the wind overhead. She half-rose to see if anyone else was awake, then huddled deeper into her sweatshirt.

"I'm going to put in for a transfer while we're in refit," she said in a low voice.

Brendan kept his face still and stayed silent.

"I think it's best—for both of us," she continued.

That part was true, at least. He closed his eyes, hoping she wasn't going to bring up the Maldives again.

The situation with Gabby had come to a head during a port visit in the Maldives.

To bolster their party boat image, they had all dined together in an expensive restaurant out on the town. The food was wonderful, a blend of French with an Indian flair, served on a platform that cantilevered out over the crystal-clear water. When the sun went down and the water darkened, the restaurant turned on underwater lights that attracted the local sea life.

The combination of the soft sea breeze, the wine, the fabulous food, and good company made for an evening to remember. It was

Dot who suggested they go dancing. Brendan shrugged. He wasn't much of a dancer, but if the rest of them wanted to go, he was happy to play the host.

The nightclub was called "The Wave," and he slipped a fifty-dollar bill to the doorman to get them a table overlooking the dance floor. Someone ordered champagne, and a silver bucket appeared at their table. Like magic, it was empty and another replaced it, although he scarcely remembered drinking any of the first one.

The pumping music made for difficult conversation, unless you leaned into the person and almost shouted directly into their ear. So Brendan drank, and watched while the rest of the crew hit the dance floor.

Except Gabby.

She was wearing a short skirt and some kind of glittery gold top that stretched tight across her breasts, but left her back bare. She slid across the leather sofa until she was right next to him and said something.

"What?" He knew perfectly well that she'd asked him to dance, but he was searching for a way out of it. Sure, they had a cover to keep, but as a naval officer he had lines he couldn't cross, and sleeping with a crew member was the biggest, brightest line he could think of.

She leaned into him, her breast resting heavily against his bicep. Her hand touched his thigh lightly, and Brendan felt himself stiffen. Gabby put her lips next to his ear, the scent of her hair and wonderful mocha-colored skin strong in Brendan's nostrils.

"Dance with me."

Her breath puffed softly against his cheek, and she might have used the closeness to nip his earlobe. Brendan stood and helped her up. She kept hold of his hand, leading him down the steps and onto the crowded dance floor.

Bodies, sweat, damp heat. The crush of dancers forced them so close together that Gabby's nipples poked him through the thin material of his shirt. A few tendrils of curly dark hair had come loose from her hair clip, and they framed her face softly. She looked up at him, and Brendan bit his lip. Her hips ground against him and his breath stuttered in his throat as his body responded to hers. He lowered his face toward Gabby, and she was already moving to meet his lips.

Then it happened. The DJ hit a strobe light; the world went freeze-frame all around him.

And Gabby's face changed. Her features sharpened, the mass of dark curls transformed into a sleek bob, and he was looking at Liz.

He jerked his head back. Gabby opened her eyes when the expected kiss didn't happened. "What's the matter?" Liz/Gabby mouthed to him in stop-motion.

Brendan gulped. He stopped dancing and put his head close to her ear. "Liz—I mean, Gabby, I can't—"

Gabby's head jerked away from him. She pushed him back into the group of dancers behind him. Brendan lost his balance, falling on his ass in a circle of Indian girls who glared down at him, looks of disgust on their faces.

The DJ started the strobe again as Brendan struggled to his feet. The combination of too much to drink and the freeze-frame of the lights meant it took him a long time to get back to the table. Brendan flopped onto the couch next to Scottie. "Where's Gabby?" he gasped.

"She grabbed her purse and left a minute ago," Scottie said in a shout. He peered at Brendan's face. "You okay?"

"Did she look upset?"

"Skipper, I've been married three times. If you want to ask a man if a woman looks upset, you best ask someone else."

It would have been funny if he wasn't so angry with himself about the whole situation. He threw a sidelong glance at Gabby. She had her beautiful brown eyes focused on him.

"Did you hear what I said?" she asked.

Brendan nodded. There was nothing he could say to make this better, so he decided to just shut up.

Gabby looked away and Brendan breathed a sigh of relief. He'd already made his clumsy apologies, multiple times. It was time to let it die.

"Who's Liz?"

"What?" Brendan's head snapped around.

"Who's Liz? That night at the club, you called me Liz. Who is she?"

"Uh, she's a friend. Someone I went to school with."

Gabby plucked the empty coffee cup from his hand. She placed a hand on his knee, the injured one. Her touch was familiar, but lacking intimacy—not like the way she'd touched him before the Maldives.

"Hey." She waited until he looked up at her. "What we were about to do on the dance floor was way beyond friends, skipper, and you called me by another woman's name. Not what any woman wants to hear."

She gave him a sad smile. "Get your head straight, sir. Liz is way more than a friend."

Brendan blew out a deep breath as Gabby disappeared into the cabin below. The sun came up over the horizon.

Less than a week and he'd be back in Minneapolis.

CHAPTER 50

Tenerife, Canary Islands
16 August 2016 — 0945 local

The Malay captain called the snowcapped volcano el Teide.

The peak was visible a full half day before they could make out the rest of the land mass that was the island of Tenerife in the Canary Islands. Rafiq stood on the bridge wing, enjoying the warm sea air and fretting about the next port of call. The trip to Tenerife had been excruciatingly slow, as the Malay breakbulk freighter made stops along the coast of South America. Even the bribe of more money would not sway the Malay captain.

"Breakbulk freighter make many stops. Act natural," was all he would say, and offer Rafiq a gap-toothed grin.

He was right, of course. Arriving at their destination early only opened them up for more scrutiny. Better to arrive the day of the event.

Jamil joined him at the railing, sleep still marking his face. Rafiq felt little need for sleep these days; time enough for that after his mission was complete.

The *Lumba* made the turn around the point of land that hid their destination. Santa Cruz de Tenerife, despite the exotic-sounding name, was a dump, a dirty port filled with ships like the *Lumba*. Cranes loomed over the edge of the concrete piers, where piles of pallets, cargo containers, and trucks sat in huddled confusion.

It was perfect. Chaos meant lax, easily bribed officials.

The tugs came out to meet them, their whistles piping sharply as they came alongside. A local pilot scrambled up the rope ladder to the deck on his way to the bridge. Rafiq and Jamil regrouped on the main deck, out of sight of the bridge, but where they could watch the approach.

The ship was being placed in a berth at Dique del Este, one of the busier piers, where it would take a half day for the Malay captain to offload his cargo from Brazil and take on fuel. Rafiq looked at the sky; they'd be gone by nightfall. Without him.

He turned to Jamil. "You have everything you need? Any final questions?"

Jamil shifted his feet on the steel deck. After nearly a decade of waiting, this was goodbye.

The *Lumba* rocked gently as the tugs pushed her close to the pier and the lines went across. A crane lifted the gangway into place and a pair of customs officials came onboard to meet with the captain. Rafiq waited until they had gone to the bridge and the pilot had left the ship before he turned to Jamil. "This is goodbye, my friend. May Allah keep you safe in your travels and shine his mercy upon your mission."

Jamil's eyes were wet, and when he hugged Rafiq, his grip was strong. Rafiq felt a tickle of worry. Jamil had been off ever since his brother had died, more emotional, softer. He wondered for a brief moment about their plan to split up. No, only he had the skills to perform this final leg of their mission.

He broke the hug and grasped the handle of the hand truck, leaning back to balance the weight on the wheels. He went first down the gangway, using his body to ease the load down the sloped walkway. He reached the bottom and met the customs official stationed there.

"Passport."

Rafiq handed him his Canadian passport, the gold crown emblem on the cover nearly worn off with use.

The customs official gestured at the black packing case on the hand truck. "What's in the case, sir?" he said in heavily accented English.

Rafiq smiled. "I'm a surveyor. The tools of my trade, *senor*."

The man nodded as he flipped through the passport pages. When he found a blank one, he stamped it and handed the booklet back to Rafiq.

"Have a good trip home, sir."

CHAPTER 51

Reza peeled back the tight-fitting black sleeve to peer at his watch. The softly glowing hands told him it was two minutes to midnight.

He'd wanted to wait until later, but Walid had insisted they launch the raid at midnight. The farm workers on the ranch started early, he said, some as early as three in the morning. Besides, security changed shifts at midnight and they could take out both sets of guards at the same time.

In the end, it was Walid's raid; all Reza could do was make suggestions. And worry.

A light rain fell, the kind that provided a nice background of white noise to mask their approach to the main house. The ranch house itself was huge, a low-slung, two-story affair of stone and timber that sprawled across the hilltop overlooking the long valley.

The earpiece crackled in Reza's ear. "I have a visual on both guards. Standing by for go."

Walid's reply came in stereo: once over the headset, and once from the man lying prone in the leaves next to Reza. "All teams, standby to go on my mark. Three, two, one. Go!"

Reza saw the two guards, sharing a cigarette in the driveway under the only lamp within a hundred meters, both do a stutter-step and drop to the ground. The team of four to his right sprang up and started to hustle across the long upslope of open lawn that lay between the edge of the jungle and the ranch house.

The door on the veranda facing them opened, and a young woman stepped out onto the wet stones. She wrapped her arms across her chest and called out in a stage whisper, "Franco?" She tiptoed across the flagstones until she could see the driveway. Her mouth dropped open when she saw the two men lying facedown in the pool of light.

Walid cursed and swung his rifle into firing position. He squeezed off a shot just as the girl turned back toward the house. The bullet nicked her shoulder and spun her to the ground. The assault team had nearly reached the veranda; she screamed when she saw them coming.

The scream was cut short by a three-bullet burst of gunfire that echoed across the valley.

Walid leaped up, dragging Reza with him, all pretense at stealth gone. "All teams, go! Go now," he shouted into the headset. He charged across the lawn. When they reached the veranda, Reza heard the deep blast of a shotgun followed by multiple bursts of automatic weapons fire. They passed the body of the young girl on the veranda, dark blots of blood on her white nightdress, her eyes staring upwards. She might have been eighteen.

They passed through a kitchen, lit only by the lights from the appliances, and into a broad hall. Walid took the stairs two at a time to where one of his men was waiting for him on the landing. He pointed to the open double doors at the end of the hall.

Nadine had managed to take out two of Walid's men with her single shotgun blast. The first body, missing most of his face, lay across the entrance to the master suite, the second had some pellets buried in his throat. The white towel pressed against the injured man's neck was dark with absorbed blood. Reza was no doctor, but he was sure this man wouldn't live either.

One of the men flipped on the light switch, flooding the room with light. Reza swallowed hard to counteract his gag reflex.

Nadine lay sprawled across the carpet, her hair splayed out like a dark halo around her head. She bled from at least six gunshots wounds in her torso, and blotches of dark red almost consumed the creamy silk of her long nightdress. Stray bullets had stitched holes into the wall behind her.

One of the other men came into the room and whispered to Walid. He turned to Reza. "Rafiq's not here."

Reza looked at the king-size bed. Only one side had been slept in.

They were too late.

Reza knelt next to Nadine. Her eyes were unfocused, and her head lolled. He gripped her chin and bent close to her. "Where is Rafiq? Where is your husband?"

She blinked her eyes heavily; her lips moved like she was trying to speak.

He leaned closer. "What?"

Her breath tickled his ear. "Fuck you," she whispered.

Reza sat back. Nadine's blood-soaked chest had stilled and her eyes stared up at the ceiling. He looked up at the wall, where a photograph of a smiling Rafiq held two squirming children.

"We need to go, Reza," Walid called to him from the doorway.

"Where are Rafiq's children?"

Walid shook his head. "We're not taking the kids. We just shot his fucking wife, for God's sake. The locals will have my head if I touch his kids."

"I need to talk to them. Alone."

Walid looked at his watch. "Three minutes. One second longer and you're on your own getting out of here."

The children were huddled together in what must have been the boy's room. The kid was clearly horse-crazy, with pictures of horses, books about horses, even a shelf full of toy horses. The boy's face was pale with fright beneath a mop of black curls, and his dark eyes stared up at Reza as he approached. He tightened his grip around his little sister.

If the boy was frightened, his sister was angry. Reza saw Rafiq's sharp features in her young face. She was clearly the stronger of the two.

Her eyes blazed and she pointed her finger up at him. "You leave us alone," she shouted.

He tried to sit on the edge of the bed, but the girl kicked at him. He remained standing. "I need to find your father," he said.

"You leave us alone," the girl repeated in a shrill voice. Her brother sat mute beside her.

Reza felt a flash of anger. He reached out and caught the girl's wrist. He squeezed until she grimaced in pain, but she would not cry. He hauled her across the bed until her face was inches from his. "I need to know where your father went."

Walid called to him. "We need to go. Now."

Reza tightened his grip on the girl's arm, and still she would not cry. His eyes flicked to her brother. "If you don't tell me, I'll take your brother away and leave you here all alone."

The girl's eyes widened a fraction.

"Papa went away," she said.

"Where? When?"

Walid hissed at him from the doorway to hurry up.

"He left in a big ship. He said he was going to sail across the ocean. Mama said the ship was called *delfin*."

CHAPTER 52

Brendan inspected himself in the mirror and let out a deep breath. Behind him he could see the pile of discarded outfits on his bed, but in the end he'd settled for the old standby: khakis, white button-down oxford, and blue blazer.

Exactly the same thing he'd worn the last time he saw Liz.

He'd been almost three weeks into his four weeks of leave before he finally screwed up the courage to call her. Brendan suspected that Don and Marjorie had both called his parents to urge him to ask Liz out.

When did it get so hard to just talk to her? Once they'd been best friends, inseparable. Sure, they dated, but life at the Academy was too busy to have a full-blown relationship.

He sucked in another deep breath to calm the butterflies in his stomach. *It's just two old friends going to dinner, that's all. Keep it cool, man. Keep it together.*

Except it was more than that. Liz was divorced now, and of all the dozens of possible FBI offices to transfer to in the entire United States, she'd chosen Minneapolis. That couldn't be a coincidence.

He spied the bottle of Old Spice that Master Chief O'Brien had given him before his last meeting with Liz and smiled. What the hell; he dabbed a splash of the cologne along his jawline.

His mother was waiting for him in the kitchen. "Oh, Brennie, don't you look handsome. Liz won't know what hit her."

Brendan rolled his eyes. "Mom, please. I'm not going to prom, just dinner with an old friend."

His father joined them in the kitchen. "Well, you can tell your 'friend'"—he waggled his fingers for air quotes—"that she's welcome here anytime."

Brendan knelt next to Champ's dog bed. "Please make them stop, buddy."

The old dog thumped his tail weakly and rolled a cataract-glazed eye in Brendan's direction. At fourteen years old, his old friend was on his last legs.

Knowing that parking near the trendy Uptown area was going to be murder this time of year, Brendan decided to walk from his parents' house in Linden Hills. It took longer than he remembered, and he arrived at the Urban Eatery a few minutes late, out of breath, and limping. Brendan wiped his brow with a pocket handkerchief as he pulled open the heavy door of the restaurant.

The interior was dim and chill with air conditioning, making the sweat under his arms freeze into clammy patches. He heard Liz before he saw her, her deep chuckle rolling out from the bar area. He stepped into the space.

Liz was leaning against the bar with both hands, facing the bartender and laughing at something he'd said. She wore a simple sheath of pale yellow that complemented her dark hair and olive-toned skin. The sleeveless dress showed off her muscled biceps and shoulders.

The bartender looked up and saw Brendan. He nodded to Liz and moved away.

As she turned around, Brendan had the sudden desire to run. He looked down at his khakis and sweaty white shirt and knew she was out of his league. She was sophisticated, mature, professional, and he was . . . the same guy she'd known a dozen years ago.

Liz's brown eyes were warm, still merry from the shared joke with the bartender. When she hugged him, he felt the strong muscles of her back through the thin dress. The warm scent of her perfume enveloped him, a subtle musk with light notes of vanilla. He thought of the cheap cologne he'd splashed on himself and tensed.

"What's wrong?" she said.

"Nothing, sorry." He clumsily disengaged from her embrace. "I'll check on our table."

"No need," Liz told him. "Tony will do it." She waved at the bartender, and he picked up the phone. Tony's eyes locked onto Brendan's for second, and Brendan thought he detected a flicker of anger in the man's gaze.

"You're on the patio, Liz," he called.

Liz took Brendan's hand and led him through the restaurant to a table for two overlooking the lake. A chilled bottle of Prosecco was waiting for them. Brendan pulled out her chair. "You seem to know this place pretty well."

Liz laughed. "I live just around the corner. I come here all the time." She accepted a glass of wine from Brendan. "What shall we toast to, Bren?"

She'd called him Bren. He fought back a rise of hope in his chest. "To absent friends?"

Liz narrowed her eyes. "How about to *present* friends?"

Brendan flushed as he repeated, "To present friends."

They eased into the conversation with small talk, mostly about work. Brendan hinted that he couldn't really say much about his recent assignment, and Liz gave him a knowing smile. "I *thought* refitting sailboats was a little below your paygrade, Commander," she said and changed the subject.

The level in the wine bottle dropped quickly as they started to get reacquainted. It was obvious Liz liked her work. She talked at length about her assignment as a special agent on the Minneapolis JTTF, and gave him some background on recent local news stories. A caprese salad arrived that Brendan didn't remember ordering, and they both dug in while laughing at a Riley story.

The empty Prosecco bottle was replaced by a pinot grigio that Brendan also didn't recall ordering. The chilled wine tasted sharp and clean. "Why did you choose Minneapolis?"

The smile on Liz's lips froze for a split second. She shrugged. "It was the first transfer I could get out of LA."

Brendan stayed silent, and Liz shifted in her seat. "That's not true," she said finally. "I planned my transfer for months before James and I broke up. I—I just needed to get away. He's a good man, but I didn't love him. Besides, I'm happy here."

Brendan's mouth went dry and he wished he hadn't drunk so much wine.

"Everything okay here, Liz?" The voice was a warm baritone.

Brendan half-turned in his seat to see Tony, the bartender, in the gathering dusk. He'd changed out of his work clothes into a pair of trendy jeans and an open-necked silk shirt. His blue eyes gave Brendan a wintry look. He moved past Brendan to stand next to Liz and rest a hand on the back of her chair.

Liz shrank away from his hand. "We're fine, Tony. I'll see you tomorrow." Tony gave Brendan a curt nod, then strode off.

Brendan sat rigid in his chair, his mind working. He flushed when Liz's eyes finally met his. "Friend of yours?"

Liz shifted in her seat. She picked up her wineglass, then put it down again without drinking. "I've seen him a few times . . . . nothing serious."

"So you're dating him?" He had a sudden image of Tony and Liz all sweaty and tangled up in the sheets of a massive four-poster bed like some cheesy *telenovela*.

Liz huffed. "I'm not a nun, Brendan! I'm a thirty-something, divorced workaholic who walked away from a man who loved her for . . . for . . ." She ran a folded napkin under her eyelids.

"For what?"

"You're serious?" The light from the candle danced in her eyes. "That Thanksgiving at Marjorie's when I threw myself at you? When I divorced my saint of a husband and moved to Minneapolis? Why would I do those things, Brendan? Are you that fucking dense?" Her voice rose and Brendan could hear the chatter on the patio die down as the other diners eavesdropped. The wine roiled around in his stomach like a sour mess.

Liz stood up. The heavy wrought iron chair stuttered against the stone patio, making a loud clatter. Her pale yellow dress seemed to attract all the light from the space around her. She placed her hands on the table and leaned toward him. The flickering candle softened the curves of her face, but her eyes glowed with fire.

"You've had some bad relationships—I know, and I don't care. You're going to deploy to someplace on the other side of the world— I know, and I don't care." Liz's parted lips trembled and she breathed heavily. Her expression looked somewhere between wanting to cry and wanting to kick his ass, but her voice was steady.

"What I do know is this: once upon a time, I said having a relationship and a career was too hard. I pushed you away. I was wrong. Here's the deal, Brendan McHugh: I love you. Always have. Always will."

Brendan tried to swallow and found he'd lost the ability. Liz's beautiful brown eyes flashed at him from across the table.

Say something, you idiot! Nothing happened. The connection between his brain and his body seemed to have shut down.

She straightened up, carefully folding her napkin, her eyes pinning him into his chair.

"I get that you're scared, Brendan, I really do. But I have turned my life upside down to be with you. I need you to meet me halfway."

Liz placed the folded napkin on her plate, slipped her handbag under her arm, and walked away. A table of three women off to his left clapped.

Brendan felt a burning flush creep up his neck as he stood, swaying slightly. He fumbled for his wallet and dropped a handful of bills on the table.

He looked at the doorway into the restaurant where Liz had disappeared.

Then he reeled toward the low railing and stepped onto the sidewalk.

CHAPTER 53

Rafiq stood at the rail of the *Ottawa*, squinting at the distant lights of Thunder Bay.

Barely a ripple disturbed the image of the half-moon reflected in the still waters of Lake Superior. Dead calm. If he believed all the songs these people sang about the Great Lake Gitchi Gumee, this was a rare condition indeed.

A flash of movement on the southern horizon caught his eye, and he snapped the binoculars to his eyes. A motor craft, running lights extinguished, was headed directly toward them. He breathed a soft sigh of relief.

The captain appeared at his elbow. "Is that him?" he said in English. The man's hands beat a nervous tattoo on the railing. For him, this was the most dangerous part of the journey. Rafiq's forged seaman's papers showed him as Indian, and the captain could plead ignorance in the unlikely event they were boarded at sea. Smuggling a person across an international border was another thing entirely.

Rafiq nodded. "Calm yourself, Captain. I'll be gone in a few minutes. You'll be well paid."

To be fair to the captain, this was a change of plans. The original plan had been for Rafiq to go ashore in Thunder Bay, but his last-minute contact with Charles Whitworth had changed the game entirely.

The luck of the draw had made Charles—he preferred "Chas"—Whitworth his freshman-year roommate at Carleton College. As the only son of a prominent Wisconsin real estate developer, Chas's life was filled with expectations, which he'd spent the greater part of his eighteen years of life not meeting. His father had tried everything: counseling, military school, rehab, Outward Bound wilderness programs, anything to make his son take his responsibilities seriously. Carleton College was the last straw. Daddy had bought his way into the freshmen class with a generous donation to some building fund and Chas was given an ultimatum: graduate or be disinherited.

To Rafiq—he went by the pseudonym of Ralf Faber in those days—the answer was obvious. The only thing Chas wanted was what his father refused to give him: his love and respect. Rafiq/Ralf saw an opportunity in this broken, spoiled man-child. The money, the political connections, the access to powerful people at the state and national level—if he could make Chas successful, Ralf would be able to use those assets someday.

His training in Hezbollah and with Hashem had taught him to watch for ways to cultivate people, and the biggest bet of Rafiq's many years of cultivation was about to reap a fabulous harvest.

To be sure, his time with Chas had not been easy. His roommate was a habitual drug user, a drunk, and read at barely an eighth grade level. Ralf got his friend clean, tutored him in his classes, and, when necessary, did his assignments for him. They were roommates and friends their entire four years of college. Chas gained the respect of his father and a fast track to becoming CEO when his aging parent passed away.

A week before their graduation from Carleton, Ralf produced a letter from a prestigious, and fictional, brokerage in London where he had landed a job. Chas's face fell; he'd hoped that Ralf would take a job offered by his father and they could stay together.

On their graduation day, Chas hugged his friend Ralf fiercely. He was near tears at the thought of being separated from his friend. "If you ever need anything—anything—you call me. Anytime. Anywhere."

Tonight, more than a decade later, Rafiq was here to collect on that promise.

He ran lightly down the ladders in the ship until he reached the small landing that jutted from the stern at the waterline. The boat approaching was a forty-footer, sleek, with a covered cabin—a rich man's pleasure craft. He caught a glimpse of the name on the fantail: *Marauder.* How appropriate.

"Ralf? Is that you?" The voice was Chas's, but coarser, roughened by years of smoking and drink, he suspected.

He slipped easily into his American accent, a vague Mid-Atlantic blend. "Chas? Toss me the line, buddy." He caught the line on the first try and secured it to the cleat on the edge of the platform. Rafiq leaped into the boat.

The ladder creaked as Chas descended from the upper-level cockpit. Even in the shadowy light, Rafiq could see his old friend had grown obese. A hug confirmed it. Chas's breath wheezed even when he was standing still. "God, it's good to see you, buddy." He paused for breath. "Why all the cloak-and-dagger stuff, anyway? I feel like a smuggler."

Rafiq laughed. "Oh, funny story, you know. I'm a journalist now and doing a story on cargo ships and working conditions. Well, wouldn't you know I lost my passport." He lowered his voice and leaned in. "I'm thinking maybe one of these guys on the ship stole it. Passports go for good money on the black market, am I right? Anyway, the idea of landing in Canada without a passport and having to go to the embassy and all that. Then I thought about you and figured why not call Chas?"

Chas had reached behind him into a small refrigerator and pulled out two beers. He cracked one open and took a long pull. He handed the other to Rafiq, who opened it and pretended to take a sip.

"Look, this actually is illegal, so how about I get my stuff and we skedaddle?"

Chas nodded and drained the last of his beer. He threw the empty container over the side.

Rafiq ran back up to the main deck. The captain was looking down on the *Marauder* from the railing. Keeping back from the rail, Rafiq extracted a smartphone from his jacket. He logged into his account and did a wire transfer of $50,000 to the captain's personal account in the Caymans. He showed the confirmation to the captain.

Rafiq could see the man's broad smile in the dim light. "Go," the captain said.

Chas was deep into another beer by the time Rafiq dragged his black packing case out onto the narrow platform. He surveyed the open water gap to the edge of the boat. It was large enough to allow the crate to fall into the water. He leaned back into the ship and called up the ladder. One of the cook's boys, a Syrian refugee, was loitering a level above. With the boy's help, he lifted the case across the gap and safely into the boat. Chas had not moved from his seated position.

"What language was that you were speaking?" Chas asked.

With a start, Rafiq realized he had spoken Arabic to the boy. He forced a laugh. "I travel a lot, so I pick up stuff here and there. Is that my beer?" He hefted the can toward Chas and took a long drink. The bitter liquid burned his tongue and the carbonation made him want to sneeze.

"Let's take off, eh?" Rafiq said in a fake Canadian accent. They used to watch the movie *Strange Brew* almost every weekend at Carleton.

Chas heaved himself to his feet and started up the ladder—after he stuffed a beer in each pocket of his shorts.

The ride to Bayfield, Wisconsin, took nearly twelve hours.

By the time the sun came up, Chas was drunk enough that Rafiq took over the pilot duties. The sight of his old friend in the soft light of morning made Rafiq sick to his stomach. The Chas he knew from college had been a slim young man with wavy brown hair and soft hazel eyes. The beast that snored behind him was a mountain of sweaty flesh with heavy jowls the color of rust and wisps of gray-brown hair swirling around his face. The eyes—when they were open—were bloodshot pools.

They'd talked for the first few hours, before Chas fell into an alcoholic stupor. Rafiq found it surprisingly easy to fabricate a backstory about his life since graduation, mixing in facts about Nadine and the children with fictional elements.

Chas responded in kind with his own tale. Two marriages, two divorces, but the family real estate company was doing fabulously well. He lived by himself in the family mansion on the shores of Lake Superior.

Perfect.

But mostly, Chas wanted to talk about the good old days. Their time at Carleton, the trips during spring break and Christmas. Rafiq indulged the urge, rolling out half-remembered stories. He looked around at one point before sunrise, and Chas was sipping from a bottle of liquor. He swung the neck of the bottle in Rafiq's direction, but Rafiq refused.

As the level in the bottle dropped, the stories became increasingly maudlin and less coherent, until Chas's chatter was replaced by a bone-rattling snore. Rafiq threw the bottle overboard.

The motor yacht had a state-of-the-art navigation system with their destination clearly marked. Rafiq kept their speed moderate and waved cheerily to other boats they passed. During the midmorning hours, he put out some fishing lines with unbaited hooks, as much for something to do as the need to keep up appearances. He let Chas sleep until he had the estate dock in sight, then he tried to wake his friend.

Chas woke in stages as Rafiq brought the boat into the slip and secured it. He stumbled down the ladder from the cockpit and made his way slowly up to the house. Rafiq locked the packing crate in the cabin of the boat and followed.

The house was silent and smelly. Rafiq wrinkled his nose at the overflowing trashcan filled with takeout containers and the sink piled with dirty dishes. Chas ignored the mess, making his way directly to a stack of food delivery flyers on the counter. "Whaddaya want for dinner, buddy?" He rubbed his face and let out a belch as he pawed through the pile.

Rafiq touched him on the shoulder. "Why don't you go fix us a drink and I'll get us something to eat?"

Chas brightened at the thought of a drink, and ambled out of the kitchen. Rafiq smashed down the trash and placed the tied bag outside the kitchen door. Then he loaded the dirty dishes into the dishwasher and set the machine on a heavy-duty cleaning cycle. He laughed to himself; here he was, cleaning up after Chas again after all these years.

He surveyed the contents of the refrigerator, settling on an unopened carton of eggs and a steak. Rafiq rummaged through the cabinets until he found a frying pan. Soon the smell of steak and eggs filled the kitchen.

Chas appeared in the doorway, sniffing the air. "Hey, that smells pretty good, Ralf. I didn't know you could cook, too." He handed

Rafiq a Bloody Mary in a pint glass.

Rafiq clinked glasses with him and pretended to take a sip. The drink was mostly vodka. Rafiq smacked his lips. "Mmm, that's good, Chas."

They ate in silence. Chas chewed with his mouth open and wheezed through the whole meal. Rafiq kept a smile painted on his face. "How about a tour, Chas?" he asked when they were done.

Chas walked him through the six bedrooms in the house and the assorted sitting rooms, study, game rooms, and so on. Everywhere they went, except for Chas's massive bedroom, there was a heavy layer of dust. They ended up back in the kitchen, Chas puffing from the effort of walking through his own house. "That's the place. Pick whatever room you like and stay as long as you like, Ralf. It's good to have you here."

Rafiq looked out into the gathering dusk. In this part of the country, it didn't get fully dark until after nine this time of year. "Can we walk outside? I'd like to see the grounds."

Chas made a pained face. "Whew, I'm pretty beat, buddy. How about tomorrow? I think I'll have a nightcap and then hit the hay."

"Good idea."

It took another hour, and three drinks, before Chas finally stumbled off to bed. Rafiq turned off the TV and sat in the gathering darkness. The living room overlooked the lakeshore, and he could make out the boats on the lake. Lots more boats would be coming for the Labor Day weekend, the official end of summer.

He listened for the even rumbles of Chas's snoring before he left the house. There was a large standalone structure, as large as a warehouse, a few hundred yards from the main house. He made his way to the unlocked side entrance, flipping on the overhead lights as he entered. The building was filled with different types of vehicles: sports cars, a pair of company pickup trucks with the Whitworth Construction logo in bold blue lettering, a small tractor. He walked past them all until he found the one he was seeking.

The Ford Econoline Heavy Duty van did not have any windows, and it looked new. Rafiq ran his hand across the blue letters of the Whitworth logo. He jogged to the steel box next to the door and pulled a set of keys off the hook marked VAN.

CHAPTER 54

Maritime approaches to Helsinki Harbor, Finland
05 September 2016 – 0800 local

Reza watched the *Lumba* through binoculars from the bridge of the FNS *Tornio*.

The Hamina-class fast attack boat idled at bare steerageway, their camouflaged hull all but invisible against the backdrop of the rocky Finnish coastline. Through the light morning chop of the Baltic Sea, an identical craft mirrored their movements from a position a kilometer off their port side. The long sleek *ohjusvene,* or missile boat, designed as a stealth platform, looked deadly in the shreds of predawn mist that hung over the water.

Reza made a conscious effort to control the tapping of his foot against the composite deck, a nervous habit he'd rather not display right now.

A commander from the *Erikoistoimintaosasto* stood next to him. The ETO, as they were called, was the elite special operations branch of the Finnish Navy. The officer issued a sharp acknowledgment into the microphone of his headset and then turned to Reza. They spoke in English, their only common tongue. "We'll be putting the pilot aboard in five minutes, sir." The officer was built like a side of beef, and the heavy hands that gripped the binoculars in front of his chest were corded with muscle.

Reza felt a stirring of hope. The solidity of this man, this boat, these people, made him believe it was all going to be okay. They could take down this ship, secure the weapon, and no one would be the wiser.

The signing ceremony for the Iranian Nuclear Accord was scheduled for noon at the Finlandia Hall, the world-famous concert hall. He suspected the terrorist plot was simple: sail the Malaysian freighter into Helsinki Harbor and blow it up there. Even if they didn't completely destroy the signing venue, the resulting political fallout would scuttle the agreement.

He took another deep breath to settle the stirring in his stomach. That ship, the *Lumba*, was the one. She had to be the one—there was no other possibility. It had taken days, but using the "dolphin" clue from Rafiq's daughter, he had identified a Malaysian freighter that had put into Fray Bentos in July. The Malaysian word for *dolphin* was *lumba*.

His meetings last night with the head of Finnish military intelligence, their Chief of Defence, and the Defence Minister had not gone well. They'd immediately wanted to call in the Americans and the other signatory nations and postpone the signing. Only a call from Rouhani himself and the comprehensive nature of Reza's information convinced them they could handle this quietly.

After consulting the Finnish president, the raid was approved. The Finns had chosen to throw everything at this problem, and Reza was impressed by the thoroughness of their response.

"The pilot's onboard," the Finnish commando called to him. "We're getting video."

The pilot, actually a commando in disguise, was wearing glasses with a camera built into the frames, and had a transmitter/repeater in his knapsack. On the video screen, Reza could see the bridge of the freighter, the worn instruments, the general mess of a merchant ship continuously at sea. The man who filled the view screen was jabbering in a mix of English, Malay, and a few Finnish words as he pointed at the charts. His straight dark hair was shaped in a rough bowl cut and a gap-toothed smile split his brown features.

The pilot asked him his last port of call.

"Gdańsk," the captain said. "I carry coal for power plant."

Reza looked at the map of the Helsinki Harbor the officer had taped to the bulkhead. The Hanasaari Power Plant was only two kilometers from Finlandia Hall, and the closest point you could get to the site of the signing ceremony from the harbor. Because there were almost no buildings between the mooring site for the power plant and the concert hall, it was the perfect place to detonate a nuclear bomb.

Reza breathed a sigh of relief. The cargo, the ship, the destination—it was all adding up. He heard the pilot ask the captain how many men he had onboard.

"Nineteen."

The commando nodded, and pressed down the transmit button on his microphone. He spoke in Finnish, but a junior officer standing next to Reza translated for him.

"All stations, this is team leader. There are one-nine hostiles on the target plus our pilot. I repeat one-nine hostiles, plus one friendly. All stations confirm."

Reza listened as the rest of the raid members called in: two Finnish Army Utti Jaeger commando strike teams onboard the helos, the sister ship to the *Tornio*, and finally the F/A-18 Hornets from the Finnish Air Force. The air strike was a last resort to prevent the ship from entering the harbor.

"All stations, stand by for go." The commander pushed the headset microphone out of the way and picked up a red phone handset. He spoke for a few moments in rapid Finnish, which was not translated for Reza, then nodded his head and hung up. He keyed his mike again.

"All stations, we are go. I repeat, go, go, go."

Reza ducked as two NH-90 helos roared over the bridge. The captain of the *Tornio* issued a sharp command in Finnish. The boat rocketed forward as the helmsman shouted a reply. Reza grabbed onto the railing as the deck tilted up. A white wave curled out from beneath the ship's bow.

Up ahead, the helos reached the *Lumba*. One hovered over the bridge and Reza watched tiny figures fast-rope down onto the bridgewings. The other helo dropped a squad of men on the main deck. The NH-90s peeled away from the freighter and took up stations to provide covering fire for the incoming attack boats. The scene from the pilot's video feed went from a professional discussion about tides and headings to a puzzled look overhead at the sudden rush of noise to outright panic as dark, armor-clad men appeared on the wings of the bridge and burst through the doors. The captain held up his hands, jabbering in multiple languages.

The ETO commander half-closed his eyes as he listened to his radio headset. "Bridge secured," he reported to Reza in a tight voice. The *Lumba* slowed in the water as the *Tornio* came alongside. Lines went across, snugging the vessels tight against each other. Additional ETO commandos scrambled up and over the side like well-armed monkeys.

The commander acknowledged progress reports as he scribbled with a grease pencil on a plexiglass status board in front of him. "We have nineteen captives, one dead." His gaze turned stony. "No immediate sign of a nuclear weapon on board. We're sending over a team to do a radiation sweep."

"Can I go aboard?" Reza asked.

The officer pursed his lips, then picked up the red handset again. He spoke without introduction in what Reza assumed was a status report. He cocked an eyebrow at Reza as he spoke again before ending the call.

"You can go aboard," he said.

Reza struggled up the cargo nets that connected the two vessels. The ETO commandos had made it look so easy. He swung his leg over the railing and stood on the deck of the *Lumba*, where another Finnish officer, armed and clad in body armor, waited for him. They picked their way across the littered, rusty deck and through a watertight door. Reza wrinkled his nose at the smell of the ship interior, a fetid mix of diesel oil, sweaty bodies, and rotten bananas.

On the bridge, the ship's crew was lined up along the front of the room. Reza recognized the captain from the video feed. He motioned for the Finnish officer to bring the captain out to the bridgewing.

The little man seemed to have regained some of his bravado. He looked Reza directly in the eye. "Who you?" he asked.

"My name is Reza Sanjabi. I'm with Iranian intelligence—"

"Iran? Why you on my ship? I do nothing to Iran, nothing to Finland. I am businessman." He thumped his chest.

Reza pulled a snapshot of Rafiq out of his breast pocket. "Have you ever seen this man?"

Reza saw a flicker of recognition in the captain's eyes.

"No, never see him." The captain folded his arms across his chest.

The Finnish officer beckoned Reza from inside the bridge. He lowered his voice. "The bomb team has done an initial sweep of the ship. No radiation and no evidence of radioactive contamination, sir. We're redoing the sweep, but it looks like they're clean."

A swell of panic made it hard for Reza to breathe. "Show me the man you killed in the raid."

The officer shrugged and led him off the bridge into the interior of the ship. Reza tried to breathe through his mouth to avoid smelling the awful atmosphere. They passed at least ten armed Finns heading down to the main deck. Already the Finnish strike teams were evacuating.

The officer led him to a hallway in one of the lower decks. A fluorescent light flickered above a body lying on the floor. Reza squatted next to the corpse as the Finnish officer handed him a flashlight.

The dead man had been shot once in the head, and half of his face was either damaged or covered in bloody gore. He was bald and seemed to have vaguely Middle Eastern features. He *could* be one of the brothers who were known to be associated with Rafiq, but all Reza had was a ten-year-old photo to compare against half a face.

"Sir?" the Finn said.

Reza gulped. The scent of blood mixed with the already close air of the ship, along with the gentle rocking, was all combining to make him feel sick. "What?" he gasped.

"You need to leave, sir."

"No, wait! We need to do an investigation—"

"Sir, it's not my call. I have orders to escort you off the ship. Now."

Reza got to his feet and followed the man out onto the main deck. Fresh air washed away the queasiness. The last of the Finnish commandos were going over the side to the *Tornio*. The other fast attack boat had already cast off, and the helos were nowhere to be seen. He climbed back down the cargo net and made his way to the bridge of the *Tornio*, where the ETO commander was wiping down the greaseboard. The headset hung loose around his neck.

"Commander, we need to detain this ship. They know where the weapon is—"

The officer stopped Reza with a wintry look. He carefully folded the rag he was using to wipe the board and indicated that Reza should step out onto the bridgewing. He slid the door shut behind them. "Do you have any idea what you've done?" he asked in a voice tight with anger. Reza saw a flush of red creeping up the commando's neck.

Reza opened his mouth, but the other man held up his hand. "We just boarded a ship in international waters and killed a man, all based on Iranian intelligence. There was no bomb, there was no evidence of a bomb, there was no evidence of any terrorist activity at all. My bosses are thanking their lucky stars we didn't involve the Americans or the other parties in this fiasco." He paused to get his breathing under control.

"I have orders to hand you over to the Finnish authorities. They will put you in the Iranian embassy for safekeeping and get you on the first flight out of the country. Are there any questions?"

Reza said nothing. *What did I miss?*

There was a car waiting for him on the pier in Helsinki Harbor, and he was back at the gates of the Iranian embassy within ten minutes. He nodded to the guard as he entered the compound. Reza walked straight through the building and out the back entrance. He jogged to the end of the street and hailed a taxi.

"Itäinen Puistotie," he said to the driver, and slunk down in his seat.

They stopped in front of the French embassy. Reza's hand shook as he paid the driver. When the taxi drove off, he marched across the street to the US Embassy and spoke to the Finnish guard at the gate.

"I need to speak to Mr. Donald Riley, please. It's urgent."

CHAPTER 55

Don sank back into the cushions of the taxi as it sped away from the Finlandia Hall, the site of the Iranian Nuclear Accord signing ceremony.

Not that he had seen much of the actual signing. From his position in the upper balcony, the Presidents of Iran and the United States, as well as the other signatory nations, had looked more like action figures than real people. Still, the Accord was signed and he'd be able to tell his grandchildren that he had been at the signing ceremony.

The two glasses of champagne he'd drunk at the reception on top of the jet lag combined to drag his eyelids down.

A rap on the taxi window jerked him awake. "What?"

He blinked his bleary eyes open. They were at the US Embassy gate. Don rooted in his hip pocket for his wallet to pay the taxi driver.

The Finnish gate guard rapped on the window again. Don lowered the glass as he fumbled for the correct change. "What?" he asked with an edge of irritation in his voice.

"Mr. Riley, you have a visitor." He pointed across the street toward the gate of the French Embassy and lowered his voice. "He's been here all evening. He goes away, then comes back again every few minutes. I almost called him in."

Don squinted through the dusk. Reza Sanjabi stopped his pacing and raised his hand to Don. The Iranian's features, normally so urbane and composed, were haggard and his hair looked as if he'd just stepped out of a wind tunnel.

Don thrust the bills into the cabbie's hand and stood in the street. He nodded to the guard. "Thanks, I'll handle it."

He could feel the guard's eyes on his back as he walked toward his Iranian friend. Come to think of it, he hadn't seen Reza at the Accord signing ceremony. There were easily a thousand people there, plus wait staff and security, so he hadn't thought much of it.

Reza gripped his hand, and drew him out of earshot of the gate. "Donald, thank you for seeing me. I need to speak with you. Please, it is urgent."

Don's mind raced as he extracted his hand from Reza's sweaty grip. Meeting openly with a foreign agent—right on the embassy doorstep, no less—was a huge mistake, but the Iranian's eyes pleaded with him.

"There's a cafe at the end of the street," Don said with a backward glance at the guard. "Let's get a cup of tea."

Reza walked with quick steps, seemingly anxious to get there as fast as possible. His gaze flickered constantly up and down the street.

"Are you okay, Reza? Are you in trouble?"

Reza shook his head and darted into the doorway of Cafe Ursula. He made his way across the room to an open table for two that commanded a good view of the windows and door. Don ordered two cups of tea at the counter and followed his friend. Reza had already taken the seat against the wall when Don reached the table.

Reza clenched the teacup. His hand shook as he took a sip. With a final sweeping glance around the room and out the window, he leaned across the table and spoke in a low voice. "Donald, I may not have much time, so I need you to listen carefully." He licked his lips and took another sip of tea.

"Additional information came to light after the discovery of the bunker with the nuclear weapons. We believe there may be another warhead." Don listened with growing anger as Reza described how he had tracked a fourth weapon that had been given to Hezbollah, and how the trail had led him to Helsinki.

Don slammed his hand down on the table, slopping tea onto the polished wood. "I knew it!" he said in a hiss. "I knew I was right. All of my information pointed to another warhead, but I didn't have any proof. Why didn't you come to me, Reza? You've wasted weeks following this trail yourself."

Reza avoided Don's eyes. "It was an internal matter. The information was not verified; I owed it to my country to make sure the threat was real before exposing us to international scrutiny." He reached into his jacket pocket and laid Rafiq's picture on the table between them. "This is the man I am looking for—Rafiq Roshed." He slid the photograph across the table, but Don didn't pick it up. His gaze was riveted on the next picture in the stack.

Don placed his finger on the second photo. "Him. He was the man in charge of the bunker where we found the three nuclear weapons."

"Yes, Hashem Aboud. He was killed by your strike team."

Don placed the photos side by side. "You say they're brothers. Hashem entrusted the fourth weapon to his brother in Hezbollah." Don tapped Rafiq's picture.

"Yes, we already know this, Donald."

Don flushed. "There is additional information from the raid which was not shared with Iran."

Reza's eyebrows shot up.

"This man"—Don plumped his finger on Hashem's picture—"said something in Farsi to one of our men before he died. Our people translated it as 'death from the north' or something like that. It made no sense. We assumed it was the ravings of a dying man."

"Was it recorded?" Reza asked. "Can I hear it?"

Don shook his head, then brightened. "But I can let you speak with the man who was with Hashem Aboud when he died."

Minneapolis, Minnesota
05 September 2016 – 1430 local

Brendan flipped through the TV channels, settling on yet another game-day projection of the Vikings matchup against Green Bay.

The new stadium and the Vikings' season opener had pretty much dominated the news for the last week. He wondered idly what Liz was doing with her holiday weekend. He tried—unsuccessfully—to block out the thought of her with the bartender.

McHugh, you are a fucking idiot.

The caller ID on Brendan's phone said DON RILEY. He muted the TV.

"Don, what's up?"

"Brendan, hi. I have you on speaker." He sounded distracted and he spoke in a stage whisper.

"Okay . . ."

"I have a friend here." Don cleared his throat. "He needs to ask you some questions about the raid on the bunker."

Brendan pulled the phone away from his ear and looked at it.

"Don, are you out of your flippin' mind? We're on a nonsecure line."

Don's voice came through stronger as he took Brendan off speaker. "Listen, Brendan, I know the rules as well as you do. This is an emergency—I think—I think it's an emergency. Please. If I'm right we could have a major national security issue on our hands."

Brendan clenched his teeth. Don was not a guy who took the rules lightly. "Alright, I'll listen to what your friend has to say, but no promises."

He could hear the calls of seagulls and the sound of a light breeze as Don put him back on speaker. The next voice on the phone had an English accent. "Commander McHugh, my name is Reza Sanjabi. I am the Iranian intelligence officer who provided the interview with the layout of the bunker."

Brendan had seen the video, the one with the older man in his underwear spilling the details about the construction of the bunker and the number of men. The video had been a key factor in the success of the raid. "Thank you, that information was very helpful to us."

"The gentleman in the video was Aban Rahmani, an Islamic cleric. We believe he funded the construction of the bunker and was planning to use the attack to seize power in Iran." The cultured voice hesitated. "There was additional information that was not passed on to you. Mr. Rahmani claimed there was a fourth warhead. He claimed the weapon was placed with a Hezbollah sleeper cell years ago."

Brendan's phone buzzed against his ear. He saw a text from Don pop up. It showed a picture of a trim man with close-cropped dark hair and a five-o'clock shadow of a beard.

"The picture Donald just sent you is of Rafiq Roshed. This is the Hezbollah agent we believe has the weapon. He was the leader of a sleeper cell in South America and was activated after your raid on the bunker. A very capable man, educated in the US, speaks English like an American and fluent Spanish, too."

"Do you know where he is?"

The Iranian's voice faltered again. "I've been tracking him all over the world. In Helsinki this morning we raided a ship believed to be carrying Roshed and the fourth weapon. Neither of them was on board. We're tracing the ship's ports of call since leaving South America, and we now believe Roshed got off in Tenerife two weeks ago."

Brendan got out of the chair and began to pace. "So, if this Rafiq has a nuclear weapon, it could be anywhere. Europe, Africa, even the US. Anywhere."

"Yes."

"And—let me guess—no one believes you after the failed raid in Helsinki."

"Yes."

Brendan blew out a breath. "So you have a questionable source and a wild goose chase. Why are you calling me?"

Don answered him. "You remember the Iranian agent at the bunker? The one you captured in Iraq?"

Brendan grunted.

"His name was Hashem Aboud," Reza said, "and Donald tells me that you were the last person to speak with him before he died."

"I was there, yes. And he whispered something in Farsi to me, but I hardly see how that can help. I've given my phonetic rendering of the phrase to the experts and they did the translating. 'Death from the north' or something like that."

"Can you tell me exactly what was said, please?"

Brendan closed his eyes. The image of Hashem's death was not something he'd ever forget: the bloody lips, the fiery eyes, the tobacco-stained grimace. It was like something from a horror movie.

"You have to understand we were on the deck of a helo and there was lots of noise, but it sounded like *doze-di-sho-male*."

Reza repeated the words softly. He paused. "Yes, I think the translation is accurate. The literal translation would be 'thieves from the north.' A more colloquial version might be 'norseman,' or 'viking,' but that's hardly a common word in Farsi."

Brendan stopped pacing, his eyes glued on the muted TV. "What did you say?"

"I said a more common translation might be 'viking.'"

Brendan felt his mouth go dry. The flat-screen TV on the wall showed the new Minnesota Vikings stadium rising above the Minneapolis skyline.

"I think I know where Rafiq is."

CHAPTER 56

Minneapolis, Minnesota
05 September 2016 – 1510 local

The traffic on southbound I-35 thickened even before he reached the Minneapolis northern suburbs.

An SUV with purple Minnesota Vikings flags clamped into both rear windows cut him off, and Rafiq had to slam on the brakes to keep from rear-ending the car. He gripped the steering wheel with both hands, taking deep breaths to calm himself. The detonation device in the weapon was ancient, the original gun-type model from the Iraqis. It was possible a collision with another vehicle might be enough to set it off—a theory he'd rather not test. The traffic started to move again and he put an extra margin of safe distance behind the car in front of him.

The new stadium rose into view as he got closer to the downtown area. He checked his watch again. He needed to make sure he was early enough to get a good parking place near the top of a parking ramp, but not so soon that his vehicle would attract the attention of security personnel. Rafiq was sure the local police would have extra patrols out to look for suspicious activity. He'd filled the back of the Whitworth Construction van with assorted tools and the black packing case blended in well.

Patience.

He'd waited nearly a decade for this moment. A few minutes more would not matter.

Killing Chas had felt more like a favor than a necessity.

The man had been drunk, of course, and it was a simple matter to stage his suicide. The only weapons Chas had in the house were a huge Smith & Wesson .357 Magnum revolver and a 20-gauge shotgun. The handgun was overkill for the job, but necessary to keep up appearances. The shotgun was on the floor of the van behind his seat.

Rafiq had stripped to his undershorts before pressing the barrel of the revolver into the mouth of his college friend and pulling the trigger. The resulting spatter against the headboard and the wall was spectacular, like a macabre piece of modern art. The beauty of it made his breath catch in his throat. It had been a long time since he'd killed a man. Too long.

Rafiq had considered typing up a suicide note, but decided against it. Anyone who walked through the filth and despair of Chas's house would conclude suicide before he even saw the body. He only needed a day's head start anyway.

After a long shower to remove any traces of blood from his skin, he walked through the house room by room, carefully wiping down anything he'd touched during his stay. Rafiq replaced the sheets from the bed he'd slept in. They were in a plastic bag behind his seat in the van. For good measure, he'd even gone outside and retrieved some of the trash to put back in the kitchen.

By the time he'd finished, there was no record of Rafiq ever having set foot inside Chas's home.

Except for the missing white van.

Rafiq circled the downtown area twice before settling on the parking garage at the corner of Park and Sixth Street, overlooking the entrance to the massive new Vikings stadium. He drove all the way to the topmost covered deck and took a spot on the side nearest the stadium.

He shut off the engine and took a moment to admire the view. Even he had to admit it was an impressive structure. Built to resemble a massive ship rising from the earth, the glass-and-steel bow of the metaphorical craft pointed almost directly at him. Rafiq craned his head to see the tip of the building around the edge of the parking garage roof overhead.

The plaza below him buzzed with people dressed in purple and gold Vikings colors. He knew from the radio reports that they expected a sellout crowd of over 65,000 spectators at this inaugural game against the Green Bay Packers. The radio reporter had also done a segment on the type of glass used to build the sheer face of the stadium front. Apparently, a group of bird-lovers were claiming the glass would confuse migrating birds. Rafiq shook his head. A billion-dollar structure erected in honor of a game and the news media talked about birds.

He would give them all something to talk about.

Rafiq smiled to himself when he saw the vans with television network logos lined up against the stadium. They would have a front-row seat to the halftime spectacle. He closed his eyes and tried to still the joyous hammering of his heart.

It was all coming together. The idea for an attack on the Vikings stadium on the same day as the meeting in Finland . . . surely this was divine inspiration. What better way to shatter this farce of a nuclear accord than to make a direct strike at the heart of the American Midwest? He looked down at the crowds of tailgaters. In his college days at Carleton, he had pretended to be one of them, drinking alcohol and consuming food to excess, to what end? He wanted to spit down on them from his perch, to rail at their American excesses and wasteful lives . . .

Today, after nine years of lying in wait, he would do more than talk. While the leaders of the Western world and the traitorous President of Iran met in Finland to sign their meaningless documents, he would turn this place to ash.

And the beauty of his plan is that they would never catch him. Even if they captured Hashem and tortured him, his brother had no inkling of his plan. He smiled at the Vikings logo on the side of the stadium; there was a certain fated symmetry to striking a symbolic Norseman in lieu of an actual Nordic country.

The atmosphere in the van started to get stuffy in the afternoon heat. Rafiq picked his way into the rear of the vehicle and cracked open the packing case. The long gray tube, the size of a fire hydrant, gleamed dully in the light that came through the windshield. He paused. When he considered all the sacrifices that had gone into making this moment possible, the surge of emotion formed a lump in his throat.

To work.

Rafiq fished two prepaid mobile phones out of his pocket. He checked that both were fully charged, and receiving a good signal. He used one to call the other. The phone gave a shrill ring before he silenced it. He stored the outgoing number in memory and slipped that phone back in his pocket. For all its destructive potential, the nuclear weapon was remarkably simple: an explosive charge fires one piece of subcritical fissile material into another, forming a supercritical mass. Although inefficient by modern standards, the bomb had more than enough power to level the stadium and all of downtown Minneapolis.

Rafiq had modified the triggering device so he could explode it using a mobile phone, technology that had barely existed when the Iraqis built this bomb. The small black box he'd glued to the side of the packing case appeared modern and out of place next to the industrial-looking nuclear weapon. He set the counter on the black box to four; an incoming phone call would trigger the device after four rings. Then he attached the remaining phone to the detonator device with a simple connector.

The nuclear bomb was armed.

Rafiq sat back on his heels, tears stinging his eyes.

Oh, my brother, wherever you are, this is a day of days.

One final touch remained. Rafiq hefted the shotgun and loaded a single shell into the chamber. He clamped the weapon into a portable vise and aimed it at the back door. Then he ran a length of wire from the trigger to a large rattrap he had scrounged from Chas's garage. He set the trap and, holding the hammer down with his foot, wedged a corner of the bar under the back door of the van. He duct-taped the entire assembly to the floor and carefully secured the shotgun trigger wire to the hammer of the trap. Then he covered the shotgun with a light blanket.

He smiled grimly. Hashem, his ever-cautious brother, would approve.

Rafiq exited the driver's side door and paused to pull a Vikings jersey over his head. Number 22, a player named Smith. A Vikings ball cap and a pair of dark glasses he'd taken from Chas's closet completed the outfit. He made his way to the street level, joining the pregame throng.

A few blocks away, Rafiq boarded the light rail bound for the Mall of America.

CHAPTER 57

FBI Minneapolis Field Office, Brooklyn Park, Minnesota
05 September 2016 – 1745 local

Liz watched Brendan's Subaru Outback pull into the visitor's spot in front of the FBI field office. He stepped out of the car and stretched.

Her gut clenched. She never intended their dinner last week to be the spectacular ultimatum she'd turned it into. All she'd wanted was a nice let's-get-reacquainted meal. There was no rush, no need to lay it all out there on their first date in years. For God's sake, the guy had taken three weeks just to call her!

But that look in his eyes when Tony had shown up . . . part jealousy, part confusion, part doubt. After all she'd done to be with him, that look was like a knife in the belly. She needed him to know that—despite whatever she'd said before—he was the one for her.

So she did it. Loud, proud, and in your face. And she scared him. The look on his face at the end of her tirade said it all: pure terror.

When he'd called her this afternoon, her heart beat faster at the sound of his voice. What followed was a cockamamie story about a rogue Hezbollah terrorist in Minneapolis with a nuclear device. She half-expected him to say "gotcha!" It sounded too far-fetched to be believed, but when she found out Don was involved she'd called Tom Trask, her SAC, immediately.

Liz pushed open the door to the security building and waved at Brendan to hurry. He jogged across the parking lot, favoring his injured leg. He was dressed in an open-necked sport shirt and jeans.

"Hi," he said, meeting her gaze for a second before brushing past her.

"Hi."

She'd already cleared him into the building. He signed the log and clipped a visitor badge to his shirt pocket. Without waiting for him, Liz started down the long walkway toward the main building.

Brendan caught up with her. "Listen, Liz, about the other night, I—"

"Brendan, I'm only going to say this once. This is where I work. Whatever this thing is between us"—she waved her finger between them—"is between us. It has nothing to do with this place. So—so just focus."

He held the door for her. There was an open elevator waiting for them. She pushed the button for the top floor, level five. She met his gaze as the door closed. "Look, Tom Trask is a good man, I trust him. Just give him the facts, and he'll make the right call."

Special Agent in Charge Thomas Trask had a corner office on the fifth floor with an attached conference room. Liz's gaze traveled over the familiar pictures on his wall: a younger Trask in a Marine Corps officer's uniform, Georgetown Law School diploma, a family photo with his wife and two kids, one in a midshipman's uniform. The man himself was a compact, fifty-something guy with an iron-gray crew cut and a more-than-firm handshake. He nodded as Liz made the introductions and he shook Brendan's hand.

"McHugh, Tom Trask. Good to meet you. Liz has told me all about you."

"She has?"

Liz closed her eyes. She had told Trask about Brendan. He was a fellow Marine and he kind of reminded her of her father. Trask winked at her and jerked his head toward the attached conference room. "Let's get started," he said.

Two other agents were already in the room: Kamen and Adams, known in the office as Cain and Abel. The light on the speaker phone was blinking red, indicating someone on hold. Liz punched the blinking button on the phone. "Don, are you there?"

"I'm here."

"Putting you on the screen now." Don Riley's round face popped up on the wall monitor.

Trask placed his hands flat on the table. "Alright, McHugh, the floor is yours. Let's hear what you've got."

Brendan took a deep breath. "A few months ago, I was part of an operation to take down an Iranian nuclear weapons site. They had three nuclear-tipped missiles on launchers, ready to strike at Israel during the Tel Aviv nuclear accord meeting."

"Holy shit," muttered one of the FBI agents. Trask's jaw tightened.

"The operation was run by an Iranian Quds officer named Hashem Aboud. I've run into him a few times over the years. Nasty character, but very well connected in the region. He was mortally wounded during the takedown; I was there when he died. He threatened me—in Farsi—but the deathbed confession never matched with any other intel. I think it's best if Mr. Riley takes it from here."

Don leaned closer to the screen. "This afternoon, an Iranian agent I've known for some time contacted me. He divulged that the Iranians believe there is a fourth nuke. The weapon was passed to

Hashem Aboud's half brother, a Hezbollah agent named Rafiq Roshed, and placed with a sleeper cell in South America. The Iranians have been pursuing this angle on their own and tracked the weapon to a Malaysian freighter that was docking in Helsinki today.

"The Finns raided the freighter this morning outside of Helsinki Harbor. The ship was clean, but it made a port call in the Canary Islands two weeks ago. After some persuasion, the captain acknowledged that one of his crew departed in Tenerife. We're coordinating with the Spanish authorities for more details on where our suspect may have gone, but if he had prearranged transport, he could be anywhere by now.

"At first blush, the Helsinki connection made perfect sense. The translation of Aboud's threat referred to activity in the north, and we know their goal was to disrupt the Tel Aviv nuclear agreement. Obviously, we were fooled." Don's voice took on an apologetic tone. "We now think the Helsinki freighter was a red herring and the real nuke is . . . somewhere else. The Vikings angle came from a side conversation with Brendan earlier today."

Trask blew out his breath. "Wow, that's pretty thin." He looked at Liz. "You've verified the translation?"

Liz avoided Trask's gaze. "I'm working from a phonetic recollection of a deathbed confession that happened months ago. Is 'vikings' a possible translation of what this Hashem character said? Yes, one of about a dozen potential meanings."

Trask scrubbed his crew cut with his short fingers. "Okay, what do we have on this Hezbollah brother and why the hell would he choose Minneapolis?"

Cain and Abel perked up. Cain pulled the keyboard close and punched some keys. The picture of Rafiq filled the split screen next to Don. Abel did the talking.

"Mr. Riley sent over Roshed's file via JWICS. This is the only picture we have of Rafiq Roshed, and it's old. Using facial recognition software and screening for gender and age, I've run a comp against all entries into the US in the last two weeks. Nothing. I also searched for a match against active US passports in the last ten years, and got no hits. But, when I ran the software on the database for student visas, I found something." He struck a key and a passport picture page appeared on the screen next to Rafiq's photo. Liz studied the photos. Side by side she could see some resemblance, but nothing conclusive by a long shot.

"Meet Ralf Faber, student at Carleton College in Northfield, Minnesota, from 1999 to 2004. Graduated with a degree in international relations. No problems with the law, didn't overstay his visa."

Trask pulled a face. "What's the degree of confidence on the match?"

"Seventy-nine percent."

"So if this is our guy and we think he's here, how did he get into the US?" Trask asked.

Cain and Abel exchanged glances. "We might have a possible lead, sir," said Abel. "When Faber renewed his visa, he put an emergency contact as Charles Whitworth, home address in Bayfield, Wisconsin. I pulled it up on the map. It's a mansion, with a big boathouse attached."

"People, this is weak stuff, barely circumstantial." Trask pressed his lips together. "That said, the possibility of a rogue nuke on US soil, the Vikings stadium grand opening . . . I guess if a terrorist wanted to make a statement, this would be a pretty good place. Washington wants us to check it out, but let's keep this out of the news."

He pointed to Cain and Abel. "Contact local PD in Bayfield. Have them get someone up to the Whitworth mansion to interview Mr. Whitworth about Roshed. Tell them we need this info yesterday. Put out an APB for Roshed to all locals and stadium security. I'll be in the ops center bringing the governor and the city officials up to speed."

Trask looked over at Liz. "Liz, this is one time that I hope you're wrong."

Brendan stood. "What can I do to help, sir?"

Trask pointed out the window to the empty parking lot. A UH-60 Black Hawk helo was setting down.

"McHugh, you and Agent Soroush are going fishing."

CHAPTER 58

Minneapolis, Minnesota
05 September 2016 – 1800 local

The car he'd stolen from the Mall of America parking lot was a 2007 Ford Taurus, silver, with 98,173 miles on it. The previous owner had been a smoker and a slob.

Rafiq headed south on Route 77 until it hooked up to I-35. He rolled down the windows to let the wind clear away the smell of cigarette smoke from the car interior. The weather was one of those perfect Minnesota days: eighty degrees, low humidity, and not a cloud in the sky. Everywhere he looked, the trees, the buildings, everything looked etched against the perfect blue of the sky.

These were the Minnesota afternoons when he and Chas would go to the lake . . . what was the name of it? A passing road sign reminded him: Prior Lake. Chas would rent them the fastest motorboat he could find and they'd race across the water, the spray and the wind whipping their faces.

The exit for Northfield appeared and he took it. County Road 19 was a rolling two-lane country road that wound east. He passed St. Olaf College, and then picked up the distinctive smell of the Malt-O-Meal factory on the breeze that blew in the window. He crossed the Cannon River, turning left onto Division Street, and drove slowly by Hogan Brothers' Acoustic Café, a favorite haunt for he and Chas.

He parked his car off campus and walked toward Skinner Chapel carrying only a knapsack containing money, two more fake passports, binoculars, and a smartphone. Anything else he needed, he could buy.

The critical phone, the one that would trigger the bomb, was in his hip pocket.

Rafiq took a seat on a shaded park bench outside the chapel. From here he could see the dorm room where he and Chas had spent their first year together. So many memories, good ones. Chas had been his first recruit. He alone had identified him and groomed him for the day when he would be needed.

But it was more than that. Chas had been his friend, too, and they'd had some good times. His nostalgic mood softened when he thought of his friend's bloated body lying in his bed with his brains painting the wall. What a waste; Rafiq had done his friend a favor.

He dozed in the warm afternoon sunshine.

Since classes at Carleton wouldn't start for another week, the campus was deserted. Anyone else was probably indoors watching the Vikings game. He smiled to himself; he hoped they were *all* watching. Rafiq rose slowly, stiff from the hard surface of the bench. He was too old for this. After this one last job for Hashem, he was finished with the Iranian side of his family. Nadine, Consie, and Javi were his family now—the rest of them could go to hell.

Nadine. He closed his eyes, trying to picture what she and the children would be doing right now. They'd be at dinner. Rafiq could almost taste the wine on his palate, a bite of steak on his tongue. Javi would be holding court with mother and little sister about his latest riding adventure. Rafiq fished the smartphone out of his knapsack. A short call, just enough to hear Nadine's voice, that's all he wanted.

No. It was little moments of weakness that destroyed great operations. He would not allow an instant of homesickness to compromise nine years of waiting and planning. His family was safe. He would be with them soon.

The sun, a beautiful globe of yellow-orange, was just touching the horizon. Rafiq checked his watch: 1915. The game had started. He opened the NFL Live smartphone app. The Vikings were already ahead by a score of 7-0. The commentators gushed about the new stadium, and nearly every commercial break featured a shot of the stadium exterior soaring into the flawless blue sky like the prow of some long-ago warship.

Perfect.

The parking lot was mostly empty on this holiday weekend. He walked slowly, as if he had forgotten where he'd parked his car. Rafiq selected a late model Toyota Corolla, dark gray, with good tires. He had some driving to do after this job.

—✕—

Minneapolis, Minnesota
05 September 2016 — 1845 local

Brendan cinched the seat belt tight across his waist as the helo lifted off.

Liz faced him from the opposite jump seat. They both wore black bulletproof vests emblazoned with FBI in yellow block letters, but only Liz was carrying a sidearm. Trask was firm on that point. She gave him a tight smile.

The crew chief passed them both heavy headsets. Liz keyed her mike. "Thanks, Chief. I'm Liz Soroush, and this is Commander Brendan McHugh. What's the plan?" Brendan turned down the volume on his headset.

The helo reached altitude and the floor tilted forward as the pilot sped toward the Minneapolis skyline.

"You need to ask Simon, ma'am. We just go where he tells us." The crew chief nodded at their other passenger, a thin man in T-shirt and jeans with a ragged haircut and the scruff of a beard on his chin.

The young man adjusted his round wire-rimmed glasses and rested his hand on the console lashed to the deck in front of him. "This is MINDS, stands for Miniature Integrated Nuclear Detection System." He pointed out the window to a meter-long tube fixed to the wing stubs where the military version of the Black Hawk normally carried exterior cargo, such as Hellfire missiles or extra fuel tanks.

"That's the detector. It can sense radionuclides and tell us what we've got down there. Radioactive elements emit a nuclear signature, so if we know what's in the bomb, we can search for those specific energy spectra—"

"What's the range?" Liz interrupted him. "How close do we need to be to the source for this to pick up a signal?"

Simon pushed his glasses up his nose. "Well, we're not a hundred percent sure. This is a beta unit for airborne platforms."

"Best guess, Simon."

"If we can do a spiral search pattern around the stadium at less than five hundred feet, MINDS should see something, then we can zoom in. We need to go slow, the photomultiplier needs about a second to process the incoming signal."

When the crew chief switched channels to speak with the pilot, Liz said to Brendan, "If we get a hit on the detector, I'm going to have him put us down. We can't risk a remote detonation if he sees us hovering over a building."

Brendan flashed her a thumbs-up.

The Black Hawk shot past the high-rise buildings of downtown Minneapolis and slowed as they approached the new Vikings stadium. The building was half as high as the IDS tower, the tallest building in the city. The rays of the evening sun turned the glass-and-steel structure a shining golden color, its triangular bulk poking out of the city skyline.

The pilot slowed the helo and leveled the craft so that they were about a hundred feet above the tallest point of the stadium, which Brendan knew from the endless newscasts was about three hundred feet. They began a slow circuit around the building. Through the glass top of the stadium, Brendan could see the game in progress. He pulled out his phone and Googled the live feed of the game. Vikings: 14, Packers: 3, with seven minutes left in the second quarter. Prince, a Minnesota hometown favorite, was the halftime show.

The helo crawled along, rounding the side of the stadium. They passed over the archways that stood in the plaza; from this height the thirty-foot structures looked like something out of a toy train set.

Liz reached across the space between them and tapped his arm. She held out her mobile phone. Brendan read the text:

Police search of Whitworth home in Bayfield, WI, found Charles Whitworth dead of self-inflicted GS wound.

"I've got something!" Simon's excited voice was loud in Brendan's headset.

He and Liz unclipped their seatbelts and crowded next to Simon. He pointed to a graph that showed a sharp peak. "I loaded in the radionuclide signature from the other similar weapons. I've been using that as a screening criteria. This spike shows high-energy gammas in the target energy range."

"Where?" Liz shouted. "Which building?"

Simon looked out the window. "That parking ramp. The one with the white roof."

Liz's voice came over the headset. "Chief, we need you to put us down on that parking ramp." Brendan looked over her shoulder as she typed out a text to Trask.

Possible detection at parking ramp, corner of 6th and Park. Proceeding on foot.

The Black Hawk pilot spun the craft around and descended rapidly toward the H painted on the topmost level of the parking ramp. Brendan swung to the ground, careful to land on his good leg, then reached back in for the portable detector unit. He and Liz kept their heads low as they ran under the whirling rotors. Liz was on the phone with Trask before the helo had even lifted off. "We're on the ground, sir, doing a search of the parking ramp. We have a handheld detector with us."

Handheld was a stretch. Brendan held an open laptop in the crook of his arm and a two-foot-long metal tube under his other arm. Simon had explained this model was usually wall-mounted, but they could use it for as long as the laptop battery lasted.

Liz ended the call and joined him. She took the laptop and balanced it on an open palm. "Okay, let's do a slow walk around the cars and see what we get."

The readings from the cars on the rooftop were all normal. Liz chewed her lip. "Let's go down a level."

Still tethered together by the MINDS gear, they moved as a pair toward the ramp. Brendan walked slightly ahead, holding the detector out in front of his chest like a rifle. At the base of the ramp was an enormous silver Cadillac Escalade wedged into a parking space labeled COMPACT ONLY. He walked slowly around the corner of the vehicle, then pulled back and flattened his body against the car.

"What?" Liz asked, barely holding onto the laptop.

A white Ford Econoline van with blue lettering on the side that said WHITWORTH CONSTRUCTION was parked on the outside row. Liz took a quick look around the side of the Escalde, then hit speed dial and pressed her phone to her ear.

She whispered into the phone, then Brendan heard her say, "Yes, sir."

"Trask is sending the EOD guys. No one believes this Roshed character is a suicide bomber, so it's probably on a timer, or maybe some sort of remote trigger. We're gonna sit tight 'til they get here."

In the background, Brendan heard the roar of the crowd through the open stadium doors. It didn't make sense. Roshed had smuggled a nuclear bomb into the United States and he was going to leave the timing of the detonation to chance? No, he would make sure every possible camera was trained on this venue . . .

"Halftime," Brendan said. "He's gonna do it at halftime." He grabbed Liz's shoulder. "Think about it: they've been advertising the halftime show for weeks. People are calling this an early Super Bowl."

Brendan fumbled for his phone to check the game clock. The Vikings were managing the clock to try to score again before the half ended. "There's less than a minute left in the half."

Liz's eyes widened. "I'm going to go take a look." She wrenched a thin strip of metal from the side of the detector. Before he could say another word, she had slipped around the front of the Escalade.

A few seconds later, he saw her head pop up near the van. She walked around the front of the vehicle, her handgun drawn. Then she holstered her weapon and slipped the strip of metal into the door of the driver's side. She was using the metal strip as a SlimJim to unlock the door, Brendan realized.

He stood up. She had the driver's side door open now, and Brendan heard the *chunk* of the power locks disengaging. He gathered up the laptop and MINDS detector and rushed toward the van. Liz, her hand on the back door of the van, called to him. "Bren, bring the detector—"

A boom echoed through the parking ramp. Liz's body flew away from the back of the van, crashing into the trunk of a sedan before sliding to the ground.

Brendan dropped the MINDS equipment.

"Liz!"

CHAPTER 59

Burnsville, Minnesota
05 September 2016 – 1945 local

Rafiq cruised up I-35, back toward the Twin Cities. He kept under the speed limit, letting the few cars on the highway pass by him.

He exited on Route 13 south, a two-lane road of strip malls and traffic lights interspersed with neighborhoods and green space. He drove conservatively, accelerating slowly away from the lights, and braking well before they turned red. The brick bulk of Burnsville High School came up on his right, and he turned into the empty parking lot. Rafiq selected a spot behind the corner of the building, next to the bleachers and out of sight of the road. He shut off the engine, letting the silence of the deserted school on a summer evening surround him.

He checked the NFL Live app again. Second quarter, three minutes left, Vikings up by only three points now. He knew from past experience that three minutes of play could take thirty minutes of actual time. Another commercial advertised the half-time show. Prince. Rafiq smiled faintly, remembering that the movie *Purple Rain* had been a popular rerun when he and Chas were at Carleton.

The squeak of the car door echoed against the brick building as he exited the vehicle. Although the sun was mostly below the horizon, there was still plenty of light. It wouldn't be dark for another few hours at this latitude. He walked north, passing the high school football stadium, the baseball diamond, and two practice fields until he reached the edge of a bluff.

The ground fell away sharply, and he looked down on a business park of warehouses. The Minnesota River glinted in the valley and he could see the lights of the cars on I-35, one lane white headlights, the other red.

Rafiq raised a set of binoculars. The Minneapolis skyline stood out sharply against the lavender of the evening sky, the high-rise towers glinting in the last rays of the dying sun. He could make out the prow of the Vikings stadium poking out of the grouping of glass and steel, a pointed shape sailing toward the cluster of downtown skyscrapers.

Perfect.

He opened the NFL Live app again in time to see the Vikings kick a field goal with four seconds left in the half. Both teams headed to their respective locker rooms. The announcers began to prattle about the halftime entertainment as the stadium went dark. Less than a minute later, a solo spotlight came up on the stage. Prince stood alone, dressed in a dazzling suit of ivory with rhinestone trim, holding an intricately shaped guitar. The music started, and Rafiq recognized the song. He closed his eyes to recall the name. It was a favorite of Chas's from *Purple Rain*—"When Doves Cry," that was it. Rafiq felt his eyes grow hot with tears of gratitude. It was as if the universe had conspired to make this moment perfect for him.

With shaking hands, he drew the second mobile phone from his hip pocket, the burner phone. He pressed the power button, watching as the screen glowed to life and connected to the mobile network. The clock in the upper right-hand corner read 20:48.

He lay on the ground, the grass soft and still warm from the sun, and positioned himself so that he could duck his head under the lip of the bluff as soon as he dialed the phone.

Prince was just finishing his first song and launching into a second. The rest of the stage was lit now, showing the rest of his band—all women, Rafiq noted. He thumbed to the icon labeled "Recent Calls."

A single number showed on the screen.

With a whispered prayer, he hit the SEND key, and ducked his head.

Parking Ramp across from Vikings stadium, Minneapolis
05 September 2016 – 2050 local

Brendan dropped to his knees next to Liz and rolled her onto her back.

The breath rushed out of his lungs. A handful of bright steel shot was still buried in the black Kevlar vest. Her right shoulder had taken a few pellets and a slice of weeping red blazed across her temple. Her head lolled to one side.

Brendan pressed his shaking fingers against her neck. He forced himself to calm down so he could feel for a pulse. It was weak, but she was still alive.

"Hold on, Lizzie," he whispered. "You and me—we're not done yet." He fumbled for his phone to call an ambulance.

A ringing sound interrupted his thoughts. He looked around.

It was coming from the van. He scrambled to his feet and peered into the back. The large-bore muzzle of a shotgun poked out from under a blanket, a tendril of smoke still leaking from the end.

The phone rang again.

There. A large black packing case occupied the center of the floor. Brendan jumped inside and flipped open the lid. A large gray tube about the size of a fire hydrant filled the case. Could this be a nuclear weapon? In his mind, he'd expected a sleek modern-looking device with red and blue wires and a fancy digital countdown clock. This? This thing looked like something he might find in a plumbing supply shop.

Next to the cylinder lay a mobile phone, its glowing green face illuminating the interior of the case.

The phone rang again. It was connected to a small black box by a foot-long length of braided wire.

Brendan frantically looked for a kill switch, anything to turn the device off.

Nothing.

With a whispered prayer, he looped the length of wire around his hand and heaved with all his strength. He let out a scream as he crashed back against the side of the van, with the mobile phone, wire, and black box dangling in his grip.

For a long moment, the world stood still around him. He could hear the roar of the crowd in the stadium, low-angle sunlight slanted through the windshield of the van painting the interior in bright gold. Liz's body lay still on the concrete.

Liz.

As he stumbled out of the back of the van, Brendan realized the phone in his hand was still ringing. He pressed the green icon and held it to his ear.

"Hello?"

The rasp of heavy breathing. In the background, he could hear an echo of the song Prince was playing in the stadium.

"Rafiq Roshed," said Brendan.

The breathing hitched.

"I know who you are. If she dies, I will find you."

The phone went dead in his hand.

He knelt next to Liz. Sirens wailed in the distance. Her eyes fluttered open, and a look of panic swept across her face.

Brendan pressed his hand to her cheek. "I'm here, Lizzie. You've been shot. You need to lie still."

"The bomb?" Her voice came out as a rasp. Her eyes widened in pain as she tried to draw a full breath.

"I—I think I disarmed it. I'm not sure." He could hear tires squealing as vehicles raced up the ramp. A helo thundered overhead. "Just stay still and hang on. I'm going to—"

She clutched at his arm. "Stay," she whispered. "Please."

Brendan squeezed her hand.

"I'm not going anywhere, Liz."

CHAPTER 60

It still hurt to turn her head. Liz angled her chair toward the front of Tom Trask's conference room so that she could see Don Riley.

The grainy video on the screen behind Don showed a stylishly dressed woman wearing dark glasses in the passenger seat of a convertible. She had her hand high on the thigh of an equally attractive man. He was laughing at something and his hand was reaching for a pair of passports.

"The driver, identified as Jose Carveza, was a Mexican national. He crossed the border into Mexico, with this, um, person, six days ago at Fabens, Texas. Mr. Carveza was discovered twenty-four hours later, shot in the back of the head, execution style. Local police considered the killing to be drug-related, given the MO. We didn't find out about it until yesterday." He switched slides, this one a close-up still photo of the woman.

"After closer scrutiny, and running the picture through facial recognition, we now believe this 'woman' is actually Rafiq Roshed."

Liz spoke first. "Five days' head start. He could be anywhere." It still hurt to take a deep breath, but it was getting better every day. The cut on her temple had healed into a thin pale streak. With any luck, the doctor said she wouldn't even have a scar. The sling on her right arm was a nuisance, but at least she was out of the temporary body brace for the broken ribs and fractured sternum. Even the bruising on her chest had faded into a pale greenish tinge.

Don nodded. "We believe he will try to make contact with his family. We have his assets frozen, of course, but we have no way of knowing what he might have set up in untraceable accounts." He gave an apologetic grimace. "The Tri-Border Region is not known for rule of law, and our intelligence assets in the area are inadequate for a search of this magnitude."

"So what's our next move?" Brendan asked. Liz spun her chair so she could see him. He sat with his back to the window and the afternoon sun cast his face in shadow.

During the week she was in the hospital, Brendan had come to see her every day. When Liz tried to apologize for the night at the restaurant, he stopped her.

"Don't," he said with a mischievous smile. "I kind of enjoyed it. It's not every day you get a beautiful woman throwing herself at you."

"If I wasn't in traction, I'd kick your ass."

The banter came easily, and they talked for hours. On his second visit, Brendan held her hand. It wasn't the grip of someone obligated to visit a friend in the hospital; it was the gentle touch of a man who knew what he wanted.

Liz smiled to herself. Brendan still hadn't kissed her yet, but they were having dinner tonight . . .

Don clearing his throat brought her back to the moment. He flashed up a satellite photo of what looked like a sizable ranch.

"Estancia Refugio Seguro," he said. "Safe Haven Ranch, Rafiq's former estate in Argentina. His wife is dead, his fortune is frozen, and we have his kids under surveillance. Long story short, we have one very pissed-off terrorist on our hands. What do we do?" He shrugged.

"We search. We watch. We wait for him to make a mistake."

CHAPTER 61

Tehran was a dirty place.

Rafiq's nose wrinkled at the smells of the tiny apartment, ignoring the scratching in the walls that could only be rats. He'd only be here a short while. Just long enough to get the final piece of information he needed.

It had been a long journey into the country. He avoided Lebanon on this trip. No sense in implicating his former colleagues in this mission. This mission was personal.

The passage through the mountains had reminded him of Argentina, the way the dry slopes swept down to long valleys and the breeze cut across the plain. There were times during the journey when if he closed his eyes, he could almost imagine he was home. He could almost imagine Nadine—or even little Javi—was riding on the horse next to him, instead of some Afghani who smelled worse than his mount.

Not so little anymore, he thought with a sad twist of his lips.

Soon. Soon he would be home again. There was just one more job to do before he could put Nadine's memory to rest.

One more loose end.

The phone in his hip pocket buzzed. Rafiq flipped it open. The text was a name, a time, and an address. He stared at it for a moment, committing the information to memory. Then he removed the battery and the SIM card from the phone, and snapped the device in half.

Rafiq picked up the motorcycle helmet from the floor next to his chair and made his way onto the darkening street.

The motorcycle was tucked into an alcove under the stairs. He snapped the visor down on his helmet and straddled the bike, the low roar of the engine startling a dog sleeping a few feet away. Nursing the throttle, he guided the motorcycle into the evening traffic, allowing the flow of cars and scooters to set the pace of his movement.

When he reached his destination, he circled the block twice, slowing as he studied the hookers lining the sidewalk. On his second pass, one stepped forward and nodded to him. She was tall and thin, with the augmented breasts and sculpted nose so common in Tehran.

"I'm Saffron," she said.

Rafiq jerked his head toward the back of the bike. Saffron pulled a long robe and headscarf from her bag and put them on before she climbed on behind him. She pressed her chest against his back and wrapped her arms around his waist.

Rafiq pulled back into traffic, weaving between cars, heading north, always north. The vehicle exhaust formed a noxious haze around them, making the back of his throat feel raw. The unending traffic slowed again and stopped. He resisted the urge to ride up on the sidewalk.

Patience.

When they reached the edge of the north Tehran suburbs, the

quantity of cars around them decreased and the quality of the vehicles improved dramatically. They were surrounded by Mercedes, Audis, even a Lamborghini. Once they passed a long section of tony high-rise apartments, the housing spread out into estates; mansions, really. Saffron indicated the exit and he made a gentle turn onto a side street, slowing his speed to match the environment.

After two more turns, they glided to a stop at a small side gate. Rafiq could see a gabled roof outlined in light over the top of the high stone wall. Saffron hopped off the bike and punched a button on the intercom box adjacent to the gate. She looked up into the camera and waved. When the lock on the gate buzzed, she pushed it open.

Rafiq shut off the bike and slipped off his helmet, following Saffron into the compound. They made their way across the courtyard to the back entrance, the gravel crunching under Rafiq's boots. Beyond the courtyard, he could see manicured gardens and the Tehran cityscape, hazy lights through a curtain of pollution.

Saffron knocked at the back entrance and it opened immediately. The man who peered out at them was dressed in a dark suit, the telltale bulge of a handgun under his arm. He gave Saffron a wicked smile. "Saffron, back so soon? He must really like you." His eyes fell on Rafiq. "Who's he?"

"My driver," Saffron replied. "We've had some trouble with girls in this end of town getting picked up by the police."

The man's eyes narrowed, then he nodded. "Okay, but he stays in the kitchen with me. Understand?"

"Whatever. Where is he?"

"He said he wants to start in the study tonight. You can meet him there."

Using her body as a shield from the guard's eyes, Saffron flashed her hand open twice toward Rafiq. Ten minutes. She pushed past the guard. "I know the way. Where's Ghassem tonight?"

"He's off. It's just me here guarding the kingdom."

Rafiq stepped into the kitchen, letting the smells of spices wrap around him. Another reminder of a home he would never have again. The guard waved his hand toward the stove. "There's tea, if you want it."

Rafiq sat at the table, facing the clock. Nine minutes to go.

Patience.

The guard sat across from him, reading the paper. He slurped his tea.

Six minutes.

"There's tea if you want it," the guard said again.

"Thank you, no."

The guard shrugged.

Three minutes.

Rafiq controlled his breathing, watching the sweep of the second hand around the face of the clock.

At one minute, the guard looked up at him with a scowl on his face. "Are you going to keep doing that deep breathing all night? She's going to be at least an hour, maybe two."

Rafiq lowered his gaze from the clock to the guard. Then he rammed the table against the man's chest, pushing him back against the stove and pinning his arms to his sides. The man tried to cry out, but the force of the blow had knocked the wind out of him. Rafiq leaped onto the table and grasped the man's head, one hand on the back of his neck, the other cupping his chin.

With a sharp twist, the man's body relaxed under Rafiq's hands.

He slipped his hand into the man's jacket and drew out his handgun, a Glock 17. It would do the job.

Rafiq walked swiftly through the halls of the mansion, his feet sinking silently into the plush of the carpet. His heart thundered in his ears.

Patience.

In the end, it was Saffron's laughter that showed him the right room. She'd left the door ajar. Rafiq peered through the crack to see the prostitute, stripped down to her bra and fishnet stockings, sitting astride a fat old man in a leather armchair. An open bottle of Johnny Walker Blue Label sat on the edge of the desk next to two glasses.

Rafiq used the muzzle of the handgun to push the door open, letting it bang against the wall. Saffron looked up, pulling her tits away from the old man's face. "Took you long enough," she said, hopping off Aban's lap.

Aban looked up in surprise when she spoke. When he focused on Rafiq's face, the color drained from his own. He reached out and grasped Saffron's wrist. "Please, go get help. This man means to hurt me."

Saffron twisted her arm away as she bent over to pick up her clothes. "That's the general idea."

Rafiq handed her an envelope as she brushed past him. He could hear her tinkling laughter as she made her way down the hall.

He stood in front of the armchair. Aban, dressed only in boxer shorts, a T-shirt, and dark socks, quailed under Rafiq's glare. His robes lay in a heap next to the chair, topped by his turban.

"Do you know who I am?" Rafiq asked him.

Aban swallowed and nodded.

"Do you know why I am here?"

Aban voice was raspy with fear. "Brother, whatever you want, I can give it to you."

"On that we agree, *brother*."

Rafiq pulled the trigger.

THE END

A Note from the Two Navy Guys

Weapons of Mass Deception probably confirms what you already knew: our world can be a dangerous place. It's always been that way. People like Rafiq Roshed and his (now deceased) Iranian half-brothers really do exist. (JR spent a twenty-one-year career as an intel officer. You don't want to know some of the things he knows.)

Thankfully, in real life, there are also patriots like Brendan McHugh, Liz Soroush, and Don Riley to balance the scales in our favor.

Although all three characters started their careers as Naval Academy midshipmen, their paths led them to different fronts in the ongoing war on terror. As this series continues, Brendan will commit to the CIA and his super-secret SIGINT program. Don will exercise his considerable brain in the service of cyberwarfare.

And Liz? I'm so glad you asked. Liz takes center stage in our second book, *Jihadi Apprentice*, a national security thriller that deals with a whole new threat: homegrown radicalism.

JR and I didn't look for this topic; it found us—in our hometown of Minneapolis.

In 2015, our local paper was filled with stories of how the Minneapolis Somali community was the number one recruiting ground for "jihadist mobilization," or young people being radicalized and leaving the country to fight for terrorist groups such as Al-Shabab and ISIS.

The idea that an American citizen—these were all American-born young people—could be manipulated in that way was troubling to us. We reached out to our contacts at the local FBI office (yes, there really is an FBI office in Brooklyn Center, Minn) and found some contacts in the local Somali community.

What we discovered was a fascinating and disturbing story of manipulation, exploitation, and youth identity. (These young people are teenagers, remember.) As *Jihadi Apprentice* took shape, we decided our favorite FBI Special Agent Liz Soroush should be given the task of figuring out this new threat. What she found will keep you reading late into the night…

Pick up your copy of *Jihadi Apprentice* and start reading now.

Happy reading –
JR and David AKA The Two Navy Guys

Visit www.twonavyguys.com for more information about us and our other books.

About the
David Bruns

David earned a Bachelor of Science in Honors English from the United States Naval Academy. That's not a typo. He's probably the only English major you'll ever meet who took multiple semesters of calculus, physics, chemistry, electrical engineering, naval architecture, and weapons systems just so he could read some Shakespeare. It was totally worth it.

After meeting Tom Clancy and reading *The Hunt for Red October* as a midshipman at the Naval Academy, he spent six years as a commissioned officer in the nuclear-powered submarine force chasing the Russians in the frigid waters of the North Atlantic. When the Soviet Union collapsed, David left the Navy for corporate life. For two decades, he schlepped his way around the globe as an itinerant executive in the high-tech sector, and even did a stint with a Silicon Valley startup before he settled down and started writing full time.

David is the creator of the sci-fi series *The Dream Guild Chronicles* and *INVINCIBLE*, the best-selling tie-in novel to Nick Webb's Legacy Fleet military sci-fi series. His short fiction has appeared in numerous venues including *Compelling Science Fiction, Future Chronicles,* and *Beyond the Stars.*

David co-authors novels in two different genres. With retired naval intel officer J.R. Olson, he writes contemporary military thrillers that look less like fiction every time he checks the news. Their latest novel, *Rules of Engagement*, was released in June 2019 by St Martin's Press (Macmillan). With co-author Chris Pourteau, David write the sci-fi series, *The SynCorp Saga*, about the corporate takeover of the solar system.

In his spare time, David enjoys traveling. He and his family have visited well over two dozen countries and almost all fifty states, but Minnesota is home (for now).

Authors

J. R. Olson

Commander, US Navy (Retired)

Jon, a born and bred Minnesotan, graduated from the US Naval Academy in 1990 with a BS in History and a commission as an Ensign in the US Navy. His assignments during his twenty-one-year career included duty aboard aircraft carriers and large deck amphibious ships; participation in numerous operations around the world, including Iraq, Somalia, Bosnia, and Afghanistan; and service to the Navy as a CIA-trained case officer. His final assignment before retirement was as the US Naval Attaché at the US Embassy in Helsinki, Finland. Jon also qualified as a Navy parachutist, logging thirty-five jumps during his career.

Since retirement from the navy, Jon has co-authored multiple novels with David. Jon has also co-authored a feature length screenplay about the Falklands War.

Jon earned a Master of Arts in National Security and Strategic Studies from the U.S. Naval War College in Newport, Rhode Island, and completed his Master of Public Affairs degree from the Humphrey School at the University of Minnesota. Professionally, Jon has served as a visiting lecturer at Carleton College and as an instructor in the School of Law Enforcement and Criminal Justice at Metropolitan State University, teaching courses on the U.S. intelligence community, terrorism and counterterrorism, and WMDs.

Jon and his wife reside on a five-acre hobby farm outside Minneapolis where they care for their fruit trees and their five rescue dogs.

53669381R00255

Made in the
USA
Lexington, KY